Chris Bradford

BULLET CATCHER

With illustrations by
Nelson Evergreen

Barrington Stoke

For more information on Chris and his books visit:
www.chrisbradford.co.uk

First published in 2015 in Great Britain by
Barrington Stoke Ltd
18 Walker Street, Edinburgh, EH3 7LP

www.barringtonstoke.co.uk

A CIP catalogue record for this book is available
from the British Library upon request

ISBN: 978-1-78112-445-1

Printed in China by Leo

Warning: Do not attempt any of the techniques described within the book. These
can be highly dangerous and result in fatal injuries. The author and publisher take
no responsibility for any injuries resulting from attempting these techniques.

In memory of Leo Joseph Street
Sakura breeze – may lead me home

CONTENTS

CHAPTER 1
GUNFIRE

The Near Future

Troy looked up from the Batman comic he was reading and locked eyes with a girl on the other side of the display stand.

The girl was geek-pretty with brown eyes, a silver nose stud and short black hair bleached white at the tips. She stopped bobbing her head to the silent beat from her headphones and smiled sweetly at Troy. Only then did he realise he was staring at her.

Troy attempted to smile back but his lips seemed to have frozen solid. He was always shy in front of girls, even girls reading retro comics on a Saturday morning in Terminus City's grand mall.

Troy stuck his head back in his comic to hide the red flush rising in his cheeks. 'Fourteen years old,' he thought, 'and I've never had a girlfriend, or been kissed! It's just embarrassing, and depressing.'

Then he heard the sound of gunfire. For a moment Troy thought it was his imagination. Sometimes he got so lost in a comic that the story seemed more real than the world around him. But as he turned the page to see Batman punch out one of the Joker's henchmen, he heard it again. Gunshots, followed by screaming.

This time he knew he *wasn't* imagining it.

The store owner – a chubby man with a ponytail and half-moon glasses – peered out into the mall. A woman ran past, wide-eyed with terror.

Troy dumped the Batman comic and ran over to the window. "What's going on?" he asked.

The store owner shook his head. "No idea."

Both of them flinched as another round of gunfire echoed through the mall. They stared as men, women and children fled in every direction. A few shoppers stood frozen in shock, while others cowered behind pillars and hid behind litter bins.

More gunshots. The fast food place opposite emptied in a flash. People knocked over tables and chairs in their rush to escape. Only one man remained. He lay across a table as spilt ketchup dripped onto the floor below.

It took a moment for Troy to realise it wasn't ketchup at all. It was blood.

Sickened at the sight, at last Troy grasped what was happening. The mall was under attack! He felt a surge of sheer panic – what to do next? His parents had gone for a coffee on the first floor. *Should he go and find them? Should he stay where he was? Or should he run?*

Troy pressed his face against the glass, scanning for his parents among the fleeing crowd. But the mall was in total chaos. He was about to give up hope when he spotted them race down the escalator and towards the comic store.

"The A.F.!" he heard his father scream. *"Run, Troy, run!"*

CHAPTER 2
ARMY OF FREEDOM

Troy knew from the TV news that A.F. stood for "Army of Freedom" – a terrorist group that launched random violent attacks on Terminus City and its people. He'd never been caught up in anything like this before. He'd always imagined that such horror and tragedy happened to other people. Not to him and his family.

Troy stared out the window of the comic store as five people in black combat trousers and black hooded jackets marched down the glossy walkways of the mall. Their faces were hidden behind blank white masks. Only their eyes could be seen through the two slits in the plastic. The lead terrorist strode along like some faceless terminator, firing his compact F4000 assault rifle at anything that moved.

Troy watched helpless as the terrorist swung the gun to point at his parents. "LOOK OUT!" he screamed.

But Troy's warning came too late.

The F4000 thundered in the man's grip. Bullets flew.

Troy's mother went down first.

His father stopped to pull her up. A bullet clipped his arm and spun him round. But he still managed to dive on top of her body to shield her.

The terrorist fired again.

His parents' bodies jerked in the storm of bullets, then lay still.

A cry of horror rose up in Troy's throat. He pounded at the window in despair. Then the terrorist turned to face him and opened fire. Troy threw himself to the floor as the store window shattered. Shards of glass rained down on him.

He heard screams as the other customers fled for the back exit. But Troy was frozen rigid with fear, too horrified by his parents' deaths to move.

The store owner slammed the front door shut and tried to lock it. In his panic he seemed to have forgotten that a glass door would be no match for an automatic rifle firing ten rounds per second. Bullets shattered the door and flung the store owner back. He landed in a bloody, broken heap by the sales desk.

The masked terrorist stepped inside.

Only now did some survival instinct impel Troy to move.

He scrambled to his feet, shoved away a comic stand and darted for the rear exit. The stand skidded across the floor and hit the terrorist. It knocked off his aim, and bullets ripped into a shelf of magazines instead of Troy.

Troy looked back and saw that the man's hood had come down. He caught a flash of shaved blond hair and a small black tattoo behind the man's left ear before the terrorist batted away the comic stand and took aim again.

But Troy wasn't the target any more. It was the cute girl who'd smiled at him earlier.

She was curled up in a ball on the floor. Troy could see that she was trembling with fear. He sprinted in her direction, flew forward and landed on top of her. The terrorist's machine gun roared and Troy felt the first of the deadly bullets hit him.

CHAPTER 3
MEDUSA

Troy woke to a strange electronic *beep ... beep ... beep ...*

His eyes flickered open and he saw that there were sensors attached to his bare chest. He lay in a hospital bed in a white room with no windows. A bank of hi-tech medical monitors displayed his heartbeat and other vital signs. The screens gave off a soft green glow.

As his eyes came into full focus, Troy saw a tall woman standing at the end of his bed. Her hair was a shock of twisted white spikes. This extreme style seemed at odds with the smart silver-grey business suit, leather gloves and long silver earrings that she wore. Her thin lips stretched in a friendly smile but the warmth didn't reach her eyes, which were as cold and grey as stone.

"How are you feeling, Troy?" she asked in a clipped English accent.

"All right ... I think," he replied, as he sat up in the bed. His muscles felt stiff and sore and he could see a dark line of bruises on his left-hand side, but that seemed to be the worst of it.

"A miracle, after what happened to you." The woman held up an ultra-thin glass pad and pressed the 'play' icon on the screen. "This is –"

"Who are you?" Troy interrupted. "Are you a doctor?"

"I'm Medusa," she said, and she thrust out a gloved hand as if she had only just remembered her manners. Then she pointed to the screen.

"As I was saying, this is from a CCTV camera at the time of the terrorist attack."

Troy looked at the screen and saw a scrawny white kid with sandy cropped hair and a gawky manner in the comic store. Himself – no wonder he had no luck with girls!

On the screen, the shop window shattered and Troy dropped to the floor.

"Fast reactions," Medusa remarked.

Now the terrorist entered and Troy pushed the magazine stand and ran for the exit.

"Good thinking to use the stand to throw off the gunman's aim," Medusa said with a curt nod of approval.

Troy hadn't meant to hit the terrorist at all. The stand had just been in his way. But he didn't correct her.

Next he saw himself dive on top of the girl.

"That was brave of you to try and save her," Medusa said.

"But I ... I didn't," Troy stammered.

Medusa smiled at him. "Don't be so modest," she said. "The girl's alive and well, thanks to you."

On the screen the terrorist's gun went on blasting out bullets. Troy's heart raced at the sight of his body shuddering with each shot.

"Turn it off! Please!" he begged. He couldn't bear to watch any more of the brutal assault. It reminded him about what had happened to his parents.

Medusa swiped the screen and the image disappeared.

"I'm glad the girl's OK, but how did we ever survive *that*?" Troy asked.

"My dear," Medusa replied, "*you* survived because you're bulletproof."

Troy stared at her. "You are joking, aren't you?"

But this mysterious woman didn't look like the sort of person who made jokes.

"You saw it for yourself," Medusa said. "That terrorist shot you at point blank range with over 15 high-velocity 45mm rounds. Not even a soldier's Kevlar body armour vest could have stood up to an attack like that."

"But that's impossible," Troy said. He now believed he was either dead, dreaming or delusional. He pinched himself but he didn't wake up.

"No, it's not impossible," Medusa said. "You're not like most humans. The cells of your skin have an unusually high carbon content and are arranged in a honeycomb pattern. When you're hit by a bullet, your skin can harden and spread the energy over a large area. This means your body can withstand ten times the impact that steel can."

Troy's jaw dropped open in shock. He remembered how he'd been hit by a car the year before as he fled from a gang of bullies. The paramedic on the scene said he should have been killed. But Troy hadn't even broken a bone. At the time everyone thought he'd just been very lucky.

"Are you saying I'm like … *Superman?*" he asked.

Medusa let out a snort of laughter. "No, dear, you don't have his strength or his looks, I'm afraid. But with the right training, we could make you into a super*boy*."

Troy frowned. "Training? What are you talking about?"

Medusa smiled her cold smile. "Troy," she said. "I'm here to recruit you as a bulletcatcher."

CHAPTER 4
BEST HOPE

"I head up SPEAR, a secret protection agency,"
Medusa explained, as Troy lay in his hospital
bed and listened with growing amazement.
"SPEAR provides security for the rich and
powerful in Terminus City. A lot of the time we
work with the sons and daughters of important
families. Our services are needed more than
ever with the increased threat from terrorists
like the A.F. That means we need more
recruits –"

"You mean there are others like me?" Troy
asked.

Medusa nodded. "Yes, but they all have
different *talents*."

Troy sank back on his pillow, stunned by what he was hearing.

"You have the natural instinct and the physical talent to be a bulletcatcher," Medusa stated. "All you have to do is sign this release form and we can begin your training."

She held out the pad again. A digital contract was on the screen. Troy looked at it and all of a sudden he realised what she was saying.

"I can't be a *bodyguard*!" he protested. He pushed the pad away. "You've got the wrong guy. I'm always the *last* one anyone chooses for sport at school. No one would want *me* as their bulletcatcher. I was scared to death in that mall. I just wanted to escape."

"That's the best response in a crisis," Medusa replied. "Escape – get yourself and the VIP out as fast as you can."

"I ... I can't be a bulletcatcher," Troy insisted. "I have to go back to school."

"And *who's* going to make sure you get to school?" Medusa asked.

"My mu –" Troy began. Then he felt his breath cut off as he remembered again that his mother and father were dead. Murdered in cold blood by an A.F. terrorist. Troy choked back a sob and stared up at the ceiling as his eyes stung with tears.

"I am very sorry for your parents' deaths," Medusa said. She sat on the edge of Troy's bed and gave his arm a soft pat. "It must be hard for you. Our records show you have no other family in Terminus City. You're alone in this world. So, what are you going to do? You can't go back to Poland. You have no family left there either. Where are you going to live? How are you going to survive?"

Troy swallowed hard and tried to fight back the tears. He didn't have any answers.

"You're an orphan, Troy, and your parents were immigrants," Medusa went on. "In this city, children like you don't last long. And no one can adopt. Not with the Council's One Family, One Child policy. But SPEAR will take care of you."

She put the digital release form in his hands.

"I ... don't know," Troy said. He felt utterly lost and desperate.

"Join SPEAR. It's your best hope," Medusa urged.

Troy looked at her. Her stone-grey eyes seemed to fill his blurred vision. She was right. *What other choice did he have?*

CHAPTER 5
SPEAR

"Welcome to SPEAR HQ," Medusa said, as her car came to a stop outside a run-down old building.

After Troy had signed the release form with his fingerprint, Medusa had taken him to his parents' tiny rented flat. They had collected his few belongings and arranged for the rest of his family's possessions to be put in storage. The only item that was of any value to Troy was a photo of him with his parents. He'd pocketed this before he left the flat to start on his new and unexpected life as a bulletcatcher.

Troy peered out the car's tinted windows at the crumbling red brick building.

"It's a library!" he said in astonishment.

"Exactly," Medusa said. "It's the perfect cover. Now everything is online, who goes to a library any more?"

"I do," Troy admitted. He felt like more of a geek than ever.

Medusa raised a thin eyebrow at him. "Why doesn't that surprise me? Now follow me."

The doors of the car opened and Medusa led Troy up the stone steps. Inside the place was deserted – there was only an outmoded library bot on duty.

The bot tracked their movements as Medusa headed over to the lift. They stepped inside and she pressed her thumb to an ID scanner. The lift juddered then went down. Troy watched the floor number drop from 0 to –1, to –2 … and then it went blank. But still the lift went down.

Troy was about to ask if the lift was broken when the doors opened onto a gleaming silver and white reception area. Discreet lighting glowed ultraviolet blue, and glass displays on the walls showed news feeds and security updates from around the world. The reception was so sleek and hi-tech that Troy felt as if he'd stepped onto a starship.

A security guard stood to attention at the desk and greeted Medusa. Behind the guard Troy spied a CCTV monitor with a video image of the library they'd just walked through. The library bot must really be a surveillance droid!

"Where's Kasia?" Medusa demanded.

"On her way," the guard replied. "I've pinged her. *Several* times."

Medusa's lips thinned in irritation. Then a girl in a pink workout top and grey joggers strolled along the curved corridor towards them. She had platinum-blonde hair, snow-white skin and bewitching ice-blue eyes. She reminded Troy of his cousin Anna in Finland. He'd only ever seen Anna in a photo, but the two girls shared the same striking looks.

"Timing is everything, Kasia," Medusa said in a stern tone. "You should know that as a bulletcatcher."

"Time is all about how you see it," Kasia replied. Her attitude was as ice-cool as her looks.

Medusa narrowed her eyes in warning. "Kasia, show our new recruit around and introduce him to the others," she snapped. "And don't be late again!"

Medusa told Troy that she would see him later and then strode off down the corridor. Her high heels clicked on the polished marble floor.

Kasia gave Medusa a salute. "Yes, your highness," she said under her breath. Then she turned to Troy. "Medusa is all right but she can be a real taskmaster at times," she said with a smirk. "So you're Troy?"

Troy nodded.

"Is it true? Did you *really* stop a bullet?" she asked.

Troy gave another nod.

Kasia whistled. "Impressive! And do you speak at all?"

Troy nodded again. He was entranced by her blue eyes, and he'd become totally tongue-tied.

Kasia laughed. "I look forward to it. Come with me. Let's get this tour over with, then we can chill."

She led him along the corridor to a door marked with an emerald green logo. It showed a graphic of a spearhead and the letters S.P.E.A.R. ran down its centre.

Troy finally plucked up the courage to speak. "What does SPEAR stand for?"

"Security, Protection and Elemental Assault Response," Kasia replied.

"Elemental?" Troy said.

"It refers to the natural superpowers a bulletcatcher like you has," Kasia said, and she pressed her thumb to the ID scanner.

The door slid open and they entered a huge round chamber. They were on an upper gallery looking down onto a sunken floor. Three circles of padded seats sloped to the centre of the chamber where there was a large hologram desk. Above this hung four mega screens.

"This is our briefing room for missions," Kasia explained. She pointed to a row of doors on the far side of the chamber. "That's our accommodation block. Your bed cell is the one on the far right with the blue border."

She walked him round the upper gallery. "Here's our main classroom ... and this is the fitness gym and combat zone."

Troy peered through a narrow window and saw stacks loaded with heavy weights, a row of resistance machines, six treadmills and a martial arts dojo. "Why do you have a gym?" he asked. "I thought everyone used Fit Pills."

"If only!" Kasia laughed. "Our combat instructor is old-school. He believes you can't get truly fit without real sweat and tears. His motto is – 'No blood, no guts, no glory.' So be prepared to *bleed* in your training. Literally!"

Troy's eyes widened in alarm. He wasn't a natural athlete, and the Fit Pills had been far too expensive for his family to ever use.

Kasia gave him a kind smile. "Don't worry, it's not all bad. The food is good and we don't ever go without," she said. She showed him a large dining area filled with the mouth-watering aroma of *real* food. Troy had forgotten what it was like – like most of the population he had grown up on synthetic meals.

Kasia carried on with the tour. "We also have a state-of-the-art Rec Room with GameChairs, a virtual cinema and even a Prism Table – but Lennox broke one of the laser cues last week."

"A Prism Table?" Troy exclaimed. "Are you serious?" He had only ever seen one on TV before.

"Well, if you like the sound of that …" Kasia said, as she stopped outside a door with a red border. "You're going to love the Reactor Room."

CHAPTER 6
REACTOR ROOM

The door slid open and a small black ball rocketed towards Troy's head. Troy had no time to avoid it. But in the blink of an eye Kasia stepped forward and caught the missile in mid-air. Just millimetres from Troy's shocked face.

"Spoilsport!" a stocky kid with an American accent called. He sat at a control desk in a small darkened room. "We all know Troy can stop a bullet, but I wanted to see if he could *dodge* one."

"Meet Lennox, the joker of our pack," Kasia said. She tossed the ball back at the boy.

Lennox ducked. But with the build of a trainee pro wrestler, he struggled to avoid the returning shot.

Kasia looked at Troy. "What are you staring at?"

Troy was still amazed at the speed of her reaction to the attack. "How did you move so fast?" he asked.

Kasia shrugged. "My talent is Reflex. I react six times faster than most humans."

"6.8 times faster, to be exact," a skinny boy with short brown hair and glasses corrected her. He was sat hunched over a computer, and his fingers flew across the touchscreen even as he spoke. "Kasia's metabolic rate is double normal levels," he explained. "She also has enhanced visual powers. Her eyes react faster and absorb three times more data in one second than a normal human's eyes. Her brain processes this data faster too, so Kasia can make rapid decisions. So, when she's on full alert, she experiences time as if it's passing in slow motion. Basically, Kasia is like a fly."

"Thanks, Joe," Kasia said. Her voice dripped with sarcasm. "You do know how to pay a girl a compliment!"

Joe looked up at her with a frown on his face. "It wasn't a compliment. It's a fact."

Kasia rolled her eyes at him and he went back to his manic typing.

"Why don't you show Troy what you can really do?" said a voice from the corner of the room. Troy spun to see an Asian girl in a purple T-shirt and dark glasses, her long dark hair twisted into a high bun.

Kasia sighed. "I'm not a circus act, Azumi."

"Joe's spent the day upgrading the Reactor software," Lennox said in a teasing tone. "I bet you can't beat the system now."

Kasia rose to the challenge. "Fifty credits says I do."

"You're on!" Lennox agreed with a grin.

A side door opened and Kasia disappeared into the main Reactor Room. Troy joined Lennox and Joe at the control desk. They peered through a window and saw Kasia standing in the middle of a circular room with a domed roof. The walls were glowing white, with thousands of faint circles dotting the surface.

The lights in the control room dimmed and the Reactor Room transformed into a street scene teeming with people and cars.

"This is a simulator," Joe explained. "It creates a real-world experience. The avatars have their own personalities and you can interact with them. We use this system to practise dealing with attacks on VIPs. With regular training sessions, the system can improve a bulletcatcher's response time to a threat by up to 50%. This could mean the difference between life and death on a real mission."

Kasia was observing the virtual crowd when a man appeared with a handgun. A hard black ball shot out from a circle in the wall, as if it had come from the weapon. Kasia had little trouble avoiding the speeding bullet.

"The scene and people may be virtual, but those balls are real," Lennox explained as Kasia sidestepped another attack. "You *don't* want to be hit by one."

"Think of this like an ultra-fast and painful form of dodgeball," Azumi said.

"Time to test the upgrade ... and Kasia," Joe said. He slid a finger across the control panel.

All of a sudden, multiple attackers appeared. But Kasia evaded them all with ease.

She bobbed and weaved and darted round the room at lightning speed.

"She's like Neo from *The Matrix*!" Troy said.

"The *what?*" Lennox asked with a frown.

"It's an old sci-fi movie," Troy said, as Kasia ducked, dived and dodged the balls flying in all directions across the Reactor Room.

After five minutes, the system ran out of ammo and the session ended. Kasia came back into the control room, out of breath but unhurt.

"You owe me fifty credits, Lennox," she said, and she held out her hand.

With a reluctant grunt, Lennox fished in his pocket for a transfer chip.

Kasia looked at Troy. "Fancy a go?"

Troy shook his head. "Looks far too hard for me."

"I'll re-set it to beginner mode," Joe said. "We can start when you're ready."

Troy realised he no longer had an excuse, and so he stepped inside the Reactor Room. A few seconds later, a restaurant scene appeared. Guests sat at tables while others chatted by the bar.

Troy could hear a piano in the background and a waiter was moving among the guests with a tray of drinks. But Troy couldn't spot any obvious attackers. Then a pretty blonde girl in a short satin dress came up to him.

"Hi, handsome," she said, with a dazzling smile.

As she waltzed past, Troy couldn't take his eyes off her.

"Excuse me, sir, would you like a drink?" the waiter asked.

Troy turned to the waiter to say no and found himself staring into the barrel of a gun. A black ball shot out and hit him dead centre in the forehead.

CHAPTER 7
APOLLO

"Not the best place to catch a bullet!" Kasia smirked the next morning as she admired the perfect circle of a red mark on Troy's forehead.

The team were gathered in the fitness gym for their first training session of the day. Troy stared down at the floor. He was still embarrassed by his swift defeat in the Reactor Room.

"Don't worry," Lennox said. He slapped Troy on the back and almost snapped his spine. "I fell for Jinx too. Who wouldn't? She's hot."

"Jinx is a program subroutine," Joe said. "She's designed to distract the user before an attack and to teach you how important it is to focus during a –"

"WHAT A BUNCH OF MISFITS, NERDS, WIMPS AND SLOBS YOU LOT ARE!" A colossal man in a red tracksuit had appeared and was thundering at them.

Troy had been warned by Kasia at breakfast that their fitness and combat instructor was a fearsome man, but nothing could have prepared him for Apollo. He had a shaven head and was the size of a bull. He looked just as strong ... and just as mean.

"You know the drill!" Apollo bawled. "You get your warm-up done *before* I get here. Now go, go, GO!"

There was a groan from the team as they got onto the treadmills and began running. Troy stepped onto his machine and searched for the start button.

"Let's see what you've got, Troy," Apollo said. He stabbed the display to life and held down the speed button.

Troy's legs went from under him and he had to sprint just to stay on the machine. When he was happy that Troy was going fast enough, Apollo moved on to Lennox. He was walking.

"Come on, Fatty, shift!" Apollo said, and he pressed the speed button.

"I'm not fat," Lennox panted. His curly dark hair was damp with sweat. "I'm double-muscled!"

"Tell that to your mama," Apollo snarled.

"It's true," Joe said, as he jogged beside them. "Lennox has the Hercules gene. It means he has muscles 25% larger and 50% stronger than an average human. If his bones were as strong, he could punch through a brick wall –"

"Save your breath for running, Joe," Apollo warned. "Strength without stamina is like a battle tank without fuel. Useless!"

They did ten minutes at full pelt on the treadmills, and then Apollo shouted, "PRESS-UPS."

Troy was relieved just to get off his machine. He dropped to the floor and lay gasping for breath. From the other side of the room, Apollo counted out reps at top volume. Troy was beginning to think that the crazy instructor could only shout, when Apollo spoke to him. "How many, Troy?"

"Errr ... none," he replied.

"NONE?" Apollo bellowed in fury. He moved to stand over Troy and re-started the count.

"One!"

Troy's arms shook as he raised himself off the floor.

"Two!"

Troy managed another press-up then collapsed. "I *can't* ... do any more," he wheezed. "I feel sick."

"I don't care if you vomit and have to dip your face in it," replied Apollo. "There's no *can't* in my gym. You won't stop until you sweat blood!"

Joe piped up. "That's not possible because –"

"Quit your science babble, Joe," Apollo snapped. "It's just a saying!"

He shook his head in despair at Troy's pathetic attempt to do a third press-up. Seeing it was a lost cause, Apollo said, "OK, time to pound those punch bags before our new excuse for a recruit bursts a blood vessel."

The team jumped up and stood in front of a row of solid leather bags hanging on hooks from the ceiling.

"I want five 30-second rounds of jab-cross-jab," Apollo barked. "Starting now!"

As they punched the bags, he went on shouting. "In an attack situation, your first plan should be to escape with the VIP."

Troy jabbed his left fist at his bag. It was like punching cement.

"But if you have to confront the threat head on," Apollo explained, "then punch to buy time. As soon as the way is clear, escape."

Troy threw his best effort at a cross. The bag barely twitched under the impact.

Apollo rolled his eyes in dismay. "That punch will buy you *zero* seconds! Put some power behind it, Troy. Hit it like you mean it! A bulletcatcher needs to build muscle memory so that your self-defence becomes second nature. JAB! CROSS! JAB!"

Troy pummelled the bag for all he was worth. His heart pounded in his chest. Sweat

poured off him. His knuckles turned red raw.
Then his wrist crumpled against the rock-solid
bag and pain shot up his arm. But he kept
going, terrified of Apollo's rage.

All of a sudden a loud THUD in the gym
brought everyone to a stop. Lennox had
punched his bag so hard that it had flown off its
hook and split. The bag lay on the floor like a
gutted pig, its stuffing spilling out everywhere.

"Lennox, that's the third bag this month!"
Apollo cried in irritation.

"It's not my fault they don't make them
strong enough," Lennox said. He tried to push
the stuffing back in.

"Leave it!" Apollo snarled. "That's the
warm-up done. Now we can begin the training
session proper."

"Begin?" Troy exclaimed. He dropped to his
knees with exhaustion. "I thought that *was* the
training!"

CHAPTER 8
ONE SECOND FIGHTING

"In a conflict situation," Apollo said, "you have 30 seconds *at most* to defeat your attacker."

Apollo had ignored Troy's pleading and Troy had dragged himself to his feet and joined Kasia and the others in a semi-circle on the padded mats of the dojo. This was Troy's first ever martial arts lesson. He had watched plenty of old samurai and ninja movies, but he had no idea what to expect from their fearsome instructor.

"It's a tactical error to think more time is going to help," Apollo went on. "First, the longer you spend fighting, the more the VIP is put at risk. Second, it's like trying to save yourself from drowning. If you can't do what you need to do in the first 30 seconds, more time will only make matters worse, not better. That's why you need to end the fight *fast* and *first*."

He beckoned Lennox to join him in the middle of the dojo.

"So today we'll go on with our *Kyusho Jitsu* training," Apollo said.

Troy turned to Azumi, who was still wearing her dark glasses. "What's *Kyusho Jitsu?*" he whispered to her.

"The ancient art of pressure point fighting," she replied under her breath. "In English, *Kyusho Jitsu* means 'One Second Fighting'."

"You mean you can defeat someone in *one* second?" Troy exclaimed in disbelief.

"Pay attention!" Apollo turned with a sharp clap of his hands. "As I was saying, *Kyusho Jitsu* works by attacking the weaker points of the human body. For example ..." He strode over to Troy and raised a rock-hard fist. "If I was to give you a light punch in the head, it would have little effect."

Troy cowered from his instructor's threat – he didn't care how 'light' the impact might be, he knew it would hurt.

"If I punched a bit harder, I might bruise your face," Apollo went on. "Harder again, and you might stagger back, or even be dazed. Full force, I'll probably break your nose and knock you out. But I might also damage my hand on your thick skull. So, what if ..."

Without warning, Apollo poked two fingers into Troy's eyes.

"Ow!" Troy cried. He jerked away and clasped a hand to his throbbing eyeballs. "What did you do that for?"

"To show you the principle of *Kyusho Jitsu*," Apollo said. It was clear he had no sympathy for Troy. "That attack was very light, but the result was dramatic. A big effect for a small amount of force. Do you understand now?"

Troy nodded his head. He didn't need another practical example.

"Good, lesson learned!" Apollo said, and he strode back over to Lennox. "We'll begin with pressure point ST-9."

Apollo placed a finger at the front of Lennox's neck, just to the right-hand side of his Adam's apple. "A strike to this point at the correct angle and force can stun and drop an attacker," he explained.

He gave Lennox's neck a light tap with the edge of his hand. Lennox collapsed to his knees as if he were a puppet and Apollo had cut his strings.

"As you can see, this is very effective," Apollo said, as he pulled Lennox back to his feet. "Anything more than 10% power will knock a person out."

"I'd like to see *that*!" Kasia said with a cheeky grin.

"I'm sure you would," Apollo replied, and he narrowed his eyes. "But I want everyone to be extra careful working on this move. At full force it can kill. Now partner up."

Troy found himself opposite Lennox.

"Take it easy on him," Apollo warned Lennox. "Remember, he isn't a punch bag."

Troy looked over at the ripped leather bag lying on the floor and began to tremble at what lay in store for him.

Lennox smiled. "Don't worry, I'll be gentle," he promised as his hand connected with Troy's neck.

The jolt that raced through Troy's body felt like a tank hitting him. His legs buckled, his head buzzed and his vision went dark. The last thing heard before he blacked out was Lennox insisting, "But I barely even touched him, *honest ...*"

CHAPTER 9
MISSION PANDORA

One month later

Troy limped out of the Reactor Room.

"Congratulations!" Kasia said. She sat with her feet propped up on the control desk. "You lasted a full minute."

"One minute three seconds, in fact," Joe corrected her. He was studying the Reactor's feedback scores. "That equals a 6.3% daily increase in survival time, while your threat response has improved by 9.4% in the last 30 days."

"Great," Troy said. He hobbled over to a spare chair.

"Not really," Joe replied. "Your overall reaction stats are still far too low. You've only got a 19% chance of surviving in any real world attack."

"Thanks for the morale boost, Joe!" Troy sighed as he slumped into the seat with dismay.

His body hurt all over from combat training and now his leg was numb from where a reactor ball had struck him. Troy had discovered early on that being bulletproof didn't mean he was immune to pain. And the past month had been very long and very painful.

Every morning Troy asked himself if he'd been right to become a bulletcatcher. During the day he was tortured by fitness, martial arts and protection training – from bodycover tactics to foot formations to escape plans. In addition to those sessions, Medusa organised classes for them in threat assessment, mission planning, first aid, radio operation and surveillance detection. And all this was just scraping the surface of what a bulletcatcher needed to master. By the time Troy went to bed each night, his mind and body were burned out.

That said, he could now do 25 full press-ups before Apollo started shouting at him for slacking. There was enough power in his punches now that the bag sometimes swung like a pendulum after he'd hit it. And he knew where the ten most effective *Kyusho* points on the human body were. One of them, in fact, was the GB-31 nerve on the upper leg where the reactor ball had just hit him.

Troy tried to rub some life back into his numb thigh.

"Heads up!" Azumi said. "The Gorgon approaches."

She meant Medusa, who was named after the snake-haired, stony-gazed Gorgon of Greek myth. The control room door was closed, but Azumi still *knew* she was coming.

Troy wasn't surprised by this. Soon after he'd joined SPEAR, he'd discovered why Azumi wore dark glasses all the time. She was blind, and her eyes were as white as milk. Yet Azumi considered herself blessed since she had the talent of Blindsight. Not only could she sense the world around her, enough to move free and unaided in it, she had the power to glimpse into the future.

At breakfast one morning, Azumi had explained that her visions weren't 100% accurate. She only received brief images, sometimes just colours, and maybe no more than a feeling of threat. But, like a canary in a coal mine, she could warn that danger was near.

A moment later the control room door opened and Medusa popped her spiky head inside.

"Briefing room now," she ordered, and disappeared again.

Lennox punched the air in excitement. "We have a mission!"

The team ran out of the control room and into the main chamber. As they took their seats, Medusa was already powering up the hologram desk.

"We've received reports that the Army of Freedom is planning an attack on the Council," she announced. "The A.F.'s target is Mayor Carlos Lomez and his daughter Pandora."

Two holographic images shimmered above the desk. One was a tall man with silver-grey hair, tailored blue suit and movie-star looks. The second was a teenage girl with hazel eyes, braided hair and golden sun-kissed skin.

Lennox nudged Troy with his elbow. "She's even hotter than Reactor Room Jinx!"

Troy had to agree. As far as he could tell from the hologram, Pandora could be a supermodel, if she chose.

"Our mission is to protect Pandora at the opening of a new 'Fresh Air Park' in the Eastern Zone of the city," Medusa explained. The hologram father and daughter were replaced by an interactive 3D map. Medusa pointed to a large green and blue dome among endless grey tower blocks. "Here's the park. Now, this is a public event, so we'll need to be on the look-out for *anything* unusual."

"Any intel on the type of threat we can expect?" Azumi asked.

Medusa shook her head. "The A.F.'s methods are hard to predict. It could be a gun assault, a bomb, a laser strike, a chemical attack or even a hoax. Whatever it turns out to be, our job is to keep Pandora safe."

Lennox put up his hand. "Can I be T.L. for this mission?"

"No, Kasia is team leader," Medusa replied. Lennox groaned with disappointment but she ignored him. "You, Joe and Azumi will form the defence ring around the VIP," she told him. "Troy will be the principal bulletcatcher."

"Me?" Troy exclaimed. "B ... but I'm not ready for a mission yet."

Medusa fixed him with her stone-grey eyes. "With your talent, you were born ready."

CHAPTER 10
TATTOO

Troy stood beside Pandora as she greeted the cheering crowd in the Fresh Air Park. He kept to her right-hand side, about a metre back at all times. SPEAR had taught him that this was the best position for a bulletcatcher – out of the VIP's personal space yet close enough to grab and shield them in the event of an attack.

Kasia and the rest of the team were dotted about in a loose circle, scanning the park for threats. Since they blended in with the other kids at the park opening, no one in the crowd paid them any heed.

Carlos Lomez walked into the park, stopping to shake hands with the cheering crowd. As the mayor and chairman of the Council he was a very powerful man, but despite this he was still pretty popular. His Fight Against Fear campaign had struck a chord with people who were worried about the rise of the A.F. and other terrorist groups. And his green policies were popular in a city choked with pollution. The new Fresh Air Park was a wonder. Under the 3-mile-wide dome was a paradise of green grass, tall trees, blue lakes and clean, fresh air.

"Troy, stay focused!" Kasia hissed in Troy's earpiece. "You should be watching the crowd, not Pandora!"

Troy blinked. He hadn't realised he was staring at her. Half an hour before, he'd been introduced to the mayor and his daughter. Shy as ever, Troy had been lost for words. Pandora had looked a bit worried.

"I thought my bulletcatcher would be …
bigger," she'd said, but then she'd put on a
cheery smile and added, "Well, let's just hope
nobody attacks us today, eh?"

Troy hadn't known how to respond so he'd
simply followed her like a faithful puppy dog.

He now focused on the task in hand and
scanned the countless faces around Pandora –
bright-eyed children, smiling mothers, excited
teenagers and cheering fathers. Flashes from
dozens of cameras blinded Troy as reporters
jostled to get the best shot for that night's
news. Cheering and clapping filled the air,
adding to the confusion.

How was Troy supposed to spot a threat in
such a huge crowd?

Then Troy caught a glimpse of shaved blond
hair and a small black tattoo. His heart almost
stopped in his chest. He could swear he'd just
seen the terrorist from the shopping mall.

Or had he imagined it?

Almost every night, Troy relived his parents' brutal murder. He would wake in a fevered sweat from a nightmare in which a faceless tattooed monster chased him through a dark maze-like mall for hours until at last Troy felt the bullets rip into his back …

Troy craned his neck to look for the man again, but the crowd had swallowed him up.

"I think I've seen an A.F. terrorist," he whispered into his mic. "The one that killed my parents."

"Where?" Kasia responded over the radio.

"To my right, 15 metres into the crowd," Troy replied.

"Draw closer, catchers," Kasia said, and the team tightened the defence ring around Pandora. "Do you sense anything, Azumi?"

"Negative," Azumi replied.

"Troy, what's the suspect's profile?" Lennox said.

"Blond hair. Heavy build. Tattoo behind his left ear," Troy told them.

"We'll need more than that to go on," Kasia said, as she scanned the crowd.

"Describe the tattoo," said Joe.

"Err, it's ... like a stick man without a head," Troy said.

"The kanji symbol for Fire," Joe said right away. "I saw that same tattoo earlier. The suspect is white, 1.85 metres, 86 kilos, and in his mid-thirties. He's wearing sunglasses, a white cotton T-shirt and a heavy black jacket with a hood. I consider that weird on such a hot day, so the odds are he's carrying a weapon –"

"You heard, Joe," Medusa interrupted. She was monitoring the situation from the mobile ops van. "Everyone, stay sharp."

Troy edged closer to Pandora as he looked for the terrorist among the crowd.

"Should we evac the VIP?" Lennox asked.

"Not yet," Medusa replied. "Do not act unless a real threat is identified. A false alarm could be embarrassing for the mayor, as well as SP–"

"Code Red!" Azumi cut in over the radio. "I've had a vision."

"Any details?" Kasia asked.

"No," Azumi said. "Just a purple colour. I think someone intends to attack."

"I can't see him," Troy said, and his voice shook with panic. "Where's he gone? He's disap–"

All of a sudden, a woman pushed to the front of the crowd and hurled a grenade at Pandora. Troy saw it fly through the air. He froze in terror as the lethal device dropped towards Pandora.

Troy was bulletproof, not bomb proof!

At the last split-second, Kasia stepped in and pulled Pandora clear. Joe, Azumi and Lennox all piled on top to shield her from the blast. The grenade struck Troy in the chest. The casing shattered, splattering black liquid all over his T-shirt.

The Council's security force went into overdrive.

"CHEM ATTACK!" one of the bodyguards shouted. He grabbed the mayor and rushed him over to a limo that was waiting on stand-by.

As the crowd panicked and screamed, two security guards tackled the woman who'd

thrown the grenade. Kasia and the rest of the team bundled Pandora into a second limo and shot off at high speed.

Troy looked down at his chest and was amazed he was still alive. At last he snapped out of his daze and sprinted after them. But an Emergency Response Squad in full-body yellow protective suits appeared and blocked his path.

"*Halt!*" they ordered, and Troy was forced to the ground at gunpoint.

CHAPTER 11
HERO GENE

"You were lucky, Troy, that woman was a protester and *not* a terrorist," Medusa said. They were having a team debrief back at SPEAR HQ. "You're even luckier that the 'grenade' was only a water bomb filled with ink. That's why the body scanners at the park gate didn't pick it up."

Troy didn't feel very lucky. He'd been held at gunpoint, stripped naked and his skin had been rubbed raw in case the black liquid was a chemical weapon, and only then did they discover it was harmless black ink! Yet Kasia and the others were still sitting a few seats away from him just to be safe.

"The mayor sends his heartfelt thanks to you all for protecting his daughter," Medusa went on. "He's requested our services again for the Council's annual charity ball next weekend."

A glittering globe with the red C logo of the Council hovered above the hologram desk.

"That's the most secure event of the year," Kasia said. "Why does he need us?"

"Because of the terrorist Troy saw at the park today, we suspect that the A.F. did intend to launch an attack," Medusa explained. "But the protester struck first and disrupted their plans. Which means they will try again."

Medusa closed down the hologram desk and walked up the stairs to the upper gallery. At the exit, she paused and turned to them. "Good work, catchers," she said. "And that was heroic of you, Troy, to stand and take the attack head on."

As the door slid shut behind her, a heavy silence fell over the chamber. Troy sensed everyone's eyes upon him.

"That's not how I remember it," Kasia said. Her snow-white face was flushed with anger. "What happened to you at the park, Troy?"

"He had brain fade," Joe said. "It's a natural response to an attack – fight, flight or freeze. He froze."

"Well, you *can't* freeze if you're a bulletcatcher," said Kasia.

"I'm no bulletcatcher," Troy replied. His voice came out flat and he couldn't meet Kasia's eye.

"Too right you're not!" Kasia said. "I had to cover for you. You failed to react and put Pandora and the rest of the team at risk."

"Don't be so hard on him," Azumi said. "We all make mistakes."

"Yeah, it's just first-time nerves," said Lennox. "Remember, he saved that girl back in the shopping mall. He'll be fine next ti–"

Troy interrupted him. "No, I didn't," he said.

"What do you mean?" said Lennox.

"I tried to tell Medusa, but she wouldn't listen," Troy explained. "I was running for the exit when ... well ... my foot slipped on a comic and I fell on top of the girl. It was by accident."

Kasia and the others stared at him in disbelief.

"Of course I'm glad the girl survived, but I *didn't* try to save her," Troy admitted. "I was trying to save my own skin." He hung his head in shame. "I'm no hero. I'm a coward."

"I knew you were too good to be true," Kasia said. Her voice was harsh with contempt.

"You're a danger to us, Troy. *You* might be bulletproof, but the rest of us aren't!"

With that, she stormed up the stairs and disappeared into the Rec Room.

Azumi followed Kasia. But as she passed Troy, she rested a hand on his arm. "We all have talents for a reason," she said. "You just need to find your reason."

Lennox shrugged. "Hey, I don't know why Kasia's making such a big thing of it. No one died. See you at dinner, Troy."

He bounded up the steps two at a time. Troy was left alone with Joe. He held his head in his hands and stared at the floor. "I may be bulletproof," he said, "but that doesn't mean I have some hero gene!"

"You're right," Joe said. "*You* don't have one."

"Thanks a lot," said Troy. "You're a real help."

"I try to be," Joe said. He put on a smile. "Listen," he said. "I've seen the CCTV film of the mall attack. It was logical for you to run. You didn't know about your bulletproof talent. Without it, there was less than a 5% chance you could save the girl."

"That's enough, Joe!" Troy snapped. "I don't need any more of your statistics. Just leave me alone, will you? What do you know anyway?"

"Everything," Joe replied. "My talent is Recall. In truth, it's just one of my many talents. I can also do advanced computer programming, mathematics and play piano to concert standard. I am also autistic. Autism used to be called a disability, but I consider it an advantage. I have a photographic memory and instant recall. I can speed-read at an amazing rate and retain 98% of the information."

Troy shook his head in confusion. "What are you trying to say, Joe?" he asked.

"There is no single gene that makes someone a hero," Joe said. "If you study history, most heroes are normal people. It's the heroic *act* that's special."

"Well, I *didn't* act." Troy sighed. He sank down in his chair as the sense of his own shame crushed him.

"No, you didn't," said Joe. "But you will act next time. You may be a bulletcatcher but you don't need a special talent to be a hero."

CHAPTER 12
DOUBLE VISION

The ballroom in Terminus City's old opera house was filled with the rich and famous. Politicians, movie stars and energy tycoons mingled with TV personalities, pop stars and supermodels. On the stage a band played old-time jazz, while guests sipped Champagne from neon-lit glasses that changed colour in time with the music. Floating tables served lobster, caviar, quail jelly and a whole roast pig – food Troy had never laid eyes upon before, let alone tasted for real.

The glamorous room and lavish food was the high standard people expected at Terminus City's most exclusive event of the year. But in the midst of all this glitz, the centre of attention was Pandora.

Dressed in a sparkling jumpsuit and a pair of diamond earrings, she was the talk of the party. And with so many people trying to get near her, Troy had his work cut out to spot any potential threats.

As Troy scanned the crowd over and over, he felt as taut as a loaded spring. His nerves were on a razor's edge. After his chat with Joe, he was no longer scared of an attack. He was scared he wouldn't react in time and so might risk the team's lives again ... and Pandora's.

There was a lull in the stream of guests, and Pandora turned to Troy.

"I haven't had the chance to thank you," she whispered. "I'm sorry I was rude about your ability to protect me. You did a great job."

Troy responded with an awkward smile. "It was Kasia who *really* saved you."

Pandora raised an eyebrow. "You're very humble, Troy. I like that."

Troy felt his cheeks redden at the compliment, even if he didn't deserve it.

"I also like the fact you don't talk too much," she added. "The boys I know just go on about themselves all the time. Of course, they just want to impress me because of who I am. You're not like that, Troy."

Pandora graced him with one of her dazzling smiles, and then she wandered off into the crowd. Troy followed a few discreet steps behind, yet close enough to intervene if he was needed. In a social situation like this one, the guests had been checked by security guards with body scanners at the door, and that meant Troy didn't need to be right beside his VIP at all times.

Troy watched Pandora greet each person in turn as she made them laugh and asked them

to dig deep into their pockets for the charity auction. He wondered why anyone would want to hurt her in the first place.

A young model in a gold sequin dress shimmied up to him. "Aren't you that mystery boy on the news?" she said, with a sweet smile. "The one who saved Pandora?"

When Troy didn't reply, she took that as a yes.

"I'm Tabitha," she said, and she rested a hand on his arm. "So what's your name?"

"Troy," he managed to reply.

'Typical!' he thought. He'd never had any luck with girls, but now he seemed to have become a magnet for them. Perhaps there was some benefit to being a bulletcatcher after all! But as pretty as this girl Tabitha was, Troy knew that he couldn't allow himself to become distracted.

"Sorry, I've got to go," he said. He offered her a polite smile and then followed Pandora across the ballroom.

"Catch you later," Tabitha said with a playful wink.

Lennox's voice sounded in Troy's ear. "Did you get her number, Romeo?"

"No," Troy said, as he took up guard near Pandora again. "Where are you?"

"By the food, of course." Lennox chuckled. "The lobster is amazing –"

"Stop thinking with your stomach, Lennox," Kasia cut in. "You're not here to enjoy yourself."

Troy spotted Kasia off to his left. She was studying one of the artworks up for auction – a tall glass sculpture of a breaking wave – but Troy knew that she was really watching the ballroom in its reflection. As he passed her,

Kasia refused to make eye contact. Even after a week, she was still angry with him.

"Any sign of your terrorist yet?" she demanded through her mic.

"Negative," he replied.

"Joe, how about you?" she asked.

Joe stood near the stage, where he appeared to be listening to the band. "So far I've spotted three men with the same build and height as our suspect," he said. "But none have blond hair or a visible tattoo."

"Maybe the A.F. have been scared off by all the security?" Lennox said.

"Don't speak too soon," said Azumi. "I've just had a vision – a knife."

Troy eyed the people near Pandora. "I see no threat."

"Nor do I," said Kasia.

"Azumi, you must be sensing the chef's knife," Lennox said. "He's about to carve up the pig."

A bearded man in a chef's hat stood over the hog roast, sharpening a long blade.

"No," Azumi responded. "I'm seeing a lot of red. Someone is very angry."

As Azumi spoke, the sound of raised voices came from the other side of the room. An elegant red-haired woman threw a glass of Champagne into a man's face, then stormed off.

"False alarm," Lennox said.

Then Troy spotted a waiter with short blond hair heading for Pandora.

"Maybe not," he said. He moved fast to cut the man off. "Suspect waiter at 12 o'clock!"

He was about to confront the suspect, when Kasia cried out, "It's not him. It's your model in the gold dress!"

Troy spun to see Tabitha make a beeline for Pandora. There was a glint of steel in her hand.

Kasia shot forward with the speed of an arrow and struck the girl in the neck at the ST-9 pressure point. Tabitha crumpled to the polished wooden floor of the ballroom.

"Something's still wrong," Azumi said. "I'm getting a double vision. There's a gun this time."

That's when Troy saw the chef slice open the belly of the pig and pull out the pistol that was hidden inside.

CHAPTER 13
SACRIFICE

For a moment, time seemed to slow for Troy. He saw everything in great detail as if he had Kasia's Reflex talent.

The ceramic gun that would have escaped the security metal detectors ...

The calm way the chef took aim at Pandora ...

The tell-tale twitch of a muscle as the chef pulled the gun's trigger ...

Troy wasn't even aware that he'd dived into the line of fire. It was pure instinct.

The bullet meant for Pandora struck Troy in the chest like a battering ram. Then the force rippled across his skin, spreading the lethal energy and saving him from harm. Winded from the impact, Troy hit the ground hard.

The chef swore in anger and fired again just as Lennox shoved the entire floating table of roast pig into him. The chef was thrown back against the wall. His aim was knocked off and his hat fell to one side to reveal short blond hair and the kanji Fire tattoo.

The second bullet whistled past Pandora, missing her by a fraction and hitting the wave sculpture instead. The priceless artwork exploded, sending fragments of glass flying across the ballroom floor. Screams filled the air and guests began to run in all directions. Kasia and Azumi seized Pandora and rushed her towards the exit.

Lennox made a grab for the chef. He got a handful of his beard, but the chef ripped his

head away and fled out the swing doors into the kitchen.

Troy was reeling from the impact of the bullet but still very much alive. He staggered to his feet and ran after the terrorist.

"Where are you going?" Lennox shouted. He was still holding the chef's false beard in his hand.

Troy clutched a hand to his bruised chest and gasped, "To catch my parents' killer."

He sprinted into the kitchen, but he couldn't see the terrorist anywhere.

"Troy, there's only one exit," Joe said over his earpiece. "Far right, to the back."

Troy spotted a door swinging shut. He ran over, burst into a stairwell and glimpsed a figure running upwards. Racing after the suspect, he took the steps two at time. He was grateful now for Apollo's painful fitness sessions.

Above him, he heard a door slam. Five flights later, Troy reached the top of the stairs where a fire door led onto the roof of the opera house. He shoved it open with his shoulder and burst out into a neon-lit night.

The blond-haired terrorist was waiting for him, with the gun primed in his hand.

Troy was blown off his feet by a second bullet.

"You don't die easily, do you?" the terrorist said as he stood over Troy's body.

Behind the man's back, Troy could see the lights of a heli-plane coming in to land. The terrorist raised his hand and signalled to the pilot.

"Why ... did you kill my parents?" Troy groaned.

The terrorist cocked his head to one side. "Did I?"

"At the mall. You shot them."

"In a war for freedom, sacrifices must be made," the terrorist replied. He pointed his gun at Troy's head. "No sacrifice, no victory."

With a squeeze of the trigger, he shot Troy point blank.

Troy fell still.

He was out cold for a good ten seconds. Then, as if emerging from a free dive deep into the sea, Troy came back to life. He saw the heli-plane making its final approach. In a last attempt to stop the terrorist escaping, Troy leaped up and punched the man's thigh with all his might.

His knuckles struck the pressure point he had aimed for.

The terrorist's leg crumpled under him. As he tried to shoot Troy again, Troy targeted the man's upper arm at pressure point P-2. The terrorist cried out in agony and dropped his gun.

Troy snatched it up.

"Are *you* willing to make the ultimate sacrifice?" Troy said. He aimed the gun and put his finger on the trigger.

"Of course," the terrorist replied. He smiled as he held up in his hands in surrender. "But you have to understand I'm just the weapon. You should be asking yourself, who is *really* pulling the trigger?"

A gunshot rang out and the terrorist slumped at Troy's feet, with a bullet in his heart.

From the roof of the opera house, Troy watched the heli-plane disappear into the night.

CHAPTER 14
BULLETCATCHER

"Well done, bulletcatchers!" Medusa said as she entered the Rec Room at SPEAR HQ the next morning.

Troy and the rest of the team were shattered from the events of the night before. They lay sprawled in the GameChairs, sipping energy smoothies for breakfast.

"Mayor Lomez is deeply grateful for our services," Medusa went on. "And Pandora has asked that Troy become her permanent bulletcatcher from now on."

Lennox elbowed Troy in the ribs and grinned. "You lucky git!"

"Doesn't matter how hot the VIP is, I'm not so lucky if she's getting shot at all the time," Troy replied. His head was still throbbing and his chest still hurt from where the bullets had hit him.

"I should hope that now your terrorist is dead," Medusa said, "the A.F. will think twice before they attack the mayor's daughter again, or anyone else in the Council for that matter." She turned her stone-grey eyes on Kasia. "Oh, and you'll be pleased to know, Kasia, that the model you knocked out cold *isn't* planning to make a complaint."

Then Medusa turned on her heels and left the room.

"Why's she blaming me?" Kasia complained. "So the model wasn't a terrorist. But what sort of idiot carries a make-up mirror shaped like a dagger?"

"It was my fault really," Azumi said. "The double vision confused me."

"We *all* make mistakes," Troy said, remembering that Azumi had used the same words the week before.

Kasia sighed. "I suppose so. I'm sorry I ever doubted you, Troy."

"Now you're a real hero," Joe said. He looked up from the gadget he was programming. "Not just a hero by accident."

Troy laughed. "You don't half have a way with words, Joe."

Troy reached into his pocket and pulled out the photo of his parents. He hoped they would be proud of him and he prayed their spirits could find peace now that their murderer was dead.

Lennox leaned over and whispered. "What I want to know is, did *you* kill that terrorist?"

Troy shook his head. "No, that wasn't me. I'm not a killer. I'm a *bulletcatcher*."

Our books are tested
for children and young people by
children and young people.

Thanks to everyone who consulted on
a manuscript for their time and effort in
helping us to make our books better
for our readers.

BULLET CATCHER

THE
MEMORY

Judith Barrow

HONNO MODERN FICTION

First published in Great Britain in 2020 by Honno Press
'Ailsa Craig', Heol y Cawl, Dinas Powys, Vale of Glamorgan,
Wales, CF64 4AH

1 2 3 4 5 6 7 8 9 10

A catalogue record for this book is available from the British Library.
Published with the financial support of the Books Council of Wales.

ISBN 978-1-912905-13-3 (paperback)
ISBN 978-1-912905-14-0 (ebook)

Cover photograph © Arcangel.com/Kerry Norgard
Cover design: Graham Preston
Text design: Elaine Sharples
Printed in Great Britain by 4Edge

For David – as usual

Acknowledgements

I would like to express my gratitude to those who helped in the publishing of *The Memory*...

To all the staff at Honno for their individual expertise, advice and help. To Caroline Oakley for her thoughtful and empathetic editing.

Special thanks to Thorne Moore, Alex Martin and Sharon Tregenza, dear friends and fellow authors, for their encouragement and enthusiasm for *The Memory*.

And to Janet Thomas, for her suport with all my writing down the years.

Lastly, as ever, to my husband, David; always by my side, always believing in me.

PART ONE

Chapter One

There's a chink of light from the street lamp coming through the vertical blinds. It spreads across the duvet on my mother's bed and onto the pillow next to her head. I reach up and pull the curtains closer together. The faint line of light is still there, but blurred around the edges.

Which is how I feel. Blurred around the edges. Except, for me, there is no light.

I move around the bed, straightening the corners, making the inner softness of the duvet match the shape of the outer material, trying to make the cover lie flat but of course I can't. The small round lump in the middle is my mother. However heavily her head lies on the pillow, however precisely her arms are down by her sides, her feet are never still. The cover twitches until centimetre by centimetre it slides to one side towards the floor like the pink, satin eiderdown used to do on my bed as a child.

In the end I yank her feet up and tuck the duvet underneath. Tonight I want her to look tidy. I want everything to be right.

She doesn't like that and opens her eyes, giving up the pretence of being asleep. Lying face upwards, the skin falling back on her cheekbones, her flesh is extraordinarily smooth, pale. Translucent almost. Her eyes are vague under the thick lines of white brows drawn together.

I ignore her; I'm bone weary. That was one of my father's phrases; he'd come in from working in the bank in the village and say it.

'I'm bone weary, Lil.' He'd rub at the lines on his forehead. 'We had to stay behind for half an hour all because that silly woman's till didn't add up.' Or '... because old Watkins insisted I show the new lad twice how I leave my books at night, just so he knows what to do...'

Old Watkins was the manager, a job my father said he could do standing on his head but never got the chance.

'...as though Watkins thinks I might not go in tomorrow.'

And then, one day, he didn't go into the bank. Or the day after that. Or ever again.

I wait by the bed. I move into her line of vision and it's as if we're watching one another, my mother and me: two women – trapped.

'I can't go on, Mum.' I lift my arms from my side, let them drop; my hands too substantial, too solid to hold up. They're strong – dependable, Sam, my husband, always says. I just think they're like shovels and I've always been resentful that I didn't inherit my mother's slender fingers. After all I got her fat arse and thick thighs, why not the nice bits?

I've been awake for over a day. I glance at the clock with the extra large numbers, bought when she could still tell the time. Now it's just something else for her to stare at, to puzzle over. It's actually twenty-seven hours since I slept, and for a lot of them I've been on my feet. Not that this is out of the ordinary. This has been going on for the last year: long days, longer nights.

'Just another phase she's going through,' the Irish doctor says, patting me on the shoulder as she leaves. 'You're doing a grand job.' While all the time I know she's wondering why – why I didn't give up the first time she suggested that I should; why, by now, I've not admitted it's all too much and said 'Please, please take her away, just for a week, a day, a night. An hour.'

But I don't. Because I have no choice. Mum told me years ago she'd sorted it out with her solicitor. There was no way she'd agree to our selling this house; as a joint owner with Sam and me, she would block any attempt we made. There's no way we could afford to put her into care either; over the years, we've ploughed most of Sam's

4

earnings into the renovation and upkeep of the place. So here I am. Here we are.

But there is another reason, a more precious reason that means I can't – won't leave this house. Rose, is here. It's over thirty years since she left us. But I still sense her next to me, hear her voice sometimes, feel her trying to comfort me. I won't leave her on her own again. I did it once before – I won't do it a second time. Not like that anyway.

'I can't go on, Mum,' I repeat. My head swims with tiredness and I'm so cold inside.

She doesn't answer. She doesn't have to most of the time. I've learned to interpret the noises: the tones of each wail, yell and cry. Even the sniffs. She was always good on the sniffs. She had a whole language of sniffs: contempt, short and sharp, lips pursed; utter displeasure, long drawn out, lip corners pulled in tight; anger, almost silent, nostrils flaring. And then there was her pleased sniff (not used very often), a long spluttering drawing in of breath accompanied by a rare smile.

She watches me. Or is that my imagination? Because as I move, her eyes don't; unfocussed, they're settled on the photograph of the three of us on the beach at Morecambe. I was six in the picture and I'm sitting on Dad's lap: the time it was taken as distant as the vague shoreline behind us; the grey sea as misty, unattainable, and as far away as yesterday's thoughts. At least to her.

Or is she seeing something else? A memory? That memory? I'm hoping that of all the recollections that linger, if any do linger in that blankness that has been her mind for so long, of all the memories, it's that one. The one that makes hate battle with pity and reluctant love. If nothing else, I hope she remembers that.

I feel quite calm. I don't speak; it's all been said.

And now her eyes move from my face, past me. It's as though she knows. I'm so close I see the criss-cross of fine red lines across the whites, the tiny yellow blobs of sleep in the inner corners, the slight stutter of a nerve on the eyelid that moves the sparse lashes.

5

And then she speaks. 'Rose?' she says. Clearly. 'Rose'. Just like that.

1963

I was eight when Rose was born. All that summer I'd watched as my mother's stomach grew larger and rounder. As she moved ever slower, each foot ponderously placed on the ground beneath her. As her face grew tighter with rage and bitterness.

'She's tired, Irene,' Dad said when I asked him what was wrong. We were in the park. It was the week before the autumn term started. The long summer days were behind us, there was a slight chill in the air, but we were making the most of the time that was left.

Thinking about what Dad said, I slowly pushed my foot against the ground. I knew it was more than that; Mum was angry about something.

Normally in summer we went for a week to the seaside. Usually Southport or Morecambe but we hadn't been anywhere for a holiday that year. Or even for one of our picnics at Bramble Clough, a dip in the hill where a tiny stream gurgled through rocks and crannies, bordered by wimberry bushes and dried heather. We'd sit on Dad's tartan blanket and eat beef paste butties and drink lemonade.

I remembered the last time we were there. I'd made a daisy chain...

Mum and Dad were lying on their backs, holding hands. I draped the daisy chain on Mum's head. It fell over her nose and she sneezed. Dad sat up and sang.

' "*Daisy, Daisy, give me your answer do.*
I'm half crazy all for the love of you..."'

Mum and me laughed and stuffed our fingers in our ears. He was so out of tune. Nanna always said Dad couldn't carry a tune in a bucket and she was right. But it didn't ever stop him singing: when he was working in the garden, when he was in the bath, whenever the fancy took him. He used to try to sing me to sleep but Mum stopped him because she said it made me too giddy to settle down.

Dad pretended to take offence so Mum and me jumped on him and tickled him until he shouted "barley" and gave in. The sun shone that day.

Bending and stretching out my legs to make the swing move, I looked around. It was that time of day when mums had already taken the younger children home for their teas. Over by the river on the far side of the large grassed area, some boys were messing about. They were hanging upside down on two tyres fastened to ropes slung over branches on the trees on the bank. After a hot summer, little water flowed over the grey boulders and shale on the riverbed. At least they wouldn't get wet if they fell in. I recognised Sam Hargreaves. He'd been my friend since our first year at Hopfield Primary School. And he helped his father deliver newspapers to our house, in holiday time.

I was so high on the swing that the chains slackened and jerked as I passed the bar they were fastened to. Arms straightened, I leant backwards so I had an upside down picture of Dad sitting on the bench, legs straightened, ankles crossed. He'd taken off his jacket and tie and pushed his trilby to the back of his head. He was cradling his pipe in his cupped hand.

'Looks like the smoke from your pipe is falling down instead of up,' I said, 'looks funny.' I saw him smile. It made me feel good. So I decided it would be all right to say what was bothering me. 'Why is Mum tired?' I asked, 'She doesn't do much.' She'd even stopped our Sunday afternoon baking cakes and biscuits times, which was something we'd done for as long as I could remember.

He'd frowned at that but only said, 'Now, now, love.'

I swung in silence, my hair sweeping the ground at the lowest point. The bit of the park we were in: the concrete area that held the swings, slide and the iron spider's web roundabout, was deserted.

'She is doing something, you know,' Dad said eventually, 'she's growing your little brother or sister.' He rubbed his knuckles on his neck, looked uncomfortable; or maybe it was the upside down image I had of his smiling mouth.

I thought it was a silly thing to say. 'Isn't she happy doing that?' I sat up, scraping the soles of my shoes on the ground to slow the swing.

'Of course she is.' But he wouldn't look at me. Instead he concentrated on his pipe and flicked the lighter into the tobacco which already glowed red. 'She's looking forward to us having an addition to our family.' He sounded odd, saying those words and I could tell he was embarrassed about something because his ears were red.

'Your ears have gone red,' I told him. 'And your nose is growing – so I know you're fibbing. Nanna said Mum has a face like a smacked backside these days; I heard her say that to her friend last week.' She'd actually said "arse" but I didn't dare repeat that, I'd never heard Dad swear, not even "damn", which I'd heard Mum say a lot over the last few months. And if I did say it, he might not let me go on my own again to Nanna's flat on the Barraclough estate.

'Enough.' His tone was sharp, sharper than he ever used on me.

My eyes stung and I twisted the swing's chains round, pushing on the ground with the toes of my shoes until I almost couldn't reach any more and I was higher than him. I didn't want him to see I was crying. I lifted my feet and was flung around and around. I was dizzy when it stopped. 'That made my eyes water,' I said, defiantly, pushing a finger under the frames of my glasses to brush away the tears.

'Time we went home,' he said. And then to show he wasn't cross, 'we'll get an ice cream.' He pointed with the stem of his pipe towards the entrance of the park where the tinny sound of 'Greensleeves' emerged from inside the white van decorated with cartoons. 'I'll race you.' He stood, took off his hat and folded his jacket over his arm. 'Go on, I'll give you a head start.'

I didn't need telling twice. I was off. He let me win, of course. I loved my Dad.

A week later I came home from school to find Rose had been born. I was surprised and pleased to see Nanna in the kitchen waiting for me. She didn't visit often; her and Mum didn't get on that well, even though they were mother and daughter. And, even better, she'd made jam tarts and had brought a bottle of Dandelion and Burdock with her.

'Calm down, wash your hands and finish this lot first.' She put the plate and glass in front of me, her hand lingering on top of my head.

I grinned up at her, jigging about in my chair so much that the pop went up my nose and I spluttered crumbs everywhere. I laughed and so did she, but there was something about her eyes that made me hesitate.

'You okay, Nanna?'

'I'm fine love.'

Later, when I look back into that moment, I see her hands trembling, hear the catch in her voice but right then I was too excited.

I raced upstairs to their room, calling, 'Mum, I'm home.' Even though she'd become so grumpy lately I'd still have a hug and a kiss from her when I got back from school. But not that day.

Mum was in bed, hunched under the clothes. She didn't move. Or speak. Perhaps she was tired; she'd been tired a lot lately. I patted the bedclothes where I thought her shoulders were and went round the other side of the bed.

The baby was in the old blue carrycot that had been mine and stored in the attic. I'd helped Dad to clean it up ages ago.

'What's she called?' Mum didn't answer. When I glanced at her she'd come out of the covers and was looking away from me, staring towards the window. Her fingers plucked at the cotton pillowcase. 'Is she okay?' I asked. The baby was so small; even though I could only see her head I could tell she was really little. I leaned over the carrycot. 'Can I hold her?'

'No.' Dad's hand rested on my shoulder, warm, gentle. 'She's too tiny.' He paused, cleared his throat. 'And she's not well, I'm afraid.'

That frightened me. I studied my sister carefully: tiny flat nose between long eyes that sloped upwards at the outer corners. A small crooked mouth pursed as though she was a bit cross about something. I could see the tip of her tongue between her lips. 'She doesn't look poorly.' I tilted my head one way and another, studying her from different angles. Nope, except for the little twist in her top lip, which was cute, she looked fine. 'What's she called?' I asked again, watching her little face tighten and then relax as she yawned, then sighed.

Turning on her back, Mum slid down under the eiderdown. 'Take it away,' she mumbled.

At first I thought she was she talking about me. Had I done something to upset her or the baby? But then I thought perhaps having a baby made you cross so I decided to forgive her. In the silent moment that followed I heard the raucous cry of a crow as it landed, thump, on the flat roof of the kitchen outside the bedroom window.

'What's she called?' I whispered to Dad, determined one of them would tell me. When there was still no reply I looked up at him and then back at my sister. 'I'm going to call her Rose, 'cos that's what her mouth looks like; a little rosebud, like my dolly's.'

Dad gathered both handles of the carrycot and lifted it from the stand. 'I'll take her,' he said, and cocked his head at me to follow.

'Do what you want.' Mum's voice was harsh. 'I don't want that thing near me.'

Then I knew she meant the baby, my baby sister. I was scared again. Something was happening I didn't understand. But I knew it was wrong to call your baby 'it'. It made me feel sick inside.

'That's mean,' I whispered.

Mum held her hand above the covers. 'Irene, you can stay. Tell me what you've been doing in school today.' She pointed to the hairbrush on the dressing table, pushing herself up in the bed. 'Fetch the brush. I'll do your hair.'

The words were familiar; it was something she said every day. But her voice was different. It was as though she was trying to persuade me to do it. Like in school when one of your friends had fallen out with another girl and she was trying to get you on her side. It didn't seem right; it didn't seem like the mum I knew.

'No, I'll go with Dad.' Suddenly I couldn't bear to be anywhere near my mother. I held the end of the carrycot, willing Rose to wake up. And then she opened her eyes. And, even though I know now it would have been impossible, I would have sworn at that moment she looked right at me and her little mouth puckered into a smile.

That was the first time I understood you could fall in love with a stranger, even though that stranger is a baby who can't yet talk.

And that you could hate somebody even though you were supposed to love them.

Chapter Two

2002: Yesterday: Noon

Mum's dozing. Cocooned in her armchair, in the corner of her room under a mountain of blankets with just her head sticking out, she looks like a big fat baby. I swear she's bloody healthier than she has been in years. She should be; she eats almost everything put in front of her. Or should I say, spooned into her. And by the time I've fed her, what with scooping up all she lets drip down her chin or has spat back at me, any appetite I had has vanished.

It's cold for September. Or perhaps it's just me; it could be lack of sleep or the fact that, even though it's lunchtime, I'm still in my nightie and thin dressing gown.

I pick up the dish of mashed potatoes and gravy. Watching her, hoping to move without her noticing, I spread my knees and push myself up into a half-crouch position. The chair creaks.

'No.' She says the word she uses most these days.

'I'm just going down to the kitchen to put the dish in the sink.' I seem to spend my days running up and down those blasted stairs. I feel the sigh deep inside me and I realise I haven't taken my daily antidepressant yet.

We did discuss moving her bed into the living room once, to make things easier for me in the daytime but that would mean we'd only have the kitchen to sit in at weekends or in the evenings if we wanted to be on our own. And, anyway, she still needs to be up here for a shower. How else would I keep her clean? So we left things as they are.

Her grip is a vice around my wrist. She doesn't open her eyes.

'I won't be a moment,' I say.

She begins to cry; the tears line the closed lids and slide down the sides of her face.

But she doesn't let go. I subside into the chair and swallow the sigh.

I think I see a shadow slip into the room. There's a warmth that surrounds me. I don't turn.

1963

Up to that year I remember that my mum laughed a lot. And I felt loved. I even put up with the hated ringlets she insisted I wore.

'Shows off your beautiful hair,' she'd say, running her hand along them and letting them spring back into a coil.

So, because I loved her as well, I put up with the nightly routine. Before tightly wrapping my hair in damp rags she brushed it fifty times like someone out of a fairy story. She'd count aloud each long sweep from root to end, until my scalp tingled and my legs began to itch through standing still, the skin on my calves mottled orange and purple with the lack of circulation.

12

I never saw her brush Rose's hair.

'Why don't you brush Rose's hair, Mum?'

'Not much to brush, love.'

'There is, she has lovely hair – all black and silky.'

The methodical strokes paused, just for a second, but, all the same, the rhythm was broken.

'Just go and put your pyjamas on,' she said. 'It's late.'

'It's the weekend. And anyway, I need to do Rose's hair.' *If you won't*, I thought, in a rare moment of rebellion. I just wanted her to love Rose in the same way she loved me. I couldn't understand why she didn't.

She sniffed, one of her cross sniffs: long drawn out, with the corners of her lips pulled in tight. I was sure she knew what I really meant, what I really wanted.

Rose was born with a shock of black hair that stood on end, making her look permanently surprised. It was a lot thicker than mine, and slippery, so, however hard I tried to fasten a ribbon in it, it didn't stay there. I envied her; at least she didn't have to go through the torture of the ringlet-making every night.

She cried a lot the first few weeks she was born. Every afternoon, when I came home from school, I'd hear the high-pitched wail and drop my satchel to hold her tight, breathing in the lovely smell of the Johnson's baby lotion that I'd smoothed onto the dry skin of her arms and legs that morning. Almost instantly she quietened and the jerky movements of her arms and legs stilled as though she had been waiting for me. She was so tiny. But right from the beginning I thought she had a personality of her own and we'd gaze into one another's eyes: me studying the flecks of white deep in her irises, Rose staring up at me, willing me to understand her needs.

I became a dab hand at folding nappies small enough to fit my sister and I'd leave some already doubled into triangles for Dad for when I was in school. Between us we learned to mix one part Carnation milk to four parts of water, something the doctor recommended for Rose because she was so little. Looking back now, the thought of the sweet stickiness of the stuff, clinging to the sides of the bottle, makes me heave. But even though she wasn't that good at sucking, and sometimes her nose was so bunged up she struggled, she did thrive on it; each day she seemed to me to grow a bit stronger. Although when she wasn't crying she didn't move much, sometimes, when I waved her rattle for her, her eyes followed the sound.

Dad took time off work to look after her by pretending he was poorly but then, when Rose was three months old, he had to go back because, after a lot of letters from the bank where he worked, his boss came to see how he was.

So Nanna moved in with us on Grove Street. I think she was happy to be with us; I knew she'd been lonely since Grandad had died the year before.

A lot of the time, Mum stayed in bed. It upset me; I wanted my old mum back. But, as the weeks went by, it also made me resent her. Nanna said it was because she was sad. I didn't see why; like I said to Sam enough times, it wasn't as though we asked her to look after Rose.

Chapter Three

2002: Yesterday: 1.00 p.m.

I think I must have slept. I have a crick in my neck, I feel spaced out and my arm is a cold dead weight on my lap. Mum is still clutching my wrist although she's now asleep – head dropped down, mouth open, a long line of saliva attaching lips to chest.

The dish of mash and gravy has tipped over on the carpet. I stare down at the mess; it'll need cleaning up.

I prise her fingers open and stand up, pausing halfway when the bloody chair creaks again. When I try to walk, my leg gives way and I cross the room in a kind of sideways, high-stepping shuffle, like John Cleese in *Monty Python's Flying Circus' Ministry of Funny Walks*. At the time I laughed till I cried. Now it's not funny: pins and needles shoot from foot to thigh. So, with both legs and one arm out of action I stand at the window waiting for the tingling to pass.

Despite feeling chilled to the bone I can see it's a lovely day out there. Lots of blue sky traced with tendrils of cloud that every now and then shadow the sun. The leaves, still thick on the flowering cherry tree outside the house, barely move. And a young girl, strutting past, sports the tiniest cropped top and miniskirt. So it must be warm. Although I suppose that means nothing – I'm not near enough to see if she's also sporting blue skin and goose bumps. A bus draws up at the stop on the road with a groan of brakes, regurgitates a cluster of passengers and sucks in the next lot who've been waiting: a non-communicating line of the patient and the impatient. I watch until I get a head-and-shoulders view of them, one behind the other in individual windows. I turn around, arms behind me holding on to the edge of the windowsill.

She's staring straight through me.

'Okay, Mum?'

She scowls and farts. Loudly. Which reminds me, I need to change the sheet on her bed; she pulled her incontinence pad out of her knickers in the night.

I leave the dish where it is for now. One thing at a time.

1963

After Rose was born nothing was ever the same again.

I'd thought that all our family outings had stopped because Mum was so tired when she was carrying Rose in her tummy. Then I thought that with Nanna looking after my sister during the daytime, so Mum could rest, we'd go back to normal. But that didn't happen.

What I missed most were the day trips that Dad's bank arranged. These outings were the best ever. Crowded coaches full of everyone laughing and shouting to one another, noisier on the home journeys when the adults were even sillier. It always surprised me that I'd slept when we pulled up at the end of Grove Street.

My favourite of those trips were to Blackpool to see the illuminations. It was one of Mum's favourites as well. The last time we went she said it was one of the best years. That was the year before Rose as well.

It had been raining all day but it had stopped by teatime. We'd already seen the lights in the daytime, the funny cartoon figures dressed like all the cards: Queen of Diamonds, Jack of Spades, all fastened to the street lamps, the village scenes on the other side of the tram tracks, the trams covered in different coloured bulbs. But it was best at night. Everything was lit up and against the blackness of the sky, the illuminations came to life.

'Isn't it wonderful, Irene? Look, look at the big red stars so high up.' Mum lifted me so I was standing on the seat, my palms flat on the window of the coach as it drove slowly along the promenade. 'See how they twist and turn. And look, a picture of an elephant.' Bulbs lit one by one to show the big animal carrying a funny man with a funny red hat on his head.

'Wait – see the double-decker trams are coming. Derek, Derek, look on this side.'

Dad was standing in the aisle of the coach, leaning on the back of one of the seats and talking to a man who was doing the same, each pointing illuminations to one another on the other side of the road. Sitting on the seats were two women.

'Derek!' Mum sounded a bit impatient but she was still smiling when I looked down at her. She kissed me on the side of my face. 'Look, Irene.' The coach stopped, halted by the cars in front of it. Dad came to sit alongside us again. He put his arm over Mum's shoulder, whispering something in her ear which made her laugh while, at the same time, reaching further to tickle me.

'Dad!' I squirmed. 'Look!' A double-decker tram trundled past us along the track covered in red and yellow lights that were arranged to make it look like a train.

'What's it say?'

'It's advertising ABC Weekend Television,' he said. 'Listen, that's the music they play, the three notes.'

A crackly "la-te-doh". It took me ages to get that little tune out of my head afterwards.

The coach suddenly started again. There were giggling screams and scuffling from some of the women behind us, pretending to fall about in their seats. Laughter and shouts of 'Whoa' and 'Hey-up' from the men. I turned to watch but Mum blocked my view.

'There's been too much drinking again, Derek. They're getting rowdy.'

'Ah, leave it Lil. No harm being done.' He bent his head to hers and gave her a big loud kiss on the mouth. 'See, we can join in and all.'

She gave him a pinch on the arm but I could tell she was pleased because she was smiling when she pointed out more pictures to me. We passed a huge board showing a scene of a family gathered together as though for a photograph: three adults, a little girl sitting at the side of the mother, a baby on the father's knee, and an older woman to one side, her hand on the baby's leg.

'It's us,' I said. 'You, me, Daddy and Nanna. Except for the baby – we don't have a baby. Shall we get one?'

Dad threw his head back and laughed. But, all at once, the humour died on his face when he glanced at Mum and he grabbed her hand. We watched the rest of the illuminations in silence. I wasn't sure what had happened but she was very quiet on the journey home.

After Rose was born, when I thought about that last time at the illuminations, it reminded me of that picture of the family. But it made me feel sad.

And, after Rose was born we didn't even go for the usual walk on

17

Sunday evenings. I wasn't always keen on those, unless it was to the park or along the river path to feed the ducks there. I used to love walking between Mum and Dad. They'd hold my hands and do little runs, swinging me up into the air, over and over again. I even missed the times when the outing was Dad's favourite, up the hill to the war memorial. I'd trail behind them moaning about my aching legs until Dad hoisted me onto his back. After Rose, I even offered to do that walk and said Dad could carry Rose instead of me. But it didn't happen.

None of my family seemed happy anymore. I missed the laughter.

And there were lots of rows. Nanna and Mum kept up a constant niggling at one another. Nanna would look ashamed and mouth 'sorry' at me as I stamped out of whatever room they were in, a wailing Rose in my arms. But Mum never even paused for breath when she was on a rant.

And, at the same time, I noticed there was something wrong between Dad and Mum.

For as long as I could remember my parents had played a sort of game every time Dad came home from work. I'd watch him creep up behind Mum, his finger to his lips telling me not to give him away. She would pretend she didn't hear him. He'd swoop, his arms around her waist and he'd twirl her round and round. She'd struggle and tell him to put her down but then laugh and give him a big noisy kiss. Watching them I used to think my laughter was like happiness bubbles inside me.

That game stopped.

And after Rose, whenever they were together, Mum constantly sniped at him, like he couldn't do right for doing wrong. I'd see her giving him sideways narrow-eyed glances, her lips pursed, her nostrils big with one of her sniffs.

Almost every night I heard them through the bedroom wall. Well, I could hear Mum's high-pitched voice, interspersed every now and then by Dad's low rumbling answers.

I hated that.

18

Sometimes I wondered if our family times stopped because Nanna was living with us. But that made me feel bad, as though I was thinking it would be better if she didn't. Of course it wouldn't have been; who would look after Rose when I was at school and Dad was at the bank?

I watched all of them and kept my head down. My only job was to look after Rose, to protect her. It upset her when people shouted. She'd cry the minute they started.

Yet worse than the rows were the silences and the watching; we spent a lot of time watching one another, waiting to see how one or another reacted to anything Rose did. Usually it was Dad and Nanna who watched Mum whenever she was near my sister; I was never sure what they thought she would do.

Chapter Four

2002: Yesterday: 2.00 p.m.

In my room I dress quickly. No time for a wash; she's crying again. A pitiful wail. 'I'm here, Mum,' I shout, 'won't be a minute. Look at the picture I gave you. It's on your knee.' A photograph of William, the Border collie we used to have. He was Dad's dog but once Rose was born he wouldn't leave her side.

I give my hair a perfunctory comb through, wincing as I tug at the day-old tangles and thanking my lucky stars the hairdresser cut it this short the last time she came to the house. I've no time to bother with it; I've got that bed to sort out...

When I sense the soft breath on the back of my neck I don't turn. In the mirror the image shimmers, the black hair like a halo around her head. I hold out my hand and touch the mirror with my fingertips.

Many of my so-called friends drifted away, stupidly embarrassed to be seen with me when I was pushing Rose around the streets in her pram. But Sam Hargreaves stayed: always there, right by my side. I knew that, in a way, he was as lonely as me with his dad out working all the time and no mum around. He never talked about where she was. If I ever asked he'd tell me to shut up. So, all I knew was that it was only him and his dad. And, like me, he loved his dad.

And I was always glad to see him when he came to sit with me on the front doorstep with Rose, when I didn't want to go inside the house because of the rows.

One of those times, a Saturday morning, I'd been sitting on the step cuddling Rose for ages. Mum was angry about something and was shouting at Dad. It was taking me all my time not to cry. Sam arrived. At first he didn't speak, but then gave me a nudge.

'Look what I've got,' he said, and pulled a crust and a couple of white bread slices from his trouser pocket. Crumbs spilled all over the step and I brushed them onto the pavement with my hanky, before Nanna saw. She was very particular about keeping the doorstep clean.

'Why were they in your pocket? Is it your breakfast?' I knew that, lots of times, he had to see to his own breakfast if his dad was delivering the papers or had gone to work in the newspaper shop.

'Nah, don't be daft, it's for the ducks. I thought we could take Rose to feed them if you were up for it?'

'Won't your dad find out you've taken the bread?'

'He won't mind. Anyroad he doesn't like the crusts, I always have them.' He jumped up and hauled me to my feet, balancing Rose against his chest so I could tie her bonnet tighter and wrap her scarf around her neck.

We shared carrying her because I didn't want to go into the house to get her pram. So we were a bit puffed by the time we got to the river and we had to sit on the low wall by the bridge to get our breath back.

Few people were on the path. Except for the occasional car passing over the bridge and the sound of sparrows in the hedges, there was little sound. The river was still, the surface reflecting the light grey sky and the thin branches of the overhanging trees. There was no warmth in the April sun but, because there was no breeze, it didn't feel cold. Even so I hugged Rose to me when we hunkered down on the banking.

There were no ducks.

'Don't worry,' Sam answered my disappointment. 'Just watch.' He ripped a chunk of crust off and rubbed it between his palms before throwing it into the water. The crumbs freckled the surface sending circles of ripples around them.

The sudden quacking and rush and splatter of ducks made Rose jump.

'Quack-quacks.' Sam took hold of her hand and waved it towards them. 'Quack-quacks.'

We watched her face as they gobbled up the rest of the bread. She didn't seem sure at first but then she laughed.

Sam chuckled. 'I knew she'd like them.' He stood brushing his hands together, letting the last of the crumbs fall onto the water. 'You okay now?'

'Yeah.'

He didn't ask what was going on in my family. When we got back home he patted both Rose and me on the shoulder.

'See you.'

I could hear him whistling even when he'd turned the corner at the end of our street.

Chapter Five

2002: Yesterday: 2.00 p.m.

Mum's cries are louder. When I hurry across the landing she's slid out of the armchair. Don't ask me how; she hardly ever moves these days and she's always a dead weight when I try to lift her from chair to bed or bed to chair. Sometimes, with my arms around her she feels strong, rigid, as though any moment she'll take her own weight and walk. Or at least shuffle. But it doesn't happen; she'll suddenly collapse and we waddle the short distance, me clinging on to her, legs bent, giant strides – while slowly but surely, she's slipping through my arms.

I check her over to make sure she hasn't hurt herself and then take my mobile out of my cardigan pocket and phone Sam to come home to lift her back into her chair. He's a painter and decorator and today, thankfully, only working down the road. I don't know how I'd manage without him at times like this.

He tells me he'll be here as soon as possible, hopefully in ten minutes. In the meantime we sit on the floor next to the dish. I notice the spilled gravy has white greasy blobs of film on it; it'll be the devil to clean off the carpet.

I manage to sit her up and get behind her, wrapping my arms around her waist to pull her closer while I sing her favourite song, "We'll Meet Again", six times in rapid succession. Every time I finish she jerks her shoulders up and down until I start again.

1964

Rose was having one of her restless nights. I thought it was my fault; I'd made her too tired to sleep.

That morning I'd taken her to the park.

Sitting on the bench near the swings, rocking the pram back and forth, I watched the families around me. There were mums with babies in prams posher than ours. I didn't care about that but some of the babies were sitting up and looking around and chuckling, waving to the sparrows as they flew past or patting their hands together. I thought some of them looked about the same age as Rose and I wanted her to do the same as them. I propped her pillow around her and wedged the doll I'd bought for her when she was born next to her, so she could sit up and watch the older children playing, notice the leaves blowing in the trees, see the flowers.

But she kept sliding sideways, looking so uncomfortable that I laid her down again. I tried to get her to hold her rattle and a daisy that I'd picked. But though she waved her arms around, her fingers spread wide, she couldn't manage to catch hold. Even when I wrapped her fingers around the stem of her rattle, it dropped as soon as I took my hand away.

Back home, after Dad and me had eaten some of Nanna's lovely Saturday potato cakes, slathered in butter, he asked me to look after Rose while he went out to do the weekly shopping.

Of course I didn't mind. I had a plan.

When he'd gone and Nanna was in the kitchen doing something, I put Rose on her back on a blanket on the carpet in the living room and changed her nappy. Then I lay alongside her, trying to get her to roll over onto her tummy towards me. I bounced the doll on the floor, making its pot legs move.

'Look, Rose, Caroline's dancing. Dance, dance, dance.' I pulled faces which, after a moment of looking puzzled, made her chuckle. In the moments in-between she made soft sounds, reaching out to me, trying to touch my glasses. But she didn't move her body. I stroked her hands, held her soft pudgy fingers in mine and gently pulled. I was sure she tried to turn over. But she couldn't do it.

In the end we sorted it by me putting the flat of my hand under her back and rolling her over myself, careful not to let her face bash onto the blanket. Then I turned her onto her back again and gently tickled her, blowing raspberries on the soft damp rolls of her neck. She loved it. In the end we were both helpless with giggling.

We played like that for ages, until my arms ached and she started to get floppy with tiredness. She hadn't managed to turn on her own. But I knew she would one day and I was determined to keep helping her.

So, like I said, listening to her crying that night, I knew it was my fault.

I waited to see if Dad got up with her as usual but he must have been so tired he didn't hear her. Throwing back my covers to go and see to her I heard their bedroom door crash open. I could tell it was Mum by the way she ran down the stairs. She had Rose with her. My sister's cries were piercingly loud at first and then muffled. I held my breath and listened. I waited for Dad to follow but he didn't. Then I heard Mum come back up. My sister wasn't with her. The door to the living room must have been closed; Rose's cries were muted but I could still hear her.

Nanna and I bumped into one another in the darkness. 'You go down to her.' Nanna's voice was quiet but in a funny way, like she was talking through her teeth.

Dad soon came. He made a bottle up for her while I walked around trying to sooth her. But by then she was so worked up it took her a while to latch on to the teat. Eventually, between us we quietened Rose but nothing and nobody would have been able to silence the row above us.

Things changed after that night. Nanna took Rose's cot into her room. Mum didn't seem to care; at least she never said anything about it when I was around.

Often, through the thin wall between my room and the bedroom they slept in, I heard Rose whimper and the low murmur of Nanna's voice. If Rose got to full throttle, which seemed to take no time at all, I'd hear the squeak of the hinges of the door and Nanna's slow heavy tread on the stairs. She never wore shoes in the house as far as I can remember. Her feet were always encased in slippers, fawn with a red criss-cross pattern and a large pom-pom on the front which wobbled as she shuffled around the kitchen. Nanna was a martyr to her bunions and, in winter, to chilblains that made her toes look like little red tomatoes.

Sometimes, if it was a weekend and I didn't have to go to school the following day, I was allowed to go downstairs as well. Nanna used to say that Rose cheered up as soon as she saw me, even from being a tiny baby. As the months passed, hardly a week went by that my sister wasn't awake some of the night. Often Dad was there too, sitting at the kitchen table with Rose, trying to get her to touch the abacus. She couldn't hold onto anything still, but Dad would guide her hand so that, together, they could give the little coloured balls a good belt. She chuckled each time they whizzed along the metal bar with a zipping sound and a loud click. She'd spend hours on that thing, given chance. Dad always got fed up first.

I loved being up in the night with Dad and Rose and Nanna.

Chapter Six

2002: Yesterday: 2.30 p.m.

By the time Sam arrives my voice is going and I can't feel my legs. She's wet herself. And me. We both need a change of clothes.

He lifts her up as though she's a child and puts her back into her armchair and tucks the thick woolly blanket around her, ignoring her cries and flapping arms; leaving me to wait until the blood supply reaches my legs so I can stand up.

He's a lovely man, my Sam; tall and broad shouldered. He's taken off his white overalls. His dark blue polo shirt matches his eyes. And although his hair is grey, it's thick and he wears it long, tied back in a ponytail. Unusual, I suppose, for a man who's almost fifty. But he doesn't look his age; his skin is clear and faintly tanned because he's been doing a lot of outside painting this summer and is almost without wrinkles, except for the laughter lines around his eyes and the creases on either side of his mouth. I always think of him as strong featured. A strong man. My man.

1965

Nanna and Dad took Rose to the doctors when she was two. I didn't know until afterwards or I would have made sure I went with them. It was days before they told me what was wrong; there was something different about her heart, they said. So we all had to keep an eye on her when she got the colds and bad chests that seemed to happen so often. I thought even Mum looked upset but I didn't understand why she hadn't taken my sister to the doctors; that's what mums should do; that's what happened when there was something wrong with me.

I loved Rose and, as I said before, I made myself responsible for her, which meant I didn't go out unless I took her with me. So I couldn't join in with the skipping or the tag games. And it was difficult playing hide and seek with a little girl who didn't know how to keep quiet. Who laughed a lot.

She made me laugh too. I didn't mind looking after her at all. I loved the soft touch of her hands on my face. I loved the trusting heaviness of her in my arms. I was just lonely.

'What's wrong with her? You've never said.'

Sam and me were sharing a bag of chips and fish bits, sitting on the kerb outside the chippy on Travis Road. Rose was lying in my lap asleep, one floppy arm dangling over my knees. William, our dog sat opposite me, panting, hoping for one of us to drop a piece of the tasty batter bits.

'Nothing,' I said, annoyed. I didn't want anyone judging my sister. I looked down at her; in her dreams – I liked to think she dreamt like me – in her dreams, expressions floated across her features. I caught a glimpse of Dad's focussed concentration when he listened to me, Nanna's smile quivering on my sister's lips. I saw nothing of my mother.

'There is. My Auntie Alice has a baby your Rose's age and she's sitting up properly. Walking as well,' he added, looking puzzled.

'Shut up!' I spoke too loudly; Rose jerked, her fingers spread wide

26

apart and she whimpered. I cuddled her to me, stroking the back of her neck; she always liked that. She quietened, her cheek warm and moist against mine.

Sam looked crestfallen. 'Sorry.'

I relented. He wasn't to know after all. I spoke quietly. 'She's got Down's syndrome.' I'd heard Mum once call her a mongoloid but Dad said the correct name for what Rose had was Down's syndrome which sounded nicer. Softer. So that's what I said.

He didn't look any the wiser and held out the greasy, almost empty bag. 'Last chip?' It was as though he didn't know what else to say, his face was flushed.

'No thanks.' I looked steadily at him; it felt important for some reason that he understood, that he accepted her as much as I did. 'She just doesn't do things as quickly as other kids.'

'Will she catch up?' He shoved the chip into his mouth and tipped the bag up to get the last of the bits. His words were spluttered through the crumbs.

I knew he was feeling awkward; I'd seen the same look on some of our neighbours' faces when Dad and me pushed Rose out in her pram. They only half-looked at her, made silly cooing noises over the prettiness of her yellow bonnet or the white lacy blanket, that Nanna had knitted. Or even talked about her doll, next to her, that was dressed in the matching woollen dress and hat. And all the time, glancing at us with pitying expressions. I didn't care about them. I did care about Sam.

'No.' I felt as though I was betraying Rose saying that. I held her closer, covered her ears between my neck and my hand, even though I knew she couldn't possibly understand. Her breath was warm on my skin.

'Never?' He lowered the bag, his eyes widening.

I tensed, stared him out. 'Never.'

He wiped his mouth on his sleeve and gave the bag to William to lick. The dog moved the paper along the pavement with his tongue as he chased the last taste clinging to the bag.

'I've never seen your mum out with Rose.'

'What do you mean?' Why would he suddenly say that? My stomach was jumping all over the place and the tang of the greasy batter rose in my mouth.

He looked awkward and then burst out, 'Is it because Rose won't catch up?' He peered round at her. 'And 'cos she looks a bit different? Is that why your mum always makes you bring her when you come out?'

I knew he was right – she didn't take my sister out. But, even though I resented her for it, something made me want to defend Mum; there were still occasions when we were on our own, when I saw glimpses as she used to be. It was true she'd rejected Rose from the moment she was born, from the moment the midwife had told her my sister was a Down's syndrome baby. I hadn't understood why that made any difference at first but I did start to understand later from the way people reacted when they saw Rose. It was as if they felt sorry for us, that it was a shame she'd been born. Mum shouldn't have felt like that, though. I always thought a mum was supposed to love her children.

The resentment, that Mum didn't love me and Rose equally, fuelled my sudden anger against Sam. 'She doesn't make me bring Rose with me. I like looking after my sister; she has a special heart and she's mine to look after. Dad says when she's older she can have her bed in my room – with me – so we can be together even more.' I held her hand, studied her tiny fingers with the even tinier pink nails. Pushed back the hot smarting of tears. 'And everybody is different in some way, aren't they? I think Rose is beautiful.'

'Sorry.' Sam lowered his head. 'I wasn't being mean.'

'I know.' I chewed the inside of my cheek. Thought about what I was going to say next. 'Shall I tell you something? Something I've not told anyone else?' He turned his head slightly, looked up and sideways at me. Questioning. 'But you've got to promise you won't ask any questions about it and you won't tell anyone else. It's a secret.'

'What?'

'Promise?'

'I promise.'

'And hope to die?'

'And hope to die.'

I took in a long breath. The words came out in a rush. 'Before Rose, for as long as I can remember, I dreamed I had a little sister. It was something I really, really wished for but I didn't say anything to Mum or Dad because...' I stopped. I didn't know why I hadn't asked them about it. 'Because it was my secret and if I spoke it out loud, it wouldn't come true.'

Sam sat up and turned to me, a strange frown bringing his eyebrows together.

I didn't stop. 'Then Rose was born and I knew – the minute I saw her – I knew – she was the sister I'd dreamed about. I mean her face; what she looked like.' I nodded vigorously. 'It was her...' I lifted Rose's fingers to my mouth and kissed them. 'I recognised her. And she looked up at me and she knew as well.' I stared at Sam. Challenging. But he didn't speak. 'So we belong to one another, Rose and me. We'll always belong to one another, as long as we live.'

I felt a bit dizzy. I didn't know whether I'd done the right thing telling him. He was my best friend but would he laugh? I'd hate him if he laughed.

But he didn't, he moved his head up and down slowly as though he understood, shifted on the edge of the pavement, sat cross-legged.

William came back and leant against us, licking the last taste of the chips from his muzzle.

'I think I get what you mean,' Sam said at last. 'And I'll never tell anybody. Ever...' He rubbed at his knees. I noticed they were ingrained with grime as usual. I always supposed his dad didn't take much notice if Sam washed or not. It never bothered me.

We looked down at my sister. As always her mouth was slightly open, her lips quivering with each breath, her eyelids flickering.

'She's dreaming,' Sam said. He smiled. 'Perhaps she's dreaming of you.'

And then I knew my secret would be safe with him. But there was something in his voice that made me ask, 'Are you okay?'

'I have a secret an' all,' he blurted. His mouth worked as though trying to get the words out.

I waited.

'I remember when my mum left us, Dad and me,' Sam said. 'I was only a kid but I remember... She wanted to take me with her, but she looked different from what she'd always looked like. I'd never seen her in the kind of clothes she wore that day – all posh, like. And she smelled different. I was frightened...' His cheeks went red and he pushed the heel of his hand up against his nose and sniffed. 'I hid in the hall cupboard. After she'd gone I heard Dad crying. So I stayed there for ages.' He rested his head on his knees, hiding his face. 'I dream an' all. I dream she comes back to us.' His voice was muffled. 'But it's a bad dream. When it started I used to wake up yelling and shouting. Dad said I was having nightmares. I never told him what they were about. I still dream that I come home from school and there she is. Like nothing ever happened. And I hate her.' He lifted his head. He was trying not to cry; his eyes all scrunched up. 'She comes between me and Dad. You know, like he doesn't have time for me anymore, like we're not *us* anymore?' I nod. 'And I hate her for that.'

I couldn't speak. There was a big lump in my chest that hurt. I leaned towards him, put my head on his shoulder for just a few moments and felt the sobs that shook him. When I straightened up and we looked at one another I knew something had changed. I felt older, somehow. And I knew that me and Sam were always going to be friends, whatever happened to us, we were always going to be in one another's lives.

A tabby cat sauntered by on the opposite side of the road, brushing against the wheel of a parked car, its tail in the air. William went mad, yelping and barking. Sam had to hang on to his collar.

Rose woke up with a start but, for once, she didn't cry. She gazed up at us and smiled.

Sam lifted her hand and put it to his own cheek. She touched his fingers with her other hand, her palm over his thumb. Get it, Rose, I thought, hold it. I watched, my breathing stilled, willing her to capture Sam's thumb. Frowning with the effort she gripped it. Tight. I laughed as she pulled it to her mouth, sucked it, her eyes squeezed together in concentration. My throat hurt. 'She hasn't done that before,' I said.

'Must be my super powers.' Sam laughed. But still, when, after a while, he asked again, 'So she'll never catch up?' I had to be honest.

'No.'

Chapter Seven

2002: Yesterday: 2.30 p.m.

The room stinks but Sam says nothing. He stands at her side, stroking her hair while I, my legs itchy with the aftermath of restricted circulation, stomp around the bed, stripping off the sheets and carrying them downstairs to shove into the kitchen sink in hot water. Once, coming back into the bedroom, I stand and watch the pair of them. I notice that, between Sam's fingers, I can see her scalp, pink through the fine strands.

Up to now, except for a few token words, we've not spoken. Now he says, 'You can't carry on like this; you need help for during the day. Carers.'

I know what he's thinking; we can't let our living here, being with her, come between us again. Once was enough. I can't lose him a second time. But still I say, 'We've tried that before, Sam. You know what happened every time. It was worse for me after they left; she'd play up even more. I'll manage. Honest.'

I drag clean sheets and a duvet cover from the shelf in the airing cupboard. 'Honest,' I say again. The tears are hot when they spill over. I look over my shoulder at him to see if he's heard the gulping sob that I've tried to swallow. He doesn't seem to. He's murmuring a few words to Mum, and she appears to be listening to him. At least she's stopped moaning while he talks. And she's not said no once.

I leave her with him while I change my clothes.

1966

I was wrong about Rose; she did catch up, it was just in her own time. When she was nearly three Rose walked on her own. She'd been able to stand for months if we held her hands but wobbled and sat back down if we let go.

I used to worry; what would happen when she was too big for me to carry? Although she was really small for her age, she seemed heavy because she was bendy. So I practised with her every day, kneeling in front of her and going backwards. She thought it great fun. But I saw the change in her face just before she flopped down on her bottom, a flicker of worry in her eyes, her little lower lip pushed out.

So the day she stood on her own, the day she took her first few steps, was wonderful. We were in the kitchen; it was a Sunday morning. Through the open back door, the warm air from outside flooded in. I could see Dad pulling weeds from the path, Mum pegging out washing that hung limply on the line in the stillness. The sky a brilliant blue, the kind that hurts your eyes to look at.

Nanna watched as I slid my fingers gradually away from Rose.

'Come on, sweetheart. Come to Irene.' I held my breath. She whimpered but I made myself shuffle back a little. 'Try? Try for me?'

Her black hair, longer but still like a halo around her head, trembled with each short breath she took, each shaky movement in her legs. I picked up her doll, Caroline, waggled its arm as though it was waving to her.

'Hello Rose. Come and get me.' Hiding my face behind the head of the doll I spoke in a squeaky voice. 'Here I am, Rose, here I am.'

And then she walked. She walked towards me, arms outstretched as I moved back on my knees. A walk that ended in a little rush before she collapsed onto me, grabbing at the doll.

'Oh good girl.' I hugged her.

When I turned to look at Nanna she was crying and laughing at the same time, not bothering to wipe away the tears that dripped from her chin.

'Mum. Dad,' I shouted. 'Rose just walked. All on her own. She walked.'

Dad ran in and crouched down near her. My sister took five steps towards him, her doll in one outstretched hand. He caught hold of her, laughing. But when he twisted around and looked up at Mum the smile faded. Arms folded, my mother leant on the doorframe. There was no expression on her face.

'About time,' was all she said.

But a few minutes later, when I was topping up two glasses of orange juice with water at the kitchen sink, I saw Mum holding on to one of Rose's dresses that was hung on the washing line. Her shoulders were shaking as though she was crying. I didn't know what to do. But then, when Dad went to her and put his hand on her arm, she shrugged him away. I turned off the tap. Sometimes there were things I didn't understand.

Nanna was with us when Dad and me took Rose to buy her first pair of proper shoes that following Monday. Before, she'd just had baby shoes – the soft fluffy type, to keep her feet warm. They were always different colours because Nanna said we shouldn't only stick to pink; girls could wear any colour they wanted. Anyway, that day was a great adventure. The shoes were red; actually they were sandals, the kind with the gold-coloured buckles and a cut-out pattern of a flower on the front. Rose chose them and none of us could refuse her.

And once she could walk, we couldn't stop her from running in any direction she fancied. And, boy, could she run fast.

But then that was an extra worry; would the running make her heart go funny again?

I worried a lot about Rose; I wanted her to have a normal life. I tried to get her to sit up on her own, to walk and talk. I could make out words that she was saying, especially when we were looking at one of her *Noddy* books that Nanna had bought. I'd guide her chubby little finger to a picture of Mr Plod or Big Ears without her showing any interest. But show her a picture of Noddy and she'd push her own finger at his hat and say "bell" clear as anything.

One thing she could do was sing. Not words, but a clear humming, notes that made tunes, sounds that soared. Crisp and clear, they made music without a recognised rhythm, but with a melody that sometimes made me close my eyes, and listen as if I'd never listened properly to anything before.

Chapter Eight

2002: Yesterday: 3.00 p.m.

Afterwards I put a towel on the bed and Sam helps me to lie her down on it so I can get her out of her wet things. Mum stares adoringly at him and her eyes follow him when he goes to stand by the bedroom window, his back to us. He doesn't turn when he says again, 'I know what you're saying, love. But you can't carry on like this.' It's his next words – especially, that emphasis on "we" – that make my skin prickle with fear. '*We* can't carry on like this. You'll make yourself ill. I can't let you do that to yourself; I can't let that happen, Irene.'

He's right, of course. But getting carers in again won't work. Mum doesn't like strangers in the house.

There are two extremely good reasons why having carers is impossible for me.

Mum screams. And when I say screams I don't mean the

occasional yelp when she doesn't like something they do. I mean a scream that doesn't stop. This woman can scream for Britain: one long loud high-pitched noise that makes your head hurt. And she doesn't stop until they leave. She can be purple in the face and still she carries on. It's unbelievable that anybody can keep that volume of noise up for so long, but she does.

And with the neighbour from hell next door I think he'd have the Council come down on us like a ton of bricks as a noise nuisance. That, or he'd try to pick a fight with Sam. He's done it before.

And I'm not sure how Sam would react the next time; we've had no end of trouble with that man.

And the other reason is the language that comes out with the screaming. I can only think the swearing was lodged in her head from years ago. I do know that she's never heard me or Sam tell anyone to "fuck off" or that we've ever said someone was "shit". It happened with the very first carer that we had; a lovely quiet woman who left in tears. I did think at the time that perhaps caring wasn't the job for her, but then two others left just as quickly. Although maybe the last one left because Mum threw a beaker at her. Quite accurately too, as I remember.

1967

Sam and me failed the eleven-plus and went together to the local secondary modern where we were in the same class until it was turned into a comprehensive school. When we were twelve, I was moved to the top set and he stayed where he was.

I was pig sick about that. We still walked to school but I struggled to fit in and he had different friends that he played with in the evenings and at weekends. I missed him.

One day, Rose and me were sitting on a bench in the park watching him with a group of other lads playing football. Rose was dozing on my lap.

I saw Sam's dad walk up to him. They talked for a few minutes and every now and then glanced over towards me.

Finally they came to the bench.

'Dad wondered if you and Rose would like to go to the lake tomorrow?'

'You'll have to ask your parents first though,' Mr Hargreaves said.

'Sounds great fun.' Dad rubbed his neck with his knuckles, so I could tell it worried him. 'Think I'll come along though, with Rose not being able to swim.'

'She can – a bit,' I lied. We'd been taking her to the local baths every week for the last few months, me and Dad.

'Aye, like a stone.' Dad lowered his newspaper and looked at me over his reading glasses

We laughed.

But still I said, '*I* can swim.' I was a bit put out.

'But you don't mind if I tag along?' It wasn't really a question. He added, 'I've got a lot of time for Albert Hargreaves; he's a good bloke. I haven't seen him in ages. I fancy asking him what plants he puts in his window boxes.'

Now that was a lie. Dad's window boxes were the best on the street; he didn't need advice. But I let that one go.

It was lovely and sunny on Saturday morning. Mum wouldn't come with us, of course, so it was just the three of us who met up with Sam and his dad at the end of their street. We hadn't told Rose where we were going – she'd get too giddy – but she guessed when we got near the park. She squealed and pulled at my hand to go faster.

It was early so there wasn't anybody else on the lake.

The man who owned the boats tugged one towards us by a rope, his hand out for the hire money.

'My treat.' Mr Hargreaves waved away Dad's proffered sixpence, holding on to the front of the rowing boat. Dad went to one of the benches and lounged back on it, crossing his ankles and smiling at Rose's squeaks of excitement.

Clutching her hand I stepped into the middle of the swaying rowing boat, followed by Sam and then his dad. I put my arm around Rose and pulled her close.

Mr Hargreaves sat on the little bench seat at the front of the boat, took off his flat cap, folded it in half and shoved it down into the top pocket of his jacket. He removed the jacket, folded it so the lining was to the outside, doubled it and pushed it under his seat. The boat was shaking all over the place. Rose was still laughing but I did wonder why he hadn't done all that before he got into the boat. Sam was grinning at me; he knew how nervous I was. I stuck my tongue out at him, shook my hair back off my face and raised my eyebrows. He covered his mouth but I could tell he was still grinning. Mr Hargreaves then turned his shirtsleeves further up his arms revealing tattoos on each. Sticking his thumbs under his braces at the shoulders he adjusted them.

'Right,' he said at last, 'let's go.' Spitting on his hands and rubbing them together with a flourish, he grasped the oars, turning the left one in small circles to spin the boat around before heaving on them to head for the middle of the water. I watched the muscles bulge and relax in his arms. One tattoo, a snake wound around a large sword, moved as if with a life of its own. It fascinated me but I did hope Rose wouldn't notice – it might have frightened her.

Dad was waving at us. I wished he wouldn't because Rose's waving back meant she swayed the whole of her body and I had difficulty holding on to her.

'Da,' she shouted, pushing hard at my chin to make me turn my head around to be sure I'd seen him as well. The boat tipped from side to side.

'Don't, Rose. I can see him.'

She must have thought me cross because she subsided onto the seat and dipped her head. I gave her a hug. She gave me one of her special smiles.

'Love Iwene,' she said.

I swallowed. 'Love Rose,' I answered.

The clunk of the oar in the stirrup and slap of water on the paddle were the only sounds. Rose leaned over the side of the boat, trailing her other hand in the water.

'Steady, youngster,' Mr Hargreaves said. I threaded my fingers through the belt of her dress and me and Sam looked at one another and smiled.

After a bit Mr Hargreaves jammed the keel of the boat into the grasses on the bank and gives us some bits of bread to throw to the squabble of ducks that rushed across to us.

A couple more circles of the lake and we were back in front of where Dad was sitting.

I was sorry it was over. I wondered how strong I'd have to be to take Rose and me out on a boat. Not that Dad would let me anyway; it would worry him to death, I bet.

We were ready for an ice cream. Dad came to sit with us on the grass by the paddling pool to eat his. Rose, as always, bit the end off the cornet and sucked the ice cream through it, making a right mess of the front of her dress. Dad said it didn't matter as he mopped at it with his big white hanky.

Mr Hargreaves produced a little blue and white plastic boat that he said he'd bought in Denholme indoor market. He and Sam took off their socks and shoes so I did the same for me and Rose, and tucked our dresses into our knicker legs.

'Derek?'

Dad laughed and shook his head. 'Your treat, Albert,' he said to Sam's dad, 'I'll just watch.'

'Look Iwene.' Rose pointed at Mr Hargreaves' legs. He had a network of varicose veins right up to his knees. She crumpled her dress up to her waist, showing her little white cotton knickers, and stared down at her own legs

'Ah, you have to have lived a good long life before you're entitled to these, young 'un,' he said. But he said it in a jokey way, so I knew he didn't mind.

He waded further into the pond, winding the key in the side of the boat. I could hear the spring inside creaking tighter.

'I tested it in our old tin bath in our backyard,' he said.

I wished I'd seen it then, because the boat promptly sank.

Rose hooted with laughter. 'Again,' she shouted, pointing to where it had disappeared, clearly thinking that was what was supposed to happen.

Mr Hargreaves picked up the boat, shook it until it was empty and, winding it up again, set it on the water. It sank. Again. And again. He did it five more times before we could persuade Rose to wade back to the banking. Her legs were blue with cold.

Dad managed to dry her with Mr Hargreaves' hanky even though she squirmed with impatience.

Both men wanted to go to the greenhouses. I pretended I didn't see them carefully putting plant cuttings into their inside jacket pockets but kept watch for the park keeper just in case. Sam kept Rose entertained by pointing to and naming the little stone gnomes in one of the flowerbeds.

Walking home we had chips in a newspaper cone from the chippy on Travis Road.

It was one of the best days ever.

Sam turned up at our house on the Sunday. Me and Rose were on a rug on the front step of our house. He sat cross-legged next to me, gave me a shove on the shoulder, careful not to dislodge Rose who settled against me with a small breathy grunt. 'Fun yesterday.'

'Yeah.'

'It's not the same playing out without you, you know. That new lot are not as good at stuff as you.'

'Huh!'

'We used to have a lot of fun. There's nothing to stop you joining in.'

'With...' I dipped my chin towards Rose; I wasn't chancing anybody saying anything about her.

39

He knew what I meant. 'I'd thump anybody who said owt.'

He would; I knew that.

We sat quietly for a while. He was right, we did have fun before. Sometimes, at weekends, we were out from first thing in the morning until it went dark. I'd pinch some bread and jam and make butties so we didn't have to go home. Sam always brought the pop.

I smiled, gave him a nudge. 'D'you remember that time we played Sardines with the Carr Street lot?' I felt the laugh rising in my chest.

'And Rose kept shouting out and we were found and—'

'Michael Shaw was really mad and he called Rose—'

'Stupid.'

'And you punched him on the nose.' I knew that had been wrong but now I laughed.

'Blood everywhere.' Sam wrinkled his nose, shamefaced.

'He deserved it.' This time I shoved him with my shoulder. 'He was horrible to her.'

'He cried—'

'Boo hoo!' I screwed up my face. 'Boo hoo – boo hoo!'

'Boo hoo – boo hoo!'

Rose woke up. I held her at arm's length and swung her from side to side. She went floppy and let her head drop backwards, laughing and imitating us. Our voices were getting louder and higher. A woman walked past, tutting and shaking her head.

We didn't care. I pulled Rose to me, holding her tight.

'He ran home to tell his mum and she came to the house. I told Dad what he'd said about Rose and he said I should punch him twice as hard next time.' Sam stroked her cheek. 'Smashing how she smells – all sweet-like.'

'It's baby lotion,' I said. 'She gets really dry skin, so I put Johnsons' baby lotion on her.'

'It's nice. Hey,' he said, grinning, 'I've just had a great idea. We could get married and then we can both look after her.'

'Don't be daft, we're not big enough. You have to be really old to marry.'

'I know that!' He flushed but grinned. 'I was only joking.'

I balanced Rose onto my knees and rocked her again. She liked that. 'Besides, I'm not washing your socks. Mum says men's socks are revolting.'

'Well, I'm not a man yet.'

His protest was wasted on me. 'Exactly – like I said, we're not old enough. And boys' socks are worse.' I had this on good authority. Sandra Sykes had once brought one of her brother's really smelly socks into class and stuffed them into Miss Lee's coat pocket. *She* hung her coat up behind the classroom door but wouldn't allow us to bring ours in even when the heating broke in the middle of winter. When she found the sock she went potty, holding it up between finger and thumb, her arm stretched out in front of her, as she dropped it into the waste-paper basket.

Sandra said she got a good telling off from her mum. And then her brother sulked at her for a week afterwards because he said it was his best pair. I can't see how he could say that; there was a great spud-hole in the heel.

Chapter Nine

2002: Yesterday: 4.00 p.m.

Sam's given up on going back to work and has gone to get us a takeaway from the all-day Chinese place, the Red Dragon, which used to be the chippy, on Travis Road. I'd just realised I hadn't eaten today, and now I'm starving. And one of my headaches is lurking behind my right eye. I've set the trays; we're going to have to eat with Mum upstairs. It happens sometimes, when the days have gone to pot. Either that, or we'll be eating at ten o'clock tonight. It must be like this sometimes when you have young children; the thought flashes through my mind and is followed immediately by the familiar stab of desolation.

She's shouting. I pick up the newspaper that Sam had brought home with him, go upstairs and drag the chair from our room into hers for Sam to sit on.

'All right?' I know I sound impatient so I try a smile; it feels stiff on my face. 'Shall I read to you?'

She doesn't answer. We sit in silence. I pick up and peer at the front page of the paper. The print blurs. These glasses aren't right. I really should have gone to the opticians last year. Second time I missed an appointment.

Just before he left Sam told me he'd booked a surprise weekend break in the Yorkshire Dales for the two of us in a four-star hotel.

'Now the foot and mouth has gone, I'd like to go back there – see for myself it's all okay. And I thought it'd be nice to support the area.'

Which was typical of Sam, always thoughtful. Still I'd said. 'We can't.'

'A posh place in Malham,' he'd said, 'Not self-catering. You always liked it round there.'

'I know.' We'd had some lovely times: long weekends, walking the Dales, in the past, years ago.

One time in particular stood out for me. It was an Easter weekend, early that year so the weather was a bit dicey: cold and windy. We'd set off the first morning with a bank of dark cloud overhead and we hadn't been walking for an hour before the rain started. By that time we were on a high ridge overlooking one of the glorious valleys that the Yorkshire Dales are renowned for. The fields, dotted with sheep and dissected by meandering stone walls, and the silver river that wound through the flatland soon disappeared behind a thick veil of rain and cloud.

'Do you want to go back?' Sam yelled above the driving rain.

'Not a chance!' Being so high with not a soul around was exhilarating. Sam tucked the map inside his coat, grabbed hold of my hand and, heads down, we marched along the narrow path. We'd walked a lot in the Dales, across moors and grasslands and I always marvelled that we were actually walking those byways for pleasure when, so many years ago, people had crossed to take their wares, their goods to markets in the nearest towns and villages. I always wondered how many thousands of footsteps we were treading in.

It was like walking in a bubble. Except for the noise of the wind and rain, there was nothing else. The calls of the sheep in the distance had long since stopped travelling across the valley.

I put my head close to Sam and yelled, 'We could be the only people in the whole world.'

Hardly had the words left my mouth when there was this tremendous roar and, through the clouds an RAF jet screamed past, so low in the valley that it was below us. I was so startled I screeched and clung on to Sam. He took a few sudden steps backwards, arms flailing, and fell with me landing on top of him. We didn't move for a few seconds then I felt his whole body shaking with laughter. It didn't take much for me to join in.

'My god, that scared the living daylights out of me,' he said, once we'd got our breath back and sat up. We were both covered in mud. He studied the sky around us, his eyes half-closed against the swirling sheet of rain. 'I think we'd better make our way down to the village. This looks set in and we're in no state to carry on. You'll catch your death in this lot.'

By the time we'd squelched our way to the road below, a pale sun lit up the edges of the clouds.

Clambering over the last wall, we stood looking around.

'I feel ridiculous now,' I said, watching a couple stroll past in their Sunday best.

'There's a pub. Church Inn.' Sam pointed.

'Can we go in though? We're such a mess.' We were wet through, our walking boots clagged with mud.

Sam was determined to have a beer. 'We'll take these off in the porch.'

Which is what we were doing when the door to the bar opened.

The largest man I'd ever seen towered over us; he was even taller than Sam.

'What yer doin'?' He scratched his stomach which was only partly covered by a tee shirt that proclaimed *"Yorkshire's Best"*.

I said nothing; it was obvious to me. But I smiled up at him.

'Are you serving?'

'Are yer suppin'?'

'If you're open.'

'If thou art suppin'.'

We could have carried on like that forever but Sam intervened.

'I'd love a beer?'

'Come in, then.' The man hitched up his trousers which were hovering dangerously low under his belly. 'An' you, lass?'

'I'd love a cup of tea?'

As I said to Sam later, using one of Nanna's sayings, he looked like a bulldog chewing a wasp.

With total scorn he said, 'A. Cup. Of. Tea?' His top lip nearly touched his nose. 'What d'yer think this place is, lass? A bloody WI? Tea an' bloody scones?' He pushed the door to the bar open, to release the malty aroma of beer, and ushered us in. 'Yer'll 'ave a proper drink or nowt at all.'

I had a lager.

It wasn't long before a crowd of locals, followed by other equally wet and muddy walkers, crowded into the tiny room to create a fug of steam, cigarette smoke and the aroma of fish and chips (that day's "special"). A heaped-up fire blazed in the large fireplace, a Great Dane panted in front of it, every now and then shifting itself to rest its head on one or the other of the customers' knees. Someone opened the lid of an old piano in the corner of the room and, before long, the place was filled with singing, laughter, the clatter of glasses and the buzz of conversation.

'What a day.' Sam stroked my cheek with the back of his fingers. I took hold of his hand and kissed it.

'And a lovely way to finish it off. You, Mr Hargreaves, are the best lover I've ever had.'

His raised himself up on one elbow. 'Out of how many?' he asked, his tone a mix of feigned anger and curiosity.

'Oh, dozens.' I pretended to think. 'Maybe more,' I added, airily.

'Well, if I'm the best, that's all right then.' He leaned towards me as though to put his mouth on mine but instead grabbed hold of my waist and began to tickle me.

'No! Stop it. No, Sam...' Laughing, I tried to wriggle away but he held on. 'I give in...'

'Tell the truth. How many?' Sam rolled me on top of him, laughing at my helplessness. 'How many lovers?'

'Oh, okay,' I gasped. 'Just you.' I collapsed onto his chest and he wrapped his arms around me. I raised my face to his. 'And you know it – I've only ever wanted you.'

'Quite right too.' In between kisses, he said. 'And me you, my love.' His lips brushing mine, he murmured, 'and who said we'd finished the day off...?'

I become conscious I'm smiling, hugging those memories to myself. This time my face doesn't feel so stiff. My mother's gazing at me. 'All right, Mum?' She continues to stare. Even though I'm not reading the newspaper, I lift it up so I can't see her.

1968

Nanna never once bad-mouthed Mum to me but I constantly heard them arguing. And I'd learned a long time ago to read Nanna's face and could always tell when she was really angry with Mum.

Mum landed herself a job in the first supermarket in Denholme. It caused such uproar in the town when it opened because all the shopkeepers said they would lose business and have to close. But it meant there were jobs for local people. And Mum was one of them.

She couldn't wait to get out of the house in a morning. She was so proud of herself that first day in her pink uniform with the name *Payless* embroidered in large gold fancy letters across the pocket over her bust. Backcombing her hair into a lump on top of her head and fastening it with a matching pink plastic comb she twisted one way and then the other, preening herself in the mirror.

'How do I look?' she asked. As if she cared what Nanna thought.

'Like somebody who didn't think of consulting anybody else in the house about what she was doing and what would happen about her kids.' Nanna didn't lift her head up to look at Mum; she was trying to dress Rose. Earlier I'd been reading *The Three Bears* to her to try to persuade her to sit still on Nanna's knee. It was a little cloth book that she could hold herself. I'd found it on a stall in the market and it was her favourite.

But I had to eat my breakfast before going to school and now the book swung in her clenched fist as she squirmed away from Nanna, trying to stroke William who obviously thought it a game and kept jumping up at her and backing away. Every time he did that she gave a high-pitched laugh and even though Nanna was losing the battle with the buttons on my sister's dress she still smiled. Just like me.

Until Nanna's words.

The room darkened, splats of rain hit the window, made me jump, glance towards it, then back at Mum. I felt a trickle of worry down my spine, aware I'd been holding my breath. Then the sudden intake of air cold in my throat.

The kitchen was thick with the smell of the toast I'd burned earlier, the knife, still covered in the black bits, glinted on the draining board of the sink, also speckled with the burnt crumbs I'd scraped off the bread. The glass butter dish and jar of strawberry jam on the drop-down front of the kitchenette seemed too ordinary, too familiar, wrong somehow for what was happening between Nanna and Mum. I wished Dad was here.

Rose had become still in that long tense moment. She stopped patting at the dog. I watched the movement of her chest with each light breath, saw the way her chin quivered, saw the frown-line on

46

her pale broad forehead as she looked down at the floor. And I wanted to pick her up and run.

I didn't move.

Mum's nostrils flared with one of her angry, almost silent sniffs. 'Consult? Why the hell should I have to *consult* you? Or anybody? Somebody has to bring extra money into this house. Anyway, you're here.' She pushed her arms into her coat. I heard her mumble, 'Worse luck,' before she said, 'With everybody who's now living under this roof, the food bill goes up every week.' She fastened a pink nylon scarf over her head and pulled the front forward in a peak to protect her fringe. 'Derek's wages don't cover a fraction of what we need, you know that. And before him and me were married you were always getting on at me to pull my weight. Well, now I am doing and you still moan. Always carping on and on, you.'

I looked down at my cornflakes. If I wasn't careful, she'd start on me. I hate you, I thought, I really, really hate you. But still I was too much of a coward to move. The worry about Rose mixed in with the guilt for not sticking up for Nanna. But there was always that fear; if it wasn't for my grandmother I didn't know who would see to my sister when I wasn't around.

The man from the house across the road started up his motorbike and revved it. The noise seemed to fill the room. I put my spoon down, pushed my glasses back over the bridge of my nose and looked up. Until the motorbike set off, the roar fading away, there was a frown of annoyance on Mum's face but she didn't take her eyes off Nanna. Her hands were on her hips: that ready-for-a-row-when-you-are stance she always adopted at times like that. They exchanged stares.

The first thing you noticed about Nanna was her eyes: so dark a brown that in some lights they seemed black. Set against her pale skin and white hair they were startling. Mum's are the same. And Rose's. Mine are blue like Dad's. But mine were always hidden behind my glasses.

I rolled the last of my cornflakes around my mouth with my

tongue, holding them long enough to soften, so that when I chewed it didn't sound in the silence. Rose let the book drop and picked up her doll to hold it close to her as she slid onto the floor to bury her head in Nanna's lap. Her dress was still unbuttoned and had slipped off one shoulder and I saw the gleam of perspiration in the small smooth rolls of fat at the back of her neck.

Nanna's face was blank but her hands were shaking as she stroked Rose's hair. 'You should be here, should have always been here, looking after this little one.'

Mum raised her eyebrows. 'Says someone who lives here rent free.' Her throat mottled until it was the same colour as her overall. It was as though I wasn't there, that only the two of them were in the room. A whole conversation was bouncing around the kitchen without either of them having to say a word. The Billy J. Kramer song, that Mum used to sing a lot, started to croon in my head, *'Little children, I wish they would go away... go anywhere.'*

I swallowed and stood, pulling my skirt away from the back of my legs where the sweat clamped the material to my skin. 'You shouldn't speak to Nanna like that. She's your mum and she's helped us a lot with Rose since she was born.'

Mum's arm moved like lightning. I felt the sting on my cheek before I even knew what she'd done. When I opened my eyes her outline was fuzzy and I blinked away the tears, trying to focus before I realised my glasses had been knocked off.

William leapt about, frantically barking. Frightened at the sudden chaos, Rose cried out. 'Iwene.'

'Here, love.' Nanna picked up my specs off the floor and pushed them into my hand. She knew I couldn't see six inches in front of me without them and I got the feeling she wanted me to see my mother's face. Her voice was calm but cold. 'Lay a finger on either of your children again, my girl,' she said, 'and I'll tell your husband.'

There was a pause.

When my mother next spoke it was as though she was forcing the words through her teeth. 'If it wasn't for you sticking your oar in, she...' she tilted her chin towards Rose, 'would be in an institution. If it wasn't for you, I'd have a life.'

Even through the shock of knowing exactly what she meant, through the hatred that coursed through me at that moment, I could still see the apprehension in her eyes.

Once, when I was seven, Mum threatened to slap me for getting my new shoes scuffed. Later I heard Dad tell her he would leave her and take me with him if ever she did. He didn't believe in smacking, had rarely raised his voice to any of us. And, in that moment I really believed he would be true to his word if ever he found out what Mum had done.

I wished again he was here. But he'd left for work ages ago. Sometimes I thought he couldn't wait to get out of the house, as though anywhere was better than here, being with us. But I told myself I was being unfair; when it was just him and Nanna and me and Rose it was lovely. He had to work, I reminded myself.

Now, as Mum pushed her feet into her black stiletto shoes, I saw her lips thin into a bitter line. She wouldn't give Nanna the satisfaction of knowing her threat had hit home. 'It's always been the same. You've always spoiled things for me.' Pulling her shiny white raincoat on, she turned and grabbed hold of the door handle, throwing her parting shot over her shoulder. 'If it wasn't for you, I wouldn't be stuck here.'

That Billy J. Kramer tune stayed with me all day.

Chapter Ten

2002: Yesterday: 4.30 pm

'I've stuck the food into the oven. I wasn't sure where you'd want to eat but I just saw the trays.' Sam stands, watching me fasten the large plastic bib around Mum's neck. 'Shall I bring hers up first?'

'Yes, I think so. See how she gets on.'

49

'Okay. Well? What about what I said?' He touches my shoulder. 'Just a couple of days away? It's all booked. You don't have to do anything but pack. Come on, you need a bit of pampering.'

I wish. I shake my head. 'We can't.'

'Why?' His voice was steady, controlled. But I saw the irritation. 'Where's Derek?'

I look up in surprise at Sam and then at Mum. There are so few days when she speaks clearly. She begins to cry. Noisily and messily.

'Derek?' She splutters Dad's name.

'Mum?' I fish for the tissue up my cardigan sleeve and lean over her, dabbing at her face.

Now she's really crying. She looks at me and then towards the door. 'No...'

Sam passes me the box of tissues from the bedside table. 'I think this will be of more use.'

I can't read his expression. I take the box and pull out a handful of the paper hankies to try to dry Mum's tears.

It's a while before I realise I'm crying too.

She holds on to me and weeps.

1968

It was seven o'clock that evening when I got back home from Sam's, where I'd been for tea. I'd dithered when he first asked me as we came out of school, because I'd worried all day that Rose might still be upset, but then I saw her and Nanna on the far side of the little park by the library. I waved.

'Iwene.' Rose was off the slide and running, flinging her arms first around my legs and then around Sam's.

'Hello, Squirt,' he said, picking her up and swinging her round and round while she laughed, clinging to him.

By the time Nanna got to us we were sitting on the library wall and Rose was munching on a Jelly Baby that Sam had produced from his pocket. Sam always had sweets.

'Hello, you two.' Nanna was breathing heavily and her headscarf had loosened so it was hanging off at the back. 'Glad we've seen you, Irene. Don't forget it's my night for the bingo.' She re-tied her scarf under her chin. 'Your dad's already home so he'll see to this one...' She smiled at Rose, who grinned back; sweet juice dribbling out of her mouth. 'Your mum finishes work at five.' She pulled a hanky out of her pocket and wiped my sister's face.

I knew what she was trying to tell me. I went to Sam's house.

Walking along Grove Street I wondered if Nanna had told Dad what had happened that morning. In a way, I hoped not, it would only cause yet another row and it would upset Rose before her bedtime. But the house was quiet when I unlocked the front door and stepped into the hall.

It was gloomy in the kitchen so I switched the light on. Dad was standing at the far end of the back path smoking. His thinking place. He turned and lifted his pipe.

I cupped and waggled my hand, making the sign to see if he wanted a drink. I saw him nod so I filled and switched on the kettle. Taking off my coat I draped it over the chair. It never occurred to me to look where Mum might be.

I just had time to nip up to our bedroom to see if Rose was awake.

Usually, in the evening, our door stayed wide open in case Rose woke up and shouted for one of us. But it was almost closed and something stopped me pushing on it. I peered through the gap.

Mum was sitting on my bed. She was cuddling Rose who was asleep but Mum was gently brushing her hair. She was brushing Rose's hair!

I stood still. The soft breathing of my sister, the faint hush of the hairbrush, the low sobs of my mother were the only sounds I heard. It felt as though I was intruding on something; I didn't know what. But I knew enough to back away. I went downstairs, tiptoeing on the sides of the treads.

In the living room I looked out through the window at the people standing under the pale yellow light of the street lamp at the bus stop. A woman was holding a buggy in one hand and a toddler in her other arm. I saw her kiss the child's head; it didn't seem to notice, as though taking that love for granted.

There was a cold lump of wretchedness in my chest. Mum didn't let herself be seen to give that love to Rose, and that hurt me in a way I didn't understand.

When I went to bed later there was a piece of paper on my pillow. It read, "Sorry about this morning."

Chapter Eleven

2002: Yesterday: 4.45 p.m.

I can't remember the last time I saw Mum so distraught.

Or maybe I can. It was when I was sixteen, a few weeks after Dad left. Nanna and Rose were out when I got home from school. I thought Mum was at work. It was when I got to the top of the stairs that I heard the sound of crying.

I knocked on her door.
    'Mum?'
    'Go away.'
    I dithered, not knowing what to do. But what I heard next made me turn the handle and open the door as quietly as I could. I recognised the wail of despair; it was the same noise that Nanna had made when Grandad died. It made my skin prickle.
    I closed the door and stood with my back to it; I didn't know what I could do but I felt I couldn't leave her on her own. She was collapsed at the side of the bed, her arms splayed out over the crumpled sheet she clutched in her fists. I watched the whole of her body heave with each outburst.

I knew Mum was causing problems between Dad and that woman he'd gone to, constantly phoning the flat and banging on their door at all times of the day and night. She didn't want Dad, but she resented that he'd left her. It was wrong of her but I understood why she was doing it. I felt like doing that myself sometimes. Or was I wrong that she didn't want him? From the looks of her, I was. She must have loved him after all.

So I knelt alongside her, moved closer, covered her hand with mine. It felt like ages before she stopped crying. I felt her fingers shift to touch mine, to curl around them. We stayed like that for what felt like ages before she lifted her head to look at me.

For some time I'd been buying the small paperback romance books that I'd seen the girls in school reading together. They were mostly rubbish: the same old, same old stories of girl meets boy, falls in love, falls out of love, girl heartbroken. Often they described the girl's face as being "awash with tears", her "features blurred". I could never picture it until that day when Mum turned her face to look at me.

'Oh, Irene.' Her words were spluttered through a stream of tears. 'I miss him.'

'I know.' I dared to put my other arm around her back and rest my head on the bed close to hers. 'I do too.'

'How could you?' Her words were thick, as though she had a cold. She scrubbed her handkerchief over her eyes and blew her nose on it.

'He's my dad.'

'I'm sorry.'

I didn't know what she was saying sorry for but it was enough. I pulled her closer. Her sobs were somehow calmer. But it was as though they were echoed in me.

Sometimes I think I'm only getting through life on memories. Usually they are of the good times. But recollecting that day has shaken me. I hold on to Mum in a confusion of feelings about her.

How the hell does Sam think I could leave her when I know there could still be times like this?

1969

'Do you think she'll be all right?'

Rose was six and it was her first day in school.

We were lucky, my old school, Hopfield Primary, had agreed to take Rose after some meetings with Dad and Nanna. I looked at the small stone building, at the window which would be her classroom. I wanted her to have friends; it was important she would have friends, that the other children were kind to her.

'It's a good school, you know that. You were happy enough.'

I didn't answer Dad. I didn't tell him I knew what it was like to be the one no one wanted to sit by in class. Or the girl who stood around, alone, while all the others played together or put themselves into teams to play rounders. I was no good at games because I didn't see that well. And that was something else to worry about; Rose had a slight squint and wore little pink National Health glasses with wires that curled around her ears and pushed them forward so they stuck out. I thought it made her look cute but it was just one more thing that made Mum sigh in an odd way.

So, when he repeated, 'You were happy enough', I didn't tell him any of that. Neither did I tell him that I was left out by the girls in the school I was now in, those who hung around in tittering huddles, giving sideways glances at the boys. Nanna said I was "big-boned". I knew I was just fat. And my eyes, which she said were my best feature, were hidden behind the thick lenses. But I didn't care; I always had Sam.

I'd decided to chance going in late to the comp the first day that Rose started school because I knew she was scared from the way she'd climbed into bed with me the night before and wrapped herself around me. I reckoned that I wouldn't be too late if I ran the half mile afterwards.

Walking alongside Nanna and Dad, my little sister clung tightly to my hand as we entered the gates. I'd brushed her hair and fastened it into two small sticky-out plaits and tied green ribbons around them to match the school uniform of dark green and yellow. She wore her new black patent leather shoes and had walked along the road lifting her feet high so she didn't scuff the toes. She'd insisted on bringing Caroline with her; the doll was tucked firmly into her little brown satchel. I hoped the other kids didn't laugh at her for having it.

Children were playing in the small schoolyard: hopscotch, chasing one another, skipping. In one corner a small boy was clumsily kicking a football against the wall. We stood by the gate, watching, listening to the shouts and screams of laughter. Nanna looked at me, apprehension clear in her eyes. Dad was running the knuckles of his hand up and down his throat, his usual nervous habit. A few of the kids turned to stare at Rose and I glanced down at her to see if she was all right but it was as if she hadn't noticed; she was watching the boy with the ball.

A woman appeared at the large green door and stood on the step surveying the scene. She held a brass bell. I covered Rose's ears – she hated loud noises, they upset her – but she squirmed away from me, letting go of my hand as the bell was rung and the children rushed to line up

Except for the small boy with the football.

Before we could stop her Rose was running across the yard to him, her satchel bobbing on her back. We saw her hold her hand out, say something. When he turned to walk with her, to follow the other pupils into school we saw what Rose had already seen; he was another Down's syndrome child. Grinning at us, Rose waved and led him past the woman.

'I'm Miss Gartside, their teacher. She'll be fine,' she called, smiling. 'Pick her up at three-fifteen.'

She closed the door. We stood staring at it in silence for a moment, then at one another.

'Well, that's that.' Dad pushed his trilby to the back of his head

55

and ran his fingers through his hair to scratch his scalp. 'S'pose we'd better get off home,' he said to Nanna.

'And you'd better run, Irene, so you're not too late.'

I nodded, gave both of them a kiss and turned away. I didn't know how I felt; I think it was a mixture of relief and sadness. My little sister was going into a world I would never enter, where I couldn't protect her. But at least she'd found a friend.

Chapter Twelve

2002: Yesterday: 5.00 p.m.

Mum's outburst, the clarity of her speech, is over as quickly as it came. She's exhausted. Once the hiccups of sobs stop she drifts off to sleep. I take the plastic bib off her and tuck her hands under the blankets.

I find Sam sitting on our bed, his head in his hands.

'Let's eat ours downstairs,' I say, stroking his hair.

He stands and we hug.

In the kitchen I take the cartons out of the oven and unwrap them. Some of the sauces have got a hardened rim along the inside of the tinfoil dishes.

Sam's quiet but I know what he's thinking; he's seen me upset. Again. And he hates it. How he puts up with this situation I'll never know. His earlier words come back to me; 'We can't carry on like this.' He's right. We've had bad times but nothing like as bad as it's been these last few months. I need to be strong. It's time for me to be strong.

1969

I skipped the last lesson to get back to Hopfield Primary at the end of the day. I knew I'd get it in the neck the day after but it was only

PE and I hated it; it was a lesson I always tried to get out of, one way or another.

I'd called home on the way and succeeded in persuading Nanna to let me go on my own but wished I hadn't; my stomach was doing somersaults with worry about how Rose had coped without me.

When the bell rang there was muffled noise inside the school long before the children burst through the doors. I remembered that joyous sense of freedom, that urge to run, shouting and laughing. But now it worried me that Rose could be knocked over. I stood on tiptoe to try to see her.

Then there she was, holding hands with the small boy we'd seen that morning and a girl, taller and older-looking than my sister.

Letting go of them she rushed across the playground and leapt to hug me around my waist.

'My fwiends, Iwene,' she whispered, turning my head to put her mouth to my ear. Just as quickly she let go of me and ran back, pulling them towards me.

'Bewyl and Mahtin,' she announced.

I swallowed the lump in my throat. She had friends. Why did I doubt that she would? My Rose always had a beaming smile and a kind heart.

'Your sister? They've made friends?' A soft voice made me turn. The woman looked almost as old as Nanna, grey hair in a tight perm, lines around pale grey eyes that had an anxious expression. But she was smiling. 'I'm Martin's mother, Mrs Althorpe. I've been so worried all day.'

'I know. Me too.' The three of them were chasing one another now, playing tag. Rose's knee socks were crumpled into folds around her ankles and her hair hung loose on one side, her plait undone, the ribbon gone.

'It's a big step for him. For both of them, I think. I never thought I'd see the day he'd be in school. Your sister...'

'Rose. Yes, I know. My dad says the head teacher is...' I tried to remember his exact words. 'Before her time.' I wasn't really sure what

57

he meant but it sounded as though he thought Mrs Scunthorpe was wonderful.

Martin's mum nodded 'Your mother...?'

I said nothing. But something in my face must have given me away.

'She doesn't manage...?' She said, looking towards Rose. 'She hasn't accepted...?'

I didn't want to be disloyal but the words blurted themselves out of my mouth. 'I don't understand why not...' The nauseous feeling of suddenly revealing family secrets to a stranger made me press my lips together tight.

'I do.' The words, spoken so softly I needed to move closer to hear them, repeated. 'I do. I've seen the looks from people. I've hidden away.' Mrs Althorpe looked directly at me, her gaze steady. 'Don't blame her, dear, she will come round. It's the shock – at first it's the shock.'

'But Rose is six...'

'People are different, dear.' It was all she said.

I shook my head. I knew that. All Rose needed was to be loved. What did it matter if she looked, was, a bit different? We're all different, was all I could think.

Another woman came towards us, pushing a pram, her eyes on the three of them still running around.

'Barbara! I'm here.'

Mrs Althorpe turned. 'Beryl's mum.' She lifted her hand and waved. 'Marion. Mrs Whitworth, my neighbour,' she added.

'Late as always.' Mrs Whitworth put a hand to her chest, her voice breathless. 'One day I'll be on time.'

'Marion, this is Irene. Her sister started school today, same as Martin?'

Mrs Whitworth smiled. 'Hello, Irene.' She nodded. 'Well, looks as if they've both settled in nicely.' She laughed as the three of them ran towards us to crowd around the pram.

'Look, Iwene, a baby.' Rose beamed up at me. 'I touch?'

'Course,' Beryl said.

'No, only look.' I spoke at the same time, not sure.

'Hold his hand, if you like.' Mrs Whitworth pulled back the blanket a little. 'He's called Nigel.'

Rose gently stroked the baby's fingers. Then she whirled away, holding out her arms and spinning, her satchel bouncing on her back.

The two women laughed when Martin and Beryl joined her.

'I think I'd better get her home,' I said. 'My nanna and dad will be wondering where we are. And Mum,' I added. Even after talking to Martin's mother I didn't want them thinking Mum didn't care.

Rose's hand was hot and sweaty as she skipped alongside me. Her glasses kept slipping down her nose.

'Caroline in your satchel?'

'Yeah.' She pushed at her glasses with the heel of her hand.

'Your ribbon came off?'

'Yeah. Miss couldn't do it. In my satch – in bag. She's nice – Miss.' Rose jerked her head up and down to make sure I understood. 'Miss Gahtside. Nice.'

'So you had fun?'

'We had singing, Iwene. I learned it. Like this. Listen.' She stood still and cleared her throat, watching me to make sure I was paying attention. ' "*Th' was a man call' Michael Finnegan. He gwew whiskers on his chinnegan.*" ' She stopped. 'Can't 'member the next. What's chinnegan?'

'His chin.' We started walking again. Soon she started singing. When I sang the next lines, remembering them from my days in the primary school, she joggled my hand.

'No, my song. I 'member.' Her forehead creased, her lower lip jutted out.

She sang the song, with odd words missing, before she let me join in. I didn't mind; I couldn't wait to get home to see Nanna's face when she could see how happy Rose was.

We were almost home before she pulled me to a halt again.

'I f'got...' She shrugged the straps of her bag off her shoulders and dropped it onto the pavement.

'Mind you don't break Caroline.' Although the doll's body was soft, stuffed with something like cotton wool, the head, arms and legs were made of hollow clay.

'I won't.' Squatting down, she struggled to open the buckles, pushed my fingers away when I tried to help. 'I do it.'

'Okay, okay. Only Nanna's waiting for us.'

'A minute.' Eventually she pulled out a square of paper and held it up to me. 'Nauwa coming.'

'What?'

'Bewyl say Nauwa coming.'

I unfolded the paper and read it. The laughter that fizzed up inside me was carried on the relief I'd been feeling the moment I saw her coming out of school with her two new friends. 'It's about the nit nurse. Nitty Nora!' I said.

'It all right?' Seeing me laugh, she grinned.

'Yes, it's all right. Remember Nanna washing our hair that time and using that little comb because she thought we might have little bugs in our hair?'

Rose pulled her mouth down in a comical way. 'Yuk!'

'Well, other people call them nits. And this is about a lady, a special nurse, who comes into schools to make sure we don't have nits. Like Nanna did.'

'Not Nauwa? Lady?'

'A nurse. Not Nora.' I laughed again.

'But not washing our hair?' She cocked her head to one side.

'No. Not washing your hair.'

'Good. I hate washing hair.' Without fastening the buckles she trailed the satchel behind her along the street. I bent down and grabbed the doll before it fell out.

Nanna appeared on our doorstep. 'Everything all right?' She called.

Rose let go of the satchel and ran towards her. 'Nanna, Nanna, I found fwiends.'

Chapter Thirteen

2002: Yesterday: 6.00 p.m.

I must have fallen asleep at the table before I finished my chicken satay and fried rice. When I lift my head, Sam's leaning back in his chair a mug of tea in his hand. There's another mug by the congealed leftovers in the white cardboard containers, pushed to one side, a thin stream of steam rising above the rim.

I run my tongue around the inside of my dry mouth. 'How long have I been asleep?'

Sam glances at the clock on the wall. 'Ten minutes,' he says. 'About ten hours less than you need.'

I cup my hands over my eyes and hold them there.

'You really don't have to do this on your own, you know.' Sam leans forward. He prises my hands away from my face. 'I mean it. Get carers in during the day to help you.'

I am so weary of him saying this. I know he means well; he thinks she would get used to strangers coming in, but I know she won't.

'She'd kick up a fuss; it always makes things more difficult for me.'

'Then,' he hesitated, 'then it has to be a care home.'

'No! We can't afford to pay for a care home; you know that. And she made sure we couldn't sell this place while she's still...'

'With us.' Sam said the words for me.

I watch him, knowing he won't remind me that I should have insisted on my being granted power of attorney at the same time as we became joint owners with Mum. But I didn't. My mother was as strong-willed then as now; she wouldn't hand over any control to anyone, especially me. And, to be honest, I hadn't blamed her at the time.

So, unless we apply to the courts for a Court Protection Order we're in the same boat as always. And then my mother's solicitor would produce that letter preventing the sale of the house and we'd be back to square one.

I break the silence. 'I'll be fine after a good sleep.'

'And when will that happen?'

I don't answer. Out of the corner of my eye I think I catch a slight movement, a flick of familiar blue. The other reason I don't want us to sell this house.

1969

I didn't go into school some days because Rose was ill. She had a lot of colds that went right on her chest. I could always tell the doctor was worried the way he frowned when he listened to her heart. Though I don't think he was pleased one time, when Rose, obviously fed up with him bending over her, snatched the stethoscope off her chest and blew down it.

So, often, I felt I was the one she most needed, even though I knew Nanna loved her as much as I did. And, anyway, I always made sure I had some homework to do while I kept an eye on her.

One time I stayed home because she had yet another of her chest infections.

Well, it was partly that – and partly because I'd started my period the day before in class. It was only my second one but I knew what was happening because I'd had the heavy ache in my stomach the night before. Just in case it happened while I was at school, Nanna had given me a sanitary towel and the piece of elastic to thread through the loops and tie around my waist. And it had, but it was in the middle of the Maths lesson and I was frightened of the teacher, who was a POW in the Second World War and had sudden and volatile explosions of anger over trivial things. So I'd sat there praying for the end of the lesson and feeling the blood trickle out of me. At the end, I'd waited for everyone to leave and for Mr Hampson to turn his back before I fled the room and, grabbing my coat from the cloakroom, I ran all the way home. I hadn't looked back at my chair; I was afraid to in case I'd left marks there.

But I knew I'd get it, one way or another when I went back. If I wasn't hauled up to the Headmaster's office, I'd be laughed at by the others in the class.

Despite the griping pains in my stomach and feeling sick, I was glad I'd stayed home.

It was a dreary day. The sky was a lowering grey. Rain spouted out of the drainpipes of the houses opposite. The guttering on one had broken and water gushed from the split. People hurried past, hunched under umbrellas. Buses sprayed water as they halted at the bus stop. Nanna had gone to the local chemist for the prescription that the doctor had given her for Rose. I'd offered to go but Nanna insisted I stay in the warm and she bundled herself up in her raincoat, wellies and her plastic 'lettuce hat'.

I watched her splash along the street from the window, while I clutched Rose to me. My sister's chest infection was bad. She was sweating, her body burning against my own hot skin and her hair was wet, stuck flat to her scalp. Her breath came in short struggling gasps of air that frightened me.

I was on my own with her. I sat on the settee rocking her and singing, singing as much for me as her, trying not to hear the desperately choking gasps. Watching the fingers on the clock move slowly; it felt as though Nanna had been gone for hours, but it was only thirty minutes.

I didn't expect to see Sam. He came through the back door shouting my name.

'I've just seen your Nan. She's had to go to the chemist on Manchester Road because the one on Station Road hasn't got what the doctor said Rose needs or something. She said you weren't so good either so I thought I'd come round...'

I burst into tears; I was so relieved to see him. Normally he wouldn't come to the house because of Mum. Over the last year his voice had gone different; it changed from a low growl to high squeak and angry spots erupted onto his face without warning. Mum teased him about both.

So Sam stayed away when he knew she was home. But that day he was there when I needed him.

'You okay?' He didn't ask me why I hadn't been in school; I felt he knew but he didn't ask and I was grateful.

I nodded.

He flung his wet coat on the floor. He was still wearing his school uniform. 'Let me have her.' He took Rose and her doll from me as though she was as light as a feather and walked around with her. I hadn't noticed before how tall and thickset he'd become. She snuggled closer to him.

I wished, fleetingly, it was me he was holding on to. 'Nanna said to give her some honey and lemon,' I said. 'I'll put the kettle on, warm some water.'

Chapter Fourteen

2002: Yesterday: 6.30 p.m.

'It's just been a bad day or two,' I say. 'Anyway, Mother wouldn't cope – not in a strange place.'

'She's already in a strange place and *we're* not coping.' Sam sits back, watching my reaction. 'You on antidepressants, me worrying about you all the time; this is driving both of us round the bend, Irene. We have to think about what it's doing to us.' He leans forward and holds my hands across the kitchen table.

The pain behind my eyes is throbbing harder now. 'You're right, of course you're right,' I say. 'But she refused to sign those power of attorney papers and it's too late now.' There, I've said it. I wait for him to blame me, even though I know he won't. 'I'm sorry, Sam.'

64

'How about we go to a solicitor? Get some advice?' He strokes my fingers. 'I've been online; there are things we can do.' He's tiptoeing around me, I can tell.

'Can we talk about it tomorrow, Sam?' I feel the panic hovering in my throat. It's always the same when he starts talking like this and the thought of my leaving Rose looms. 'You can show me then. I've got such a headache—'

'And why, love?' He lets go of my hands and sits back in his chair. There is a note of exasperation in his voice but, when I look at him, his eyes show how worried he is.

'I'm sorry.' How many times, how often do I say those words?

'I know.' He still holds my hand. 'But you've done your bit, more than your bit.' He drains the mug, stands up to rinse it under the cold water. 'Let's face it, love,' he says, 'you were never that close, you and her.'

He was wrong about that but I was too tired to argue.

1970

I was sitting on the back doorstep, one eye open, squinting at the wisps of clouds disappear from vision and then opening the other eye to watch them float past. Dad and Rose were in a deckchair on the grass at the back of our row of houses. The sudden clatter as Caroline fell onto the path and Rose's cry of 'Iwene,' startled me, but when I saw what had happened I laughed and jumped up. 'I'll get it, Dad.' But as I handed the doll back to my sister, I looked up at my father and I knew something was wrong. His head was tilted to one side and he was shaking. 'Dad?' It was as though he couldn't hear me and when I crouched in front of him I couldn't get him to look at me. 'Dad!' His arms hung down at his sides and Rose slipped off him. I caught her; she was getting really heavy and I had to put my knee under her bottom to hitch her up to my shoulder. I looked along the communal land. There was no one in sight. Then Mrs Rhodes at the end house came out, carrying a basket of washing.

'Mrs Rhodes. Mrs Rhodes.' I ran towards her. Rose was crying. 'It's Dad – he's gone funny.' Rose was slipping. 'And Nanna's out.' I struggled to keep hold of my sister and I fell to my knees on the ground. Her arms were so tight around my neck I could hardly breathe. When I looked up Mrs Rhodes was running towards us. And then past us. I twisted round to see her bend over my father.

'Get Mr Rhodes,' she shouted. 'Hurry up.'

He was a big, fat man and I had to push him from behind to hurry him along which made Rose laugh. I wasn't laughing; I was frightened. But when we got to our patch of grass Dad was sitting up again drinking a cup of water. Or at least trying to; his hands were trembling so much the water was sloshing all over the place and Mrs Rhodes had to hold the cup for him.

'He's fine, now, love.' She turned her head to look at me.

Dad gave me a wobbly smile. 'I'm all right, sweetheart,' he said, 'just had a bit of a funny do.'

The doctor said afterwards it was a minor stroke.

So that meant I had two people to worry about.

Chapter Fifteen

2002: Yesterday: 6.45 p.m.

Sam was wrong when he said Mum and me were never close. We were. Before Rose. I feel ashamed saying that, as though it was Rose's fault. It wasn't.

It's a long time ago, and the memories are sometimes vague. But they are there for the days when all this is too much for me; I dredge them up in the worst moments. It helps.

The shopping trips for clothes when all we bought were things for me, Mum and me going to the baths for a swim, the Saturday morning matinees at the local picture house on Boardman Street, birthday parties.

The one I remember the best was my sixth birthday party. Well, it was really an extra treat; I'd already had a sort of party at home with Mum and Dad and Nanna. That was the last one I remember Grandad being there. Sam was with us as well and we had sausage and chips and the grown-ups had fish and chips. Afterwards we had ice cream and Nanna had made me a cake with white icing and those little hard coloured balls scattered on top. I didn't much like those but I didn't say anything because the cake itself was yummy. Grandad got some of the balls stuck under his teeth and had to take his top set out. It was like his lip disappeared under his nose. Sam and me got the giggles but Nanna pretended she was cross with him for doing it. I could tell she was only pretending because her eyes crinkled at the corners and she sucked on her mouth.

Anyway, like I said, I had an extra birthday treat: a trip to the pictures. Mum sorted it out by herself because Dad was staying with Nanna. I didn't know at the time it was because Grandad had started to be poorly.

I was allowed to take three friends with me: Cherry Smith, Marilyn Morgan and Jean King. Sam wouldn't come because he said it was a soppy film.

Cherry and Marilyn were best friends and Jean was mine (well, best friend who was a girl). Sam was my really, really best friend.

'He's a boy anyway,' Cherry said, on the way there. 'We don't want a daft boy with us.'

'No,' I said. I felt a bit disloyal to Sam.

We studied the poster on the wall of the Astoria while we queued for the manager to open the doors.

'*One Hundred and One Dalmatians*,' Marilyn read aloud.

'I wonder where they found a hundred of them,' Jean said.

Cherry and Marilyn shoved at one another, rolling their eyes and sniggering.

I didn't join in. I hoped Jean hadn't noticed.

'I don't like the look of her.' Cherry pointed to a woman in the picture dressed in a fur coat and with long red nails and red sneery lips.

'Cruella de Vil,' Mum said. 'She's the baddy.

We shrieked in a dramatic way.

It started to drizzle just as the doors were opened and everyone squashed into the entrance.

'One adult, four children in the balcony.' Mum pushed her money under the glass and waited for the man in the box office to tear off the five pink tickets.

'Can't we go in the stalls?' Jean's lip trembled. 'I'm frightened of being up high.'

'Certainly not.' Despite her words, Mum smiled, her voice gentle. 'You'll be fine.'

'I'll hold your hand,' I said, giving Jean my new handkerchief when I saw the tears spill over. I always felt a bit sorry for Jean; her clothes never quite fit her. Her mother found them at the Methodist weekly jumble sale. Dresses with huge thick hems turned up a few times, cardigan and jumper sleeves halfway up her arms

'Thanks,' she said with a shaky smile, offering my hanky back after she'd blown her nose on it.

It was all snotty.

'No, you keep it. I had six of them in a box from Nanna for my birthday.'

'But it's so pretty.' She touched the red embroidered rose on one corner. 'You sure?'

'Yeah.'

We jostled against one another at the sweet counter.

'Anything up to sixpence each, girls,' Mum warned.

I chose Alphabet Letters even though the man behind the counter wouldn't let me pick the letters. Marilyn had a liquorice wheel with a pink middle and a packet of pretend cigarettes. Cherry had a bag of her usual Cherry Lips and Jean, Jelly Babies.

We settled on the seats in the balcony and Mum sat by the aisle and lit a cigarette. The smoke swirled blue in the dimmed lights when the gold curtains were drawn back. Marilyn pretended to smoke hers.

We waited, impatient, for the boring news to finish.

Twice during *One Hundred and One Dalmatians*, the manager stopped the film: once because the kids in the stalls made such a racket, and again, because some boys were climbing over the seats and the usherette shouted at them.

We were cross because it took ages for them to settle down.

Marilyn leant over the rail of the balcony to see what was happening. 'It's Benny Robinson and my brother being pests. Just wait 'til I tell Mum.' She sat back. 'Did we miss any of the film?'

'I think it does skip a bit each time,' I said. 'It was juddering at first.' She scowled.

At the interval Mum stood up and looked towards the back of the balcony where the usherette stood with her tray.

'Anyone for a tub of ice cream?'

As soon as she left, Marilyn fumbled around in her cardigan pocket and took out a peashooter and a handful of hard peas.

'Watch this.'

We stood at the side of her. Even Jean was brave enough to peer over the balcony.

Leaning over the rail Marilyn took aim at her brother. Despite the clamour of noise we still heard the yell. She grinned at us.

We grinned back.

Marilyn's brother was glaring upwards but not at us. He was staring at a boy who was standing at the balcony rail on the opposite side of the aisle.

'I'll get you,' he shouted.

We slumped back into our seats.

I hoped Mum hadn't seen what had happened; I knew if there was any bother we wouldn't be going to the café on Curzon Street and have the Knickerbocker Glory afterwards.

'Aren't you scared he'll find out it was you,' Cherry asked Marilyn, grinning in admiration.

'Am I 'eck. I can wallop him no problem. He's as soft as muck.'

At the end of the film the manager let us out before those in the stalls.

'My mother says it's because people on the balcony are posher. We always sit up there,' Cherry whispered, blowing a big pink bubble with her bubblegum. It burst, covering her mouth and nose. She picked it off her face as we hurried down Curzon Street to claim our Knickerbocker Glory.

Sam's forgotten the times before Rose. I don't remind him. But I do try to smile.

He doesn't. In fact he looks undeniably annoyed

The depression that has been my shadow for so long now envelops me. I hear the small sigh behind me, smell baby lotion. For once I don't feel comforted.

1970

I went through a stage of refusing to wear my glasses when I was fifteen because Sam said my eyes were beautiful. The world became a blur of colours and shapes but I was too vain to admit it. And, anyway, I knew the streets around where we lived like the back of my hand; it didn't occur to me that I'd also need to see what was going on. Stupid.

And of course I came a cropper one day; I lost Rose. Well, I didn't exactly lose her, I just couldn't see her after she let go of my hand and ran off in the park's playground. I could hear her laughing so kept moving in that direction, bumping into people. Once I tripped over a dog and fell to my knees and a man helped me to my feet, leaving his hand too long on my bottom. He smelled funny so I mumbled my thanks and stumbled away from him. When I needed to stop and listen for Rose I made myself move on, thinking he was following me.

It was then I heard the splash and the scream. The river!

Panicking, my heart thudding, I ran, shouting her name through my sobs, my arms stretched out in front of me. I slid down the banking and into the rushing water that dragged at my legs and filled my knee-length boots as I waded further in, swirling my hands under the surface, sliding on slimy rocks. It was cold despite the sun making sparks of light on the water, so bright they hurt my eyes. I turned around and around, gasping for breath, hoping to catch the flash of Rose's red dress and making a frantic mental pact with God that I would never be vain ever again; that I wouldn't leave my glasses at the side of my bed ever again – if only he'd let my sister be safe – not drowned.

I was screaming her name so loudly I didn't hear my own being shouted. The first I knew that Sam was there was when I felt his hand on mine, pulling at me, leading me out of the river and on to the path.

'What the hell were you doing?' He was angry, grabbing my shoulders and shaking me.

'I've lost Rose.' I shivered; the hem of my miniskirt clung, wet, to my thighs each time I moved. I felt the sloshing of water inside my boots. 'I thought she'd fallen in. I can't find her.'

'What're you talking about?' His hands dropped away.

As he spoke I felt Rose's fingers entwine mine, warm against the chill of my skin.

'I played.' Her voice quiet, frightened. 'Iwene?'

My legs wouldn't hold my; I sank to my knees and clung to her.

'Where are your glasses?' Sam moved away from me, turned towards the river, scanning the ground.

'No,' I said, 'they haven't fallen off, I left them at home.'

'Again?' I heard the anger in his voice. 'It's daft Irene; you can't see your hand in front of your face. You've got to stop being so stupid.' I saw the movement of his hand towards Rose's head. 'Especially when you have her to look after.'

'I know. I'm sorry.' Somewhere to my left I could hear boys laughing and jeering. 'You're with your mates?'

'It doesn't matter. Let's get you two home,' he said, pulling his jumper off and giving it to me.

He walked between Rose and me. We didn't speak until we stood outside our house.

'Promise me you'll stop doing this, Irene. You could get hurt.'

I felt ashamed. Even so I said. 'They're the only thing that I like about myself – my eyes. You said yourself you liked them.'

He lifted my sister up into his arms and gave her a squeeze. 'You okay, kid?'

'Yes.' Her voice trembled. 'I's sowwy.'

'S'okay.' He set her on her feet and poked his face closer to mine, our noses brushing. 'Can you see me?' he asked in a deep ghostly tone and grinning.

The relief, the realisation that both my sister and me were safely home, coursed through me. I smiled at him. 'Yes, you daft ha'porth.' I yanked his jumper over my head and handed it to him.

'Well listen to me. I like you, all of you. Now go in and get dry. And don't be such a drip in future.' He stopped, looking at my wet sleeves and skirt, both of us realising at the same time what he'd said. We began to laugh. Rose joined in with her lovely chuckle. When we'd calmed down he said, 'And put your glasses on; it doesn't matter that you wear specs. It doesn't stop you having fab eyes.'

Chapter Sixteen

2002: Yesterday: 7.00 p.m.

These days, the only time I don't wear my specs is in bed. Sam says he loves to look into my eyes when we lie close to one another, sharing a pillow, his arm under my head. He says the colour reminds him of a clear blue sky. He says I'm beautiful.

I joke that he's looking at me after one too many pints of beer but he doesn't drink that much and besides it's not funny. It's as though I'm rushing towards old age before I've actually lived.

We hear a thud upstairs. When we get to Mum's bedroom her plastic beaker is on the floor in the doorway and she beams at us.

'Think someone wants something,' Sam mutters, but there's a smile in his voice.

'You hungry Mum?'

She waggles her head.

'I'll warm it up. You stay with her, stick her bib thing on.'

By the time he's back I've got her sitting up and ready.

She won't let me help her to eat, keeps pushing my hand away. It's going to be a long session.

'I'll go and clear up in the kitchen,' Sam says. 'Will you be all right?' Mum has ketchup all around her mouth. In one hand she's clutching a couple of squashed chips, with the other she's busy poking at the peas that have fallen into the pocket of her plastic bib.

I twist around in the chair to smile up at him. The corners of my mouth quiver with the effort. 'Course.'

'Sure?'

Sometimes it's as if time stops. We're still looking at each other, Sam waiting for me to answer again when there's a cough, a choking noise. I half-stand, look at Mum, but Sam's quicker. She's smeared the chips all over her face but some dangle from her mouth and she's gone pink. He leans her forward and thumps her on her back, sticking his finger between her lips and pulling the bits of the chips out. When she stops choking he picks up a cloth and wipes her mouth, but when he tries to dry her with a towel she swats at him.

She's messed herself again. I can smell it.

1971

Everything changed when I was sixteen.

Irene, I'm sorry. I hate leaving you and Rose but it really is for the best...

Best for who? I stared at the piece of paper covered in Dad's writing. He'd left. Just like that. I came home from school and there was the letter on my bed.

...you know how things have been between your mum and me, it's impossible.

But what about us? What about me and Rose? I feel sick.

I should have told you last night I was leaving but I chickened out. I'll be honest with you, I've met someone. Well, really I've known her for a few years.

What did that mean – known her? Did it mean he'd been shagging this – this woman for years? Having sex? I knew all about sex, well I knew what we'd been told in biology in school. I sat on the bed, feeling uncomfortable. I didn't want to picture that: old people having sex, making love.

She's called Susan Wilson. She's a widow. Come to see me when you can and I'll explain everything. Bring Rose. Susan lives in a flat on Beech Drive on the new housing estate. Number 14.

Love Dad xx

Explain everything? How could he explain to Rose that he won't be here when she wakes up in the night, when she's poorly or sad, when she falls and he's not here to pick her up, to cuddle her? She won't understand what's happened. And there wasn't anything else to explain to me. Somehow, despite being ill and having to leave work, he'd also managed to have an affair with some woman over the last year or so and now he'd left us. A cold chill ran through me, tightened my scalp. What were me and Rose supposed to do now? For a moment the anger took over and I hated Dad. I wondered if Mum knew and what she would say.

Chapter Seventeen

'She needs changing again.'

'I'll help you stick her in the bath.'

'I could get in the shower with her?'

'No, I'm here; it'll be easier for you and take less time if we just give her a bath.'

He shows no sign of embarrassment when he helps me to undress her, not even when I clean the mess from her buttocks, not even when I take off her vest to reveal her flaccid flat breasts and she hugs him.

I watch him trying to extricate himself from her grasp; see how gentle he is with her. I know how much he regrets agreeing to buy into the house to live with her. And yet he still has this compassion. He's such a good man.

She's clinging to him like a limpet, her arms wrapped around him, her head on his chest. Hugging him.

She used to hug me once. But that was before Rose was born. After that, because she wouldn't hug my sister, I refused to let her hug me. Nanna cuddled Rose and me at the drop of a hat. Nanna used to say she couldn't get enough hugs. I remember how much she missed Grandad after he died. He was a short man, as wide as he was tall. His loud laugh somehow seemed too big for his body. He loved to throw his arms around Nanna and swing her round and round, while she shouted for him to put her down. But she always laughed as well. She was sad for a long time after he'd gone.

Once, a while after she came to live with us, Nanna said me and Rose were the best thing that happened to her in her life: after Grandad, of course.

Mum won't let go of Sam's hand even when she's sitting in the bath. It's easier to bath her when he's here. Other times, I have to go in the shower with her and that's a right palaver. But he's content to perch on the side while I wash her.

She's looking adoringly up at Sam from under her sparse grey eyelashes; I wonder who she thinks he is. For a moment I feel a pang of sadness for this woman; once so pretty, so sure of her attractiveness. When I wipe her face she pushes my hand away.

'No.'

I'm stopping her gaze on him.

Ten minutes is as long as I usually take bathing her; she gets cold quickly. But, tonight she refuses to get out.

'No.'

I pull the plug out and she looks, baffled as the water drains off her. Then cross. But, when Sam holds out the towel and wraps it around her she allows him to lift her up and stand her on the mat. She wobbles as I dry her. He holds her steady while I fasten the incontinence pad into her knickers and then slip the nightdress on.

It's early for her to go to bed. 'Do you think she'll still be hungry?' I hold up her dressing gown, unsure what to do.

'Better not chance giving her anything else after her choking do,' Sam says. 'Let's just get her into bed. Then you can have an early night as well.' He picks Mum up and takes her to her room. Putting on her bed socks I think Sam needs his sleep as much as me; he has an early start tomorrow. After the hours he lost today from work, he has a lot to catch up on.

He gently slips his hand from hers and, with a couple of grunts, she snuggles down under the covers.

1971

Of course she knew. As soon as I walked into the kitchen I could tell she knew from the set of her mouth and the heavy silence that seemed to still the air.

'Thought you were getting changed out of that uniform?' She wouldn't meet my eye as she peeled potatoes. The blade of the small knife in her hand kept catching the gleam of sunlight from the window and sending flashes on the wall next to me.

Rose had her thumb in her mouth and was looking from Mum to me, a frown creasing her wide forehead. Nanna was fussing with the buttons of her cardigan. 'I'll take Rose into the other room.' She squeezed my shoulder when she passed me.

Rose clung to my hand. I kissed her fingers. 'See you in a bit.' I smiled, trying to reassure her.

I'd crumpled the letter in my fist; I could feel the sharp edges of the paper digging into my palm.

I swallowed. 'Dad—'

'I don't want to talk about him.'

'But—'

'Didn't you hear what I said?' She threw the knife into the sink and whirled around to face me. Her lips were thin and turned down, her eyes puffy and red.

Perhaps I should have felt something for her: concern, compassion even, but right at that moment her distress didn't touch me. The only thing I felt was bewilderment. 'I don't understand what's happened.'

'All these years ... all these years I stuck it out. I could have gone – left – but I didn't. I had my chances – offers.' The words were harsh but her voice trembled. 'But I didn't leave. I stayed...'

'Why?' It would have been so much better if she had gone. 'Why stay, Mother? If you hated being here with us so much?'

'It's as much my house as his.' She flung out her arms as if to take in the whole place. 'Why should I leave it all to him?'

'But now *he's* gone. He's left us. Because of you—'

'And good riddance to bad rubbish.'

'That's my dad you're talking about—'

'Oh for god's sake, he's not even your dad. He's not—' she stopped.

The room shifted around me. 'What?' I clenched my fist, felt the letter being crushed tighter. 'What do you mean?'

Her sniff was long, drawn out. Her eyes closed. She bit down on her lower lip as though trying to hold back her next words. But still they came out. 'I said he's not your dad, not your real father anyway.'

'I don't understand...' How could she say that? The anger seeped away, replaced by panic. 'I don't believe you.'

She shrugged the hard mask back in place. 'Please yourself.' She picked the knife out of the sink and started to cut up the potatoes. The melted lard in the pan began to smoke. She lifted the wire basket and filled it with the raw chips before lowering it into the fat. Her next words were lost in the splutter and hiss as the fat rose over the wet potatoes.

'What?'

Her face was red and shiny with the heat. 'I said—' she overemphasised the words. 'You're real father buggered off as soon as I found out I was pregnant.'

'I don't understand,' I repeated.

'And you the little clever clogs who thinks she knows everything.' She shook the basket in the chip pan. 'Work it out for yourself.'

There was a loud buzzing in my ears. My legs crumpled and I felt behind me for a chair. Sitting, I put my head between my knees.

Mum continued as though she hadn't noticed. 'The chap who got me pregnant did a moonlight flit the day I told him I'd missed my period – the bastard. But I'd always known Derek liked me; he'd chased me for years, so it was easy enough. He couldn't believe his luck when I said I'd marry him. I was young, pretty – some said I was beautiful.' Her voice was loud, harsh. 'Getting Derek was easy – he couldn't wait to get me down that aisle, even got a special licence. He was so desperate for me not to change my mind. And he was over the moon when you arrived – six weeks early.'

Only I wasn't early was I? Not if I wasn't his. Did he know? And did he really believe what she said. He wasn't stupid. And if he knew I wasn't his why hadn't he told me? I wasn't a kid anymore.

I felt Rose's snuffly breathing next to my cheek. 'Iwene?' Then she was gone, leaving behind the smell of Johnson's baby lotion.

Nanna's hand was on my shoulder. 'Lilian, how could you...?' I looked up at her. Her face was ashen. 'Are you all right, Irene?' I managed a nod. Out of the corner of my eye I saw Rose scurry into

78

the living room where she hid under the pile of cushions on the settee. 'I didn't know, Irene. I swear. She told me Derek was your dad.'

Mum lifted her chin, her mouth twisted. When she spoke there was a challenge in her voice. 'I didn't – you just assumed.'

'I thought—'

'Like *you* always think *you* know everything, as well.' Mum lifted the chips out of the fat and propped the basket against the rim of the pan. 'You didn't care who her father was. You were quick enough to get me married off.' She turned off the cooker ring. 'Don't say you weren't.' Her voice rose. 'What? Your daughter – the unmarried mother? What would the neighbours say?'

'It wouldn't have mattered – not to your Dad and me – you know he idolised you.'

'Huh!' Mum puffed her lips out in a scornful gesture.

'He did. But he'd be ashamed of what you've done to Derek. And to Irene. You should be ashamed.'

'Me? Ashamed? He's the one that's been having the affair. He's the one who's gone off to live with some floozy. He's the one to leave me with...' She waved a hand towards the living room where I could see Rose's bottom jutting out from the cushion, Caroline, dangling from her hand over the side of the settee.

The anger rushed through me. 'You're cruel and horrible. I don't blame Dad for finding someone else. If I was him I'd do the same. And as soon as I'm old enough, I'll leave as well.'

I avoided meeting Nanna's eyes but I sensed her sadness.

There are images that always come to mind when I remember the moment I found out that Dad wasn't my biological father; Nanna's eyes, filled with misery, and my sister trying to hide under the cushions to get away from the harsh sound of my mother's voice, with only her arm sticking out and clutching hold of Caroline.

I've still got her, Caroline. Before I lived with Sam I took the doll to bed with me. Nowadays she sits on the top of the set of drawers

79

in our room. In the gloom I look across towards her. I think she still smells vaguely of Johnson's baby lotion. Or it might just be my imagination.

Chapter Eighteen

2002: Yesterday: 8.30 p.m.

I've cleaned the armchair and put a different cover on it so I'm on the seat and Sam is perched on the arm while we wait for her to go to sleep. Her eyes are open and I know if we move she'll start thrashing about, trying to get up. It's always the same.

My eyelids droop and I jerk awake, hurt my neck.

'Come on,' Sam says, 'I'll stay with her while you go and get into your night things.'

Mum struggles to sit up. Now, when she looks at Sam there's fear in her eyes and she's holding out her hand to me.

I go to stand by the bed, squeeze her fingers. 'I'm here.'

I hate the nights. I don't think it's too strong a word. The doctor's given me sleeping tablets for Mum but getting them down her is a nightmare. She has a talent for holding them under her tongue and spitting them out when I've turned my back, however long I sit waiting for her to swallow the damn things. I've tried crushing them in her night-time porridge (even though you're not supposed to), I've hidden them in a spoonful of her favourite rice pudding and in the strawberry jelly she normally wolfs down. Once, in desperation and to my shame, I even forced them into her mouth and tried to make her have a drink of water. She nearly choked.

After that I gave up.

So now I wait with Sam.

This woman will be the death of me.

Or me her.

1971

'Did you mean it?'

It was Friday; the evening of the last day of the summer term. Sam and me were sitting on the path just outside the back door. School had finished and the long summer holidays stretched in front of us. Well, stretched in front of me before the autumn term started and I'd have to get my head down to study for my GCEs. Sam had already left school and was working as an apprentice with a local firm of decorators. He was also on a two-day release course at the college in Manchester, thirteen miles away from our village, which meant I didn't see all that much of him.

'Mean what?' I tilted my head back on the garden chair to watch the glint of the sun flashing through the leaves of the apple tree that Dad had planted years ago that had never produced apples.

'That you'll leave as soon as you can?' His voice had a rough edge to it as though it was a question that he'd bottled up. 'You know how I feel about you, Irene...'

He leant forward in his chair, his head lowered, his hair flopping so I couldn't see his face. But his neck was scarlet. 'I love you – always have. And I know you feel the same...' I saw his Adam's apple jerk rapidly up and down his throat. 'It'll take me three years to finish the apprenticeship. I'll be on good money if they take me on proper. Or even if I go to another firm.' He lifted his head, gazed towards the end of the garden. 'We'll both be nineteen then and I'd like us to get married. Nobody can stop us.'

It wasn't what I expected him to say.

'I know. And I love you, Sam.' I stroked his lovely strong fingers. 'But you know I want to stay on in school, hopefully go to university – or, at least, teacher training college—'

'That could still happen.' He straightened up, faced me. Smiling. 'I'd be earning. I'd keep us until you're qualified. I would never get in the way of your career, whatever it was you wanted to do. But...'

'But?' I felt uneasy.

He stopped abruptly, his smile fading. 'That was a right battle you had with Rose.' He'd waited outside while Nanna and me had struggled with her in the house.

'She didn't want to go to bed.' I was immediately defensive. I opened my eyes, challenging him. 'It's not often she has a tantrum as bad as that.'

'She's strong.'

I raised my hand to my cheekbone; there was already a small lump where her head had collided with it. 'This was an accident.'

'I know it was, Irene...' He rubbed at his nose with the back of his hand. 'But she's a strong little thing. And stubborn...'

'She's in bed now—'

'Only because your nanna is lying down alongside her. And you said you didn't manage to get her undressed.'

He was right. We'd given in and let her keep her vest and pants on, her pyjamas having been thrown in the corner of the room.

'Well, like I said, it doesn't happen often.' I sat upright in the chair, folding my arms and hunching my shoulders. 'You know she's missing Dad. She doesn't understand why he's not here anymore. It's difficult for her.'

'What if she never understands? What will happen then, Irene?' He lowered his voice. 'With your dad gone and your mum hardly ever here...'

He was right about Mum. Since Dad left, she'd started to work long hours. At least she said she did. Sometimes I saw one of her best frocks and a pair of shoes tucked under the cover of her basket when she went out to work in the morning. And, once, waiting up for her to come home, I'd peeped through the window to see her in a car with a man. I almost missed Sam's next words.

'And your nanna's not getting any younger...' He tried to take hold of my hand but I kept both of them tucked under my armpits. 'What happens when she can't cope with Rose? What if Rose has these paddies when she's older and bigger if something doesn't suit and is too much for her?'

'She won't.' He'd never talked like this before.

'Or when your nanna isn't here anymore?' He touched my cheek, tried to turn my face to his. I resisted, the anger in me refusing to accept what he was saying. 'It's been bothering me a bit. Well...' his forehead furrowed. 'A lot, if I'm honest.' He gently pulled my hand away from my body, held it between his fingers. 'You know I love her as much as you do. But you – we – need to talk about this. We have to be sensible—'

'Sensible?' I huffed out a breath, sneered. I'd always taken it for granted that he'd help with Rose whatever happened; that we'd manage somehow. But obviously not.

'I'll always want to help with Rose—'

'Who says I'd let you? And, listening to you now, why would you want to?'

'Because, like I said, I love her as much as you do and she'll always come first, I know that. But look at us. You've already said you want to leave, to get more qualifications to teach. I don't know where I'll go once the apprenticeship finishes, or if I'll have a job at the same place. What happens then? And where will Rose fit in when your nanna—'

'Stop it! With me. She'll be with me. You can please yourself, Sam Hargreaves. I'd give it all up; find something to do around here...'

There was a slight noise behind us. A scuffle of a slipper on the lino on the kitchen floor. I looked round. Nanna had come into the kitchen. She was holding Rose's shoes and a cloth and polish.

'If I can pass, you two, I'll clean these outside. She'll need them for morning.'

She gave me an odd little smile that only curved her lips and didn't reach her eyes. I knew she'd heard us.

Chapter Nineteen

Mum's asleep at last. Her hand drops out of mine and I move away.

Sam touches my cheek, gives me a kiss and says, 'Come on – bed.'

Mum whimpers and struggles to sit up. I go to stand next to her again but he holds on to my hand. 'I'll see to her.'

'You have paperwork to do. Go on downstairs.' His books and his jobs are piling up because I've been asking a lot of him in the daytimes these last few months. Every time Mum has fallen, each time she's been stroppy at bedtime, he's been there for me. He never lets me down. 'I'll cope.'

'"I'll cope" will be on your headstone if you don't start looking after yourself.' There was a hint of frustration in his voice. 'You'll be in that graveyard before her if you're not careful.'

I persuade her to lie down and flop back in the chair. The next thing I know Sam's lifting me to my feet and holding me. 'Bedtime,' he says. Still with my eyes closed I cling to him.

'You all right?' Sam's palm, on the back of my head as I lean into him, comforts me and I breathe in the familiar faint smell of paint and Hugo Boss aftershave. 'You've not got those palpitations again?'

'No. And I'll be fine.'

'You sure you took all your tablets today?'

'Yes.'

'You're out on your feet.'

And I am. I feel the shifting plates of my world tilt under me again. But still I say, 'I'm fine,' suddenly wishing we were alone, craving his lovemaking. When was the last time that happened? I can't remember. We stand like that for a while until I'm swaying, lulled into drowsiness.

Am I imagining the slight pressure on my back, the warmth of breath on my hand? Is that what always persuades me Rose is here? Whatever it is, I'm comforted for a moment before it's gone and I shiver.

'Irene?' His voice is low, urgent. 'Come on, love, you need to get to bed.'

I do. Another one of Dad's sayings was that he could sleep draped over a washing line and that's just how I feel now. One more minute and I'll be out cold against Sam. Pushing myself upright I stare out of the window at the sky. Dark clouds, pulled apart by high-flying winds, show pearlised pinks and silver, the glow of the daytime sunshine already vanished. The nights have started to draw in. I can't stand the thought of going through another long winter behind curtained windows.

I'm glad to get undressed and climb into bed.

'Let's hope you get a good sleep.'

I don't utter the words that immediately spring to mind, that chance would be a fine thing.

'I will.'

1971

We tried hard to fill the gap that Dad left but Rose cried a lot for him. I hadn't taken her to see him at the woman's flat but, without telling Mum, I agreed to meet him in the park. I wondered how Rose would react.

There was a tingle of nerves in my stomach. I wanted to show Dad how furious I was, how I didn't understand how he could leave us. All I really wanted was to feel his arms around me; to have him hold me tight and tell me everything would be okay. Tell me what Mum said was a lie. I was his daughter, he was my real dad.

I'd put Rose in the baby swings although, at eight, she was getting too big and it was a struggle to ease her legs through the bar. She leaned as far back as she could so she could see me, her spiky black hair flattening and rising, each time I gave the swing a gentle push, the little twist in her top lip making her smile even bigger.

Dad was only a few feet away from us by the time she saw him. I made a mental note to tell Nanna we needed to take her back to the opticians, her sight could have gone worse since her first visit and I hadn't thought to ask if the small fold of skin at the inner corner of each eye stopped her seeing properly. Our doctor hadn't suggested anything about that when we'd taken her the last time she had a chest infection. I promised myself I'd talk to Nanna about it later. When Rose did see Dad she yelled with delight, 'Da', struggling to get out of the swing.

'Wait, wait,' I cried, untangling her from the seat and chains. Dad put his hands under her arms and lifted her out.

'My, you've grown,' he said, in an over-hearty voice.

'It's only been a month, she hasn't grown that much.' I knew I sounded sulky but didn't care. It was actually five weeks and two days since he walked out on us. It felt like years. I wouldn't look at him. I gazed over at the river where Sam used to play on the rope swing. There was another group of young lads there now, laughing and skimming their feet over the water.

'Thanks for the letter, Irene. Thanks for seeing me.'

'Just for Rose's sake.'

He flushed. 'You've every right to be angry with me. Susan said I should have—'

'Don't – don't talk to me about her.' This was the cow who'd taken our Dad away from us. Why would he think I'd want to know what she said or thought?

When I turned back Rose had her face pressed close to his. I avoided his outstretched hand, giving Rose her doll instead.

'Da.' Rose looked from one to the other of us. Her smile froze, the corners of her lips slowly turned down. 'Iwene?' She frowned as she said my name, pressing her mouth to Caroline's hard head.

'It's all right, love.' I stroked her back. 'You could at least have rung,' I said, hating myself for even showing him how much I was hurting.

'I did. Four times. Your mother put the phone down on me.' He kept his voice even.

'Well you should have written then.'

'I did that too. I'm presuming you didn't get those either?'

'No.' Mother must have kept or destroyed them. I walked over and sat next to him. 'Sorry,' I said quietly. 'It's just with us losing the dog last year – and now you've disappeared – Rose soon gets upset. She doesn't understand. All she knows is that anyone she loves disappears.'

'I know. And, for what it's worth, I'm sorry as well.' He carried Rose to the bench where he'd always sat when he brought me at her age. Clutching the doll she settled against him and closed her eyes.

'How's her...?' He mouthed the words, tapping his chest.

'The doctor says okay. For now,' I added.

Rose slowly raised her hand and stroked his cheek, her eyes still closed.

'She's pleased to see you, at least,' I said.

'And you're not?'

'No – yes – I suppose so. You left us.' The anger was quick to return.

'Irene, I am sorry.' He was pale, his eyes bloodshot. 'I really am. And I wish I could have taken you with me.'

'Why couldn't you?' Would I have gone to that woman's place anyway? I knew the answer before the question finished in my head. There was no way I'd have taken Rose there, no way I'd have left Nanna. 'Forget I said that.' The words were abrupt and, for a second or two, I took satisfaction from hurting him. But it didn't last long; he really did look dreadful. I wondered if he thought he'd made a mistake moving in with that woman. Or had another funny turn.

He didn't acknowledge me. Instead he mouthed above Rose's head. 'It's not that cut and dried – I wish I could explain better – but I couldn't take Rose away from all she knows. Susan's – the flat—'

I turned away, straightened my mouth, hoped he saw my anger. If he did he ignored it. 'It's only a small place. There's no room—'

'For us,' I interrupted. Too loud, Rose squeezed her eyes tighter. 'There's no room for us in your life.'

'Don't put words in my mouth.' He spoke sharply. My sister twisted to look up at him. He smiled at her, dropped a kiss on her forehead. 'Sorry, love.' Rubbing his knuckles against his throat he whispered, 'I didn't say that, it's not what I mean. After I was ill I started to think about things. Like what was I doing living with a woman who hates me?' I opened my mouth to protest. 'You know, as well as I do, she does.' Rose whimpered. He rocked her. I watched him, waiting. 'Susan's been patient, she didn't push for me to leave your mother but she's had a hard time over the years. She has no one. You have Mum and Nanna.'

'We have Nanna,' I corrected. Did he expect me to feel sorry for the cow? He'd have to wait a long time if he did, I thought. Yet there was a faint understanding as well; this was so like Dad. He always weighed thing up; "balancing the books" he called it.

He took hold of my hand. I let him. 'If there was any other way...' the words floated away. 'I'm sorry,' he said again.

I felt the resentment seep out of me and rested against him, the fierce heat of tears behind my eyes. 'I know.'

Two council gardeners were weeding the flowerbeds on the other side of the park. Another was pushing a lawn mower over the grass. The roll and spin of the blades made a comforting, familiar sound. Everything seemed so normal. But it wasn't.

'We have the same colour of eyes, don't we?' I glanced up at him. 'Our eyes are the same?'

'Yes, I suppose we do, love. I suppose they are.'

'Which is odd – because Mum told me you're not really my dad.' I heard the intake of breath. 'That's not why you left us, is it?' He didn't answer. 'Dad?' I was scared; if he'd gone because of me, then it was my fault Rose had lost her daddy. I couldn't bear to think it might be my fault.

A woman came to the play area with a small girl and a pram. The girl climbed the steps of the slide, the woman followed her.

'No. It wasn't, you must never think that. I've known I wasn't your real dad for a long time.' Even though he spoke quietly, his voice was firm. 'I didn't know until you were a toddler, sweetheart, but by then it was too late. I loved you like you were my own – you are mine.' He turned to me. 'I want you to always know that. In every way that matters, you are my daughter and I love you.' His face was red.

'Are you angry?'

'Not with you. With your mother.' Rose gave a little snort and he relaxed his hold on her, let her sink down onto his lap. 'I always thought I'd be the one to tell you when the time seemed right. It never did. I suppose I was scared, scared you'd reject me. I should have plucked up the courage.'

I watched Rose. In her sleep she put her thumb in her mouth and sucked on it. A little dribble of saliva glistened on her chin. 'You won't tell Mum we've met, will you? Or that I've told you what she said? She'll go mad.'

'I won't. But I'm glad it's come out.' His smile made me feel better. 'Because, like I've said, you also know how much I love you. So...' He gave me a small nudge with his shoulder, 'it doesn't make one jot of difference to me, one way or the other. And I hope you feel the same.' His voice rose on the question and I nodded. He pressed his lips together. 'So, no, I won't say anything to your mother.'

'You won't be coming back though, will you?'

'No, Irene, I won't.'

'Okay,' I said slowly, 'so what happens now?'

'I promise I'll see you two as often as I can. We'll sort that out between us. And we can find out the numbers of the telephone boxes nearest to us and arrange when to call one another.' He hesitated. 'And you can always come to the flat. You've got the address?' I nodded, hating the thought of that but knowing he was right. 'It's a ten minute walk from Grove Street, love. Five if you have to run.' I lifted my face to his, puzzled. 'What I mean is – if it's that urgent, I'm only minutes away.' As though to emphasise what he was saying, he put his finger under my chin. 'I will always – always be here for you. You must never forget that. Understand?' I nodded 'Good.' He sighed and leaned back.

We sat like that for a long time. But I knew that, really, it was up to me to look after Rose.

Chapter Twenty

2002: Yesterday: 9.15 p.m.

No sooner do I pull my duvet over me than Mum starts shouting.

Dragging my dressing gown on, I hurry in to her before Sam leaves his paperwork to come upstairs again.

She's taken off her nightie. When I feel underneath her, there's a wet patch on the sheet. I'll have to change the bedding again. She laughs, spit dribbling.

Sam comes upstairs anyway. 'I'll help.' From the determined look on his face I know there's no point in arguing.

We work in silence.

1972

'Don't want you to go.' Rose pouted, her forehead lined with her frown.

'I have to, love. I need to catch the bus.'

'No. Want you to stay. Stay with me.' She wound her fingers tight around the strap of my shoulder bag. Her jaw was set in that stubborn way that exasperated me and yet I loved. It was that determination that had helped her overcome so many obstacles in her life. I couldn't help smiling but I knew I had to be firm.

'Now listen. I need to go, Rose.' I tried bribery. 'Remember, Saturday I work at the place where I buy your chocolate éclairs?'

I could see her wavering; she loved chocolate éclairs. But she still didn't let go of the bag.

'I come too.'

'Oh, Rose, I wish you could but you can't.' I checked my watch;

if I ran, I could still be on time for the bus. I liked my Saturday job at Littlewoods. It gave me some spending money and, to be honest, I liked getting out of the house.

'I be good.'

'You're always good, sweetheart.'

Her eyes grew large with tears.

'Tell you what. How about I bring you a chocolate éclair tonight and I promise to take you swimming tomorrow?'

She'd missed her swimming; it had been a good month since she'd been to the baths. The last cold had, yet again, gone onto her chest and it had only been a week since the doctor gave her the all clear, saying the exercise would do her good. She'd been mithering ever since to go.

I gave her a quick kiss, gently peeling her fingers off the strap.

'Pwomise?'

'Promise.'

She laughed and clapped her hands. 'Okay. Love Iwene.' She jumped up and wrapped her arms around my neck. I staggered back with the weight of her but managed to hold on while she gave me a long wet kiss.

'Love Rose.'

I'd been taking her swimming since she was five and now, at eight, she could do a pretty decent doggy-paddle.

She was frightened the first time we went. She held her hands over her ears against the echoing noise of the other kids playing and yelling that bounced down from the domed ceiling of the building. And she didn't like the smell or taste of the chlorine in the water. More than anything she hated getting undressed in the little cubicles at the side of the pool with only the thick, damp, flapping canvas curtain for cover from prying eyes.

But, after a time, she looked forward to our weekly Sunday visits and couldn't wait to get into her pink ruched costume and rubber swimming hat with the white plastic flower attached and the strap that tucked under her chin. Her little double chin.

One week she'd slipped out through the curtain and escaped before I could put my own costume on. When I heard the shriek and then the splash I knew it was Rose. And I knew she'd jumped into the water opposite our cubicle. Into the deep end. The screaming instantly followed. I pulled the straps over my shoulders, kicked my clothes to one side and, dragging the curtain back, ran out onto the poolside.

I gulped against the lump of fear in my throat. My sister was being held up by Sam and she was giggling and squirting water at him from her mouth.

He lifted his chin and formed the words, 'You okay?' at me.

I nodded, went back into the cubicle to pick up our clothes from the damp floor and put them into the tray on the wooden seat, my heart thudding. I held my towel to my face, forcing back the nausea and tears.

By the time I dived in, Rose was having a great time being passed back and forth from Sam to another lad, laughing and loving the attention.

I surfaced next to him. 'Thanks, Sam,' I said, pinching my nose against the sting of the chlorine and treading water. 'I didn't know you were coming to the baths today. Good job you were here.'

'Couple of mates fancied a dip.' He reached over and touched my arm, his hand slipping down to my fingers. 'It's fine. She's fine. She saw me. That's why she jumped in.' He jerked his head towards the lifeguard who was chatting to a girl I recognised from school. 'Not that he noticed. Blummin' useless idiot.' He scowled.

He helped me to take Rose to the shallow end and then swam away with a leisurely front crawl. It was the first time I'd seen him swim for a while; the muscles in his shoulders and arms were like a grown man's. There was an odd feeling in the pit of my stomach.

'Iwene?' Rose wound her arms around my neck. 'Cold,' she said.

She was; I could feel the pimples of goose bumps on her skin and her lips were turning blue.

'Come on then.' I clutched her tightly to me and, hanging on to the rail, hauled us up the metal steps. 'Enough's enough for today.'

'Enough's enough for today,' she repeated.

Chapter Twenty-One

2002: Yesterday: 9.30 p.m.

Mum starts to whimper. Before she can get to full throttle I get up. No Sam hovering at the foot of the stairs, I hear the low murmur of music from the radio in the kitchen. I kneel at the side of her bed and hold her hand for a few minutes until she settles again.

1972

The store was busy that day but I couldn't get Rose's face out of my head. I hoped Nanna or Dad would bring her into work like they did sometimes. Then I would hear her shriek of excitement when she spotted me, not caring who she ran into, her words, the sing-song 'sowwy', sowwy' running into one long phrase, as she pushed through the shoppers to hug me tight around my waist. And giggle when I kissed the end of her little upturned nose as usual, her lovely dark slanting eyes shining behind the lenses in her glasses.

When I started my Saturday job at Littlewoods I was on the jumpers counter but before long the supervisor told me to work on the clothes rails. Knitted dresses were all the rage then and I was slim. Each week she chose one for me to wear. I was supposed to swan about, showing all the worn-down housewives that were buying kids' clothes and big knickers for themselves, what they could look like if they pinched some money out of the housekeeping and bought a Littlewoods frock.

But they weren't all like Mum, who spent a fortune on her wardrobe, and the idea was soon dropped. I wasn't sorry; Sam used to come and laugh like billy-o when he saw me in some of the dresses. He said I looked daft – cheeky beggar. As though he knew anything about fashion.

That day my mind wasn't on the job; I felt guilty leaving Rose and I hoped she wasn't playing up for Nanna. Her tantrums were really something; she'd lie on the floor and scream, kicking anyone who went near her, or she'd throw things. It didn't happen often but it was upsetting.

And, that morning, when I ran along the street to catch the bus, despite the fact that she'd agreed to let me go, I was sure that I'd heard Rose shouting for me. I knew I should have gone back. But I needed my Saturday job money, all two pounds of it; Mum said I had to make my own spends. By then I'd long since realised she was jealous of the closeness Rose and me had. Sometimes that made me sad. She didn't need to be jealous; she could have accepted Rose as she was, and Mum and me could have gone back to how we were before.

I caught the bus to work.

It haunts me at night, even now.

Chapter Twenty-Two

2002: Yesterday: 10.00 p.m.

Mum's moaning again. I get up, light-headed. I stumble, holding on to the wall as I cross the landing.

1972

There was a lovely children's department in Littlewoods. In my coffee break I went to look at the shorts and tee shirt I'd had put away for Rose until I'd saved enough from my wages to pay for them. The lady in charge, Miss Philbin, let me give her ten pence a week and was keeping them for me. I'm not sure it was store policy and I have a feeling she'd already paid for them herself when I look back. I'd told her about my sister and she'd helped me to choose the clothes.

'Age five?' she'd said, holding the shorts up and tilting her head, looking from me to the label on them. 'You sure?' She smiled at me, folding them up and sliding them back into the plastic packet. 'I thought you said your sister was eight?'

'She is. She's small for her age.' I hesitated. 'Rose is Down's syndrome.'

'Ah.' Miss Philbin nodded. 'I see...'

I could feel the easy anger burning my cheeks before she added, 'My nephew is, too. But he's twelve now, a big lad. I'm sure your sister will catch up.'

Everyone always talked of Rose catching up as though she was always running behind everyone. It made me mad. But seeing as how I could tell the supervisor was trying to be kind, I swallowed the irritation.

'These are for the sports day at our local primary school.'

'She goes to school, then?' Miss Philbin raised her eyebrows. 'Danny, my nephew wasn't allowed. He's in a special institution.'

'Rose is going to no institution,' I said, thinking *however special*! 'The school was glad to have her.' I didn't say she was still in the first class with the five-year-olds, just like her friend, Martin. 'Anyway,' I checked my watch. 'I'd better get back to my department.'

'Right!' Miss Philbin opened a drawer and, after putting the shorts and tee shirt in, locked it. 'Another week and these will be yours – Rose's. I'm sure she'll love them.'

'She will.' I smiled. I remembered the year before when Rose had insisted in joining every race. And winning. Even against the eleven-year-old girls. And nobody had minded.

Nobody had stopped her.

But then something else came to mind, a race I'd almost forgotten. Rose was way out in front in an obstacle race when there was a loud cry. One little girl had fallen. Rose stopped and turned to look. Then she ran back past the other girls to the one who was on the ground, helped her to her feet and gave her a huge hug. Hand in hand they ran towards the finishing line to loud applause from everyone.

Rose, always pleased when she knew she'd done something right, was beaming from ear to ear.

And, in the end, when she'd shared out the little medals and sweets that she'd won, one of the older girls had carried her off the field on her shoulders and into school. It sounded as though everybody was cheering for her and all the adults, including the teachers, were clapping. Rose loved the attention. I was so proud of her; I thought my heart would burst.

Chapter Twenty-Three

2002: Yesterday: 10.30 p.m.

Mum screams. The noise goes right through me. I get up. Each time I feel that the scream in my head will burst out. I flap my hand towards Sam who is halfway up the stairs.

'I'll see to her,' he says, raising his voice above Mum's noise.

'No, I'm up now.'

'Have you had any sleep?' His face is taut with anxiety.

I nod.

'I've nearly finished this month's accounts. I'll be up in a minute.'

I nod again.

The screaming stops. I watch Sam go down the stairs and half-turn to go back into our bedroom. She starts again; obviously she was just drawing breath before her next outburst.

My jaw is clenched so tightly it aches.

1972

I was allowed half an hour for a lunch break in Littlewoods. There wasn't much time to go around town to the other shops, so I usually went into the canteen. Sometimes I sat with a girl called Sophia, another Saturday girl who went to some sort of college in the week to learn shorthand and typing, though she told me it was only to pass the time. She didn't need to work because her father owned one of the largest cotton mills in Manchester.

'So why are you here at Littlewoods? Doing a Saturday job?'

Sophia pulled her mouth into a downward grimace. 'Mummy thinks I should see what the real world is all about.' She stressed the words. 'And I use the money to buy bits and pieces without going into my allowance – and without Mummy knowing.'

I wasn't sure what she meant by "bits and pieces" but didn't want to show my ignorance, especially as she winked when she said it. So I said, 'My Nanna used to work in a cotton mill. She was a weaver.'

'Really?' Sophia looked at me as though I was some sort of interesting insect species. 'How fascinating...' She took a bite of her sandwich. I'd noticed she chewed with just her front teeth, her mouth pursed. I assumed that was how all posh people ate and tried it myself sometimes at home until Mum noticed and asked me why I was pulling stupid faces. After that I only did it when she wasn't looking, and just to make Rose laugh.

I unwrapped the cellophane on my sandwich. 'I love egg and cress butties,' I said, taking a bite.

'Butties?' Sophia raised one eyebrow which I thought made her look a bit silly. 'Oh, you mean sandwiches.' She laughed. But when I scowled she looked down at the table.

Her tone was conciliatory when she next spoke: 'You haven't said much about your family, Irene.' She carefully placed her sandwich down and sipped at her glass of water. 'Do you have any brothers or sisters?'

'A sister. She's eight.' I thought of the way I'd left home earlier and felt bad. I wondered if I could just say I was ill and ask to go home.

But I was supposed to be washing and pressing jumpers and cardigans that customers had returned. Secretly, I thought it wrong that they were put back into plastic sleeves and piled on the counters as though they were new, even though my supervisor said I was so good at the ironing she wouldn't trust anyone else to do it.

'Irene?' Sophia's voice interrupted my thoughts. 'Your family? Your sister?'

'Rose. She's called Rose.' I bit into my butty, wondering whether to tell her about Rose. And then I felt ashamed that I was thinking that, as though I was being disloyal to my sister. 'She's Down's syndrome.' I knew I'd made a mistake as soon as I said it. The girl stopped chewing in that daft way, swallowed hard, choked. She reached for her glass and gulped water, her face crimson. When she could speak she said, 'Oh, how awful for you. Does it run in the family?'

My chair crashed to the floor when I stood. I found it difficult to breath. Placing my hands flat on the table I bent over her. 'You stupid...! You are so stupid.' I knew my voice was loud; that others in the canteen were looking at me, but I didn't care. 'My sister – my sister is worth ten of you – with your silly voice and your thinking you're better than anyone else just because your dad owns a mill.'

She shrank back in her chair and, for a moment I was horrified that I'd scared her. But then Rose's trusting face flashed into my head. And I straightened up, pulling back my shoulders, struggling to keep my voice from trembling. I looked around. 'My sister is Down's syndrome and is one of the nicest, kindest, most generous little girls that I know.'

No one spoke. I glanced around; not one person met my eyes. There were a few uncomfortable coughs, a shifting in seats. And then there was an arm around my shoulder.

'Come on, dear.' It was Miss Philbin. 'Let's go and get those clothes for Rose. I think you could take them home today, don't you?'

As she led me out of the canteen and away from the hushed whispers, I knew it would be the last time I'd go in there. And that it would probably be the last day I would work at Littlewoods.

I wasn't sorry. At that moment I hated everyone in that room.

Chapter Twenty-Four

2002: Yesterday: 11.00 p.m.

I've been up five times in the last three hours. I feel like I'm sleepwalking.

I stand, half-asleep by her bed, my hand on hers. There's a strange sensation in the room, almost as if someone is standing next to me, a low murmuring. 'Rose?' I murmur. Mum quietens.

1972

'I know exactly how you feel, Irene. Some people don't understand about Down's syndrome. You just have to feel sorry for their ignorance.' I was stopped from answering when Miss Philbin gave me the tee shirt and shorts. 'Take these when you go home today. Give me the rest of the money when you can.' She'd wrapped them in pink paper with red roses printed all over on it.

'Thank you, Miss Philbin.'

Before I knew it I was being held in her arms while I cried.

After a moment Miss Philbin said in a brisk voice, 'That's enough now. Let's get back to work.' She held me away from her, her hands on my shoulders.

'Thank you for wrapping them so beautifully.' I lifted the parcel to examine the paper again. 'She'll love these for sports day.'

'You're very welcome. Oh, I nearly forgot.' She reached back into the drawer and pulled out a small red woollen dress and bonnet. 'I had some wool left over after I'd knitted my father a jumper,' she said. 'So I made these for your sister's dolly you told me about last week. Do you think she'd like them?'

'I think she'll love them.'

'I'll wrap them,' she said, neatly ripping off some of the tissue paper piled on the counter. 'And tell her to have a good sports day from me.'

'I will.' I took the second small parcel and, without thinking, kissed her cheek. 'Thank you, Miss Philbin. You're one of the nicest people I've ever met.'

I watched as her face turned pink. 'Go on with you! Now,' she folded her hands at her waist, self-consciously looking around the store, 'back to your department.' But I saw the way her lips trembled when she repeated, 'I hope you all enjoy Rose's sports day.'

I didn't care about the Sophias of this world. I didn't care what anyone said about Down's syndrome children, Rose was a thinker. And she had all the love in the world to give.

And I was desperate to leave the store and go home to tell her I loved her. Perhaps she wouldn't remember I'd run out that morning while she was still shouting for me.

Chapter Twenty-Five

2002: Today: 12.05 a.m.

The next time Mum starts shouting out again we both fling the covers back.

I'd forgotten to prop her up in bed; she's had a bit of a cough lately and the doctor said to try her with more pillows. I don't want that bugger next door shouting the odds again because of her coughing. He works shifts and yells at us through the wall sometimes if she's too noisy.

She fights with us as we put our hands under her armpits and haul her higher in the bed. My head is pressed against her shoulder; I feel the warm clamminess of her skin above the neckline of her nightdress.

'No. No.' She yanks at my hair. It hurts.

Sam stops her, gently freeing me. 'No yourself, Lil.' He shakes his head, his voice firm. 'You okay, Irene?'

'Yeah.'

My mother pushes out her lower lip. Sniffs.

'I'll stay with her a bit.'

'I'll get your dressing gown and slippers.'

It takes ages for her to settle. Despite the dressing gown, I'm frozen. Eventually I shuffle to the side of the bed and let myself drop onto the floor on my knees. I wait, taking in long slow breaths. No movement from her so I crawl to the door, only straightening up when I'm on the landing, cursing that damn floorboard that always creaks. I put my hands on the middle of my back and stretch, rolling my neck.

In our bed, Sam's warm. I snuggle up to him. He gets hold of my arm and pulls it across his chest.

'You'll get as cold as me.'

'Doesn't matter. And I'll get up next time,' he says. 'No arguing.'

1972

All afternoon, alone in the laundry room, I washed and pressed those woollens and I have to say I was proud of how good they looked when I fastened the bags; no customer would ever tell they were sort of second-hand.

But I was uneasy. I felt something was wrong.

I should have relied on my instinct. It was as though Rose and me had an invisible cord that joined us.

Once, in an English lesson, I think I was around fourteen, we were studying *Little Women* and one of the girls was reading aloud to the groans and sighs of the boys in the class. To me the words became large and bold: ' "Leaning low over this dearest of her sisters, she kissed the damp forehead with her heart on her lips, and softly whispered, Goodbye, my Beth. Goodbye!" '

The panic made my skin icy though my palms were damp. Rose; she needed me, I was sure. I raised my hand.

'Irene?' Mrs Ellinore lowered her text and looked at me over her glasses

I loved our English teacher and hated knowing that I was going to lie to her.

'I need to go out, Mrs Ellinore, I think I'm going to be sick.' I put my hand to my mouth.

'Me too,' muttered David Scofield behind me. 'Soppy book.'

There were a few titters and some gagging noises from the other lads.

'Well, you'd better go to the school nurse.' She seemed concerned; she actually believed me, knowing how much I liked English. 'Hurry,' she added, as I grabbed my satchel and ran past her, along the corridor and out of the school.

I didn't stop running until I reached our street. The doctor's car was parked on the road outside our house.

I burst through the door. 'What is it? Rose? Her heart?'

'No. Calm down, she's fine.' Nanna was in the hall talking to the doctor.

'She'll be fine, now.' The doctor repeated Nanna's words.

'Now?'

'She had a little...' Nanna's voice quivered.

'A little what?' I flung my satchel on the floor, my blazer followed.

'A fainting—'

'A fit.' The doctor corrected Nanna.

'She's never fainted – or had a fit.' (I'd seen one of the older girls in school have a fit once; Rose had never been like that.)

'When? When did it happen?' I was already taking the stairs two at a time.

'About an hour ago. Calm down, Irene.'

I knew it! An hour ago; when I was in class.

I made myself stop and take a breath before opening the bedroom door.

'I was dizzy, Iwene. I was wanting you to come home. I wished so hard.' Rose wrapped her arms tight around my neck, she was hot and sticky. I climbed onto the bed beside her.

'That's all you'll ever have to do, love,' I said. 'You wish hard and I'll always, always come.'

The end of that hateful day eventually arrived, the store closed and my supervisor let me go. I collected my coat and Rose's parcels from my locker, picked up the meat and potato pies and the chocolate éclair that I'd bought earlier from the food counter and sprinted out the staff door.

It felt as though people were deliberately getting in my way. I dodged around them: running, running along the crowded, wet streets, ducking under umbrellas, sidestepping lines of home-going shop assistants, avoiding late shoppers.

Buses passed, but I couldn't see mine.

And all the time Rose was pulling me home by that invisible cord.

Chapter Twenty-Six

2002: Today: 12.55 a.m.

She's crying.

Sam did get up the next time but now he's asleep so I stumble downstairs to warm some milk for her and pour a tablespoon of brandy into it.

'Let's get you pissed, Mother,' I murmur to myself. 'Then we can both get some sleep.'

Back upstairs. 'Come on, Mum,' I say, sliding my arm around her shoulder and sitting her up a bit more, 'drink your milk.' She closes her mouth tight. 'I've put a drop of brandy in it,' I coax. Now she purses her lips and, encouraged, I lift the sippy beaker higher. 'That's it.'

She finishes the lot, smacking her lips in between each slurp, her eyes fixed on me.

Sam is awake and watching me when I get back into bed.

'Okay?'

Nodding, I lie without even saying a word.

1972

At last I was able to get on a bus, but it moved so slowly, caught up in the evening traffic. Stop, start. Stop, start. My legs jiggled with an impatience that made my skin tingle. *Come on, come on.* The words went round and round in my head. Each time we set off I let go of the breath I'd been holding in my chest, only to pull in another stuttering intake of air when we slowed to a crawl.

Finally, shops gave way to the houses of the roads leading to Grove Street.

For a few minutes the bus picked up speed. Sitting in a window seat, I stared through the smears of rain at my pale hazy reflection in the glass.

I couldn't get rid of the unease that had tormented me all day. *Be with you soon, Rose. Be with you soon.* I gazed at my image in the bus window and blinked; it was my sister's face I was looking at. And, as I watched, her expressions changed one after the other, copying all her emotions in rapid succession: one moment thoughtful, even sad, the next gleeful, laughing – in the sudden way she reacted to everything and everyone around her.

Then it seemed as though her eyes met mine and we were in a world of our own.

Be with you soon, Rose. Be with you soon…

Chapter Twenty-Seven

2002: Today: 1.20 a.m.

Mum's yelling and coughing, flailing her arms around because, somehow, she's tangled up in the duvet and she's panicking. By the time I've settled her down again it's turned two in the morning, my back's aching and my head's still pounding. I throw two more paracetamol down my throat.

There was a time when, if I wasn't careful to keep the door locked, she would wander off and I'd chase around the streets looking for her. At least, then, she'd tire herself out and sleep for hours at a time. At least then I'd get a decent rest.

At least then, we didn't have the thumping on the wall from next door.

1972

'Rose?' Rose's dark eyes looked into mine. We held one another's gaze in the rain-streaked window of the bus. She smiled. I loved the way her eyes sloped up at the outer corners, it always made her look so happy.

She tilted her head as if to ask me a question, in the way she did when she was puzzled about something.

It's all right, Rose, be with you in a few minutes. I tried to push the words out from my mind to hers. *I'm almost home.*

But the bus kept stopping: people getting off, more getting on, laughing and talking about the bloody weather to the driver, to the conductor. Taking their time to sit down, to settle in their damp rustling raincoats, arrange their bags, umbrellas, kids. *Hurry up. Hurry up. Move. Move.*

*I'm sorry I left you this morning, Rose. But it will be okay, I'll be there in a few minute*s. I thought I saw her nod her head slightly. Still she kept her eyes on mine. The rumbling engine of the bus, the clicking of the indicator as the vehicle turned onto a road, the chatter of the other passengers, all faded away.

Chapter Twenty-Eight

Sam's snoring. I've left the landing light on and, in the subdued glow, I can see him lying in his favourite position, one arm folded under his head. I lie on my side of the bed. It's cold. I slide across until I feel the warmth of him, put my feet on his legs. Wonderful! And he doesn't wake.

1972

I lifted my hand towards the window then let it drop as I saw tears hover on her lower lids and then spill over. 'Rose.' I spoke her name aloud. The guilt stabbed, icily cold, in my stomach. 'I'm sorry, love, I'm sorry...'

I couldn't take my eyes away from her image. Slowly the tears slid down her cheeks and her lips turned downwards. I couldn't stand it; I felt my own tears slip unbidden from my eyes as well. 'Don't, Rose. Don't cry.'

The bus ground to a halt again. I looked at my watch, grabbed hold of the back of the seat in front of me and peered through the window at the front. A tractor trundled along, two warning lights flickering above the cab. The road was too narrow to overtake. I tried to see where we were, if there was anything I could recognise. Would it be quicker to get off, to run home?

Chapter Twenty-Nine

2002: Today: 2.45 a.m.

I must have catnapped. Anyway, I'm warm and I think I can hear soft off-key singing; the words to 'Here We Go Round the Mulberry

Bush'. I'm not frightened, why should I be? It was Rose's favourite nursery rhyme and it comforts me. I lift up on one elbow and stare into the dim light off the landing. Is that a soft rustle, as though someone is moving slowly to the door? I let my head drop back onto the pillow. 'Rose,' I murmur. Sam shifts in his sleep and I put my hand on his. Does *he* feel my sister's presence at all?

Does Mum? I've asked her often enough when we're on our own. She doesn't answer of course. They say it's the long-term memories that stay but I can't tell, however much I study her face when I ask the question. I wonder if that day, that memory has stayed with her.

It's never far away from me

1972

'You all right, dearie?' A hand pressed on my shoulder. It took me by surprise and I partly turned my head to glance at the woman in the seat behind me. 'Dearie?' Her fingers dug in, insistent. I shrugged her off. I heard her whisper and then another voice, deeper this time, a man murmuring, before the woman asked again, 'You all right?'

'Fine,' I said with impatience. Leave me alone, I thought. Leave us alone. 'I'm all right.' I didn't look around. When I looked back at the window Rose's image had disappeared. I'd lost her. The muscles in my stomach tightened. I grabbed the rail, tensed, ready to stand.

Chapter Thirty

2002: Today: 3.30 a.m.

She's moaning now. I'm gritting my teeth, tightening my fists so hard my nails are hurting the palms of my hands. There's a crash. Now what! Sam gives a sudden snort and turns on his side away from me. I give him a shove in the hope he'll wake and see to her. Don't be mean; I remind myself he has to work tomorrow. Today. So I sit up and push the duvet off my legs. It has to be the sippy beaker. I left it on the bedside table.

It's behind the door, which is at least six foot from the bed. She's slumped a bit but is still mostly sitting up against the pillows and turned towards me. Her hand is on top of the little table.

'Did you just throw that?' I ask, knowing she won't answer, thinking that surely that's not possible. She looks away, closes her eyes. But a slight smile moves her lips and she sniffs, a long spluttering drawing in of breath.

I leave the beaker where it is and go back to bed.

1972

I stood, grasping the rail with both hands. Then, on shaking legs and grabbing the back of each seat as I moved, I stumbled down the aisle towards the conductor.

'I need to get off,' I said.

'What?' He was leaning against the rail at the bottom of the stairs that led to the upper deck, swaying with the movement of the bus.

'Get off,' I said again. 'Just stop the bus. Please. I need to get off.'

'You sick or summat?'

'Yes – no, I just...'

'Can't just stop between stops, lass.' He frowned, bent towards me, holding on to his ticket machine. 'Where did you want to go?'

The scream that was waiting somewhere in my chest was threatening to erupt. 'Grove Street.' It was all I could manage. Even to me my voice sounded strange, forced.

He twisted around to look through the front window. I saw him exchange a look with and the driver. His frown changed, he looked concerned. 'You can get off in a minute, love. Someone meeting you?'

Without looking at him I nodded and grabbed hold of the bar

near the door. As soon as it opened, I leapt onto the pavement and began running.

Chapter Thirty-One

2002: Today: 4.25 a.m.

I'm jolted out of my doze by Mother's scream. The skin on my scalp tightens and my heart is going sixteen to the dozen.

By the time I'm by her bed the man next door begins thumping rhythmically on his side of the bedroom wall. He must be on days this week and we've obviously woken him too early.

Mum stops and looks around, eyes and mouth wide open. She's scared by the noise.

'It's fine Mum, don't be frightened.' I don't realise I'm crying until I sense the warm wetness trail off my chin onto my neck. I lie alongside her, holding her until he stops banging. Finally she's asleep again. I slip off the bed, stand up and wait, watching her, listening for him.

It's quiet.

1972

I ran, head down against the rain that trickled down my neck. Water streamed into the drains at the side of the road, passing cars sending it high in the air, drenching one side of me. It didn't matter; all I wanted to do was to get home, to end this feeling of dread

Normally I'd burst through the front door and shout, 'I'm home. Rose? Irene's home,' and wait for the squeal of delight and the thunder of her footsteps on the stairs or the crash of one of the doors as she flung it open. But the house was silent. There was no answer to my call.

And normally, Nanna would have lit the gas in the oven in

readiness for the heating of the pies. The kitchen would be warm with the heat from the stove. But that day the room was chilled.

Chapter Thirty-Two

2002: Today: 4.55 a.m.

Wiping my nose I stuff my hanky in the pocket of my dressing gown and, as quietly as I can, go to the bathroom to use the loo. Washing my hands I rest against the washbasin and look into the mirror. It shocks me to see how old I look. I touch the lines around my mouth, see the slackness of skin on my neck. Sam says I'm still beautiful but, except for my eyes, I see little of the girl I was.

She's made me old before my time. So I'll just keep on hoping that, one morning, when I go in to her, she'll be dead.

I can hear her whimpering. Not again. Please. Not again. Before long it will be a full-throated cry. Reminds me of Rose when she was a baby. I take in a quivering breath. Was this how Mum felt about my sister, this resentment? And, for a dreadful moment, I understand why. She must have wished her dead from the minute she was born.

1972

That evening wasn't normal. The whole day hadn't been normal. It would be a long time before anything was normal again.

It was as though the whole of my skin was crawling.

'Rose?'

No answer. I pushed my wet shoes off and hung my coat on the back of one of the kitchen chairs to drip. I'd dropped my bag onto the kitchen table. One of the parcels for Rose had fallen out. I left it there. Slowly, I walked out of the kitchen into the front room. No one. 'Nanna?' No answer. 'Mum? Rose?' Silence. I went to the bottom of the stairs. Holding my breath, I listened.

The wooden bannister was smooth under my fingers except for the small dents where Rose had bitten into it when she was having one of her rare tantrums as a toddler.

I waited on the landing, breathing slowly so I could hear if there was any sound. But there wasn't. Nanna's door was closed. I found myself willing her to come out, to tell me everything was all right. But I couldn't make myself knock on her door.

I could almost feel the silence all around, closing in. The door to my bedroom was partly open. Something was wrong. I didn't know what. Ice trailed down my spine but I told myself that if I breathed in and out slowly I – it would be all right.

I put the flat of my hand against the door and cautiously pushed. Mum was standing by the side of Rose's bed.

'Mum?' At first I thought she hadn't heard me but I saw her back stiffen. And, on either side of her, I saw the ends of the pillow she was clutching to her stomach. How long had she been standing there? 'Mum? What's happened?' I peered around her. My sister was lying on her back. That was wrong for a start, she hated lying like that. From being a baby she'd insisted on wriggling around until she was on her front. I was always frightened she'd smother. Now the cold was deep inside me and I couldn't stop the trembling. Rose's chubby legs lay tidily side by side. But when I looked at her feet, one sock dangled off her toes. Looking down at the floor I saw her red sandal on its side.

'What have you done?' My heart was hammering.

'Nothing!'

'Nothing?' I shouted. 'Nothing? The pillow...?' I pushed Mum out of the way and looked down on my sister. 'Rose? What's wrong? Wake up.' I bent over and shook her. 'Rose. Rose! Wake up!'

Her head flopped from side to side. I screamed, turned back to my mother, yelled at her, 'What did you do to her?' She didn't speak. I pushed her. 'Get an ambulance. The doctor! Do something...' She didn't move. 'Mum! Go!'

She dropped the pillow and ran from the room

111

'Nanna,' I shouted. 'Nanna!' I fell to my knees by the side of the bed, put my head to Rose's chest. Listened. No sound. No heartbeat. 'Nanna. Rose,' I whispered. I placed my cheek close to her mouth. Waited. Thought I could feel her breathing. Leaned back and looked at her. Not breathing. Touched her face. Her skin still held a slight waxy warmth but it didn't feel like her anymore.

Tears fell on her hand. I swiped my arm across my wet face.

'Rose? Sweetie?' I could hear the pleading in my voice. A wave of pain rose up from my stomach to my head and swept down my back, knocking the breath out of me.

She almost looked as if she was asleep except that her eyelids were slightly open. Always struggling with a blocked nose, her lips were parted as usual but bluer and I could see that instead of the tip of her tongue just resting on her lower lip, it lolled to one side of her mouth. And there were tiny red marks covering her chin. I shook her. 'Rose.' I pulled her to me. Her head flopped against my arm.

I laid my sister carefully back onto the bed and stood up.

I was going to be sick. I stood, heaving. Tried to drag air into my lungs. Throat tight. I turned, my legs shaking.

My mother was standing by the door.

'I found her like this.' Her voice, harsh and quivering, cut into the silence.

'Liar,' I screamed. 'Liar!' I pushed her out of the way and stumbled across the landing to Nanna's room.

Chapter Thirty-Three

2002: Today: 5.15 a.m.

Mum's whimpering gets louder. I perch alongside her, stroking her bony forehead, hoping it will send her off. But each time I slowly lift my hand away her eyes snap open and she moans.

So I rock her to sleep.

She tucks herself into me when I do that. It's a strange sensation: a cuddle coming from a woman who stopped hugging me years ago, who I loved once, and whose hugs I yearned for. Until that day. And, despite the hatred that was born from the memory, still there is that sliver of pity, of love, for her that I cannot help. Cannot dismiss.

She sleeps.

I cross to our bedroom. I'm shivering when I take off my dressing gown and slide into bed. I can feel the warmth coming from Sam. I tuck my knees up and put my cold feet on his back.

1972

'Nanna, Nanna.' I flung myself towards her. The panic took the strength from my legs, made me collapse before I reached the bed. I crawled on hands and knees. 'I don't understand. Didn't you hear? Didn't you hear me shout for you?'

'I couldn't—'

'Couldn't what?' I flung out my arms. 'Why are you lying on the bed? Why didn't you stop her?' It hurt my chest to scream out the words but I couldn't help it. 'I saw her. Why didn't you? Why?'

'Hush. Hush, child.' Nanna was lying on top of the eiderdown on her bed, eyes closed, when I flung her door open. Now she sat up, swung round and held out her arms. I half-rose, half-fell. She caught hold of me, rocking me. I felt the wet of her tears on my neck.

'We should get the doctor.' I nodded, emphatic. 'Have you? Have you sent for an ambulance?' I pushed myself away from her. Why did she seem so calm? But when I looked into her eyes I saw the anguish. The bleakness.

'It's too late.'

'It shouldn't be. You should have done something. Stopped her.' I didn't understand. The great gulping drawing in of breath, made my head swim.

'Rose's gone, Irene.'

'No!' I swung my head from side to side. 'Send for someone...'

'I've asked Mrs Rhodes to send for the doctor.' She pulled me close again, spoke softly. 'Her hubby's gone for your dad.'

She gathered me to her. Together we wept.

Nanna held on to me when the doctor banged on the front door.

'Let your mum go, love,' she whispered, her voice hoarse, when I tried to untangle myself from her arms. 'You stay with me.'

'I want to tell him. I saw her—'

'You didn't.'

I listened to Mum's hurried footsteps as she passed the door, went downstairs. To the slow creak of the treads as both her and the doctor came up the stairs and stopped on the landing. My mother's words were muted and it was impossible to hear what she was saying with Nanna breathing so close to my ear.

'I should go... Be with Rose.' I struggled to sit up, the great thumping of my heart starting again.

'No.' My grandmother's grip tightened. 'There's nothing you can do. Leave it to your mother. She found Rose.'

'She did it. You know that.' I twisted my head to look at her. 'How can you let her be in there with Rose? Telling her lies. With Rose lying there. All alone.'

'She'll tell Doctor Harris anything he needs to know—'

'Lies. She'll tell him lies. You know that.'

'I don't...' There was a slight hesitation. 'She won't.'

They were such a long time with my sister. When I heard the soft squeak of the bedroom door opening and the hushed conversation, I strained to listen.

'Her heart ... weakened ... so many chest infections ... not long since I last examined her ... won't need a post-mortem.'

I felt Nanna's quick intake of breath and knew she'd heard as well.

'Do something, Nanna. Stop him. Tell him.'

Mum was sobbing.

Pretending, I thought. She's just pretending. I ground my teeth tight together.

'You mustn't blame yourself, Mrs Bradshaw. Children like your daughter are prone to heart problems. It could have happened at any time...'

'Nanna?'

'No, Irene, stay here.'

I heard a sharp click as though the doctor was fastening his bag. 'I'll ring the undertaker when I get back to the surgery.' Again the squeak of the stairs.

'He's gone.'

Dad hadn't come yet. He'd promised he would always come if there was something wrong. There couldn't be anything more wrong than this.

Chapter Thirty-Four

2002: Today: 5.45 a.m.

I wake in the middle of that dream again, the one where I get home ten minutes earlier on that day and stop my mother smothering Rose. My pillow is wet. The sheet under me has come away from the corner of the mattress and rolled up under my chest. I rise up on one elbow and try to force the sheet back into place. It's hopeless and I swear in exasperation.

'Your mother?' Sam mumbles his question.

'No, shush.'

I think he's asleep before I even answer him. I feel my lips press together in resentment. I have no right; he has to get up for work in an hour. But there, in that moment, I do resent him. I reach out, cover his fingers with mine. I relax in the comfort that gives me. Welcome the oblivion.

Now it seems I'm standing on a clifftop looking down at the

115

waves colliding with slabs of rocks far below. Rose is holding on to my fingers. Sam's gripping my other hand because I'm leaning forward into the wind, challenging the centre of gravity in my body, daring myself to bend forward a little further. Each squall flings sea spray over me. I feel the cold mist on my face, see it settle on the fibres of my coat as I look downwards. See Rose fall over the edge.

1972

Later, something woke me. The street lamp outside our house flickered on and off. Headlights swept across the room together with a rumble of an engine, a swish of tyres. There were no sounds in the house. I turned towards Nanna; she was awake, her dark eyes seeming so large in her face, were fixed on me.

There it was again, someone hammering on the front door. Dad? But surely he still had his key?

'That'll be Dad. I'll go and let him in.' I slid off the bed but her next words stopped me leaving the room.

'No. He's here. I heard him a while ago.'

'Why didn't you tell me?'

She didn't answer that. Instead she whispered, 'It'll be the undertaker, love.' She pulled back her bedcovers. 'Come back in here with me, your Dad will let them in.'

I closed the door and lay next to Nanna. We listened in silence to the subdued mutterings and scuffling in my bedroom.

'I can't let them take her, she belongs here with us.' I struggled to sit up but Nanna held on to me.

'Don't, Irene.'

'But—'

'She can't stay here.' Nanna tugged on my arm. I curled up next to her thin frame again, listening to a slow and careful thump of feet on the stairs, the whispers. 'It's best she's not here.'

'Why?'

'It just is.'

'Listen, they're being rough with her.'

'No they're not. And nobody,' she spoke fiercely, 'nobody can hurt her anymore.'

The front door slammed. Outside, more doors clunked shut, an engine started and a car rumbled away and once more there was silence in the house.

Nanna moaned. The shaking in her body was so severe I moved with it. And then I was holding her, as though I was the adult. I became aware of how fragile this woman, my lifelong protector, suddenly felt against my own robust body. It was as if our roles had abruptly reversed. I wasn't ready for that.

I needed to see if Dad really was here. As gently as I could, I slid my arm from under her arm and got off the bed. 'Try to have a sleep, Nanna.'

She didn't answer at first. As I pulled the door to I heard her whisper, 'I doubt I'll ever sleep again.'

I heard the gasping cries as soon as I opened the living room door. Mum was by herself on the settee. In the kitchen, Dad was sitting in the dark at the table. He was rocking to and fro. It was his sobs I'd heard. I went to him, touched him on the shoulder and kissed his cheek. It was wet. He didn't even notice I was there.

Chapter Thirty-Five

2002: Today: 6.45 a.m.

I'm awake and blinking in the brightness of the bedside light. I look over to Sam's side of the bed. He's awake.

'You okay, Irene?' he says, rising up on one elbow. His face is crumpled from sleep but there's no missing his concern.

'Yes.' I glance at the clock. It's ten minutes since I last looked. I listen. No sound from Mum; the relief rushes over me.

'You stay here while you can,' he says. 'I'll make a cup of tea.'

117

I watch him pushing his arms into his dressing gown and fumbling for his slippers with his feet.

When he's gone I turn off the light and let myself sink back down.

I think I hear a soft sigh.

1972

It was cold in the kitchen and I could see Dad shivering. I didn't speak. Mechanically I laid the fire and lit it. When the coal took hold I swivelled around on my heels to look at him. In the dim glow I watched my father shrinking into a little old man right before my eyes.

I went to kneel in front of him, leaning against his legs, trying to work out how to say what I'd seen.

The living room door crashed back against the wall.

'Derek. Oh god.' Mum crossed the kitchen floor in a second and threw herself against him, unbalancing me so that I fell backwards. I stood, watching them clutching one another in their grief. How could he? He knew how much she resented Rose. How could he be comforting her now?

It didn't make any difference anyway. Rose was gone. My sister was dead but I didn't understand.

I went across to the table, opened my bag and took out the pies and chocolate éclair. I threw the pies in the bin and carefully put the chocolate éclair on top of them.

Chapter Thirty-Six

2002: Today: 7.00 a.m.

Spoke too soon. I can hear her moaning. Up again! I can't stop yawning. But she can't start crying again and annoy the man next door, though it must be time for him to get up for his shift.

118

He's not a nice bloke; I know that much, even if I don't know his name. One shriek, one shout, one cry from Mum and he thumps out his anger. Yet we hear him all the time, living his life on the other side of the wall: the throb of music, the loud television, the irritating tune of his phone, the high screech of women's laughter, the clatter of crockery.

Sam's often said he'll go and have a word with him but I don't let him. I don't think he's the kind of bloke you can reason with. It's not worth the trouble it'd stir up.

I met him once, just after he came to live next door, and after a particularly bad time with Mum.

'I'm sorry about last night,' I said. 'My mother – she can't help it—'

'Bloody racket!'

'She's not usually so bad, it's—'

'That's the third sodding night in a row I've had no sleep. Some of us have to work, you know.'

'I know and—'

'Look, keep her quiet or I'll complain to the fucking Council about the noise.'

'There's no need to be like that—'

'Fuck off.'

I haven't bothered with the bloke since.

1972

On the day of the funeral the sun shone. I didn't go to see Rose but Nanna said the undertaker had put her in her Whitsuntide clothes. The white cotton dress with small red strawberries dotted all over it, the white cardigan Nanna had knitted for her, the silver bracelet I'd bought for her out of my Saturday wages. She said he'd also tucked one of her white handkerchiefs under the bracelet, folded to show the embroidered "R" in one corner, just below the lace edging.

119

As the hearse and our car drew up outside the chapel, I saw the crowds of people gathered in strange half-circles on each side of the gravel path outside. They huddled, holding their kids close in front of them, their arms held protectively over each child; almost as though we could contaminate them with our grief. It made me angry. Out of the corner of my eye I saw some of the girls who went to my school and a couple of the women from Littlewoods. They all seemed to be holding handkerchiefs. I'd screwed mine into a wet ball in my fist before I got out of the funeral car. Head down, I wrapped my black cardigan around me and crossed my arms over my waist. I waited while they slid Rose's coffin from the hearse.

I'd sat between Nanna and Dad in the car, refusing to look at Mum who sat on the small tip-up seat opposite us. She'd keened under her breath from the moment the hearse arrived on the street outside our house. Now I could see the black veil on her hat quiver.

There was a spray of lilies on Rose's small white coffin. Dad and Sam carried her into the chapel, tears trailing down both their faces. Holding Nanna's elbow I followed as close as I could, cutting in front of my mother. I didn't care.

I didn't hear the words the minister spoke. I didn't sing the hymn. "*Jesus bids us shine...*" The music flowed around me, only remembered hours later. The sense of detachment lasted until I was in bed, that night. Then it was replaced by a mixture of panic and grief. I suddenly realised that what had happened to Rose; the ending of all the breaths that made my chest lift and fall, would one day stop. Just as it would for all the people who had crowded around us in that small chapel, that place filled with the sickening smell of sweaty bodies and flowers already dying on top of that little white coffin.

I didn't go to see Rose put into the ground.

Sleepless, in the darkness I lay with my eyes stretched open. I wondered if she was as cold as me. As lonely.

Chapter Thirty-Seven

2002: Today: 7.20 a.m.

I've slept a little at the side of her. The light comes through the curtains; I've been meaning to change them for thicker ones for ages in the hope it'll make her sleep longer but haven't got round to it. I lie, listening for a moment. Every now and then a bird stutters out a note or two. There's a faint hum of traffic travelling in the air from the motorway on the far side of town and occasionally a car swishing past on our street. It's raining.

1972

In the weeks that followed the house was silent. It seemed worse because Nanna spent a lot of time at her church. I used to tease her about the time she went to a morning service dressed up to the nines but forgetting she still had her slippers on. It wasn't funny anymore, she didn't appear to care what she wore to go there after Rose died; sometimes she still had on her pinny under her coat. Once, I just managed to remove her hairnet before she left the house. It was as if she didn't notice.

She didn't go to see the doctor, even though Dad said he'd told her that Doctor Harris had asked that she make an appointment

At mealtimes we pushed the food around the plate. Swallowing a piece of bread or a spoonful of soup past the tightness in my throat was hard. Often Nanna left the table before she'd managed even one mouthful.

I sensed Mum watching me. I couldn't decide if she looked guilty or defensive or if it was just me, clinging on to the memory.

Without asking Nanna or me, Mum went through the house like a whirlwind clearing my sister's things from every room. There was no stopping her. I saw the tears. I ignored them.

By the time of the funeral, everything that was my sister's had gone...

Except for the doll, Caroline, dressed in the red woollen dress and bonnet Miss Philbin knitted, and the abacus. I hid those. I've still got them.

Chapter Thirty-Eight

2002: Today: 7.25 a.m.

I'm not asleep but the shock shoots though me, sits me bolt up in bed. The bass notes from next door crash around the room. Dizzy, I press my fingers into my ears and stagger from the bedroom.

'What the hell?' Sam is running up the stairs; still in his dressing gown, a mug of tea for me in his hand which he leaves on the landing windowsill.

Mum is wailing a silent howl, eyes tightly closed and mouth stretched so wide she looks like that painting, 'The Scream'.

1973

The following year I stayed mostly in my room studying for my A levels. It was the only way I could keep the memory out of my mind. That and planning for when I'd go to teacher training college.

Mum never mentioned Rose again. It was as though she'd not existed. At least to my mother. Sometimes I thought I could feel my sister so close to me, that if I reached out I would be able to stroke her silky black hair.

When I could, I'd talk to Sam about Rose. Not about the day she died; not about what I'd seen. I was afraid he'd think I was making it up, making it up because I hated Mum for telling me Dad wasn't my real father. I did hate her. But I was also bewildered: all those times I'd caught her watching my sister with sadness in her eyes, the crying, that first day she went to work at the supermarket and I came home to find her cuddling Rose and combing her hair, in our bedroom. Had I imagined that; misread it all? But then I remember her with that pillow and the hatred returns. I saw the look on her face when she turned as I ran into the bedroom. I often caught her watching me with her eyes narrowed and we'd stare at one another before, with a long sniff that made her nostril flare, she'd turn away.

So I didn't talk about it to Dad or Sam even though we spoke about my sister, the funny things she'd done or said. In an odd way it made me both happy and sad at the same time. And I'd stopped trying to talk about Rose to Nanna, it upset her too much.

I remember the day we were sitting on a blanket on the grass at the back of the house. Sam was helping me to revise for my English Literature exam. We were studying *Antony and Cleopatra*; you know, that bit where she's coming down the river in the barge. I was struggling to memorise it.

'It's hopeless.' I threw the book down and lay back watching a black cloud of starlings twist and dart around in the sky. 'Wonder why they do that?'

Sam leaned back on his elbows and stared upwards, his arms taking his weight. 'I don't know. They just do, it's their nature.' He glanced down at me. 'It'll be okay, you know. You'll sail through the exam.'

I shrugged. 'Perhaps I'm trying too hard.' I tipped my head backwards so I could look back at the house. Mum was sitting at the kitchen table, a cup in her hand. 'I just need to pass – I need to get my A levels. I need to get into teacher training college – to get away from here.' I saw the corners of his mouth turn down. 'We'll be all right, you and me,' I said. 'We'll still see one another.' I folded my arms under my head. 'There'll be the holidays.'

'But will you come home for them?' He lowered himself next to me, faced me.

The starlings curved into an "S" shape, separating and then coming together in a black mass. 'Course I will, I'll want to be with Nanna – and I can put up with her,' I moved my eyes upwards in the direction of the kitchen again, 'for a few weeks.'

'How is your Nan?'

'I don't know. Since Rose – since Rose died it's as though she's lost all interest in anything.' I held the bridge of my nose between thumb and forefinger, pressing hard to stop the tears. 'You know what she was like, Sam, so full of life, so – jolly, even when things were difficult here.' I kept my eyes closed. 'Even then she'd make the best of things. And she always tried to protect me and Rose from Mum's tempers.' I laughed but even to my ears it sounded bitter. 'And there have been a lot of them.' I rolled onto my stomach so I could be closer to him. Despite my thoughts I still felt my skin tingle and an odd sensation between my thighs when I was near him. We hadn't actually done "it" yet but, when we kissed, he sometimes held my breasts, ran the palm of his hands over my nipples. It drove me mad for more but I knew we had to be careful; I didn't want to spoil my plans to become a teacher.

'Stop it.' He gave a soft chuckle and moved away; he knew how I felt. 'I know that look.' His face grew serious again. 'Have you had Doctor Harris to your Nan?'

'She won't let him come to the house. She says she goes to the surgery.' I was worried, she'd lost more weight but she just said she'd lost her appetite and that was true; I'd watch her pretending to eat, push around the food on her plate. I often did the same. 'She's stubborn, says she's fine.'

'Have you spoken to your Dad about her?' Sam knew there was no point in asking if I'd discussed it with Mum. Though she was her own mother, Mum showed no interest.

'Yeah. He says it's taking her a long time to get over losing Rose. But she won't even talk about Rose, it's like she clams up.' I sighed. The starlings floated away towards the trees on the far side of the common land. I watched as they settled, noisy bobbing shapes on the branches. I sat up. 'I've had enough for now.' I flicked the text closed. 'Let's go to the pictures.'

Sam pulled the cuff of his shirt up and studied his watch. 'It's a bit late.'

'If we run, we should catch the main film.'

'We don't even know what's on.'

'Who cares, so long as it gets us away from here.' I jumped up, held my hand out to him. 'Come on.'

He picked up my books and the blanket. 'Okay.'

'You go round to the front of the house. I'll meet you there.'

I carried the blanket and the books up to my room. When I peeped in at Nanna it looked as though she was asleep. Without saying anything to my mother, I slipped out of the front door.

We ran hand in hand to the local picture house on Boardman Street. When we got there the newsreel was just finishing. We settled in our favourite seats in the stalls.

'Do you remember the last time we brought Rose,' I whispered, 'to see *Mary Poppins*?'

'Do I!' Sam grinned. 'She danced in the aisle to the music.'

'"Spoonful of Sugar."' I squeezed his hand. 'And she sang the words – well, her version of them. And everyone laughed.'

'And some of the other kids joined in...' The flickering light of the screen lit up his face. I saw his smile. 'I miss her too, you know, Irene.'

I loved him even more for saying that.

Chapter Thirty-Nine

2002: Today: 7.30 a.m.

The noise stops. Mum doesn't, the silent scream becomes one of her loudest yells. I'm holding her tense body against me and slowly she calms.

'Like a bit of hard rock in a morning,' our neighbour bellows through the wall and it starts all over again.

And so does Mum. She's terrified.

'Right, that's it.' Sam's hopping about, trying to get his socks on.

'No, Sam,' I shout above the noise. 'Please.'

'Yeah, yeah, yeah,' the man shouts, the words screeching through the beat. It goes on and on. The booming bass, the high-pitched words and Mum's screams are so loud my head is filled.

'I'm not putting up with that.' The muscles in Sam's jaw stand out. He's dragging on his clothes.

'Let it go. Please, Sam.'

And then the noise stops. And for a few seconds so does Mum.

But Sam is now fastening his shoes. 'Has he done anything like this before? In the daytime?' He lifts his head to look at me. 'When I'm not here?'

I've never dared tell him half the things that bugger's got up to in the past months. 'No. Don't. You'll only make things worse,' I plead. I hold Mum. Tears and snot mix on her face. I grab her towel from the back of the chair, and wipe it all away.

The man now starts a rapid succession of short bursts of the noise. On off. On off.

I hold on to Sam's sleeve, gripping it for dear life. I can see the frustration shaking his whole body but he won't shrug me off, he won't push me away, I know that. 'Stop it,' I shout in between the noise. 'Stop it,' I yell at the wall, over Mum's head.

'I'm sick of all the bloody wailing. Night after night. Keeping me awake.'

'I'm sorry.' It's stupid: this man and me shouting at a wall. 'I'm sorry, she can't help it.'

'Why don't you just put the bloody old cow out of her misery once and for all? Make us all happy.'

'Irene, let go. He's not going to get away with that. I'm going to kill the bastard.'

I tighten my grasp. I've rarely seen Sam lose his temper. Never with me. But still, it's frightening. I have to do something. And then I hear myself shouting back, 'And why don't you shut the fuck up once and for all.'

Sam laughs out loud, incredulity on his face. I've shocked myself and right away glance down at Mum. Her eyes are open, fixed on my face. She sniffs, a long slow sniff and I swear there's a smile trembling on her lips. I dip my head and kiss her forehead, this woman I've had a strange kind of relationship with for so long. The knot of rage dissipates.

She reaches up, a brush of her fingers on my cheek. There's a rush of something inside me but, when I look again at her, her eyes are blank, slide away from mine and her body goes slack.

1973

Over the weeks that followed, I barely spoke to my mother unless it was to argue with her. Sometimes, in the night, I thought about how she was before Rose; how close we'd been for those few years, and I wondered again if it would have been different if my sister hadn't been born. But then it really should have been me she resented; I was the cause of my mother marrying Dad on the rebound. Perhaps she'd never been really happy. Perhaps what I remembered was wishful thinking.

And yet I knew it wasn't; Mum and me *had* been close. That much was true. Just as it was true that now I couldn't wait for the day when I could go to teacher training college; college would be my passport away from Grove Street.

'And I'll need more help from you now she's not fit enough.' Mum spoke as if she was continuing a conversation. She jerked her head towards the ceiling as she bumped the vacuum cleaner into the settee where I was sitting. 'And something towards your keep.'

I looked up from the text of George Eliot's *The Mill on the Floss* that I was studying for a test at the end of the week. 'It's not Nanna's fault she's not well, and I help when I can.'

'When you feel like it, you mean. And you chose to pack in your Saturday job.'

'I couldn't go back there.' The thought of going back to

Littlewoods was unimaginable for me; it was all tied up with that last day, the day Rose died. 'And I haven't asked you for any money, have I?'

'No, but you're spongeing off your father.'

'I don't ask for much—'

'Money that I should have off him.'

'It'll be the exams soon. I need to revise.' I knew my tone of voice would annoy her but I wasn't ready for her next words.

'Well, we can soon alter that. You can pack in the highfaluting idea of going to college. In fact you can pack that lot in right away. You can get a job right now.' She spoke above the noise of the Hoover, her face flushed as she nodded towards the book. 'If you think I'm going to keep you until you swan off you've another think coming.' She switched the vacuum cleaner off and wound the cable around the handle in quick impatient movements.

'But I've only another few weeks before I take my A levels.'

'Not if I've got anything to do with it. You've burned your boat, madam; I'm not paying out good money to feed someone who treats me like dirt. You've hardly had a civil word to say to me in a long time—'

I snapped the book closed. There was a moment of stillness between us.

'You think you're better than me, don't you?' Pushing the sleeves of her cardigan further up her arms she said, briskly. 'Well let's see, shall we?'

There was a knock on the door. 'Irene?'

'Dad?' I ran to the door and flung it open. He'd tell her what for; he knew I needed to stay on in school, take my exams. It was the only way I could escape this house.

But he looked past me at Mum. 'I've only called to see how your mother is. Is that all right?'

I looked back at her. She shrugged.

Since his last stroke he dragged his foot. It took him a moment to balance on the step before coming in.

'Tell him,' I demanded, 'tell him what you've just said.' She didn't. 'She wants me to get a full-time job,' I said to Dad. 'I can't. You know that. I want—'

'You want. You want,' Mum interrupted. 'Always what you want, madam. Now I'm telling you. I don't just want you to get a job, I'm telling you to—'

'No!' I shouted her down. 'No, I won't.'

Dad put his hand on my arm. 'Stop it. Both of you.' He gave me a squeeze. 'We'll sort it,' he said to me. 'What's the problem, Lil?'

'What's the problem? What's the problem? You must be joking. And don't "Lil" me.' Mum hauled the Hoover into the kitchen and slammed it down on the floor. Then she came back into the living room, her hands on her hips. 'The problem, Derek...?' She emphasised his name, oozing sarcasm. 'The problem? Could it possibly be that my husband left me for some bloody tart?'

I saw Dad's jaw set but he didn't speak.

'Or could it be that I've got a mother who takes to her bed when she feels like it? There again, it could possibly be that I've got a lazy cow for a daughter...' She took in a long breath and steadied herself against the doorframe. 'And I'm up to my eyes in debt.'

I looked from her to Dad. It was obvious from the expression on his face he knew no more about the debts than I did.

'I've been giving you money.'

'A pittance.'

'It was enough to keep both of my girls – and your mother. And extra.' Dad spoke quietly. 'Where's it all gone? What have you been spending it on?'

They glared at one another. Something else was going on between them. It made me uncomfortable, as though this wasn't something I should be part of.

'It's nothing to do with you.' Mum glanced away from him and moved to tidy the cushions on the settee. She didn't look up. 'Whatever the money goes on, it's not your business. But I can't manage everything on my own. It's not fair, leaving me to sort everything out by myself.' I was surprised to see tears. I felt a tremor of sympathy for her but then she contradicted herself. 'What happens in this house – my house – is nothing to do with you anymore. You moved out to be with your floozy, remember? So keep your bloody nose out. And what I do about my daughter – *my* daughter...' She glared at him. '...is my business, not yours.'

'We'll sort the money business out afterwards,' Dad said. 'But now, if you don't mind, I'll go up to see your mother.'

Mum's face tightened. 'Oh, I've no doubt she'll want to see you. And no doubt she'll have a long list of moans about me for you to listen to.' She turned away from him.

'I'll come with you,' I said.

As I passed Mum she caught hold of my arm. It hurt. 'I meant what I said; you find a job.' Her eyes were narrowed. 'You find a job and start paying your way,' she repeated quietly. 'I'm not keeping this place going on my own anymore.'

I shook off her grip on me. She meant it. I saw all my plans vanishing. But I didn't want her to think she'd won. 'Okay, I'll get a job,' I said. I didn't take my eyes off her. 'I'll work something out, even if I have to go to night school to get my qualifications.'

'Which you'll pay for yourself,' Mum said, a look of triumph on her face.

'Twist the knife, why don't you?' They were the last words I spoke to my mother for a long time.

I got a job in Woolworths in town on the stationery counter. It was good money so it kept my mother off my back, and the college let me take my exams even though I'd actually left. With a pass in two A levels, and the GCEs I already had, I was accepted into the teacher training college in Manchester.

Chapter Forty

'She smiled.' Sam's anger vanishes as quickly as it had arrived. He laughs. 'Well, now we know what we need to do; you'll have to swear more often.'

My laugh is a little shaky. The scene with our neighbour has upset me more than I can admit.

'Mind you, I'll still be having a word with that nasty sod when I see him next. He can't get away with doing that.' He studies me. 'You okay?'

'I will be. And I think Mum will be as well.' She's plucking at the duvet cover and humming tunelessly, the fear instantly forgotten. 'Will you make us another brew, love? The last one'll be cold by now.'

He hugs me. 'Course I will.' He gathers back his hair and loops a band around the ponytail. I watch him leave the room. 'I'll put your mum's in her beaker with the lid, shall I? Easier for you?'

'Thanks, that's great.'

1973

'I've been assigned a room in one of the halls of residence.' I pulled my coat tighter around me watching the yellowing leaves eddying around our feet. Autumn had come early. 'They all seem much the same as one another. The one I saw when I went to the college was okay.' I glimpsed Dad's look of worry. 'Honest, Dad, they're fine.'

'Do you have enough money?'

'Yeah, it's a good maintenance grant—'

'One good thing about me not working.'

I grinned. 'Mum wasn't too impressed about being sent that form for her to declare her wages.'

Dad allowed himself a low snort of amusement. 'I think she

thought you'd fall at the first hurdle, not be able to afford to go to college. I did tell her your amount of grant would depend on us being means tested. She wasn't impressed.'

'Anyway, I'm packed and ready for Saturday.'

'Are you sure I can't come with you? See you settled in?'

I gave him a quick kiss on the cheek. 'I'll be absolutely fine. Honest.'

Except for Dad and me, the park was empty. From the bench where we were sitting I could see the playground. The swings moved slowly, pushed by the strong wind that swayed the almost-bare branches above us. The grassed area was churned mud now, the result of weeks of rain. The ducks huddled together on the banks of the river

'Have you told your mother when you're going?'

'No.' I grimaced. 'There's only one thing, I'm worried about leaving Nanna with her.' And the sense that I'd also be letting Rose down by leaving her again; I often talked to her in the darkness of the nights.

'I'll keep an eye on Nanna, love.'

'Thanks, Dad, I know you will. I must be honest, I'll be glad to go. I can't stand it there anymore.'

'I know.' I heard the tightness in his voice. 'She wasn't always like this, you know. She was very popular; I didn't think I stood a chance – I thought I'd be last in line.'

I kept quiet. Dad hadn't talked to me about this before. In fact I knew little about my parents' life before I came on the scene.

'And when we first got together she laughed a lot.' Dad paused. 'She was a great one for laughing – she was fun.'

We stared at one another, me in disbelief, Dad – well; I couldn't make out how he felt. The cold had given his face a pinched look. We really should be walking, not sitting on this damp bench.

'When you came along she was content for a long time.'

'Was she? Were you?'

'Yes.' He paused. 'And if you're meaning because you weren't really my child…' He looked determined when he said, 'I want you to know once and for all that, as far as I'm concerned, you've always been mine.' He ran his knuckles over the scarf at his throat. 'But if ever you want to find your – real father – I'll do all I can to help. I made her tell me his name once, it's —'

'Don't.' I covered my ears. 'Don't tell me, I don't want to know. I'll never want to know and I'll never go looking for him. He's nobody. You're my dad.'

He hugged me. 'Thank you, Irene. But it was something that needed to be said, that should have been said years ago.' He looked upwards and I followed his gaze. Streaks of charcoal-grey clouds raced across paler patches of sky. Rooks were blown along like scruffy rags, battling against the wind. 'I should have said.'

'No. I'm glad I didn't know any sooner.'

'We had some good times when you were little.'

'I remember.' And I did.

But then, suddenly, I had a memory I'd never had before, of running hand in hand with Mum and Dad along a path in a park. They were swinging me between them and she was laughing. We passed the stall where a woman twirled long wooden sticks into a shiny tub full of pink candyfloss and I remembered breathing in the sweet sugary smell. I could hear music, whirligig music, like on television. And when we turned a corner, there it was: a carousel, just like the picture in the interludes on the telly. I had another flash of memory; an image of sitting, holding on to the hard ears of a black shiny hobby horse on a roundabout, and the stink of sweat from the man who worked the carousel; who hung on the pole of our horse and whispered in Mum's ear. Leaning back against Mum, her arms around me as she held on to the reins, I'd felt her laughing.

Dad was talking again and the memory vanished. 'But I always knew I wasn't enough for her. I was a disappointment.' He shook his head, dismissing my protest. 'I wasn't what she thought I'd be, Irene. Either as a breadwinner – or as a husband.'

'You've been a good husband. Nothing excuses what she's like with you.' Or with Nanna, her own mother. Or me. Or how she was with Rose, especially not with Rose.

It was as though he read my mind.

'I've always felt guilty about Rose, you know...'

I stiffened.

'That maybe what happened...' Dad swallowed, 'wouldn't have, if I'd been there to keep an eye on her. Made sure she was safe.'

There was a long moment when we didn't speak. Then I said, 'How do you mean?'

'Well, she struggled sometimes with her breathing. And she was always getting chest infections. Perhaps that's what—'

'No!' I could tell him what I knew; Mum standing over Rose with that pillow. But then I saw the distress in his eyes. It would do no good raking it all up again. What if it made him ill, even made him have another stroke? I couldn't bear that thought. 'No.' I made my voice softer. 'There was nothing you could have done and I want you to promise me you'll stop thinking like that. Please?'

'All right. But ...'

'But nothing.' I stood and waited while he did the same. I was as tall as him. I tucked his scarf more firmly around his neck and kissed him on the nose. 'Come on, Susan will wonder where you are. We've been ages.' I didn't feel the resentment that usually came with her name; I knew she'd look after him when I wasn't around even though I'd never seen or spoken to her. I knew it because I could see how happy Dad was. 'And it's time for me to face the lion in his den. Or should I say the lioness?'

We laughed and I put my arm through his.

A boy appeared on a bicycle at the gates to the park. Standing on the pedals he weaved his way along the path followed by a man who was laughing. 'He's just learned to ride,' he called to us, 'found his independence. Leaves me behind every time.'

Dad and me looked at one another. And smiled.

Chapter Forty-One

2002: Today: 8.15 a.m.

I listen to the comforting sound of the kettle boiling and the rattle of cups, waiting until I'm sure there will be no more noise from the neighbour from hell.

When I hear the loud crash of his front door and the whine of the car engine I take my arms from around Mum and settle her down on her pillow, covering her up. Right away she's asleep. I sit on the edge of the bed watching her, wondering why I have such difficult, disparate feelings for this woman who has caused me pain in so many ways. As a helpless human being she needs protecting. But when I think about who she is, what she was like with Rose, I burn with anger. And then there's that memory: that image of her by my sister's bed.

1973

'Manchester isn't that far away, Dad, we can still see one another. We can sort something out, I won't be studying or at lectures all the time.' Anxious, I looked over the heads of the people milling around us. The train hadn't come in yet but Sam was nowhere to be seen.

'He'll get here in time.' It was as though Dad read my mind.

'Still, we might as well go through,' I said, 'we can stand just on the other side.' We pushed our way through the barrier and onto the platform.

I'd never liked this railway station, even when I was little and we were going by train on holiday to Cornwall. It was an echoing place, filled with the oily-smelling warm backdraught of departing trains. I gazed around. Above us, rain pounded on the dirty glass roof and pigeons squatted on the steel girders. One swooped down and strutted along the edge of the platform, head bobbing, skittering out of the way of hurrying feet. 'Sam should be here by now.' I didn't need an answer and he didn't give one. 'You can get cheap day returns, if you don't feel like driving in the city.' He had his profile to me; I couldn't tell what he was thinking. 'Dad...?'

He leaned back to look into my face. There were tears brimming in his eyes. 'You just get on with your life and make the most of college. Rose would want you to be happy.'

I cried then. Loud, gasping sobs. Dad held me until I was still. Then he repeated my earlier words. 'Manchester isn't that far away. Like you said, love, we can still see one another.' He handed me his handkerchief.

There was a sudden rush of noise: the rumble of the train coming into the station, the indecipherable words from the loudspeaker, people shouting.

And then I saw Sam running towards the barrier. 'He's here.' The relief flooded through me.

'Just remember what I said, Irene. Be happy.' Dad gave me a kiss on the cheek. 'Sam's a nice lad, you could do worse than sticking with him.'

'Don't you be marrying me off just yet. I've got at least the next three years to get through first.' To find out what I want to do with my life, I thought, however much I love Sam. I tried to smile but my lips trembled.

'I'm not. But you could do worse, he's learning a trade and he thinks the world of you.'

'I know.'

I held out my arms, waiting for Sam to hold me. Dad stepped to one side as Sam gathered me up.

One day we would get married. Just not yet.

Chapter Forty-Two

2002: Today: 9.00 a.m.

Mum's yelling. Sam's late for work and was just leaving the house but he pounds back upstairs and follows me into her room. She's kicked off her covers and is struggling to sit up, her face contorted with fear.

'It's okay, Mother.' I try to hold her but she fights me.

'Help!' She looks past me to Sam. 'Help.' She gives me a huge push. I fall to the floor.

Sam lifts me up. 'I'll see to her,' he says. 'You go downstairs.'

My legs just about hold me.

In the kitchen I sit at the table, my head on my arms. The next thing I remember is Sam stroking my hair.

'She's gone...'

I look up at him. A moment of chilling hope goes through me. My face obviously gave away my thought, because he shakes his head.

'She's gone back to sleep,' he says. 'For now,' he adds.

1973

I was eighteen and in college in Manchester and I was afraid of nothing and no one. I threw myself into being a student that first term. I didn't miss a lecture or a group discussion with the others in the student union and I was looking forward to my first teaching practice in a local primary school in November. My social life was pretty hectic as well – so many impromptu parties and debates. Though I met and enjoyed flirting with many of the lads there, I was never unfaithful to Sam. I was happier than I'd been in a long time. I lost weight and persevered with the contact lenses Dad had treated me to as a going away present. Pretty painful at first, those hard lenses, but boy did I think I was the bee's knees. I wore my hair short and angular with kiss curls at the side that I fastened with kirby grips at night. Sometimes, when I couldn't sleep because the grips dug into my face, I'd remember the agony of the ringlets and the irony of it made me smile in the darkness.

I'd already discovered I liked making my own clothes so, when I found I didn't need my Olympia typewriter, I swapped it for a sewing machine that one of the girls, Carol, owned. It wasn't long before everyone found out I could sew. The Simplicity patterns I picked up in the market were being passed from one to another and the orders came in thick and fast. By the end of the third week I had a good little business on the go and I'd already bought a pair of purple patent platform shoes from Freeman, Hardy & Willis. Difficult to walk in, but I thought they made my legs look good.

Most Sundays were spent with me sewing in the small kitchen in the middle of the corridor with Rod Stewart belting out 'Sailing' and 'Maggie May' or with an LP of Simon and Garfunkel setting the mood of the day.

'Can you make me a skirt out of this?' Patricia, the girl who had the room opposite the kitchen was always first after I'd lugged in the sewing machine and put it on the table in the middle of the room. She moaned constantly at weekends about the smell of the cooking we did, with the canteen being closed Saturday and Sundays.

I looked up from the pinafore dress I was hemming. 'There's barely half a yard. I'm not sure.'

She held up the pink and white checked material. 'A miniskirt?'

'It'd have to be a micro.' Carol from the room next to mine, and a good mate, wafted in on a wave of Youth Dew. 'You'd struggle to get that round your beam end.'

Patricia stamped out.

'You shouldn't be mean, Carol.' I cut through the thread with the sharp Quick Unpick.

Carol shrugged. 'She's such a drag.' She lit the gas on the grill, unwrapped the slices of white bread and slapped them haphazardly on the wire tray. 'Toast?' She pushed three slices on without waiting for an answer and started wrestling with the can opener on a tin of beans. After a moment she glanced over to me with an ashamed smile.

'Actually, I think I have a couple of yards of something to spare. It's bright pink. My mother gave it to me, she says I look good in pink.' She puffed out her cheeks. 'Er, I think not.' She did a twirl, still holding knife and toast. Her black leather skirt and black polo neck jumper showed off her slender figure.

'I'll go and get her. Tell her what you've said.' I smiled at Carol. I was fitting in well at college. And I was making good friends.

The only problem I had was that Sam hadn't come to see me. There had been four weekends and still he hadn't. We spoke from one of the four telephone boxes outside the halls almost every night. But there was always a queue waiting to use them so it was all very hurried and I felt there was never enough time to say what I wanted to say. And, to be honest, he never sounded at ease using the phone. I missed him and I was getting worried.

Chapter Forty-Three

2002: Today: 9.30 a.m.

Sam's been gone thirty minutes; it feels like hours.

When I go back into the kitchen I see the blasted pilot light on the boiler's gone out. For the next five minutes I struggle to relight it but it's having none of it which means the heating's gone off. It hasn't been serviced this year – something else I keep forgetting to sort out. I sit on the nearest kitchen chair.

In her bed, Mum is singing. 'Jesus bids us shine in a fuck, fuck, fuck.'

1973

I needn't have worried: I found out Sam had been working all hours to get in front with his jobs for the firm where he was an apprentice and with his college work. He was in his last year, and, conscientious as usual, wanted, as he told me on the last phone call, "to clear the decks" for when he did come to see me.

I was so excited it hadn't occurred to me to think where he would stay.

'With you, of course.' Carol's eyebrows disappeared under her fringe.

She brought home a different chap every Saturday night. Most of them didn't think it necessary to put any clothes on when going to the kitchen to get a glass of water, or to stick their heads out of the hall window for a post-coital cigarette. Carol didn't like smoking in her room, which made me laugh; even though she was always immaculately dressed, her place was a tip more often than not.

'Oh. Well, to be honest we haven't gone all the way yet. We've got near to it but, you know...'

'What? How long have you been going out with him?' Carol perched on the worktop in the kitchen, crossed her long slender legs and leaned back, blowing cigarette smoke out of the open window.

'Always, it seems.'

Carol pursed her lips, took a drag on the cigarette. 'I need to sort you two out.'

'You *need* to keep your neb out of my love life,' I said.

When Sam did come to stay we had a night trawling the clubs and got back to my room in the early hours of Sunday morning.

I was suddenly self-conscious. We'd been smothering our laughter, sneaking into the building, but when Sam closed the door behind us it dawned on me that we were alone – I mean really alone – for the first time that evening.

I waited for a moment, trying to form the right words in my head then turned, slowly to look at him.

'I think we've waited long enough, don't you, Sam? Have you got...?' I couldn't bring myself to say the word Durex.

'Got? Got what?'

'You know...'

Sam grinned. 'No. What?'

'Things. You know...' The sod was going to make me say it. 'Durex.'

He laughed and patted his jeans back pocket. Then his other pocket. Then his jacket inside pocket. The smile faded. 'Oh, bugger, they're in my other jeans.'

I didn't know whether to laugh at the disappointment on his face or to swear. I sighed. 'Next time then,' I said.

'Next time,' he agreed, ruefully.

I laughed when, with a flourish, he gave a mock impression of being a gentleman and turned his back so I could get undressed. Once I was in my baby-doll pyjamas and under the covers he got undressed as well. I wasn't supposed to look but after I took my lenses out and put my glasses on, I did. He looked funny in his white string vest and Y-fronts. We tucked into that narrow bed like spoons in a drawer. We got so close to making love but, in the end, it was Sam who moved away. I was relieved he had more self-control than me. I knew he'd wait until I was ready and I was so afraid of getting pregnant. Getting pregnant wasn't in my plans – then.

Later, with toe-curling embarrassment I listened to Carol in the next room. The creaks of the bed and the loud gasps could be heard clearly through the wall. I hoped Sam was asleep but after a few minutes he muttered, 'Noisy neighbour you've got.' I could feel him laughing and although I was hot with embarrassment I couldn't help joining in. Soon we were shouting out in laughter and as Sam flung an arm out, gasping for breath, he forgot how narrow my bed was and, arms flailing, fell out with a yell. Through the wall came a cry of triumph. 'Well done, Irene, you finally broke your duck then?' Sam thought it hilarious.

Chapter Forty-Four

2002: Today: 9.45 a.m.

She won't let me get her out of bed; she keeps pushing me away. She won't stop singing and, all the time, she's watching me. I could just leave her. I will. I'll leave her. I turn my back on her. I'll walk out and leave her there. I pretend to tidy the shelves in her wardrobe, making myself breathe evenly, pushing down the frustration. Then I hear her puffing and panting and the sound of Velcro ripping. It can only mean one thing; she's struggling to take off her incontinence pants to throw. It wouldn't be the first time.

'Don't even think about it,' I say, without turning around. Too late, the sodden cotton pad hits my shoulder. She always could throw straight, Dad can vouch for that; he was on the receiving end often enough.

I pick up the pants without speaking and walk out. In the bathroom I shove them in one of the plastic bags and drop it into the bin on top of the one already there that I've forgotten to take out to the dustbin.

I wash my hands and sit on the side of the bath. She's shouting now instead of singing. After a few moments there is silence. And then I hear the sobs. Guilt overwhelms the anger. I go back to her.

1973

It did seem daft that we'd waited so long and done nothing about it. I had no trust in a Durex and Sam understood, so once I was registered with the doctor near college I asked the GP to prescribe the contraceptive pill for me. After a month of religiously taking it and the anticipation of Sam's next visit, when he was actually standing in front of me in my room, I was filled with anxiety. However close we'd come to making love, we hadn't actually gone the whole way.

'You okay?' Sam was pale; he shifted from foot to foot. Held out his hand.

'I am.' I took hold of his fingers; they were trembling.

'This is silly.' His laugh was a short breathy sound.

'Just hold me,' I said. I moved closer, wound his arm around my waist.

We stood still for a few moments. I felt the heat of his body, the need in both of us. The rooms on either side of us were quiet; it was the middle of the afternoon, it seemed everyone was out on campus. Rain streaked the windows, blurred the grounds, the buildings outside. We were alone.

We kissed.

'You okay?' Sam touched my lips with the tip of his finger.

The same words he'd used earlier, a lifetime ago.

'Wonderful.' I loved the feel of his skin on mine. I ran my fingers along the length of him: his shoulder, chest, stomach, thigh. I'd known him, his body for so many years but not like this. The rain beat harder on the glass. 'We can't go out in this,' I said, looking up at the window, pretending disappointment and kneeling up I straddled him. 'We'll just have to find a way to pass the time.'

But then the firm Sam worked for went bankrupt and, even though he was, by then, fully qualified, he had to find jobs where he could and sometimes he couldn't make it to Manchester. When one of the girls shouted up the stairwell that he was on the phone in the telephone box outside the hall, I knew it would be one of those times.

'Sam,' I said, leaning against the dusty glass wall of the box. 'You've got a job on?'

'I'm sorry. I'll miss your birthday.'

'Don't be daft, love, it can't be helped. Anyway, I'll be too busy to celebrate. I need to get some more stuff ready for my teaching practice next week.'

The static from the line hissed in my ears in the few seconds. He didn't say anything but I knew what he was thinking. Or rather hoping. It was a break in the term; I could have gone home. Even though I'd have loved to see Nanna, I didn't want to be anywhere near Mum. I knew I was being selfish, but I had no intention of going back to Grove Street. Besides, I really was looking forward to my first time in an actual classroom.

Chapter Forty-Five

2002: Today: 10.30 a.m.

I've left a message for Sam on his mobile to tell him about the heating. I don't want him to come home to find me like this. But I still don't move. I'm lying on the floor in Mum's room. It's simply easier than standing up. The carpet smells dusty; there are rolls of fluff under the bed. I raise my head to see her and hope, wish, that the slight movement of her chest would just stop.

1973

Greenworth Primary School was an old Victorian gritstone building, surrounded by green-painted iron railings.

My classroom was two smaller rooms knocked into one with a beamed ceiling and windows so high that, although they were large and let in plenty of light, even standing I was unable to see the playground outside.

I'd been told to expect a large class but seeing four rows of thirty tiny five-year-olds behind their desks that first day made my legs quiver. It seemed to me that we watched one another with the same curiosity and apprehension. It didn't help that one of my lecturers had ensconced herself in the far corner of the room with a notebook and pen on her lap.

I took a long breath and smiled, hoping the nervous twitch in the corners of my mouth didn't show.

'Good morning everyone, I'm Miss Bradshaw.' I clasped my hands behind my back, tightening my fingers together. 'Now, I don't think I'm going to be able to remember all your names on our first day so this is what I suggest...'

Five minutes later, amid a lot of giggling, I'd pushed the two front rows of desks and chairs as far back as I could and we were all sitting in a circle at the front of the classroom.

'Right. Everyone sitting comfortably?' There was a lot of shuffling, crossing of legs and laughing again. I could feel the tension drain away inside me.

I drew the large bag I'd brought with me from underneath my table and, with great flourishes, produced all the dried oak and sycamore leaves, scraps of material and wax crayons I'd collected over the last fortnight and placed them carefully in the middle. I kept the Copydex by my side; I didn't want to be responsible for thirty lots of fingers being glued up to high heaven.

Some of the children leant forward to touch. I didn't stop them.

'Can we pick some up?' The question came from a little girl with bright red hair.

'Of course you may. What's your name?'

'Gillian, Miss.' She lowered her head. Shy.

'Well, Gillian – everyone...' I delved again into the bag for the circles of paper I'd made from a roll of old wallpaper Sam had got for me. 'If you turn these over so you have the white side upwards...' I started to pass them around, 'And when I point to each you, would you please tell me your name and then you may choose one leaf, one piece of material and two crayons. There are enough to go around so no one needs to feel left out.' I looked at them. 'Everyone understand?'

They nodded, a chorus of 'Yes, Miss Bradshaw,' rippling through them.

'Well done.' It was a good start.

During the first break I watched the general expressions of distaste as the children drank their milk. Quite a few of the boys chewed the tops of the straws flat and pretended to suck hard while the level of the milk in the little bottle stayed the same. I sympathised with them – I'd hated the stuff when I was in school, especially in winter when the bottles were put on the radiators to thaw the milk out and it was half-frozen, half-lukewarm. So I ignored it when some of them furtively slipped the almost full bottles into the crate before going out into the playground or coming back to sit in the circle to look at the leaves or draw.

Later, when I'd could tell they were thoroughly tired out, we had story time. By the end of the day, I learned their names, we'd had fun and they had some lovely montages to take home after hours of cutting, sticking and copying.

That was my most favourite age group. The noisy, barely contained excitement as each day went by in the lead up to Christmas was infectious. Colourful paper chains were made and hung across the walls, balloons were blown up and pinned around the blackboard. Images of Father Christmas were drawn and glued onto the large strip of paper I'd spent one evening fastening along the length of one side of the room. It was wonderful to come into the classroom each morning knowing that the red, green and white decorations that transformed the dull magnolia walls were my idea.

I looked forward to going into the school every day. As the end of term grew nearer, we split the time into tasks and rehearsals for the nativity play.

On the morning of the final rehearsal, I decided they should make Christmas cards. It was difficult to contain them but I enjoyed it. Conscious that it was my last day, I treasured every moment.

One boy, Alan Frobisher, had arrived in full shepherd's outfit.

'Perhaps a good idea to take off your headdress, Alan?'

'No, thanks, Miss. Mam said I'll never get it right if I do and she said it'd taken her all her time to fasten it on this morning, so it stays on.'

146

'Oh. All right. Perhaps tie it back a bit while we make the cards?'

'No, it'll be okay.'

By the time the thin cardboard had been cut into squares, decorated with drawings of Father Christmas or Christmas trees and glued with sprinkles of gold and silver stars, Alan's headdress was looking decidedly festive. But he seemed happy enough as, with tongue poking out in a way that reminded me of Rose, he laboriously wrote "Happy Christmas" on the inside of the card; so generously spaced that the words "Mam and Dad", ended up on the back.

There was one panic when we discovered we had lost baby Jesus: a doll that Samantha Carter, as Mary, had brought from home. When we found it hidden in the Wendy house, I saw that someone had crayoned a pair of glasses on it. Despite much rubbing with soap and water it didn't come off completely and baby Jesus was presented to the audience with two black eyes, concealed by a shawl pinned so tightly by me that only its nose was showing.

All the other girls on our corridor went home. I had no choice but to do the same; the college closed and I had nowhere else to go. Besides, I'd had a short note from Nanna saying how much she was looking forward to hearing all my news and having a belated celebration for my birthday. She'd added a strange bit at the end of that last sentence in wobbly capital letters: "WITH YOU SITTING IN FRONT OF ME SO I CAN SEE THAT YOU ARE REALLY HAPPY". That bothered me; I'd written every other week to her, telling her what I'd been doing and putting in as many funny bits as I could think of. What was worrying her?

Chapter Forty-Six

2002: Today: 10.40 a.m.

She starts grunting and I know what she's doing. I scramble to my feet. 'No!' It's too late. What in god's name has she been eating? Nothing I haven't given her but something obviously hasn't agreed with her; there's shit everywhere. She's covered in it, her back, her legs, her feet. The smell is awful. She's watching me. She looks frightened. Oh god, she's frightened of me.

1973

Sam met me on the station, a huge self-conscious smile on his face and a red rose in his hand, which he thrust at me as soon as I stood in front of him.

'Hi.' He breathed the word, wrapped his arms around me, nuzzling into my neck. 'I've missed you.'

'And me you,' I said. 'But not this place.' I felt his body tense and was immediately sorry for the words. 'Where are we going first?'

'Dad says if you fancy a bit of something to eat with us? Bit of a homecoming and late birthday bash combined? He's made a cake – your favourite – chocolate.'

'That would be brilliant. But I want to see Nanna first...'

'Of course you do.' Sam picked up my case and I linked his arm.

Outside the dreariness of the station, Denholme was looking quite festive in the darkness of late afternoon. The council office windows were lit up with strings of white bulbs and a star was perched above the large front doors. Coloured lights hung from lamp-post to lamp-post along Ashton Street. Each of the small shops cast a rectangular glow on the pavements and, as we passed, the displays of pretend wrapped presents, tinsel and tiny Christmas trees covered in multicoloured baubles and topped with winged angels, gave me an unexpected flicker of excitement.

'Have you seen Nanna lately?' My breath hung white in the cold air. I tucked my red tartan scarf firmly around my neck and hugged Sam closer for warmth.

'I met your dad by chance on his way to your house last week and called round with him.' He gave me a quick kiss on my cheek. 'She looked a bit tired. But thrilled you were coming home,' he added hastily, when I glanced at him. 'I'm not sure, judge for yourself.'

'I will.' His hesitation worried me. But then I had a sudden thought. 'If she's up to it, would your dad mind if Nan comes with us to your place?'

'Course not.'

Whether it was because I hadn't seen her for a while or whether she was ill, I wasn't sure. She looked frail when she came to the door. 'You all right, Nanna?'

'I'm fine, love. Just a bit tired. I've been bottoming the house; getting it all spick and span for you coming home. And doing a bit of baking, what with missing your birthday and it being Christmas. You know me.'

I hugged her. 'I do. And you shouldn't have.' But Mum should, I thought. 'Where's Mum?'

'Eee, I don't know. I don't see her for dust most days. She's out that door whippet quick in a morning.'

'No change there then.' Despite my irritation at Mum – I suspected it wasn't the first time Nanna had been left alone in the evening as well as in the daytime – I had to laugh. I'd forgotten how my grandmother sometimes resorted to these quirky phrases.

'Tell you what, Nanna, Sam's dad's invited us to go to their house for something to eat. Belated birthday tea. You up for it?'

'I'll get my hat and coat. And that cake.' She raised her arm for me to help her out of the low armchair. No hesitation.

I laughed. 'Great. Carry on like this and I'll be the size of a house by the time I get back to college.'

149

'No more talk about going back when you've only just got here. I want to savver every minute.'

'Hear, hear,' Sam said, helping Nanna into her coat.

Outside the house, Sam put himself between us and crooked his elbows. Nanna and me slipped our arms through his and off we marched. Frail or not, my grandmother could still manage a good pace.

That night was one of a few at their place. Though she soon was tired, Nanna was always on top form. She loved to make people laugh even when she was also laughing at herself.

That first time we were at Sam's house, after she'd admired their new electric cooker, she told us about her and Grandad when they first moved into their place on Barraclough.

'We reckoned the Council thought we were going to have a large family from the size of the boiler they supplied us with in the kitchen,' she said, flushing. 'It were months before we found out from a neighbour that we were supposed to boil clothes in it and not potatoes and veg.'

'I don't believe you...' Sam's dad spluttered out the words.

'It's true.' Nanna was pink with indignation even as she laughed at herself. 'I did. Mind you, I'd have given my back teeth to use it again for the spuds we needed all the Christmases we had in those days, when every one of our neighbours piled into our place. Good job I didn't though; they'd all have frothed at the mouth from the carbolic soap.'

Mr Hargreaves roared again at that, which encouraged her to tell us about other funny times when her and Grandad were first married. I loved watching her face light up at the memories which always finished with the phrase, 'Eee, we did laugh.' It made me happy to listen to her low chuckle. I was grateful to Sam's dad for making such a fuss of her. More so when he took me on one side the last time we were at their house, and he told me he'd keep in touch with her.

It wasn't too bad a Christmas, better than I expected anyway. I realised it was as much an effort for Mum to be civil as it was for me, but I was glad we succeeded in being polite to one another.

I even found myself giving Mum a hug and a kiss on the cheek as I left. 'Look after one another,' I said, holding Nanna close when the three of us stood on the doorstep in the awkward moment of leave-taking. I glanced back once to wave. Only Nanna was still there.

Chapter Forty-Seven

2002: Today: 10.40 a.m.

'It's okay,' I say. 'Don't get upset. I'm not angry.'

She closes her eyes, holds up her arms.

'Wait.' I don't know what to do. It's like my feet won't move. I can't think straight. I can't leave her like this, I know that...

1974

I'd thought a lot about the way I wanted to teach, and who, while I was at home. Perhaps it was because I felt so near to Rose. The idea grew, and by the time I got off the train in Manchester, I'd made up my mind.

Everyone, except me, came back with so much food from home that we decided to throw a belated New Year party and invited some of the other students. One of the girls had dropped out because she was missing her boyfriend. Her absence allowed Patricia to move into that room, which meant she was away from the kitchen, so was doubly happy; I hadn't realised she was a vegetarian and the smell of grilling bacon or sausages sickened her.

I studied her over my glass of Mateus Rosé. 'You've lost some weight? You look great.'

A pink flush coloured her cheeks. 'I'm trying. Wasn't easy over Christmas.'

'I bet.' I frowned in sympathy. 'I lived on those Limmits biscuits when I first came here.'

'I couldn't do that, the ingredients, you know… '

'Of course, I didn't think—'

There was a small cheer around the fondue set that Carol had brought back with her. After inspecting the pot, she'd declared the cheese melted.

'You can have cheese, though?' I asked Patricia.

'Oh yes.' We joined the rest of the gang and speared the chunks of bread. There weren't enough of the proper fondue forks so we made do with metal knitting needles and took turns to swirl them around in the cheese in a figure of eight, which Carol told us was the correct way to dip.

I soon got fed up with the jostling around the worktop to get past the lads to the fondue and retreated to the other food. Patricia followed me.

'Are you all right?' She reached across the table to scoop up a handful of raisins and peanuts, avoiding the fish paste and ham and pickle butties. 'You seem to be preoccupied?'

'I'm fine.' I paused, dithering over whether to have a sausage roll or cheese and pineapple on a stick. In consideration of Patricia and her sensitive nose I chose the latter. 'I know it's nearly three years away and we've only done one teaching practice, but have you decided what age group you want to teach?'

'Oh, little ones, definitely. I said right away at my interview but I was told there was some flexibility to swop my education course if I changed my mind.' She gave a little shudder. 'I couldn't teach teenagers. I doubt I would be able to deal with them. Especially boys. I've got four brothers at home and I've had enough of boys.' She laughed. 'Why? What age are you going to teach? Have you? Thought about it, I mean?'

'Yes. But I need some advice about it—' I didn't get the chance to explain.

'Wotcha, girls.' One of the lads from the student union group flung his arms around our shoulders. 'Hogging all the food eh? Come on, move over, let the dog see the rabbit, as my granny would say.' He let go of us and grabbed two of the butties in each hand. 'How are you, Tricia?'

I saw Patricia go bright red and took the hint.

'Think I'll just...' I waved my hand towards the door. 'Things to do...' I winked at her. She went even redder, opened her eyes wide and shook her head. Fancies you, I mouthed. Go for it. 'See you later,' I said. He was too preoccupied with my friend to even notice me leaving.

In my room, I made a note of all the lectures I wanted to attend during the year and those I thought I could safely miss without jeopardising the idea that was beginning to formulate in my mind. I wanted to talk it over with my tutor as early as possible, so the next day I made an appointment with her.

Maureen Wintor was a wonderful eccentric and I loved everything about her. Tall and aristocratic with white hair piled carelessly high on top of her head, a long baggy grey cardigan flung over an assortment of colourful full-length dresses, she would sweep into the lecture hall with a smile and would always start her lectures with the same question: 'What is the correct method of teaching?' Before answering it herself: 'The one that takes each individual child into consideration.' She was passionate about teaching and wanted all of us to feel the same.

I knew she would listen and give me the best advice she could.

I spent the first ten minutes talking to her about Rose.

'You do know that teaching in a special school will require you to take an extra course after you qualify, don't you?' she said, a few thoughtful moments after I stopped speaking.

'Yes, of course.'

'Good. It hasn't always been so. Once, it wasn't the job of teachers to help children with special needs. And it wasn't particularly important or even worthwhile. But, thankfully, we've moved on...'

A kind smile accompanied the slight frown on her face. 'So it will be a while before you will be earning a decent wage.'

'I hadn't thought of the money,' I confessed.

'No, I guessed that wasn't your first priority.' This time her smile was wider. 'But if that's your plan, and I understand why, I suggest that the best thing you can do is to finish your course, and become qualified to teach anywhere first, just in case you change your mind—' She held up both hands as I began to protest and laughed. 'Okay, I can see you won't, Irene. So, the more you learn about child development and children's thinking and the theory of education today, the better equipped you'll be.'

She pushed a baggy cardigan sleeve up her arm and checked her watch. 'Now, we'd better get on, we both have places to be.' When she stood, she held out her hand to shake mine. 'Keep your head down these next three years and work hard. I know, whatever you do in the future, Irene, you will make a success of it.'

I held on to those last words and there were many times I needed to repeat them to myself.

Chapter Forty-Eight

2002: Today: 10.45 a.m.

Shower. She'll have to go in the shower. Which means I'll have to get in as well. But with no heating on we'll both be cold.

And it'll be yet another struggle.

At one time Mum constantly washed her hands and left the water running. I can't count the number of times she flooded the bathroom. These days I have a fight on my hands just washing her face.

1974

I took a seat on the back row of the chairs in the student union. There were a larger number of students than usual for the discussion. Over the weeks I'd missed very few; they were always lively and I enjoyed the debates.

This one had been advertised on the union noticeboard as,

"Education, like any other public service, is answerable to the society which it serves and which pays for it. Discuss."

I'd looked forward to it for days and thought most of the others from my corridor had as well but, looking around, I couldn't see any of my friends, which surprised me. I thought that Patricia, at least, would have been interested but, as the room filled up even more, there was no sign of her. Then I remembered, she was finishing the essay on the philosophy, sociology and psychology of education from my notes she'd borrowed in return for the music and art notes I'd cribbed from her: lectures I'd missed. I loved both subjects, but they were two of the ones I knew I could safely miss occasionally without risking my plans.

People were still streaming through the door. Most of the chairs were occupied and so some lounged against the walls. I searched for Carol; it wasn't like her to miss these things. She always said it was the one place she was sure to pick up some talent.

As usual three third-year students were leading the debate, and the one who was acting as chairman stood. I recognised her from the times she'd sat at the back of the room in some of our English lectures from Mr Eastmore. She tucked her long straight hair behind her ears, pushed the wire-rimmed glasses over the bridge of her nose and cleared her throat before speaking.

'Hi, everyone. I think I know a lot of you here tonight but for those who don't know who I am, my name is Julia. On my left is Tony and on my right, Phil. We're chairing the debate tonight. Now,

I'll read out an article that has been doing the rounds in some of the Red Tops lately.' She waved the sheet of paper in her hand, held it close to her and read, '"There is a feeling that the educational system is out of touch with the fundamental need for Britain to survive today both economically and competitively in either the industrial or the commercial world."'

There was a rumble of disgust throughout the room, some jeers. As it died down, one loud question rang out.

'So, are you saying we're wasting our time on this course? That what we're learning to pass on to pupils is useless?'

Carol! I spotted her further along my row, an older lad next to her, his arm slung casually along her shoulders. I saw him grin and dip his head towards her, whispering.

'No, if you'd listened you would have noticed I said it was in the newspapers. It's not my opinion. I copied the article.' The girl held up the paper in her hand. 'I'd like the thoughts from the room about it, please.'

I saw the colour rise in Carol's face, then lost sight of her as she slunk down in her seat.

Julia waited. When no one spoke she said, 'Okay, I'll paraphrase some of the article. It says there is no set national curriculum in schools, no set subjects taught. The present curriculum, it says, pays too little attention to the basic skills of reading, writing, and arithmetic, and is overloaded with fringe subjects.'

'What are they calling "fringe subjects"?' A male student's voice rose above the mumbling that had started again.

'We presume, PE, Music, Art...'

'Nature walks? Dance?' From behind us.

'Anything like that.' The call came from the other side of the room.

I held up my hand. The student called Tony behind the desk touched Julia's arm and pointed to me. I felt the panic, heard the shake in my voice when I spoke. 'These so called "fringe subjects" are vital, not only in giving a rounded education but to form a connection with the children, surely? In the more relaxed atmosphere of these lessons, we will be able to form good relationships – not only to keep discipline within the class that comes from the teaching of the core subjects, but to instil in the children the importance of hard work, good manners – caring for those around them.'

My last words were drowned out by the clapping. But then I heard: 'Rubbish! Kids need to be aware of the importance of industry to our society. We aren't told how to get that over to them on this course. The schools I've had practice in have been overloaded with these weak subjects. Literacy and numeracy...' He paused, presumably for him to get maximum effect for his argument, 'Literacy and numeracy, the building blocks of education, are being neglected.'

I turned around to face him.

'So, why are you here? I mean, why are you on this course, if that's what you think? Here, we're being taught that all the subjects are important – core – and the so-called "fringe" – which, by the way, I think is a phrase that is an insult to both teachers and children. Children especially. We're learning to pass on our belief that the whole of education is important in making them rounded individuals, and for them to have as much knowledge as we can give them in order to face the world, their futures.' I stopped; what was the point? I would be taking a different route from the majority of the people in the room. The children I wanted to spend my time with in the future would be oblivious to any world other than their own.

The weeks flew by in a round of lectures, long talks with Maureen Wintor about the way forward, how to follow my ambition to teach in special schools, and reading books on the development of children with learning difficulties. Without realising it, it kept me too busy to think much about home apart from writing to Nanna, Sam and Dad and receiving the weekly letters from them, at least from Sam and Dad. For some reason, I just accepted that Dad wrote instead of Nanna. When I did think about it, I suppose I thought it had become too much of an effort for her.

I didn't go home for the Easter holidays either; I had lesson plans to prepare for my next teaching practice – Sam was working away and Carol and Patricia were staying in Manchester as well. To salve my conscience I wrote a short note to Nanna every other day, letting her know what I was doing.

Chapter Forty-Nine

2002: Today: 10.45 a.m.

I can't see how I'm going to get her into the bathroom; I can't walk her there, even her feet are covered in shit.

She's waiting. Watching me.

Think!

The folding wheelchair! I go down and dig it out from the cupboard under the stairs and slowly lug it step by step to the landing. At the top I hit my shin on one of the footrests. I bite my lip. Bloody hell, that hurt.

When I get my breath back I try to get it into her room; it just fits through the door. It's one the social services gave to us years ago, before it was too difficult to take her outside. But they didn't come back for it and I couldn't be bothered to ring them, so it's just one more thing gathering dust.

1974

Carol and Patricia had gone home, so I found myself traipsing around on my own one weekend. I was standing on Oldham Street, looking through the window of C&A's at a lovely green and purple minidress and wondering if I could afford it, when I noticed the reflection of a man standing next to me.

'Dad! What are you doing here?'

He laughed, giving me a hug.

'We came to see you. We were on our way to the university. But here you are...'

It was the anxious way he glanced past me that made me realise something was wrong and I turned.

The woman behind us looked about forty years old, was tall and slender and wore a paisley-patterned maxi dress with long flowing sleeves and a scoop neck. Her brown hair was fastened into a French pleat. She looked ... elegant.

'Irene, this is Susan.'

'So glad to meet you at last,' she said, smiling. 'I thought it would never happen.' She had perfect white teeth.

'Hi.' My smile felt stiff on my lips, but I tried for Dad's sake.

'Well now.' His ears glowed red and he cleared his throat, rubbing his neck with his knuckles. 'Now it has – have you time for a bite to eat with us? We thought we'd go to the Berni Inn on Peter Street.'

'I don't think—'

'Please Irene. I've been meaning to come over for a couple of weeks now.'

'Oh?' There was something in his voice that worried me all at once. 'Okay. I suppose I could.'

We walked in silence.

When the waiter showed us to the table I slid along the red bench opposite them. Dad's left hand, resting on the table, was trembling. Susan covered it with hers, almost as an automatic gesture. And then I saw the look he gave the woman. Not a look I ever saw him give my mother and for a split second I almost felt sorry for Mum. But I knew it was her who'd tossed aside the love from Dad.

'Shall we order?' Dad said. 'And then we can talk?'

'Okay...' I glanced at the menu fastened into the plastic stand in the middle of the table 'I'll have the melon boat without the maraschino cherry and then the gammon, I think.'

There was an awkward silence while we waited for the food to arrive but I kept that smile fixed. People bustled about close to us, settled at their respective tables and the waiters buzzed back and forth bringing drinks. When we were finally served with the starters and the large schooners of sherry Dad said, 'There's something I need to tell you, Irene.' His spoon shook against the glass dish that held his prawn cocktail. 'It's bad news, I'm afraid.'

'What's wrong?' Alarmed at his obvious distress I stopped separating a piece of melon from the rest. 'You're not ill are you? You haven't had another scare?'

'No. I'm sorry.' He rubbed his forehead. 'I should have at least waited 'til we'd eaten.'

'Too late now.' I tried to keep my tone light but there was an uneasy quiver in my stomach. 'Go on.'

Susan looked at me over the rim of her schooner; her eyes were soft, sympathetic.

'Dad? What is it?'

He gave a small cough. 'It's Nanna. They've found out what's wrong with her...' I couldn't breathe. 'It's leukaemia – she hasn't been going to the doctors – she just pretended to. She said she knew all along she was very ill – just wanted to go on as normal for as long as she could.'

As long as she could? She'd seemed to be unwell ever since – ever since Rose died – but I'd always assumed it was the shock of losing my sister. Or that she was getting old. But she must have been really poorly all the time. Suddenly it was as though everything around me was in slow motion; waves of sound came and went. My jaw slackened, but I couldn't form any words.

'I didn't want to tell you before the doctor and hospital were sure.'

'You should have.' I finally found my voice. 'Nanna—'

'Didn't want me to tell you.' He was pleading with me, obviously hoping I'd understand.

'You should have told me. I had a right to know.' I was angry with myself. 'Mum should have told me.' Even as I spoke I knew why she hadn't. There'd been hardly any contact between us, even when I'd gone home: as much my fault as hers. I'd always believed she was envious of the closeness Nanna and me had. 'That's why Nanna hasn't been replying to my letters,' I said, 'and why you write the letters for her.' Self-recrimination rumbled away inside me. I should have known something was wrong.

'She still loves getting them. She said I shouldn't tell you – not then anyway. She didn't want you worrying.'

'I'll come home.'

'Can you do that?'

'Yes. No. I don't know.' I held his hand. 'But I will.' I wanted to ask him what Mum had said about Nanna; she was her mother, after all. But I knew that was pointless, Nanna wouldn't accept any help from her after all the years of their estrangement. And she was my nanna, she'd looked after both Rose and me for a long time; it was my turn to look after her. But, at the back of my mind I was already wondering whether the college would let me take an extended leave, if they would keep my place open. Despite myself, knowing I was being selfish, I felt that all my plans were slipping away.

'Thanks, Irene.' He was near to tears. He'd always been close to Nanna. I could understand him being so upset but he was a private man. To be almost crying in public made me see how scared he was for her. And it frightened me. I grabbed my shoulder bag.

'Look, I can't finish this. And I don't want anything else—'

'No, you must eat—'

'No, honestly. I think I'll just go and pack.'

'Well – if you're sure? I have to say I'm not hungry now, either. But I need to go to the lavatory first.' He blew his nose and stood up. Susan and me watched him make his way through the tables to the other end of the room.

I didn't feel any need to say anything to her.

Chapter Fifty

2002: Today: 10.45 a.m.

I stand in front of the airing cupboard, trying to choose two old towels. There's a faint scent of Johnson's baby lotion. 'I know, Rose.' I nod. 'But I'll be all right.' I nod again in determination. 'It'll be okay.' I pull two towels from one of the piles and take them to the wheelchair, spreading them on the seat. I go back for a clean sheet. The smell of the lotion has gone.

'Come on then, Mother. Let's get you up.' I wrap the sheet around her so I don't get covered in crap. When I try to pick her up so her feet don't touch the carpet she goes floppy. 'Straighten up, Mum. Please.' She slumps lower onto the bed. 'Come on, Mother,' I say. My heart is thudding. Bloody palpitations! 'You have to help. Please.' She doesn't. 'Please Mum,' I yell. I'm at the end of my tether. She stiffens, grunts, and looks up at me, bewildered. I'm ashamed...

1974

After a long moment of silence Susan said. 'I said he should talk to you alone. And before now.'

I lifted my shoulders. I didn't trust my voice.

She fidgeted with the silver bangle on her arm, biting her lip. She looked across the restaurant in the direction my father had gone. 'I don't think your father ever told you how we met, did he?'

'No.' What was the point of knowing that now? 'Ancient history.' I knew how rude I was being, but couldn't help it.

It didn't stop her.

'We literally bumped into one another. I dropped my shopping. The carrier bags split and everything spilled out. He carried it home for me.' She waited, her eyes fixed on me. I said nothing, it was the kind of thing Dad would do: always a gentleman. 'It was getting late, the shops had closed. He only had a thin jacket on so I asked him in for a cup of tea.' She must have seen the cynicism in my eyes because she added, 'It wasn't like that. It was the first time I'd forced myself to go out of my flat since my husband died. I just looked at everything scattered all over the pavement and burst into tears. Your poor father didn't know where to put himself.' She smiled.

I didn't. I stared at her. I let her squirm, fidget with the clip on her bracelet. The part of me that was the distraught sixteen-year-old girl still blamed this woman for taking my dad away when I needed him so badly.

It was as though she could read my mind. 'Look Irene...' The sympathy was there again. 'I understand why you're angry. But you couldn't feel worse than your father did when he had to leave you.'

'Had to?' I hoped I looked as incredulous as I felt. What the hell did she mean?

'Your father is a very quiet man.'

'Tell me something I don't know.'

'From what I can gather, your mother worked hard at making him feel useless. When he had his second stroke and he stopped working at the bank, she made him feel good for nothing. He had to get out from your house, you must understand that?'

'He left us behind.'

'I know, and I'm sorry. But when he first came to me he was in bed for over a fortnight. He did try to phone you and I posted some letters he'd written to you but, most of the time, he slept. The doctor said he was on the verge of a breakdown. If he'd stayed he would have been no use to you anyway. He couldn't look after himself just then.' She rummaged for a tissue in her handbag and dabbed at her eyes. 'Sorry, it brings it all back.'

It felt like we were on opposite sides of a wall. Neither of us saw anything other than what we wanted to see. I didn't want to believe what she was trying to tell me and she didn't really understand me.

I spoke abruptly. 'Tell me about Nanna.' My heart raced, the pulse in my ears thudded so loudly it sounded to me as though I was speaking in a tunnel. 'How is she really?'

'I haven't seen her.'

Obviously. The thought of her turning up at the house – Mum would have had a fit.

'But from what he's told me, your dad spoke the truth. He's thought long and hard about the situation...'

The situation? I raised my eyebrows. I was, probably unfairly, quite pleased to see the way she flushed. 'He's struggled with what to do for the best. Your grandmother is very ill but she really didn't want you to know. Derek told me she said she's never wanted you to be tied down.'

'Tied down? How?'

'I suppose she means you looking after her, stuck at home. But your Dad persuaded her it was your right to know and to choose what to do about it. He doesn't think your mother wants to.'

The woman knew an awful lot about us. But, even though I was aware I was acting like a spoilt brat, inside the resentment lessened. She'd obviously brought a lot of comfort to Dad, and I was being unreasonable. He was right, we couldn't trust my mother to look after Nanna properly.

'I had no intention of coming between your mum and dad, you know.' She pushed her sleeves up and leant forward, her arms resting on the table. She looked earnest. 'I truly didn't.'

'There wasn't much you could come between.'

'I love your father and I'd do anything for him. He needs me. But he loves you and your nanna. He hasn't known what to do. He's been calling almost every day to see her. It's hard for him ... he's not well a lot of the time himself.'

Two long-haired, black-leather-clad rockers hovered in the doorway. One of them had his transistor radio in his hand. 'Resurrection Shuffle' blasted out. The waiter rushed towards them, flapping his hand. 'Out, out!' One of the lads lifted his chin, challenging. I noticed the waiter kept his distance, his tray clutched to his chest. 'Out!'

The one holding the radio ran his finger across a dial and the volume rose and, completely out of tune, he sang along, making a V-sign in the air. He winked across at us and backed out slowly.

A smile quivered on my lips but I watched Susan, waited for a withering remark.

Instead she burst out laughing. 'I know just how that feels,' she said. A couple of bricks in the wall between us crumbled. I joined in her laughter.

She held out her hand. 'I'm glad you're coming back with us. Can we call a truce?'

I nodded. Her fingers were warm between mine. 'Glad to,' I said. And I meant it. Almost.

Chapter Fifty-One

2002: Today: 10.55 a.m.

Somehow I get Mum into the chair and drag it backwards. She starts to slip on the towels. I hold on to her shoulder. The wheels seem too wide to go through the door. I turn the chair around and reverse, dragging it into the bathroom. Grabbing the sheet I pull her up and balance her on the lavatory seat while I quickly undress. I've already switched the immersion heater on and turned the shower to warm. The room is full of steam.

1974

'I can't guarantee there will be a place here for you when you are able to return, Irene. It all depends on the Education Department.' Professor Milton studied my record file. 'But you have certainly excelled in both your term and day teaching practices. I'm only sorry you will be unable to carry out your next one. Although,' she tapped her pen on the pile of sheets that were my lesson plans, 'you do have admirable and ambitious ideas for the pupils. It's obvious you have a good grasp of what teaching is about these days. If you ever apply to re-enter the course, I could present these to strengthen your case.' She sighed, dropped her pen, placed her hands on her desk and linked her fingers. 'And there is definitely no one else who can care for your grandmother?'

'No.' I blinked hard to stop the tears. To be truthful the sorrow for Nanna was mingled with the sadness I'd been bottling up for days; my dreams of teaching, of hoping for a future helping children like Rose, were slipping away.

'Well...' Professor Milton stood and held out her hand. The interview was evidently over. 'I can only reiterate that I am sorry we are losing you and I hope that, one day, you will find a way to resume your studies.'

It was harder saying goodbye to Carol and Patricia. Despite protestations of keeping in touch, I already knew I had, in their minds, left the companionship of college life, the shared friendship. I watched them walk away along the platform, arm in arm. They didn't wait for the train to set off.

Chapter Fifty-Two

2002: Today: 11.00 a.m.

I'm holding her around her waist as we shuffle into the shower. I aim for the plastic chair in the middle of the tray to plonk her in it. She slips through my arms like a huge, pink lump of soap. Trying to stop her falling, I find myself face down in her naked lap. The thought flashes through my mind that Mum and me have never been this close in all my life and bubbles up until it explodes in a great hysterical hoot of mirth.

I extricate myself from the mound of flesh that's her stomach and look up at her. She looks down at me, startled. The shock that stretches her mouth open is replaced by a softening of her features and her lips puff out with a sudden titter. I sit back, legs sprawled out on either side of the chair. She clings on to the arms of it, still giggling.

We stare at one another. I have the sudden image of how we must look; two plump women, both blinking against the water pouring down on us, both pink in the heat, both with flattened wet hair, both laughing. Ridiculous. I'm laughing and I can't stop.

The tears soon follow the hysterical laughter and I can't stop those either. Mum soon joins in.

1974

Those first weeks back at Grove Street passed in a daze of sleepless nights and distressing days. Nanna tried not to show how much pain she was in, but I could tell when she needed her tablets more than usual. And when they were not enough to ease her.

As soon as I'd come back from Manchester, Mum had told me she couldn't help with Nanna; that she needed her sleep if she was going to be the only one to bring money into the house. She'd been promoted to senior assistant at the supermarket. A rapid rise up the ladder, I believed, thanks to her affair with the manager who picked her up in his red Vauxhall Viva every morning.

I didn't care; it was a relief not to have her at home and Dad helped as much as he could. Often he slept on the settee. I was grateful to Susan for understanding how much I needed him with me.

'I thought you'd gone up to bed.'

I looked up at Dad from resting my head on the table. He'd been staying with us for the last three nights and looked as weary as I felt.

'I didn't make it, obviously.' I looked around, blinking and smiled up at him. I stretched. 'I'll make another brew.'

'I'll do it.' His slippers squeaked on the lino as he crossed the kitchen, shoulders slumped under his old navy blue dressing gown, the hem uneven. 'I've just been up to Nanna.' He rolled his neck stiffly from side to side.

'How is she?'

'Rough. I've given her some more of the tablets the doctor left.' He ran his fingers through his hair, already mussed and standing on end.

'She can't carry on like this, Dad.' I rubbed the circulation back into my arms.

'I know.' He poured hot water into the teapot and swished it around. 'But she's always said she wouldn't go into hospital.'

I looked past him, through the window where streaks of paleness split the dark. It was just starting to get light even though it was only four o'clock in the morning. It was warm already and would be welcomed by everyone except Nanna, bathed in her own sweat. 'She has no choice now. Neither do we. All this isn't doing you any good; you're going to have another one of your do's if you're not careful.' I saw him sway. 'You're not feeling so good now, are you?' I said. When he turned to me, his face was grey. I jumped up. 'Right, back on that settee with you.' He let me take off his dressing gown and help him under the covers. I stroked his hair off his forehead. 'Get a good sleep. I'll watch Nanna.'

When I went upstairs Mum was sprawled on her back, her arm flung across what used to be Dad's pillow, her face furrowed: discontent even in sleep. I pushed at her. Turning on her side she grumbled, 'What time?'

'Time you got up,' I said. 'That's if you're working today.'

In the bathroom I filled the washing-up bowl and found a clean flannel in the airing cupboard.

Nanna's room smelled vaguely of lavender. I'd tried to ward off what I thought of as the stench of illness by using the soap and talcum powder she'd always been fond of. It didn't always work but wasn't too bad when I went in.

For a moment, I gazed at her dressing table where the only

168

photograph of Rose and me was propped up against the mirror. Then, crossing the bedroom, I sat down in the chair next to her bed.

'You awake, Nanna?'

She slowly opened her eyes. 'Hello, love.'

'Do you feel like a wash?' I lifted the bowl.

'Eee, I do that,' she whispered. 'And a comb of my hair, I feel like I've been dragged through a hedge backwards.'

Her skin was loose folds over her bones. Seeing the wasted muscles made me want to cry. Although small, she'd been a strong woman in the past. Even though I tried to be as gentle as I could, she still winced as I smoothed the soapy flannel over her.

When I'd finished, I changed the top sheet for a clean one and folded the duvet over, so it covered her feet. However warm she got they were always freezing to touch. I sat forward in the chair, resting her thin fingers in mine. I thought she'd gone to sleep but, when Mum started to bang around, Nanna's eyelids flickered and opened.

'Stop with me a bit Irene, I want to talk to you.'

I nodded but at the back of my mind I was listening to Mum going downstairs and hoped she'd leave Dad alone; he was doing her as much of a favour as me. Nanna was her mother after all. Not that you'd know it.

I heard Mum bang the front door. She hadn't even come in to see Nanna.

'She's gone.' Sweat was already beading on my grandmother's forehead.

'Yes, I know.' In her fancy suit I thought, bitterly, with her fancy man.

'Don't hate her, Irene.'

There was nothing I could say to that.

'I need to talk to you.' The air crackled inside her chest and was puffed out in short bursts.

'Let the tablets do their work, Nanna. Wait until you've had another sleep.'

'No. It won't wait.' Her fingers plucked at the top sheet. 'I wrote it down ... I put it in—'

'It'll wait, love.' I covered her fingers with mine. 'Hush, now.'

'I need to—'

'You need to rest,' I said, firmly. I stood up and pulled the sheet higher under her chin. 'Have a little nap and I'll come back in half an hour.'

'Irene...' Her voice faltered.

'Rest,' I said. 'I promise I'll be back soon.'

Chapter Fifty-Three

2002: Today: 11.00 a.m.

She holds out her hand to me, still sobbing and giggling at the same time. Unable to believe that she understands I need help, I grab hold of it and scrabble to get leverage on the slippery floor, twisting to get onto my knees. I stay like that for a moment, my backside up in the air, tittering again. I hear her grunt above the splash of the water. The next thing I feel is the slap on my bum. It stings but I carry on sniggering as I grip the legs of the chair and try to straighten up. The chair slides and I collapse again.

She shouts, 'Whoops!'

I echo her. 'Whoops!'

We're watching one another, cackling uncontrollably while I reach out through the shower curtain and feel for the mat on the bathroom floor. When I find it I drag it in with us and shuffle onto it. With the rough material under me, I manage to stand, holding on to the arms of the chair, my breath coming in short spluttering gasps.

She's still laughing, her eyes never leaving my face.

'Right, Mother,' I say, 'Let's get on with what we're here for.' I run my hand across my head, flattening my hair and do the same for her. The hysteria still bubbles up in silly cackles and she copies me. Knees against hers for balance, I take the old soft loofah off the corner shelf and rub soap on it.

The laughter dies in her eyes.

From the yells you'd think I was scraping her skin off with a scouring pad.

1974

The kids from four doors up were kicking a ball around the common land when I went to hang out the washing on the line. I hoped they wouldn't come this far down; I'd had football imprints on the sheets before.

Dad appeared at the back door. 'I'm okay now, so I'm off home,' he said.

'You're dressed! Sure you're okay?'

'Sure. How's Nanna?'

'Tired out. She was almost asleep the whole time I was up there.' I'd pushed away the niggles of concern. She'd wanted to talk to me about something. Now the worry returned; should I have let her tell me what it was?

'I'll be back later.' Dad folded his jacket over his arm.

I went with him to the front door.

He kissed me on the cheek. 'See you tonight.'

I watched him walk down the street. He was limping worse than usual. Perhaps Susan would make him rest again for a bit once he was home; funny how I thought of her flat as his these days. Funny how you've grown to accept her, I told myself. I looked around. Every day over the last week the pavements had shimmered in the heat, windows were flung wide open, the strands of the plastic multi-coloured curtains, hung in the doorways to keep out flies, barely moved. Two of the neighbours were chatting next door.

'Our Freda, what works at the doctor's, says Olive Carter's had that fungal infection on her big toenail for as long as she can remember.'

I stopped to listen; Mrs Gregory's gossip could always lighten my mood.

'I thought she walked funny. And her always acting as if she's better than the rest of us.'

'Fungal infection.' Both women lifted their folded arms up under their bosoms and slowly nodded at each other.

I smiled. Brilliant! Until Mrs Gregory called out, 'How's your Nan, Irene?'

I shook my head, unwilling to answer in case my words floated up to my grandmother in her bed.

In the kitchen I made a fresh pot of tea and poured some into the cup with a spout that she now used. Even with her usual splash of whiskey in it, it would be too hot for her, so I sat to drink mine at the table staring out of the back door at the piece of land Dad used to call his lawn. It was a weed-covered patch of earth now. A cat came and crouched in the middle of it.

The smell of lavender was strong when I opened Nanna's door. I carried the cup to the little bedside table and went over to the window. Two lines of a spider's web, glowing orange and green in the sunlight, swung across the corners of the frame, swaying in the slight movement of air coming in through the open sash. I broke the thread and wiped my hand on my skirt. The neighbours were still there, arms crossed as they leaned against the house.

I thought I heard a sound, a whisper, and turned back into the room. After looking out into the brightness it took me a few seconds to focus. 'Feel better for that little sleep?' There was no answering lift of her hand, no small murmur. 'Nanna?' I don't know what caused the ripple of goosebumps to rise along my arms, what stopped my feet from moving. 'Nanna?'

By the time I forced myself to touch her face there was no warmth of breath against my fingers. I pulled back, my legs rubber under me. I sat at the side of her, fighting down the waves of panic. I wished Sam wasn't working. I should get Dad.

Someone rattled the doorknocker and I jumped up. Glad to be

out of there, I was halfway down the stairs before I realised it would be the doctor on his rounds. I flung the door open and, pulling on his sleeve, almost hauled him into the house. 'She's gone, she's dead.' The hysteria made my voice thin and high-pitched.

'Stay down here.' Doctor Harris made sure I was sitting on the settee before he went upstairs. When he came back down he looked wretched. It dawned on me he must be nearly retiring age; we'd been his patients as far back as I could remember. 'I would have liked her to go into hospital months ago,' he said, 'but she was a stubborn old bird.' There was a smile in his voice. 'She's been living on borrowed time for a long time.'

'Did she know?' It didn't sound like my voice.

'Oh, yes.' His head moved up and down, slightly. 'She knew.'

'I didn't.'

He nodded, this time more definite. 'She protected you. She was adamant about that. She said she wanted you to have the freedom to live your life in the way you should.'

I didn't understand. But he'd known her a long time, seen what she'd done for our family, what she'd done for Rose and I realised how fond of Nanna he was. He put his arms around me. 'You and your Dad did as much as you could. You must never reproach yourself for anything, Irene. She's out of pain now.'

Later, I remembered I hadn't asked Nanna what she wanted to tell me; what it was she'd written.

I promised myself I'd look for whatever it was soon.

Chapter Fifty-Four

2002: Today: 11.45 a.m.

I haven't bothered dressing her: no point, she's going nowhere. She'll be warm enough in her flannelette nightie and woolly dressing gown. And I'm back in my dressing gown. I'm trying to get some

173

breakfast into her but she's clamping her gums around the spoon each time I shovel the porridge in. She moves her mouth around and then pushes most of it back out with her tongue.

'Come on, Mother,' I say and wipe her face with the cloth. She hits out at me, knocks my glasses skew-whiff. For a moment the world is a combination of fuzziness and sharp clarity. She's flapping her arms about. I lean away from her, pull my specs off and press on the side of my nose where the bridge had dug in. I put the cloth and the porridge on the floor and try to catch hold of her. 'Stop it.' I stand up. 'Stop it.' The rage feels like a hot fire inside me. I can't stop shouting. 'Stop it, stop it, stop it, stop it.'

I walk away and don't look back. Sitting on the stairs I rock, my arms crossed tight across my waist, head on my knees. The dry sobs fill my throat. I think I'm going to choke. Or scream.

Where did you go, Rose?

1974

We buried Nanna next to Grandad. I liked the idea that they were together, but couldn't help thinking how different it was from Rose's funeral. There were only us, her family, a few of our neighbours and three of Nanna's friends from the Barrowclough estate.

Nanna had planned her own funeral with the minister. It was a short service with no hymns but the chapel organ was played quietly in the background all the time, even as he spoke. Somehow that was soothing and he said some lovely things about her and then read a psalm that he said was one of her favourites:

'"And I shall dwell in the house of the Lord for many long days".'

When his words and hushed music drifted away on the echo of the old building, the numbness that had been in me for the last week cracked open and I wept in great noisy bursts. I couldn't stop.

Clutching on to Sam I sank onto the pew.

'Take a deep breath, love,' he murmured, holding me to him and wiping my face with his dry handkerchief. But the wailing waves of noise kept coming out of me, hurt my chest, my throat – my mouth – stretched wide open. I cried for Nanna, for Rose, for me.

I felt a cool hand take hold of mine. Mum. When we'd filed into the chapel, she'd placed herself at the end of the pew. Last in, first out, I remembered thinking, in bitterness. It was as though she couldn't wait for it all to be over so she could escape. But she'd made her way past my father to get to me, to comfort me. And looking towards her in that moment I saw the wretchedness in her eyes, the trembling lips. The shock of that sudden insight into my mother halted my sobs.

'It will be all right, Irene.'

I barely heard the words. 'I'll miss her,' I mumbled.

'We all will.' Then the mask of indifference returned and she took her hand away. 'But we must go on. Life doesn't stop for the rest of us.' She stood, pulled on her black cotton gloves and adjusted her hat. 'Come on.'

Sam helped me to my feet. When I glanced around, everyone's gaze was fixed on Nanna's coffin. They all looked uncomfortable.

'I've made a right show of myself,' I muttered to Sam.

'Rubbish,' he said, giving me a squeeze and looking at Dad who nodded at me and mouthed the words.

'All right?'

'Yes.'

Mum had left the pew. We followed. The long spray of white carnations and ferns on top of Nanna's coffin wobbled as the bearers shuffled up the narrow aisle.

I was glad to get out of the chapel; away from the smell of old wood and musty carpet, away from the strong spicy tang of the lilies that someone had placed near the altar. Out into the day where the breeze was bending the leaf-laden branches of the trees and the sky was a veil of pale clouds.

No one spoke. The gravel crunched under our feet. At the far end of the small graveyard, a man was cutting the hedge that surrounded the chapel. The steady clip-clip of the shears carried towards us and

I imagined I could smell the cut wood and leaves. A couple, standing by a headstone as we passed, flicked a look at us. The woman was crying, her face flushed. The man lifted a hand. I heard Sam make a low sound of greeting.

And then we were standing by the hole in the ground.

I let the minister's words, the intakes of breath and low sobs from those around me, float over my head; afraid, if I heard them, the helpless wailing would take over again.

There were no arrangements for refreshments afterwards; Mother had said she didn't want any of the neighbours or Nanna's friends back at the house. To be honest I wasn't sorry; there was something I needed to do.

I searched Nanna's room from top to bottom. But I didn't find anything.

Chapter Fifty-Five

2002: Today: 12.15 p.m.

I don't know how long I would have stayed sitting at the top of the stairs if the courier hadn't knocked. A large box. Mum's incontinence pads and knickers from the social services. I don't look at him and I don't care what he thinks; he's seen me before like this. Loads of times.

I drop the carton on the floor in the hall and listen at the bottom of the stairs. No sound.

1974

'How do you fancy a few weeks away from here?'

'A few weeks? I know you said you've saved up for a holiday, but a few weeks?'

Sam nuzzled my neck. 'Hmm? Get away from around here for a while?'

We were walking along the path at the side of the river. For once it wasn't raining but the trail was muddy and we splashed through puddles in our wellies. The weather had, over the last two weeks, reverted to the cloudy coolness we had in the North and I was wearing jeans and my chunky white sweater. I had my hands tucked inside the sleeves and Sam was holding me close to him.

'Sam?'

'Ah...' He turned on that sheepish grin of his that I knew so well.

'What's the catch?'

We stopped, stepping off the path to let a family with a wailing toddler pass. The mother, a fraught look on her face, nodded her thanks; the father, ignored us.

'Ignorant beggar,' Sam murmured in my ear, but I could tell he was smiling and his voice held a hint of enthusiasm when we set off walking again. 'No catch. Well not really...' He grabbed my hand. 'Not a lot – but you'll like it,' he said in a high-pitched voice, mimicking Paul Daniels, the magician.

I laughed. 'Come on. Spill.'

'Mate of mine in the business has been offered this job in Wales. A big house that needs completely doing up and it's too much for him on his own. The family are going away for about a month or so. Apparently, they have a place in France. Anyway there's couple of dogs and some cats they need looking after according to Brian, my mate, and he's taking his wife. So, I wondered if you fancy coming along?'

'What's she like?' I immediately thought of the girls I knew in school; apart from Carol and Patricia I hadn't had much luck with friends.

'His wife? Pauline?' Sam looked puzzled, then his face cleared and I could tell he knew what was worrying me. 'She's okay. You'll like her, I think.'

'Sure?'

'Yeah. What do you say?' He gently pulled on my arm and we stopped. The river was high on the banking and moving swiftly. I presumed it was because of all the rain we'd had. The water was different shades of darkness, reflecting the overcast sky and I shivered, despite my thick sweater.

Sam must have noticed because he immediately said, 'And I bet it's warmer in Wales.'

I wasn't sure I believed him.

'It'll be a few weeks away from your mum.'

I thought about that. To be honest we were getting on a bit better, the few times we were home at the same time. If ever she was a bit stroppy, I remembered the moment she'd held my hand at Nanna's funeral and I tried not to snap back at her.

'Things aren't that bad at the moment,' I said at last. 'But let me think about it, huh?' I should really have got some sort of a job to pay for my keep but, strangely, it wasn't something my mother had mentioned. Very out of character. Perhaps it was because I was doing all the cleaning and the meals for when she came home after work, I thought. Still, if I wasn't at home, it was one less to feed or use the electricity.

And I hadn't heard anything from the college to let me know if I would be allowed back on my course. I was sick to death of running to the letterbox every time I heard the postman.

'Okay, then.'

He laughed, picked me up and spun me around. 'It'll be great. Just you and me together, on our own.'

I knew he was thinking of those few times we'd achieved that. But I couldn't resist laughing and adding. 'On our own ... in Wales ... with another couple ... and some dogs and cats.'

Chapter Fifty-Six

2002: Today: 12.45 p.m.

I dozed off. The thumping wakes me. It sounds as if she's stamping her feet on the floor. I listen, rubbing my eyes. She is; she's stamping her feet. I grit my teeth.

1974

The letter from the college arrived the day we left. Professor Milton was true to her word and had submitted my lesson plans and a letter of recommendation. I was surprised to see that, according to the letter, Maureen Wintor had also added her support. I'd be back in college by the end of September and, while we were away, I'd decided I would write to Carol and Patricia, who were already renting somewhere, to see if there was a room for me.

Mum seemed pleased; at least she gave one of her rare pleased sniffs. Though I wasn't sure if it was because she'd get the house back to herself, or just because it was what I wanted.

I rested my hand on the old stone pillar at the end of the wide driveway. Well, it would have been wide if the rhododendron bushes hadn't overgrown and tumbled over the walls at either side. The garden had the same unkempt look.

'Looks as if it's been empty for years,' Pauline said. 'Brian didn't tell me what a state it was in. We might be taking on more than we bargained for, Irene.' Her smile was wry.

We'd travelled down in separate vans, me and Sam in his, them in Brian's; there was so much stuff to carry. So, except for a quick loo break and a sandwich just past Chester, we hadn't had much time to get to know one another, Pauline and me. But I silently agreed with her, and wondered what we'd let ourselves in for.

'Inside might be better.'

'Let's hope so.' She nudged me. 'Brian's caught me out before with his mad schemes.'

Mad schemes? That didn't bode well. 'Good money though, Sam says?'

'Oh, yeah, should be worth coming all this way. And I love animals, so it'll be fun,' she said, looking over her shoulder at her husband who was unloading the van. 'And, if I'm here, it'll stop Brian drinking all the profits away at some local pub.'

We stared up at the house. The red brick was covered in ivy, some of it even curled around the tops of large bay windows downstairs. A flat porch roof with a fancy stone trim at the front was held up by columns. The door, set back in the porch, had long rectangular panes of coloured glass. The curtains on all five upstairs windows were drawn. There were two smaller windows standing out from the roof, which sported chimneystacks at either end with at least four chimney pots. In the guttering I could see grass.

'Come on, girls, give us a hand.' Brian passed us carrying a stepladder and tins of paint. 'Grab the paste buckets and wallpaper, eh?' He grinned. 'It's not as bad as it looks if you go round the back of the house. That's where the hens are kept.'

'What?' Pauline spun round to look at him. 'You didn't say anything about hens,' she said, her tone indignant. 'You said dogs – and cats.' Fists on her hips she looked at me. 'Did Sam say anything about hens?'

'No.' I almost laughed. I would have if I hadn't seen how upset she was. When we'd arrived at their house that morning she was dressed as if she was going on a fashion parade: multi-coloured maxi dress, pink wedge-heeled shoes and a large pink hat. 'Perhaps it won't be that bad. You have brought other clothes, haven't you?' I looked at the large suitcase pushed alongside the decorating table and tins of paint in Brian's pale blue Morris Minor van.

'Well, yes.' She followed my gaze. 'But nothing that I can see myself cleaning a hen place out in.' She looked towards the house and then down at herself. 'Perhaps I should have put jeans on.'

'Don't worry,' I said, 'I've brought wellies and a couple of pairs of Sam's old overalls – just in case we were asked to help with something other than looking after the dogs.' I could hear deep barks coming from the inside of the house. Both men had disappeared. 'Sounds as though the boys have met the dogs.'

Pauline heaved at her suitcase and put it on the path. 'They sound big.'

'Sure it'll be fine...' I'd barely finished speaking when three black and white Newfoundland dogs came lumbering down the drive, chased by Sam. Pauline shrieked and turned. She'd almost climbed into Brian's van when the first one reached her and leapt, pinning her to the door and frantically wagging and licking her face.

'Get it off me, it's bloody heavy.'

Sam threaded his fingers through the wide collar around the Newfoundland's neck. 'He's quite friendly,' he puffed, dragging the dog away, 'he only wants to play.'

'Well, not like that.' Pauline produced a hanky from up her sleeve and wiped her hands and face. She tilted her head and surveyed the dog, smiling. 'He is gorgeous though.'

I noticed one of the other dogs was cocking its leg against her suitcase. Raising my eyebrows I looked at Sam and indicated with my head. He made a grab at the dog, letting go of the first one which promptly chased the third Newfoundland down the lane.

'It'll come back,' Sam said, a hopeful look on his face.

'There's something else.' Brian plodded towards us grinning. 'There are two tiny pigs in a pen at the far end of the back garden.'

'Pigs? Pigs! You knew!' Pauline screeched, pointing her finger at him. 'You bloody knew.'

We stared at each other. Pauline was outraged. Brian arranged a mock apologetic expression. I watched the mirth grow on Sam's face and felt mine responding. I couldn't help it – I dissolved into laughter.

It was obvious Pauline was struggling to stay serious but before long we were all doubled up.

'You swine,' she said to Brian, when we calmed down a little.

That set us off again.

'Come on, Pauline,' I said, laughing and linking arms with her. 'Let's go and see what we've landed ourselves in.'

Chapter Fifty-Seven

2002: Today: 12.45 p.m.

I am so tired. I sit on the chair in Mum's room, telling myself I'm keeping her company while hoping that *Loose Women*, with all their chatter, will entertain Mum for a few blessed minutes. I watch them myself, envying the way the presenters are so at ease, with their nice hair and clothes.

But Mum keeps banging on the arm of her chair and staring at me. I know she doesn't want me to sleep.

I must do, though, because in my dream I see Rose waving to me from a window. She's back.

1974

'They said they're ripping out the kitchen and bathroom so we don't have to touch those,' Brian said, as we wandered through the house. It was cold and felt a bit creepy; all the furniture downstairs was covered up with white sheets. There were spare ones folded on the floor, presumably to protect the carpets when the decorating started but now occupied by cats, three tabbies and two black, who raised their heads to watch us for a second or two. The three downstairs rooms were square with high ceilings, ornate picture rails and large old-fashioned sash windows. The décor was so dated: flock wallpaper and dark brown paintwork.

Upstairs we identified which two of the five bedrooms we would sleep in. I chose one which looked out over miles of countryside:

through the window I could see misshapen fields of different shades of green bordered by wandering stone walls, clusters of houses, lines of trees on the horizon, black against the sky.

'Isn't it gorgeous?' I leaned back against Sam, my head tucked under his chin, loving the feel of the muscles under the skin of the arms that held me. 'I'm going to love being here.' I shifted so I could look up at him. 'We'll manage to get out for walks together sometimes, d'you think?'

'Don't see why not.' He kissed the corner of my mouth, his hand over my breast. 'Hmm?' He shuffled us towards the double bed.

'We can't,' I whispered. 'Not now.' I could hear Pauline opening drawers and wardrobe doors; getting organised. 'That's what I should be doing – unpacking.'

'Huh. Boring.' Sam drawled the word out.

Brian appeared at the doorway, dragging Pauline by the hand. 'Come on you two. Sam, bring your notebook, we'll make a list of what wants doing and where we're going to start.'

Nice chap though he was, Brian seemed to me to be someone who liked to delegate. He proved me right when we went downstairs. But Pauline was more than a match for him

'This flock wallpaper's going to be a bugger to get off.' Brian made a wry face, looking around the large dining room 'Sorry girls, you're going to have to help.'

'We'll give you the mornings.' Pauline winked at me. 'We'll swop you jobs. We'll scrape this stuff off...' she picked at an edge of the red and silver paper that covered the walls of the large dining room, before ripping off a strip of it with a flourish. 'And you clean out those pigs – oh and the hens,' she added as her husband opened his mouth to protest. 'Otherwise, you're on your own. Eh, Irene?'

I shrugged and peeked over at Sam to see his reaction; I'd have been quite happy to help but I did admire Pauline's tactics.

Sam raised one eyebrow and grinned at me but said nothing.

We all waited for Brian's answer. 'Okay.' He gave in, evidently used to his wife's bargaining. 'It's a deal.'

We hadn't minded being given the task of feeding the hens but the first time we found out what the pigs were supposed to eat we drew the line at that.

'What do you mean we're supposed to make them special meals?' Pauline said. We stared down at the two piglets.

I thought they were rather cute.

The owners had left lists of what to feed the animals on: all ordinary dog, cat and hen food as far as I could tell. The pigs were a different matter.

'Curry!' Quiche?' Pauline ran her finger down the page. 'I'm not cooking for two pigs.' She looked at me, raised an eyebrow. 'Not the four-legged kind anyway.'

We went to the nearest supermarket and bought the curry and quiche out of the money the owners had left in an envelope "for contingencies."

Once it was agreed what our daily tasks would be, that was the routine we followed over the weeks. Sometimes, studying my sore hands and broken nails, I questioned if Pauline and me had landed ourselves with the rough end of the deal. But the men were grateful and, bit by bit, each of the rooms was transformed.

Except for the weekends, when Sam and me went out walking, the afternoons belonged to Pauline and me and the dogs. After we'd fed the cats and done our stint at the wallpaper scraping, we explored the countryside with the dogs firmly on leads.

We'd go down the lane, over a stile and across the fields. The dogs were well trained but we kept them on leads until we passed the fields where the sheep were. Rose used to call them 'Baas'. Dad sometimes took us on the bus to one of the villages on the edge of the moors for a walk and a bite to eat in one of the cafés there. My sister was entranced by the sheep and always wanted to hug them. I'd often had to chase after her when she saw them in the distance.

The sheep in Wales looked a lot cleaner than the ones back home.

Once Pauline and me had crossed over the small stone humped-backed bridge that forded a fast-flowing stream, we headed towards the hills where we let the dogs run around as we trudged up the hill to the top. The scenery was glorious – so impressive. Even on the days when it rained it didn't matter. But on fine days, when the breeze was sharp enough to whip our hair around and sting our cheeks, it was wonderful.

Those weeks were some of the best times Sam and me had.

I was sorry to leave Stoneswood House, but I was also excited; I was going back to college to complete my course in a week's time. Sam had made contact with a firm that needed painters and decorators for a huge council estate that was being built on the outskirts of Manchester. We were going to live together at last.

Chapter Fifty-Eight

2002: Today: 1.00 p.m.

I wake with a start to a noise rising above the rapid rush of blood pulsing in my chest. I'm slumped on the chair and I know Mum's probably staring at me, so I keep my eyes closed and listen. At first I think it's someone outside, even somebody at the door but then I realise it's her. She's singing again. Bloody singing. I mean, actually singing two bloody words. It's mumbled but I can make it out. *'Little children...'* Over and over, like a stuck record player. I can't stand it anymore. I'm stiff but I launch myself from that chair and go downstairs. Billy J. bloody Kramer has a lot to answer for.

1974

I had a dream about Rose the first night home. She was in the lounge of Stoneswood House, sitting on the maroon moquette settee surrounded by the five cats, stroking each with her small chubby hands.

The sun poured in through the wide bay window, contrasting the brightness of the white ribbons and the dense black of her hair, tied into two thin plaits. She picked up the cat that had become her favourite, a large sleek ginger one with a long fluffy tail.

Holding it in her arms she twirled round and round, singing one of her strange little tunes to soft music playing somewhere in the background. I recognised the instrument as a clarinet, which was the cat in 'Peter and the Wolf'. It was a record that Nanna had bought Rose and, strangely, became her favourite, even though I'd thought it scary. There was an expression of complete concentration on her face, a small smile, slightly crooked because of that little lift in her top lip. Beautiful. The cat didn't fight to escape as I expected it would but gazed up at her with its unusually round yellow eyes.

There were other children there, children who were actually in her class at the primary school. To them, Rose was no different, and in this dream each one took a cat and copied her, doing exactly as she did.

Chapter Fifty-Nine

2002: Today: 1.35 p.m.

I wake up with my head in a pool of spilt tea on the kitchen table. How I got to the kitchen, I don't remember. I rub my hair dry with a towel.

My mobile rings. I can't find it. I'm running around like a headless chicken, swiping my hands along the worktops, opening cupboard doors, the fridge. Listening to the persistent ring tune. Running into the living room I throw cushions off the settee and feel down the back of the armchairs. Hopeless. I stand looking around. Feel the vibration of the phone in my dressing gown pocket. It stops.

1974

It was strange being back in college in September. Because I had missed the whole of the summer term before I went home to look after Nanna, I needed to start again. I didn't mind, even though I knew no one in my year, and I soaked up everything: the lectures, the group meetings with Maureen Wintor who was still one of my tutors and the political discussions in the students' union, though I wasn't ever quite sure which party I particularly followed.

I did miss Carol and Patricia though, who were now into their second year and shared a place with their boyfriends so, one way or another, we didn't manage to get together much.

The other thing that hadn't worked out was finding somewhere for Sam and me to live; the flats we liked we couldn't afford, and the ones we could afford were either too far away from the college, or were in an area that Sam felt wasn't safe for me to be in alone when he was working long days.

So, for the time being we lived in a rented tiny bedsit, part of a converted shop. We saw little of one another during the week so flat hunting was often relegated to the weekends when Sam wasn't on the building site, or I wasn't preparing for my teaching practice.

My placement was in a larger junior school in a part of Manchester I'd never been in before. My time there would last for six weeks so I was quite daunted, especially as the children were older. I had no experience of nine to eleven-year-olds. When I was planning the lessons, it often occurred to me how much I'd enjoyed being with the younger children; how much they were like Rose in lots of way with their willingness to try anything.

That first Monday morning after half-term I faced twenty-five kids in serried rows; an atmosphere of suspicion emanated from the lot of them.

'Good morning child— er – all, my name is Miss Bradshaw. I hope you are looking forward to our time together.' I doubted it, looking at them. 'I won't be able to remember all your names at once but, as I read out the register, I'll try.' I fixed my widest smile and cast my glance around to cover all of them.

Silence.

'Right.' I moved to sit behind my desk, immediately feeling more comfortable there, and I opened the registration file. The answers to the names were given in varying tones; guttural from some of the boys, who actually looked older than eleven, to bright responses from the girls, who had obviously decided to "be on my side", going by the smiles and small waves they aimed in my direction.

I opened what should have been the lesson plans; I'd thought to start with maths, then concentrate on reading or writing practice with projects in the afternoons. Casting a glance over them, I changed my mind.

'I want to talk about what we'll be doing during the time I'm with you this term. The two lessons of the morning will be spent on arithmetic, spelling and composition writing.' I saw the rolled eyes, heard the low groans of a few of the boys and laughed. 'Yes, I know. But knowing your tables, being able to add and subtract and all that goes with maths will be something you all need to know before going into your next school. And correct spelling, reading and writing, being able to express yourself, will be essential to the rest of your lives.

So, class, that's what our mornings will look like.' I heard the low grumbles, chose to ignore them, focussing instead on the encouraging nods from most of the girls. 'However...' I looked around to make I could see all eyes were on me. '... However, our afternoons will be your choice. I'll list the choices on the blackboard later so you can discuss them in playtime after your dinners.' That stopped the grumbles; I saw the boys glance at one another, some laughed. One punched the arm at his classmate next to him. I held up my hand. 'Your choice, my rules. Starting tomorrow. As for who will go first, the boys or girls...' I took a five pence piece from my purse. 'I'll toss this and one of you will call. Show of hands who wishes to call.' Hands were raised amid cries of 'Me, Miss', some waving energetically. 'You, please.' I pointed to a boy in the middle row. 'What's your name?'

'Roger, Miss.'

'Okay, Roger. Are you ready? He nodded. I tossed the coin in the air, caught it and placed it on the back of my hand, covering it with my other palm.

'Heads,' he said.

I lifted my hand. 'Heads it is. The boys will have the first turn. You will need to appoint someone to speak for you but the activity has to be an agreement with the majority of you and it has to be different each time.' I smiled before saying, 'And it can't always be football.' This brought cheers from the girls and mock groaning and slapping of foreheads from the boys.

I looked through the window. The October sun was weak but there was no breeze, quite warm enough for them to go out with their coats and hats on. And, from the look of them, what this lot needed was fresh air. 'But for today we're going to go out to walk along the lane that runs by the school and find some of the leaves that are coming off...'

Only a few stifled groans, no eye rolling, I noticed with satisfaction.

'Those who don't want to do this may go carefully...' I paused, '... carefully alongside the little stream, to look for interesting small stones. Then when we return at breaktime, I'll tell you what we're going to do.'

An hour later, during the first break, after listing the activities from them to choose from on the blackboard, I was tearing newspapers into strips for the papier mâché and mixing the flour and water in a large bowl to make the glue.

By the time the bell went for start of class again, the glue was ready. I added a sprinkling of salt to stop it going mouldy and I handed one of the girls the wooden spoon.

'Mandy, is it?' She nodded, her eyes fixed on the liquid. 'If you

189

would keep stirring for me please?' I smiled at her when she almost snatched the spoon from me and stirred vigorously. 'We're going to make a collage of nature,' I announced, giving out the ten brushes I'd found in the class storeroom and the strips of paper to the rest of the pupils. Indicating the squares of cardboard on my desk and the egg boxes and toilet roll tubes I'd been collecting for week, I said, 'Watch what I do first.' Pulling apart an egg box and arranging a few of the oak, sycamore and small green privet leaves in front of me, I spread the glue on the strips of paper. 'Choose one of these,' I waved my hand over the eggs boxes and rolls, 'To make the shape you want, sort out the leaves and stones you need. And make sure you all have your aprons on before you start building your picture.'

It was a messy but very successful morning. By dinnertime we'd covered everything, including fingers, with the glued paper and flowers and leaves. They enjoyed it, even the boys from what I could make out. Though I did see them sneaking peeks at the list on the board, heard their furtive hurried whispers.

So that afternoon set the pattern for the rest of the term. I had included various craft and nature projects alongside team games, sports: football, netball, rounders. As I expected, we began with a game of football. The girls joined in with enthusiasm knowing, I suspect, that the boys had to go along with their choice the following day.

I was glad that I'd gone with my instinct. The idea that they had some control over a part of their day in school worked both for them and for me. I felt that by respecting their wishes they responded in the mornings by working at what the Head called "real learning".

I soon learned who struggled with arithmetic and who didn't. At first I wrote sums on the board which would start off easy and get harder. But I also had boxes of graded sums which I had written out by hand for the pupils who struggled. I was careful not to draw attention to them. There was one boy, Bernard, I was particularly worried about, so used the cards more and more.

'Take your time, everyone. It's not a race.' I placed a card in front of Bernard. He looked at it and then at me and smiled.

'Thanks, Miss.'

I smiled back at him and raised my voice. 'Anyone who has any trouble with any of the sums, please do not hesitate to ask.' That day the only child who didn't raise their hand was Bernard. Afterwards, while marking during the lunchtime, I left his card until the last. He'd got every sum right and, at the end he'd written, "easy-peasy". I laughed and suddenly an old familiar sensation of happiness mixed with relief made my skin tingle. It was the same emotion that I'd felt when Rose clapped after she'd succeeded at something. I wrapped my arms around myself and squeezed my eyes tight.

Working with that one child convinced me that the decision I'd made, to work with children who were labelled as "special", was the right one for me. As soon as I was qualified, I would find the school where I felt I was most needed.

Chapter Sixty

2002: Today: 1.36 p.m.

I'm holding my arm out full-length to see who called. These days I need reading glasses as well as my 'seeing' glasses to read anything. I've often joked that my arms just aren't long enough, that's all. It's a joke that went stale months ago but I keep saying it. And Sam still laughs.

1974

Sam had a letter from his dad asking him to go home for a couple of days. It didn't sound urgent but with his contract finished on the first phase of the building site and the new one not due to begin until after Christmas, he went back to Denholme.

We'd agreed that once my teaching practice was completed, I'd follow him. I knew Mum would be away; I'd had a rare note from her to tell me she was going to stay with a friend. I tried not to think too much about that.

Sam met me at the station but, despite his smile, I knew something was wrong: he held me too tightly and too long when I first stepped off the train.

'Let's go to the Anchor,' he said right away, taking my duffle bag from me and slinging it over his shoulder. 'We need to talk.'

He was quiet all the way to the pub. He held my hand close to him as we walked along the orange-lit streets in the drizzle. I knew him well enough to leave him alone until he was ready to speak but the worry built up with every footstep.

'I'll get some drinks,' Sam said. I watched him battle through the crowds around the bar of the Dropped Anchor, still unsure what was happening.

The pub had only just reopened and was now themed. Bits of boats and nets hung everywhere, even from the oak beams, and a brass bell hanging from one of them just missed Sam's head. Every wall was covered in pictures of ships and, for some reason the staff wore sailor hats. All a bit odd for a northern town on the outskirts of Manchester; I registered the thought even while I was anxiously waiting to see what was wrong with Sam.

Carrying his pint and my Babycham back to the table, he sat down on the bench next to me and picked up my hand. He wore his hair long and I couldn't see his face from the side so I reached over and tucked it behind his ear.

'What is it, love? What's wrong?'

'Dad's dying. He's got prostate cancer.' The word were abrupt, stark. He took off his leather jacket and dropped it onto the seat next to me. I couldn't take in what he'd said. I stared at him, not knowing what to say.

It was Saturday night and it seemed everybody we knew had swarmed to the Dropped Anchor to check it out. A few were looking over to where we were sitting. I saw a couple of Sam's mates start towards us. I moved my head – warned them off.

I gripped his fingers. 'When did you find out?' It was months since I'd seen Albert but I'd always liked him; I had never forgotten his kindness to me, Rose and Nanna.

'Last night. He said he's known there was something wrong for weeks. He's been having all sorts of tests, apparently, and the doc told him. That's why he wrote. He said he didn't want to tell me before, the daft old sod.'

First Rose, then Nanna, and now Sam's dad. I looked out of the window, trying to think what to say that wouldn't sound banal. The day's rain had knocked most of the remaining leaves off the trees. While I watched red, white and blue lights flickered on, lighting up the bare branches. In the end I decided there was nothing I could say other than, 'I'm sorry Sam.' When I kissed him his beard was soft against my lips.

'There's nothing they can do,' he said at last. 'It's gone into his bones.' I knew what he was going to say even before he spoke. 'I can't leave him, Irene.'

'Of course you can't.' Sam and his father had always been so close; Sam needed to stay in Denholme for however long he was needed. I hesitated before I next spoke but it had to be said; he couldn't live on fresh air. 'What will you do about your work in Manchester, Sam?'

He shrugged, his fingers tightened on mine. 'I'll have to pack it in. They'll understand.' His eyes were bleak when he looked at me. 'I could pick up jobs when and where. See how it goes, eh?'

'Yes, love. We'll see how it goes.'

Chapter Sixty-One

2002: Today: 1.40 p.m.

It was Sam. I phone him back. My hands are shaking. With the cold? Or tiredness? I can't think straight.

He says he's on a job way over the other side of Manchester and he'll be really late home; can I manage without heating until then?

I tell him yes, don't worry about it; I've plugged in the little blow-heater in Mum's room and she's got thick gloves and socks on. I've yanked the duvet off her bed and wrapped her hands and feet under it. He asks what about you? I'm fine, I say, looking around at all the mess: the pots, the bedding, the overflowing rubbish bin by the sink.

1975

'And you're sure there is no other way?' Professor Milton sat back in her chair, hands folded in her lap.

'I've thought about it, Professor, there isn't.'

Of course there was; I knew Sam wouldn't want me to finish college yet again. And I realised I had to do it before I told him; he would try to persuade me to stay in Manchester. But I'd made up my mind. After all the support Sam had given me in the past – with Rose – the difficult times with Mother, when Dad left, and when Nanna was ill, this was something I could do for him. He loved his father and he'd told me that the doctor had said he had to be prepared for Albert's illness to get a lot worse before the end. I didn't want Sam to face that on his own.

The professor's words interrupted my thoughts.

'I believe you wished to train eventually as a special educational needs teacher. With qualified teacher status and a programme of initial specialist teacher training that would enable you to do that.'

I knew that, of course I did, but that would take time: too much time. It was now that I was needed, as far as I was concerned.

So even seeing the disappointment and disapproval that was etched over Professor Milton's face didn't sway me from what I'd decided. Still, I felt obliged to say, 'I am sorry. I know that I was only accepted back here because of you—'

'And Miss Wintor, don't forget. I presume you're going to tell her?' I had the feeling that, in the past, the professor had allowed nothing and no one to get in her way of her career. Well, that was not what I wanted to be like. There would come a time when I would be able to work with children like Rose, but it could wait.

'Of course. I'm grateful to both of you—'

'But you won't change your mind?'

'No...'

'Well, it's a shame.' She leaned forward and put both palms on top of her desk and stood. 'You would have made an excellent teacher.'

I was being dismissed.

'I'm sorry.'

That slight lift of her shoulders could have been a shrug. She didn't understand and there was no point in saying anything else.

Making my way along the corridors, weaving unobserved through the lines of earnest-faced students clutching files and books, it struck me that this was a world I would probably never be part of again. And I was all right with that; I knew what I wanted to do.

Even so, by the time I stood in front of Maureen Wintor's office, my face felt hot with the effort of holding back the tears.

'I already know,' she said, when she opened her door and drew me in. She enfolded me in her arms and patted my back. 'The professor has told me everything and I am so sorry, Irene. But I do understand, which, I gather, is not her point of view. Here,' she led me to the chair in front of her desk, 'Sit here and I'll make us a cup of something... Smoke?' I shook my head. 'Mind if I do?' She lit her cigarette without waiting for me to respond, drifting in her inimitable way, across the office, towards the kettle. 'I have an idea I want to put to you.'

A vague sense of excitement was making my skin tingle, when I left an hour later. Maureen had made a suggestion that I volunteer to work in a special school, called Clough Fields, which was in the grounds of a mental hospital in Neygrove. Her cousin was a teacher there. It was something I could do, even if I got some sort of job to pay mother for my keep at the same time.

'For you, Rose,' I murmured, walking away from the college with my head held high. 'For you.'

Chapter Sixty-Two

2002: Today: 1.50 p.m.

Rain clatters on the window. A door bangs. A dog barks. I hear people running, the swish of the wheels of the bus as it pulls up at the stop. Without going into the front room I can't see what's happening but I can imagine them all pushing and shoving to get on and out of the rain. I wish I was going somewhere too.

Can't hear any noise from upstairs. If she's asleep, I'll have a lie down.

1975

'I don't want you leaving college because of me.' Sam paced up and down in front of me. I was glad Mum was out; she'd have loved seeing us arguing, I'm sure. She hadn't received the news well either but for a totally different reason; she didn't want me under her feet, spoiling her so-called love life, I imagined.

'It's not because of you,' I said for the umpteenth time. 'It's up to me what I do, Sam, and up to you to accept it. You won't change my mind and, anyway, it's too late, I've done it.' We'd been going round and round in circles for the past hour. 'I love you. I want to be here, where you are—'

196

'See! It is because of me.'

The long breath I took in gave me the chance to think. Whatever I said next needed to end this quarrel.

'Look, Sam, when Nanna was ill I came home to look after her. It was the right thing for me to do – for me. You've made the same decision for your dad and it's the right one. I respect that. Now you just have to accept my decision about this. And that's an end to it.' I held out my hand. 'Come and sit down, love. This is the last thing we should be falling out about. We should be working out how we're going to manage with your dad to make things as easy as possible for him.'

'You're right. I'm sorry.' He clasped my fingers, sat on the settee next to me. I leaned on him. 'I just worry that I'm spoiling—'

'Nothing. You're spoiling nothing. Plans are on hold, that's all. I've got a job lined up in the newsagents at the other end of your street...'

He looked at me in surprise. I nodded.

'It's only four days a week, Thursday to Sunday, so it doesn't bring in much but it'll more than pay for my keep, which will keep Mum off my back. And I have an interview to be a volunteer at this special school in Neygrove. So I could be there the first three days of the week. Or perhaps not that much – I could help you with your dad sometimes?'

'We'll see.' Sam took me in his arms. 'I want to spend as much time as I can with Dad...' I heard the catch in his voice, felt him swallow. 'It'll be good having you here, Irene, but I know this volunteering is something near to what you've wanted to do...'

'For Rose,' I murmured.

'Yes, love. For Rose. So...' He sat back, held me at arm's length and smiled. 'So – one way or another we'll manage.'

'I love you.'

'And I, Irene Bradshaw, love you. And always will.'

Chapter Sixty-Three

2002: Today: 2.00 p.m.

Her chin is resting on her chest. Her head moves with each breath; bobs up and down, up and down. It's quite relaxing watching. I close my eyes. Breathe. Breathe.

I stumble sideways, trip over my dressing gown belt. I'm still in my dressing gown. I hadn't noticed.

Has she eaten today? I can't remember. I'll sort out some food for her, so I'll be ready for when she wakes up.

Then I'll have a lie down.

1975

I knew as soon as I walked up to the gates of the hospital school it was where I wanted to be. It was a three-storey red- brick building with large windows, every one of them plastered with colourful drawings of houses with stick people standing in front of them and pictures of large balloons with words such as "Waving", Hello", "Hi", inserted in them. I could hear laughter, children' voices. Despite the chill in the air the large blue doors were wide open, a mat with the word, "Welcome." written on it.

'Hi.' The woman who came towards me was tiny with long white hair that spread out over her shoulders, and wore a pink twinset and A-line black skirt. Her grasp was firm, warm, as we shook hands.

'I'm Christine Widdecombe, Head Teacher. You must be Irene...?'

'Irene Bradshaw, Mrs – er – Miss...Widdecombe.' I couldn't see her left hand; couldn't tell if she was married or not.

She laughed. 'Christine please, we don't stand on ceremony here. And it's Mrs Widdecombe, just in case you ever need to know.' She ushered me along the corridor. 'Come into my office and we'll have a chat.'

'Do sit down. Tea?' She closed the door.

'Please.' I sat in a large black squashy armchair while she switched on the kettle and arranged cups and saucers on a tray. There was a quietness about her movements; she was comfortable to be with.

'Tell me a little about yourself,' she said, glancing over her shoulder.

I gave her a quick resumé of my qualifications from school, about the teaching practices I'd done. I said nothing about what had happened at home other than to say I hadn't completed the teaching course at the college for personal reasons and that Maureen Wintor had suggested I try for a place at Clough Fields. By the time I'd finished there was a cup of tea and a plate of biscuits in front of me and Christine Widdecombe was settling in the armchair at the other side of the small coffee table.

'Maureen Wintor is a relative of one of my teachers. Margaret Jones.' Christine smiled and, resting her elbows on the arms of the chair, threaded her fingers together to hold them under her chin, her head to one side as if studying me.

'Yes, she was one of my tutors at the college.'

'She recommended you highly.'

'I'm very grateful to her. This – or something like this is what I wanted to do ...' I wondered how much Maureen had already passed on. I picked up the tea, the cup rattled slightly in the saucer. I balanced it on my lap to stop the noise. Outside the door there were sounds of footsteps, chatter.

'Classes changing over.' She glanced at the clock. 'We have a drama teacher coming in now. The children love it.' The wrinkles at the corners of her eyes deepened when she smiled again. 'You say you gave up college for personal reasons? I'm sorry if I this is intrusive, but would you like to tell me something about that?'

'Mainly because of illness in my family.' Her brown eyes behind the rimless glasses showed nothing of the curiosity she might be feeling. 'It was my own decision.' Too late I realised my tone was defensive; but I needed her to know I was not someone to pity.

199

'But you wanted to teach?'

'Initially, yes. But I knew in the first year at college I wanted to be with...' I faltered, 'To help mentally handicapped children at a school like this.'

'It is a shame that you were not able to attain the qualification which would have enabled you to teach here. We have two teachers who already had Training Council Diplomas and who took a year's conversion course to be able to teach but it doesn't work the other way around, I'm afraid. Not since our special children have been part of the school system.' Her expression was sympathetic.

'I already have a job, but it's part-time; I just wanted to volunteer here. I want to support the children within the school system. To support the teacher,' I added hastily. 'I know I wouldn't be allowed to teach.' I halted for a moment. 'I had a sister. Rose. She died...' I waited for the image, the memory to go as quickly as it flashed into my mind. 'She was Down's.'

'I'm sorry for your loss.' She waited a moment before saying, 'We do have another helper here whose son, Martin, is Down's. Barbara. He's a nice lad, Martin. He's come on well.'

Martin? Barbara? 'I think I might have already met her. Martin Althorpe was one of Rose's friends at their primary school. It's a long time since I saw them– if it is them,' I added.

'Good gracious. Really?' She looked pleased. 'Tell me more about Rose, about you and Rose.'

'I was eight when she was born...' I hesitated; should I tell her about my mother's attitude to her? 'My mother found it difficult...'

'Yes, many parents do.'

'My father didn't, nor my grandmother. We looked after Rose between us. Mostly me, because at first my father was working and then wasn't well.' I wouldn't tell her he left us. 'And my mother worked and my grandmother needed me. But I didn't mind. To me Rose was special in so many ways. She was clever. As she got older she understood most of what we talked about, she laughed a lot and went to an ordinary school. Like I said, she had a lovely singing

200

voice. And she was my little friend as well as sister.' I knew I was gabbling and stopped. 'She was lovely...'

Christine Widdecombe laughed. 'I'm sure she was.' But then she said. 'But tell me how you felt. You were very young to take on that responsibility. Didn't you resent that?' She raised her eyebrows.

I knew I had to think carefully before I answered. 'I don't think so. I resented how people judged Rose – even when they didn't know her – just by how she looked...'

'That's not what I meant, Irene. I meant didn't you begrudge looking after her so much? What about your friends? What about how you felt when you were older, perhaps wanted to go out on your own, to parties or the cinema? She was how old when she died?'

'Eight. I was just seventeen. I always wanted to protect Rose, to keep her safe, happy. There was just ... something between us.'

'I see.' She paused. 'Well, I think that's all for now. I will, of course, need more references. And then, all being well you will be asked to come to another interview with myself and one or two others from our management team.' She smiled. 'I'm sure you'll appreciate we need to be extremely careful who comes into contact with our special children.'

'Of course. I understand.'

We stood at the same time and shook hands. All I could do now was wait.

Chapter Sixty-Four

2002: Today: 2.15 p.m.

I've found some cooked mince in the fridge and the mashed potato left over from yesterday. I can't be bothered to think of anything else for her and she doesn't care either, as long as she has something to eat. It's guesswork whether she'll spit it out, gobble it up or bite the spoon. I swear she smirks, whichever. I've made gravy for the meat from a tub of granules. I hadn't used them for a while; I'd made yesterday's from stock cubes and cornflour but there's no cornflour left. I checked the sell by date on the bottom of the tub – still two weeks to go, so they're okay. She likes her gravy thick.

She's shouting again.

1975

Working in the newsagents wasn't the most brain-taxing work and some of the customers drove me round the bend with their constant carping about the weather or the neighbours' behaviour but, once I got used to it, I began to enjoy chatting with whoever came into the shop.

After a few months Mr Wardle, who owned the newsagents with his wife, gave me the keys to the shop door and asked me to let myself in at five in the morning to collect the papers from the suppliers and sort them out for the paper lads.

'I'm getting too old to get up at that time,' he said, tilting his head to one side and adjusting his hearing aid that had begun to hiss and crackle. 'If we could find someone to buy the place, me and the missus could be more comfortable in our old age. 'Appen even move to Morecambe – wife always wanted to live there. So,' he said, 'early morning shift? What do you think? I'll pay double time – five 'til nine? 'Til shop opens? After that, your usual money?'

To be honest I was relieved; I was getting tired of all the complaints from the customers that they were getting the wrong papers. Besides his hearing, Mr Wardle's eyes weren't that sharp either and he'd often pack the bags with the papers all mixed up. And I rather liked the silence of the streets when I walked to work, especially when the summer months came, when it was light at that time in a morning and the only sounds were those of the sparrows waking, the far hum of the motorway and the rattle and whine of the milkman's electric float.

I had been a bit worried when Mr Wardle said he wanted to sell. I was sure that whoever bought would want to run the place for themselves and I'd probably be out of a job. But he seemed content to let things plod on. Often he'd shuffle into the shop around seven to bring me a cup of tea and check that the paper lads had collected their bags and gone on their rounds, his braces dangling, collarless shirt undone at the neck to show his scrawny throat. Satisfied, and with a wave of his hand, he'd go back up to the flat where he and Mrs Wardle lived. Sometimes I wouldn't see him all day. I liked that, I liked pretending it was my shop; I liked pretending I was in charge of Vera Morris, the woman who worked alongside me in the afternoons, even though we got on well and I wouldn't have dreamt of giving her any orders.

Chapter Sixty-Five

2002: Today: 2.30 p.m.

I can't shovel it in fast enough. She fixes her eyes on me and gets hold of my hand to guide the spoon in. Something she hasn't done for ages. Her head's bobbing about, her mouth's wide open. I swear she looks the spit of a baby bird when she does that. When it's finished she starts to shout.

'I'll make some more,' I say. She won't let go of my hand. 'Mother, if you let me go, I said I'll get some more.' I prise her fingers open as gently as I can. My head swims with tiredness.

She finishes the next lot off as well. I think, if I can fill her up, she'll sleep. Which means I can too. We both sit back for a breather. I shiver. I'll get dressed.

1975

The chat I'd had with Christine Widdecombe was a walk in the park compared with the second interview I had at Clough Fields. I was sure the warm flush that had started at the base of my throat had now turned my face scarlet. And my mouth was so dry, I wasn't certain I'd be able to speak. I made myself sit still in the hard chair opposite the long oak table, behind which three people shuffled papers and whispered to one another. It felt like it had been a long time since I'd walked into this office, one more spacious than Christine Widdecombe's, but I knew it was really only a minute or two.

And when they all looked up at me and smiled, I felt my shoulders drop from around my ears and I smiled back at them and lifted my chin.

'Good Morning, Miss Bradshaw. I'm Mr Clayton, Chairman of the Management Committee.' The man gestured to his right. 'This is Mrs Ebsworth.' Then to his left, 'And Miss Middleton. Members of the committee. You've met Mrs Widdecombe.' She smiled at me from an armchair at one end of the table, but didn't speak at all after that.

'Hello.' My voice was a squeak. I coughed.

'Please don't be nervous, we're not ogres. Mrs Widdecombe, here, has told us you wish to help in the school here as a volunteer.'

'Yes. Yes I do.'

He clasped his hands on top of the table.

'Could you tell us why, please?'

'I had a sister, she was Down's. We were very close and I looked after her a lot and I learned how to understand her needs and the way she wanted things to be done, what she wanted to do. She was very strong-willed.' I couldn't stop the smile. 'She gave me the gift of patience...' Oh hell, did that sound pretentious? 'I mean I learned how to do things with her, in her time.'

I was relieved to see them smile again, each scribbling notes on the pads in front of them.

'Obviously you understand we need to be careful who comes into contact with our special children.' This from Miss Middleton. She was staring, studying me from behind thick-framed black glasses.

'Of course.'

'We do have other volunteers. All have had to be checked.'

'Yes, I understand completely.'

She moved her head as though satisfied and I saw her make a tick in a box on a form in front of her.

'We have received two more references, Miss Bradshaw. One from...' The chairman put his glasses on and read, 'from a Mr Wardle, proprietor of the newsagents where you work. He speaks highly of you: calls you a "people person", "very reliable and kind," oh, and "good at time-keeping".' I saw the corners of his mouth twitch. 'And one from Miss Canon, the Head of the Greenworth Primary School...' He pulled his glasses down his nose and peered at me.

'I did teaching practice there.' I nodded. 'It's a lovely school.'

'What did you learn from teaching there?' The woman who'd been introduced as Mrs Ebsworth spoke for the first time; she had a lilting Welsh accent that took me right back to the time I'd been in Wales with Sam and the others.

I decided I liked her and leant forward in my chair, trying to think what to say. 'I think what I most learned, from the short time I was there and from the other school I was in, where the children were slightly older, was that all children have different needs.' I stopped, trying to work out how best to say what I meant. Mrs Ebsworth smiled and waited. It encouraged me. 'Each one needs to be allowed to trust you in their own time, in their own way. There were one or two children in those schools who had their own challenges.' Rose's face came into my mind. 'I needed to use different methods to get to know each one and it took longer with them than with the other children. I had to adapt and be flexible with the way I presented what I planned to teach. In college, we studied child development and children's thinking and the theory of education today. Actually, you know, although it was good to have that knowledge, being with the children is completely unlike any theory.' They glanced at one another. I rushed on. 'If only because, as with any of us, they are not made to always conform to theories.'

That seemed to please them. At least I thought so from the way they huddled together and nodded to one another.

'It's a shame you didn't complete the teaching course,' Mrs Ebsworth said, lifting her head to look at me. 'Perhaps one day you'll be able to go back to college?'

'Perhaps. But in the meantime I'd love to be helping here. In any capacity.' I looked down at my fingers which were knotted in my lap. 'I think it's what my sister would have liked me to do.' I'd blurted that out without even thinking.

'You do understand what would be asked of you? The essential areas? Above all else you will be caring for the children's physical needs: keeping the children safe, feeding some of them...' Miss Middleton tilted her head before adding, 'changing nappies, keeping them clean. There is really no room for sentimentality—'

'I don't think Miss Bradshaw meant it that way.' Mr Clayton looked from her to me. 'I'm sure she is not under any illusion about our special children...'

'I'm not.' I was grateful for him recognising what I'd been trying to say for the last half hour.

'Working, volunteering here, can be challenging. We try to be as flexible as possible within the remits of the Education Department but each child is, as you said and as in any school, an individual. In some cases, the main difficulty is speech as well as understanding certain situations. Those children have lower cognitive development. But we always find ways around that,' Mrs Ebsworth said, cheerfully. 'We use any means we can of communicating: play, music and movement, drawing, allowing the children to express themselves in their own way. Their trust is won by praise rather than judgement or chastisement.'

'I understand.'

There was a moment of silence. I could hear a buzz of chatter in the background.

'Anything else, ladies?' Mr Clayton glanced from one to the other. 'No? So, Miss Bradshaw, I think that's all. If you would be kind enough to step out for a little while, while we make our decision?' He reached forward and pressed a button on the phone on the desk. 'I'll ask the secretary to make you a cup of tea.'

'Of course. Thank you.' My hand was sweaty on the door handle. I was glad to sit down on one of the chairs in the corridor. I could hear children laughing. I crossed my fingers. Let this be the start. 'Please,' I whispered. Let me fulfil my promise to Rose. I'd let her down once; given this chance, I wouldn't do it again.

I couldn't drink the tea the secretary had handed to me with a smile; I was on pins.

Within minutes they called me in.

My legs were shaking when I turned back at the gates to look at Clough Fields. The drawings in the windows, the houses with the stick people standing in front of them, the pictures of the large balloons with the words in them seemed to be just for me: a welcome. I looked at the balloon that had "Waving" written in it. And I waved back.

Chapter Sixty-Six

2002: Today: 3.00 p.m.

When I go into our bedroom, there's a faint smell of Johnson's baby lotion and I take it in deeply, savour its comfort.

Hello Rose, love.

And then it's gone.

I should get dressed. I flop onto on the bed and let myself slide sideways until my head is on the pillow. Close my eyes. I feel that slowing-down sensation; that lovely giving in as all your body relaxes.

'No! No. Whoops!'

I stuff my fingers in my ears.

1976

Being at Clough Fields filled a need in me that I'd had since I lost Rose.

The lessons ran as long as the children's concentration lasted so the set timetables were flexible. One subject, though, was always popular in the class: Mrs Taylor's storytime in the afternoons. And then she would concentrate on the subject of the day...

'So what can the boy do?' Mrs Taylor held up the large picture book. 'The cat is stuck in the tree but John is not tall enough to reach it.' She waited. 'What will John do to rescue the cat stuck up the tree?'

'He's too short.' The little girl sitting next to me pointed at the book and then hesitated, turning to me.

I nodded.

'Quite right, Karen.' The teacher smiled. 'Well done. He's too short.'

The girl beamed. She leaned over and gave me a hug.

'Well done,' I whispered. It had surprised me how quickly I'd become accepted by these children in the hospital school, all special in their own way. Somehow it made me feel closer to Rose.

'So what should he do?' Mrs Taylor shook her head. 'He's too short, as Karen said.'

I got another hug.

There were a few moments when none of the children spoke. The only sounds were the scrape of chairs on the wooden floor, sniffs and coughs.

'He needs to get taller, doesn't he?' Mrs Taylor smiled. 'Remember what we did earlier to make ourselves tall. Perhaps Miss Bradshaw will remember?'

The whole class turned their eyes towards me. I stood up and stretched my arms into the air. There was a lot of laughter, someone clapped. Before long they were all clapping. I sat down.

'Okay everyone.' Mrs Taylor held up her hand until the clapping stopped. 'So what should John do?' One of the younger children stood and stretched upwards, followed by a few of the others. The teacher turned the page of the book to show the boy reaching up but still unable to touch the branch the cat was on. 'John isn't tall enough, is he?' She nodded towards me. I went to stand next to her. 'Miss Bradshaw is going to show you some pictures. Which of the things in the pictures will help John to be tall enough to reach the cat?'

Each time I held up pictures to show various things, Mrs Taylor turned the page to show that the boy in the book still couldn't reach the cat.

'A box?'

'No!' they shouted, laughing and pointing.

'A dustbin?'

'No!' Some of them were now leaning forward, elbows on the desks. They really did enjoy the storytimes. I had to admit it was my favourite time as well.

'A table?'

'No!'

'Still not.'

'Not tall.'

I laughed, deliberately slow in choosing the fourth card showing the ladder. When Mrs Taylor turned the page there was a collective, 'Yes!' of triumph and much clapping.

I loved watching the way the children began to understand the difference.

'Well done, everyone. And thank you, Miss Bradshaw.'

Karen came to stand by me, took hold of my hand and led me back to my chair.

I had been so nervous the first day walking into the classroom and being faced with fifteen children and the watchful eye of the teacher. I'd wondered how different it would be from previous times in schools. But any concerns I had melted away under the relaxed and friendly atmosphere of the place.

Chapter Sixty-Seven

2002: Today: 3.00 p.m.

It's no good; I can still hear her.

'No! No. Whoops!'

I swing my legs over the side of the bed and sit up reaching over for the heap of clothes I'd taken off the night before. The blue jumper's inside out so I fumble with the arms as I move, dragging it over my head. I bang into the door frame and fall, land heavily on my right knee. 'Bloody hell!' Pain. I wait. It subsides. I stay still, my back against the post at the top of the stairs.

She's stopped shouting and is watching me from her armchair.

Or is she watching me? Or through me – seeing something I can't? She looks frightened.

Pity vies with anger.

My jaw aches; I'm clenching my teeth.

1977

It took a year before Sam admitted he couldn't manage; he was turning work down and he wasn't coping at home. Even though the district nurse was calling every day to make sure his dad was comfortable and out of pain, there were still times Sam had to leave him on his own. I helped as much as I could by staying with Albert when I wasn't in the shop or the school. Some weeks, the only time we saw one another was in the evenings when Sam had settled his dad for the night.

But Albert was frightened when he was left alone. Things had to change.

'I'll help,' I said. 'I could move in with you until...' I didn't finish the sentence but we both knew what I meant.

'What about the shop?' Sam stroked his hair from his forehead, a sure sign he was worried. 'And the school?'

I made sure he didn't see the regret that battled with my wish to take some of the burden away from him. 'This is more important, Sam. And I'm sure there will still be days when I can go to the school. I'm part-time at the shop anyway and I'm guessing Vera will welcome more hours since her son left home. I think she could do with the money and she says she gets lonely. I'll ask Mr Wardle if I can just do the early morning shift – and perhaps, sometimes, later in the day – before the shop shuts, the days I'm there.' I waited to see his reaction and was relieved when he nodded; to be honest I wasn't sure I could manage being stuck in all day again, not with someone so sick.

'That'd be great,' he said, taking hold of my hand and bringing it up to his face. 'Thank you. But I'd pay you – for the hours you look after Dad – I'll pay you.' His forehead creased with anxiety.

'Don't be daft. I'll be eating here – and sleeping here.' I saw a smile quiver at my last words and nodded. 'See? There's an upside to everything.' I covered his fingers with mine and moved closer to him. 'We'll get through this, love. We'll get through this together.'

'Thank you, Irene.' He leant his head against mine. 'We could get married, you know? But I don't want you to think I'm asking you now just because I need your help.'

'I don't. Now's not the right time anyway.' I'd put him off so many times it always amazed me whenever he asked again. 'How about I come to live with you and your dad, see how it goes?'

We came to an agreement. I left Grove Street and moved into their house. I kept my days at Clough Fields; I had built up a relationship with the children and the teachers there and didn't want to lose that. And by working the very early shifts at the shop before Sam went to work, I was still earning. My money went towards the food and Sam paid all the other bills for the house.

We juggled looking after his dad. It was a practical decision all round.

When I told Mum what I was going to do, we had a strange conversation that I didn't understand until years later.

'We've not got on for a while, Irene.' She actually looked sad. 'My fault...' She stopped herself. 'Mainly,' she added.

I didn't know what to say. The memory of her standing by Rose's bed that day was etched in my mind forever. I swallowed. Was she going to finally tell me the truth?

'Mainly?' I finally said. 'Mum—'

'You never gave me a chance. You and Nanna. I never got a look in—'

'We did. You didn't want—'

'Don't tell me what I did or bloody didn't want, Irene.'

This could easily turn into another row.

'Just say what you wanted to say, Mum.' I tried to speak softly.

But she seemed to be stuck on her resentment. 'Nanna didn't want me to...'

'Don't drag Nanna into this.' I couldn't help myself. 'Please – don't...'

Her face closed up into a scowl. She turned back to the cooker where she'd been scrambling eggs for her tea. 'Huh, these have gone like rubber now.' She scraped the contents of the frying pan into the bin.

And that was it. End of the conversation. The moment had gone. I went upstairs to pack. I got nothing but a curt nod when I left an hour later.

And something else happened that I didn't expect. I hadn't long been living at Sam's house when Susan turned up with a casserole. It had been a particularly hard day with his father; I looked like nothing on earth. Or, I thought, swallowing the lump in my throat, like Nanna used to say – I'd been "dragged through a hedge backwards". When I opened the door, it took me a moment to register it was her standing on the doorstep. 'I won't come in,' she said to my stumbling invitation. 'I don't want to intrude.' She handed the dish to me. 'You've enough on your plate without visitors.'

'It's very good of you.'

'You're family,' she said, quietly. 'The only family I have. I was hoping you felt the same.' She flushed, turned on the doorstep and then stopped. 'There's something I've wanted to say for a while.' She fiddled with the buttons on her white crocheted cardigan. 'I'll always look after your father, you know that?' She moved from foot to foot on those stylish stilettos of hers. Her smile hovered on her lips.

'I know that, Susan.' I'd watched her fussing over him like a mother hen whenever I saw them together.

'I realise there's always a danger that he could have another stroke.' She bit her lip. 'He gets tired very quickly. But please don't worry about him. If anything ever did happen, you'd be the first person I would send for.' Then she straightened up, ran her hands over her immaculate hair and smiled. 'But nothing will happen to him. I won't let it.'

In that moment I knew Susan and me wouldn't be just civil to one another, we would be friends. On impulse I bent down and hugged her with my free arm. 'Thank you.'

'Just make sure you don't overdo things yourself,' she said, putting both arms around me. I breathed in the faint perfume I'd become used to whenever she was around and realised it was what had lingered on Dad's coat whenever he'd stayed with me to look after Nanna. For some reason it comforted me, as though I understood, at last, that someone was watching out for him.

When I went home to check if there was any post for me, I'd sometimes go to sit on Rose's bed which was still there, stripped of bedclothes. If I stayed very still I'd feel the bare mattress dip slightly at the side of me. If I was very lucky I could imagine the warmth of a small hand slip into mine on my lap and feel comforted.

Chapter Sixty-Eight

2002: Today: 3.10 p.m.

Rain clatters on the landing window, startles both of us. A draught whines through the gap between the frame and the wall where the seal has broken. Past the glass, the sky is like a slab of dull gunmetal.

When I look back to her, I see her tears through mine. I should get up, go to her. I'll just stay here a moment, close my eyes...

She shouts. My head jerks back. Hits the post. Pain.

I scramble to my feet. Hold her. Shouting becomes loud crying.

1977

In the first year or so after I'd moved in, it was just a case of Sam or me being there when the doctor called, or keeping Albert company and making sure he took all his tablets. So many pills. We spent lots of time talking, him and me. I'd try to make something tasty for his meal in the middle of the day, the only time he ate. He loved my chicken pie; he insisted on having it even though he could never finish it and the pastry always gave him indigestion. Who was I to argue with a man facing what he had to face?

We'd eat together in front of the telly, trays on knees, catching up on the news.

'I like to know what's going on in the world.' Albert swirled the mashed potato around on his plate and belched.

'Give over, you'd watch Angela Rippon and Anna Ford if they sat there saying nothing.' I tried not to let him see I was keeping an eye on him; there were times when he just played with his food, breathing in the smell of it.

He chuckled. 'You're right there, lass. Nowt like a pretty woman to warm the cockles of your heart.' He sobered. 'I can look, can't I? At least I can do that.'

'Course you can Albert, nothing wrong in that at all.' I hated watching this once strapping man shrinking into skin and bone. He looked at me, unable to hide the bleakness in his eyes, his hand, still holding the fork, resting on the edge of the tray. I put my own knife and fork together on the plate. 'I'm full,' I said, 'and if you've finished, I think it's time you had a lie down.'

'I thought I'd stay here on the settee, like? Have a lie down here?'

'Okay, I'll get a couple of blankets.'

When I got back to the living room Albert was stretched out. I turned off the television and covered him up. 'I'll let you have a rest then.'

'No.' He caught hold of my fingers. 'Stop and have a natter, Irene.'

I was hoping to get a breath of fresh air in the backyard; with the electric fire on all day in the room, it was always stifling inside. But I couldn't refuse. 'What shall we talk about then?'

'Your favourite subject? Sam?'

I grinned. 'Good.'

'Did I tell you about the time he got stuck on his granny's lavvy roof?'

'You did.'

'The time we thought we'd lost him and searched all over, just to find him under the bed asleep?'

'Yeah, that too.'

'How about his first day in school, when he walked out with nobody noticing him and he came all the way home on his own with a stray dog following him?'

'And that.' I chuckled.

'Hmm, I'll have to think hard then.'

There was something I'd wanted to know for a long time. Sam always clammed up if I tried to ask. I wondered if his father would do the same. I chanced it. 'Will you tell me about when his mother left?' The lines on his forehead deepened, his mouth pinched in. 'Not if it's upsetting for you, Albert. I only want to understand. But if you'd rather not...'

'No, it doesn't upset me anymore; it was a long time ago. It's

215

better you know anyway – just in case she turns up one day. I don't know how he'd be. You'll be the one having to deal with our Sam, then, I doubt I'll be around.' He shook his head at my protest. 'Don't be daft, lass. And don't pretend. Please. We both know how this is going to end. It's important you know about … her. I don't know why I didn't think of it myself.' His fingers twitched on the hem of the blanket around his chest. 'Where to start,' he said.

I waited. The reflection of the room in the mirror above the fireplace shimmered and flickered with the stream of heat rising from the three glowing bars.

'She's called Ada. When she left, Sam was only four, poor little bugger.' Albert spoke abruptly. 'She worked weekends on a carpet stall on the market in town and one day she didn't come back home. I reported it to the police on the Monday. I'd been up two nights expecting her here any time. Worrying. Later in the day they came back. Told me she was all right but she didn't want me to find her.' He glowered. 'They looked at me as though they thought I'd been knocking her about, but I hadn't. I'd not touched a hair on her head, lass. You know?'

'I know.' And I believed him.

'They said she didn't want to be with me anymore and she'd send for Sam when she was settled.' He was breathing heavily. I heard the hollow rush of air going in and out of his chest, watched his Adam's apple slide up and down his throat.

'Stop now, Albert. It's enough. I understand.'

'No, I need to finish this. Later on, I found out she'd run off with the market trader she worked for. When she finally came for Sam, he refused to leave me. He hid in the pantry in the kitchen. She didn't seem that bothered, just shrugged and got back into the other fellow's car. Flash bugger it was an' all, big black saloon.' He didn't look up at me. 'I couldn't compete with that. I didn't trust myself to go out an' tackle the bastard. I stayed in the house. He came round to let her in the passenger side an' looked up at the window. Smiled. Like he was bloody making fun of me.' I stayed very still until he spoke again. 'He dripped in gold.' He waggled his hand. 'You know, fancy signet ring, fancy watch, poncy gold bracelet and what have you. Camel coat. Posh shoes. Trilby – he even lifted his hat to the cow as she got in. I remember thinking the Brylcreem made him look as bloody oily as he was.' Albert was really struggling to speak now and I was sorry I'd asked.

'That's enough for now, Albert. We can finish this another time,' I said, when he protested. 'Thanks for telling me all this.'

'It's fine, lass. It's better you know,' he said again.

Chapter Sixty-Nine

2002: Today: 3.25 p.m.

She won't stop howling. Loud ear-splitting howls that judder through me. I'm sitting on the arm of her chair, holding her, rocking her.

What I *want* to do is shake her...

1978

'There's one thing I really want, Irene.'

Albert and me were sitting in the backyard. It was a mild day so I'd heaved his armchair from the living room and wrapped him in blankets to enjoy the fresh air. Now we were sipping tea and sharing a plate of bourbon biscuits.

'What's that, Albert?' I was on the wooden bench, leaning against the wall of the house, eyes closed and savouring the chocolate taste of the filling.

'I'd like you and Sam to be wed while I'm still here to enjoy a knees-up.'

I sat upright and took a gulp of tea.

'Really?'

'Really.' Albert chuckled. 'Your face, it's a picture. It's about time my son made an honest woman of you.' He watched me. I saw his face change, set into seriousness. 'Really. It's my dearest wish, Irene.' He reached out for my hand. His fingers in mine were bony and cold. I put my cup onto the bench at the side of me and slid to my knees next to him.

'Is it?'

'I'd like to see the two of you settled. I could go in peace, then.'

'Don't talk like that, Albert.' Tears smarted behind my eyes. I'd grown fond of this man.

'Just saying the truth, love.' He let go of my hand and stroked my cheek before resting his head on the back of the chair and looking up.

I followed his gaze. The sun was a buttery yellow filmed by a gauze of thin cloud. Birds, too high to see what they were, circled above us.

'Well,' I said, standing and resting my hand on his shoulder. 'Well, when he comes home from work, we'll have to let your son know what we've decided, won't we?'

Sam stopped washing his hands in the kitchen sink. He looked from me to Albert and back again to me. 'What did you say, Irene?'

'I asked you to marry me. Your dad thinks you should make an honest woman of me, that we've been living over the brush for too long.'

'All the years I've asked for us to be married...' His voice, husky, trailed away. He coughed, came towards me, his hands dripping with soapy water. 'And now it's something you've decided between the two of you? Huh.' He glared at us in mock anger before grabbing me and swinging me around until I was dizzy. Dizzy and, in that moment, happier than I'd been for a long time.

'I told her, if you didn't hurry up and ask her, I would.' Albert grinned at us. I saw a shadow of the man he once was, a shadow of Sam in him.

'I've been asking her since we were ten, Dad, you do know that?'

Ignoring the wet handprints on my blouse, I curled my arm around his shoulders and pulled him towards me to kiss him.

'My turn.' Albert lifted his face.

Sam kissed him on the cheek.

'Not you, you daft bugger.' Laughing, Albert took a swipe at his son.

I bent down and kissed his other cheek. 'Thank you, Albert,' I whispered. 'Thank you.'

It had taken a long time and an elderly and ill man for me to know when the moment was right.

Chapter Seventy

2002: Today: 3.30 p.m.

I can't stand it. Need to walk away. I stand up so suddenly she slides sideways in the chair and stops the noise. She tries to grab me. I pull her upright again, tuck the blankets down the sides of the armchair cushion. Walk away.

There's a pulsing in my throat. I put my hand to my neck. I feel the beat. Beating ... beating under my palm.

1978

A month later, we were married. Our wedding day was lovely, even though it rained buckets.

I went to Susan's to get ready. I loved the feel of the long satin dress as I slipped it over my head.

'You've lost weight since the last fitting.' She turned me around, a look of concentration on her face. 'Take it off and I'll tack it at the waist. It won't show.'

The bedroom door opened. 'Tea?' Dad was already in his best

suit even though there was still another three hours before we were expected at the registry office. He ran his finger around his collar.

'No thanks,' Susan and me chorused.

'But a small sherry would be most welcome, darling,' she added.

'Babycham for me if you've got one, Dad?'

'And why wouldn't I have? Knowing my little girl would be with us?'

As soon as he came back with the drinks Susan shooed him away. 'Go and keep Albert company. Watch the horse racing on the TV,' she said. 'And take your jacket off – it'll not be fit to be seen.'

'And your tie, Dad, you look uncomfortable and you're going to have to wear it all the time anyway at the registry office.' I'd not seen him so nervous since the first time me and Susan came face to face.

I wondered if Mother would come to the wedding. She'd said nothing when I asked if she would. With a tingle of apprehension I thought, what if she came and caused a scene?

I sat sipping the Babycham, worrying about that as I watched Susan expertly stitching the seams of my pale blue dress.

'There. Done.' She bit through the thread. 'Try it now.' She glanced through the window. 'Too much to ask for a fine day...'

'Doesn't matter.' It really didn't. At long last I felt ready to be married. And have a family. I knew if we had a little girl, I'd call her Rose.

I'd had a dream about Rose the previous night. I dreamt she was eight and a bridesmaid at our wedding.

She wore a long pink dress with a pink Alice band in her hair, decorated with a row of tiny rosebuds. Every time I glanced around she was laughing and looking at the pews of smiling people watching her as she walked behind me, the train looped around one wrist and a small posy of white carnations in the other hand. She looked so happy.

When I woke my pillow was wet with my tears.

The rain didn't stop but I didn't care. I didn't even mind that my white stilettos heels were ruined by mud and green stains from the patch of grass outside the registry office, where we had the photos taken. Or that a lot of the pictures Dad took just showed mine and Sam's bodies with our heads hidden underneath the large black umbrella we'd borrowed from one of the staff.

And I found out later the matching blue lace bolero had transferred its damp pattern onto my shoulders. Lying back against the pillows after we'd made love, Sam gently kissed the patterns and said I looked like a tattooed lady from a circus. I told him, as long as it wasn't the fat lady, I didn't care.

Mum stayed away; somehow that made me sad, though I knew she wouldn't be able to stand seeing Dad with Susan without creating a fuss, so perhaps it was for the best. There were only the seven of us. Pauline and Brian were our witnesses. And, even though Albert was almost skeletally thin and hunched under covers in his NHS wheelchair, he looked more content than he had in months.

After the ceremony we went to the Dropped Anchor for a drink. We thought we'd surprise all our friends but they'd turned the tables on us and the bar was packed.

A lot of Albert's friends were there as well and he did his best to be the life and the soul of the party for a while. When we could see he was tiring, Dad and Susan took him back to Tatton Street for us.

'Sure you'll be all right with him, Dad?' I said.

'We'll all be fine. We'll give him his tablets and I'll get him to bed. This is your day, stay and enjoy yourselves.'

Albert caught hold of my hand when I went to him.

'Thanks, lass,' he said. 'Best day of my life...' His breath came in shallow wheezes. 'Well, 'cept when yon mon was born.' He gestured with his head towards Sam who was walking across the room towards us, a pint in his hand. 'I can go happy now—'

'You're going nowhere for a long time yet – Pops,' I said, using Sam's name for his father.

Albert chuckled. But then we looked into one another's eyes. His were a pale watery blue. We both knew the truth.

'Come on, then,' I said, tucking his scarf firmer under his coat and settling his cap straight. 'Off with you, and no speeding in that thing.'

Sam gave his dad a hug and we watched the three of them negotiate the pub doorway, cheered on by Albert's mates.

'He'll be fine with them, love.' I kissed Sam's cheek. It was wet.

'I know.' Sam sniffed and rubbed his palm over his face. 'I know.'

'Hey up.' Arms enveloped the two of us. Brian squeezed us together in a huddle. 'Okay you two?'

'Fine,' we choroused, turning to him and Pauline.

'So, how soon will we hear the patter of tiny feet, then?' Brian leered. 'Ouch!' He rubbed the back of his head where Pauline had clipped him with her hand.

'Don't be so personal.' But she was grinning and tipped her head to one side as if she was asking the question.

'We're hoping to start a family as soon as we can.' Sam held me close to him, sensing my embarrassment. 'There's nothing to stop us, is there, love?'

He was right. Setting up on his own was the best thing that Sam had done and his business was thriving. We'd even talked of one day asking Mr Wardle if we could rent the newspaper shop.

Like I said, it was a lovely day.

Chapter Seventy-One

2002: Today: 4.10 p.m.

Breathing steadier.

She's quiet. I'm dressed!

Don't remember getting dressed. My stomach flips. This sudden not remembering is new. Am I going like her? I rap my knuckles on my forehead – come on brain.

I wait, hoping to see the shadow, the slight movement in the air that tells me Rose is in the room. Nothing.

1978

'I need to try my new camera out.' Sam nodded towards the furthest headland from the long beach where we'd lain for the last hour. 'I want to see what's past that. Coming with me?'

It was only the second day of our honeymoon in Tenby. Before we were married we didn't think we'd be able to go away and leave Albert, but Dad and Susan insisted on moving in to look after him, "as a wedding present", they'd said. It was wonderful to be on our own after so long.

'I can't be bothered to move. You go,' I said, 'I'll just lie here and top up my tan.'

'Well mind you don't burn.' Sam tossed the suncream towards me. Grains of dry sand scattered around the bottle. 'Watch it.' I brushed them off my stomach. My flat stomach. I'd starved myself for weeks to be able to look decent in my new bikini and I knew I did. I wriggled, fluttering my eyelashes at him.

'Tease.' Sam threw himself back down on the blanket next to me, sliding his hand down the waist of my bikini bottom. Even as I grabbed his fingers to stop him I instinctively arched my back. 'No,' I protested but couldn't help smiling. 'Not here.' I sat up to see if anyone around us had noticed.

'Well, come with me then,' he said again.

'What about the sea?' The sandstone cliffs at the end of the beach had a definite dark line running along them that showed how far the tide rose. 'We might get cut off.'

Sam shielded his eyes, squinting against the glare of the sun. 'It's well out; it'll be hours before it comes back in. Come on, put your shoes on.' He jumped up and held out his hand. 'I want to take some photos. And you have to be in some of them, make the lads jealous of my beautiful new wife.'

I laughed as I let him pull me to my feet.

The beach on the other side of the headland was deserted. It was as though the rocks cut off all other sound except for the distant quiet roll of the waves. Our feet sank deep into the soft sand, still damp in the shade of the cliff. We held hands, leaving behind us two close lines of footprints.

'Up there should be good.' Sam pointed. Scooped out by time and explorers, a narrow path led to the clifftop.

I was drawn, protesting, all the way to the top. But when we stood amongst the yellow budding gorse, I was stunned by the view. The sea changed from navy to turquoise with the currents but it seemed so still. A seagull flew overhead, but it was its floating shadow on the water I watched, as it disappeared into the distance. A line of silver light highlighted the horizon.

Out of the corner of my eye I saw Sam turning this way and that, trying to catch the changes in the sky and sea. A rumbling above me made me look up; an aeroplane passed unseen beyond the blueness. When I looked back at Sam he was watching me.

'Happy?' he said. Smiling.

'Ecstatic,' I said. When he came towards me I knew what he wanted.

Chapter Seventy-Two

2002: Today: 4.15 p.m.

Standing by her chair. Watching. Even in her sleep she's not still; her fingers are twitching, her feet rub against one another. And she's scowling. Even in her sleep, she scowls.

Room's stifling. Stuffy. Too hot. Electric heaters blasting out.

Legs feel odd. Head pounding.

Want to sleep.

Better go downstairs first; think I forgot to lock the back door.

1980

Once home from honeymoon, we settled into a sort of routine. Albert and me never talked about Sam's mother again. In the months that followed he grew worse and took to his bed. The nurses came every day to wash and put ointment on his buttocks to stop him getting bedsores. He didn't like me doing things like that for him – I only did it the once and never again –- we were both too embarrassed.

He was in a lot of pain. We'd hear him crying out in the night. Sam went in the first time but his dad bellowed for him to get out. So he didn't go in again. I lay in bed, holding Sam as he wept as well. It went on for a long time.

Without even noticing time going by, I was twenty-five. Sam's dad died the day before my twenty-sixth birthday. There were many times we'd thought he was on his last legs. When he did finally go we were grateful; he'd been in such pain at the end.

It was a long hard dying.

Chapter Seventy-Three

2002: Today: 4.25 p.m.

Dirty crockery is still in the sink. Ignore it. I open the back door, lift my face upwards. The rain is light, like cold spray, on my face. I want to stay here. Forever.

1980

The day of Albert's funeral Sam's mother, Ada, turned up.

I'd noticed the large woman watching from a distance on one of the paths in the graveyard. I noticed her because she was wearing a red dress and hat, and a fur stole around her shoulders; one of the those with a fox's head and tail attached. I remembered wondering if she was at the wrong church; whether she should actually be at a wedding somewhere.

The boom of the organ music grew louder when we halted behind the coffin at the entrance. There was a rustle of clothes, a few coughs as people stood to 'Jesu, Joy of Man's Desiring'.

'I know Dad wasn't religious, but this is what's expected isn't it?' Sam whispered.

'It's fine,' I whispered back to him, squeezing his arm while, at the same time, wishing this was all over. I preferred the small chapel on Hillrise Road but this church was nearer to Albert's house and easier for his neighbours and friends to attend.

And there were a lot of people for the service, the pews were packed; Albert had been well liked. I recognised some of them as Albert's pals who'd called at the house to chat to him in the early days; in the months when he was fit enough to sit in the living room and have a bit of a laugh. I hadn't appreciated how popular he was.

I held on to Sam's arm as we followed the men carrying the coffin. The sun shone through the mullioned windows, the colours reflecting across the polished wood as they walked slowly along the aisle: rectangles of muted blue, red and gold sliding along, gone, then there again, at the next window.

I couldn't tell who was shaking more, him or me. The memory of the other two funerals in my life became a physical sensation, made me falter as I walked, a huge sob stuck in my throat. I gulped and gripped Sam's arm tighter.

'You okay?'

I didn't look at him. 'I'm okay. Sorry.'

I was glad when we reached the front pew and I could sit down. Behind me there were deep muffled clearings of throats and soft snuffles.

The six men settled the coffin on the trestle and moved away. The minister stood by the side of it and began to speak.

I heard little of the service; I remember even less of that hour,

226

only that I could feel each heave of air going into Sam's chest, each shaking release. I was relieved when it was over and we were able to file out behind the coffin into the fresh air.

The woman was there again, but this time she was standing by the church steps, her back to the afternoon sun, so that I was unable to see her face.

'Samuel,' she said, putting out her hand, preventing him from following the procession. 'Samuel?'

He stumbled, still wiping his eyes. I had my arm around his waist and I held on to him, not understanding why she'd stopped us, frowning at her. 'Please, not now,' I said, my voice sharp with a sudden apprehension. There was something about her, a vague similarity that I recognised. I glanced over my shoulder, saw the people waiting in lines in the church to follow us and urged Sam on. 'Come on, love.'

She didn't let go of his arm.

He hadn't heard her at first but now, looking down at her hand and then slowly lifting his head to look at her I saw his eyes widen and felt his back become suddenly rigid under my grasp. But he didn't speak.

And I knew who she was.

There was a commotion from behind us. Someone brushed past me.

'You've got a bloody cheek.' It was one of Albert's friends. He looked at me. ''Scuse the language, missus.' He touched the front of his hair as though raising a hat. 'Ken Whitlow.' He shifted his gaze from me to her and glared. 'Just what the hell do you think you're doing?'

The woman ignored him, adjusted the fur stole around her shoulders with her other hand. 'It's me, Samuel,' she said. Although her accent was the same as mine and Sam's there was a coarseness about it, a harsh curtness. 'Yer mam,' she said. 'Yer don't recognise me?'

I felt my senses sharpen; I heard the muted mutterings, saw the curious glances as everyone filed past us, smelt the cloying perfume coming from the nearness of the woman. I waited.

'Like I said, you've got a bloody cheek.' Albert's friend knocked her hand away and pressed Sam and me forward. I noticed the pall-bearers, unaware of what was going on, had stopped by a freshly dug rectangle in the ground. 'We've got a dear friend – to say our goodbyes to...' He jerked his head towards Sam, his expression softened with compassion. 'Pay our respects to his father.'

'My husband,' she called after us. 'He was still my husband.'

Sam forced us to a halt and, pulling away from me, turned and took a few steps. 'He's not – wasn't your husband.' The words were ground out through his teeth. 'You've been no wife to him in years. And you're not my mother.' He lunged towards her, face red, his arm outstretched, finger pointing. 'You. Are. Not. My. Mother. What are you doing here? You've no right.'

Sam's rage was frightening. Yet *she* didn't budge. There was no fear, no alarm in her expression. If I had to put a name to it, I would have said she looked annoyed.

Then she turned and walked away.

Ken had grabbed Sam. 'Come on, lad,' he soothed, 'she's nowt a penny, never has been. She's not worth getting upset about.' His hand on Sam's shoulders he led the two of us towards the open grave, where everyone was waiting. 'Allus one for bother,' he said to me. 'We'll have seen the last of her now.'

Why did I doubt his words?

Chapter Seventy-Four

2002: Today: 4.30 p.m.

Grey and purple clouds scud across the sky. Heavy splats of rain land on the path. Each splash turns the grey concrete black. I count them.

'One. Two. Three.'

Got a great wodge of rage in my chest.

I was right to doubt Ken Whitlow's words. Sam's mother turned up at the house on Tatton Street the following day in the same red coat and horrible fox fur thing that we'd seen her in outside the church at the funeral.

Sam was out.

After the funeral, we'd held the wake at the Labour Club. It had been a surprisingly cheerful event that we both enjoyed. Months ago – with great foresight typical of Albert – he'd arranged through a friend for balloons and photos of him to be placed around the room. Sam and me were amazed to see how many charity fund raising events he'd organised there down the years through the club. We'd known him to be a staunch Labour member but that was a side of him that took us by surprise. And he'd even left money for drinks behind the bar for anyone who could tell a funny story about him. The cash soon dried up; there were many stories, and the tears that flowed were an equal mix of laughter and sadness. Albert would have really enjoyed the evening as well.

Walking home late that night, Sam and me had a long talk. I hadn't broached the subject of Ada but, when Sam did, I knew I needed to listen.

'Dad never knew but I watched her drive off with that flash git,' he said. 'I hid because I didn't want to leave him.'

It had been raining earlier in the evening and the orange pools of light from the street lamps marked our progress through the streets. Each time we passed one, I looked to see his face; his jawline was set taut and he was fighting to keep his words even.

'I didn't understand what was happening, but when the police came I sat on the stairs and I heard them tell him she didn't want to come home, didn't want Dad – us – to know where she was. I was only a kid and to me that said she didn't want either of us. I couldn't understand what I'd done to make her not want me. I thought for a long time it was my fault she'd left. After they'd gone,

I watched Dad cry. But I didn't go to him because I was afraid he'd blame me.'

There was nothing I could do but to squeeze his arm closer to my side, rest my head for a second against him. Our footsteps echoed on the empty pavements. Except for the occasional blue blur of television screens through curtained windows, most of the houses were in darkness. It was as though we were totally alone and somehow our isolation made his words even more heart-rending.

At the house we stopped on the pavement in front of the door.

'We leave all that here,' he said. 'I don't want any mention of her in our home – or anywhere – ever again.'

So when I opened the door and saw his mother standing on the step, jaw jutted belligerently, I was ready for her.

'You saw how upset Sam was yesterday. He doesn't want to see you.'

She moved up onto the last step, so close to me I could smell the staleness of cigarettes on her breath and strong cheap perfume..

'He'll want to see me when he hears I'm the tenant of this house now.'

'How?' It was a shock but I tried to keep my voice calm. 'What do you mean?'

'I was still Albert's wife. Now I'm his widow.' There was a glint of sickening triumph in her eyes. 'We never divorced. Rent book was – is – in joint names, so I'm entitled to live in this house'

'I don't believe you. And, anyway, why would you want to? Haven't you got your own place?' I saw her tighten her mouth into a thin line when I said that. 'Have you been kicked out by the man you ran off with? Or have there been more men since and the last one got rid of you?'

If looks could kill! But I kept my stare steady.

'This is my place now,' she said. 'I'm entitled to live here.'

'Like hell.' But a niggle of worry stirred in me, trying to remember if Albert had ever said anything about a divorce. If what she said was true, if she did actually have a right to this house, how would Sam react? What would he do?

Sam had an appointment to see Albert's solicitor, I knew that. He'd waited until after the funeral. I'd supposed Albert had written a will. It wasn't something I'd ever talked about with him; it wasn't my business. But what if he hadn't? What if what the woman said was right, that the tenancy would go to her as Albert's widow? Did that happen with privately rented property? Sam had sent a cheque to the landlord to cover a month's rent and written to explain about Albert and to say that we'd like to take tenancy of the house within days of him dying But we'd heard nothing back and presumed it was all okay.

She must have seen my hesitation because she tried to push past me. 'I've a right to come in...'

I held on to the door. 'There's nothing for you here.'

I saw her look at my fingers. 'You married to my son, eh?' She held her top lip with her teeth; they were stained with nicotine. 'So you're my daughter-in-law.'

'I'm nothing of the sort. And it's nothing to do with you.'

'But this is.' She waved her hand upwards, indicating the house. 'And *this* is between him and me, nothing to do with *you*.' Narrowing her eyes, she prodded my chest. 'Now get out of my way.'

'How dare you.' I knocked her hand away and pushed her. She staggered back onto the pavement.

'You need to go,' I said. 'Now – before Sam gets back.' I slammed the door shut. Through the frosted glass panel I could see her still standing on the pavement.

'You'll be hearing from our solicitor.'

I didn't answer. Turning my back I leaned against the door, looking along the hall. I felt sick. What if this really wasn't our home anymore? What would we do?

Before I moved in Sam had told me he'd wanted to ask the landlord to tidy the place up, or at least let him do it. But Albert had been adamant; he'd said he didn't want the man "sticking his nose in"; he was happy with the place as it was. "I haven't set eyes on him for years – soft bugger lives down South somewhere, lad, and that's how I like it. He gets his money through t'bank and I ask for nowt." He'd winked at me. "Anyhow, he'd catch his death of cold if he came up North." He and Sam had laughed at that.

And then, when Albert became so ill, that had been the end of any thought of doing anything. So the hall floor still had the brown lino that had long lost its pattern and the walls, painted in magnolia, had the permanent dark smudges of fingers around the light switches, and the ceiling light shade was a murky cream with a fly-spotted bulb inside it.

I'd become used to it all. It hadn't mattered. We were all together.

"Our solicitor"? So was she still with the same man? Or was there someone else? And how much did I need to worry? I knew I should tell Sam.

When I peered through the glass there was no dark shadow there anymore.

For now I would keep it to myself.

Chapter Seventy-Five

2002: Today: 4.45 p.m.

Drops too many to count now. I could put my hand out to feel them. I don't. It's outside. I know nothing of outside, haven't for months. All I know is inside my head. All I know is this house. And the people in it.

1980

That night I didn't tell Sam about his mother coming to Tatton Street. I hoped her threat was an empty one and she'd stay away. I would have been happier if we'd had a letter back from the landlord but told myself it would be okay; if we could just hang on at the house until we could put a deposit on the newspaper shop and get a mortgage, it would all be fine.

So I pushed the worry of Sam's mother to the back of my mind.

During a visit to give us his condolences the day Albert died, Mr Wardle had asked us if we were willing to look after the shop for a month once we'd got through the funeral. He was kind: he said it was so we could get a feel of the place, to find out whether we could manage the business. But I knew how fond he was of Sam; he'd known him since his days as the paper lad, of course, and Mr Wardle confided in me that he thought it would take Sam's mind off things. And after the visit from Sam's mother, I was glad to be away from the house.

The shop was only small but, believing it was going to be our future, we rearranged things to suit the way we were going to work in it. The glass jars of sweets along the shelves: aniseed balls, barley sugar, fruit chews, pear drops – all in alphabetical order, so I could find them easily. I dusted the red lids every other day, arranged and filled the layers of chocolate bars in order of size and shape, made sure the card stands were neat and tidy, the magazines and newspapers laid properly one after the other in order, and the ice cream cabinet lid wiped twice a day.

Vera and me managed the shop between us most of the time. But when he wasn't working Sam helped out. He was brilliant with the children, flirted with the old ladies, talked football with the old men. And it comforted him to chat with some of his dad's mates, even though I saw the sadness in his eyes.

I loved the sound of the shop doorbell, loved coming through the curtain from the private little stockroom at the back when customers came into the shop.

With a few more weeks we'd have enough to put the deposit down and it would be ours. Life was good.

It was the end of the week and we'd planned to go out the following day, for a long walk on Sheepfold Hill and a pub lunch, our occasional Sunday treat.

We were chatting while I made tea. Sam had washed and changed out of his overalls. He looked as contented as me.

'Anything I can do?'

'Not yet.' I jiggled the basket in the hot fat in the chip pan. 'These will take a while yet. 'Sit down. I've done sausages and peas, that okay?'

'Great.' He kissed the back of my neck, put his arms around my waist. 'Love you.'

I felt the stir of his body against mine and the familiar wave of happiness. Turning my head I pressed my face to his. 'Love you too. But tea will get cancelled if you carry on like this.'

He laughed, his breath hot on my skin, and gave me another kiss. 'Okay.'

'I gave Vera the money to bank into the shop account.' I put two plates on the grill to warm. 'I think Mr Wardle will be pleased with what we've taken this week.'

'Did you give Vera her wages?'

'I did. And mine are in the drawer.' I waved the fork I was using to push the sausages around in the frying pan towards the cupboard. 'I'll bank it Monday.'

'We're nearly there, Irene. A couple more months and we'll have enough for the deposit on the shop.'

'I know.' We grinned at one another. 'Oh, there are a couple of envelopes on the side there, addressed to your dad. And one for you.'

'Thanks. 'Sam picked them up and dropped onto the armchair. I heard him rip one open.

'Can you set the table, love?' When he didn't answer I turned around. 'Sam?' he was pinching his nostrils, his eyes squeezed tight. 'What's wrong?'

'Dad's not been paying the rent.' Sam let his hand drop away from his face. There was a white line around his lips.

'What?' Almost without thinking, I lifted up the chip basket and rested it on the rim of the pan, pushed the frying pan away from the hot gas ring. Turned off the cooker.

'This is from Dad's landlord, Parker.' He scanned through it as though he needed to make sure what it said.

'Sam?'

'He says he's heard about Dad and sends his condolences. And he's sorry but he wants the house back for a relative of his. He says he used to get cheques from Dad but hasn't had any for over twelve month. He's prepared to write some of it off but wants rent from us...' He looked up from the paper, his face ashen and then carried on reading, '"as you've been living in the house as well."'

'Can he do that?' If we weren't the official tenant, could he make us pay? 'Sam?'

'I don't know.' He looked across the counter to me. 'He obviously thinks we've been ignoring everything and refusing to pay. And we have been living here. The rent is owed. Dad hasn't been paying it.' He lifted the letter, his hand shaking. 'He wants twelve hundred and sixty pounds. Besides the cheque I sent. He says he's cashed that and is giving us the month to move out.'

I swallowed, too stunned to say anything. But I felt the twisting panic crawling along my scalp. 'That'll be nearly all our savings, Sam.' My legs went from under me; I sat down opposite him on the settee.

'And it's still less than Dad really owed.' Sam reread the letter. 'He could have asked for the full amount.'

'I could swear your dad said ages ago it went directly from the bank by standing order.'

'Apparently not...' Sam closed his eyes, shook his head.

My mouth was dry. I swallowed fear. 'But if there was a problem we would know about it. There would have been letters, surely?'

'Well I've seen nothing. Have you?'

I moved my head. 'No. But we've both been run off our feet these last few months...'

'I don't believe this. How can this be happening?'

'Do you think he'll take part payments? Mr Parker? Monthly payments? So we don't have to use all our savings.'

He shrugged.

Now I knew why we hadn't heard from his mother; she must have discovered what a state everything was in and disappeared back under her stone. The sudden anger dissolved into resignation. At least I'd no need to tell him about her now.

If only Albert had told us, we could have sorted it.

'We need to look in Dad's room – see what else is going to jump out and bite us on the arse.' Sam scowled, his voice harsh.

It felt intrusive going into Albert's room. I'd stripped the bed but not turned the mattress. I wish I had. Because, there, pushed right under the top end of the bed, were envelopes. Mostly unopened. The demands for rent arrears. Bank statements. And one or two letters of thanks from charities.

Sitting on the edge of the bed Sam studied the bank statements. 'Monthly standing orders to at least ten charities.' He threw the papers down. 'What the bloody hell happened to charity begins at home?' He jumped up, paced the room, as though he didn't know what to do with his anger. 'Well, at least we know where his pension went.'

'Don't, Sam. Please.'

'How have they got here? Dad was hardly downstairs for months.'

'I don't know.' How had I missed this? I saw the post every day. Didn't I? 'The nurses? Do you think he asked them to bring up his post?' Was this my fault? Should I have noticed? 'I should have seen what was going on.'

'You can't blame yourself, Irene. I was here as well.' He flattened his palm on his forehead, pushed his hair back.

Sam saying that didn't make me feel any better. 'What are we going to do?'

'There's only one thing to do. We have to pay. Otherwise Parker will take us to court. If we get sued, it'll go on record. We'd never get a mortgage – if we ever could afford the deposit,' he added, bitterly. He swung around to face me. 'You do know what this means, Irene?'

I couldn't stop the smarting tears even before his next words.

'Buying the shop is out of the question now.' Sam sat down next to me. We didn't speak for quite a while. But then he said, 'I am so sorry, love.'

I stared around the room that still held the stale smell of illness. 'It's not your fault, Sam. And please don't be angry with Albert. He wouldn't know what he was doing. Not for months, probably.'

'Huh!' He shook his head, his shoulders slumped.

'He wouldn't have realised. Or he hid his head in the sand.'

Sam didn't answer.

We neither of us slept much that night.

Chapter Seventy-Six

2002: Today: 4.50 p.m.

'Come,' Rose says.

'Rose?' I half-turn my head. This is the first time she's actually spoken to me. 'Rose? Where are you...?'

'Come. Mummy needs you.'

'No.' I hold on to the door frame. The wood is wet, slippery under my hand. I think I might slide down onto the step. 'I'm so tired. I've had enough.' I can't believe I'm talking to my little sister after all this time. 'I knew you were here, love,' I whisper.

She doesn't answer me.

'Come. Mummy needs you.'

'No. I can't. She's asleep. Let me sleep.'

But all she says again is, 'Mummy needs you.'

1980

'We'll put things back the way they were,' Sam told Mr Wardle.

'No, don't. I think you had the right idea, it's a lot better like this.'

Mr Wardle held out his hand. 'And I'm sorry things didn't work out for you. It's been nice thinking I'd be handing over to a lovely young couple.' He sighed.

'What will you do now?' I asked him.

'Not sure. Not sure I want to hang on until I find someone else.' He chewed on the corner of his moustache. 'Don't suppose you want to rent it off me?'

A sliver of hope flared and died as he added, 'Course I can't let you have the flat, me and the missus are upstairs. We were thinking we might like to move to Morecambe but now...' He trailed off as we both shook our heads.

I felt even worse then; we'd obviously spoiled their plans as well.

'Sorry, Mr Wardle, we'd have to find somewhere to live. We couldn't afford two rents. But thanks for the offer.' Sam smiled at him. 'It was kind of you.'

The man waved away our thanks. 'I'm only sorry I can't help more.' His shoulders moved up and down with another great sigh. 'Probably cut our losses and shut up shop if someone doesn't come along in the next month or two. Both me and Betty are getting a bit long in the tooth for this malarkey now. Getting up at three every morning to bring in the papers and sort 'em ain't doing our old bones much good.'

He tried to laugh about that but I knew his grin was as false as our smiles when we walked out. And away from our dream.

Chapter Seventy-Seven

2002: Today: 4.50 p.m.

'What do you care,' I say, 'after what she did?'

Nothing. She's gone. I close the back door, leave the kitchen. Stand on the first tread of the stairs. 'Rose? I'm right, you know. What I saw? Rose?'

My legs are heavy. The stairs are steep.

'It was lovely while it lasted, love.' I looked up at Sam; he seemed to have aged since his dad died. There were lines at the edges of his eyes and mouth.

'Lasted all of a few months, Irene. I'm sorry.'

'It's not your fault. And don't go blaming your dad either.'

So, less than a year after we were married, we faced being homeless. We searched around for somewhere else to live. We couldn't afford to buy; we hadn't enough for a deposit. We put our names down for a council house but the waiting list was over a year long and that for a house not even in our area. We scoured the papers and walked for miles looking for somewhere to rent. Finding something we could afford in Denholme was impossible. I hadn't known before how many scruffy, bug-ridden flats and bedsits there were around the town; we were desperate but I still couldn't bring myself to live like that.

The problem was that most of Sam's work was local. If we moved away he would need to build up a reputation and that would take time. Something we hadn't got.

When I finally opened up to Dad he was as devastated as we were. He paced the blue carpet in the living room of his and Susan's flat. 'I'm just sorry I can't help, love. I should never have signed the house over to your mother. You should have had a share in it. If I'd done that – if I had some say in it still I could—'

'Don't.' If he didn't stop he'd wear the pattern off the carpet, I thought. 'Don't Dad.' I held on to his arm, as he paced past me again. 'You thought you had no choice; you were being kind.'

'Or salving my conscience.' He stopped, shook his head. 'After what I did...' He glanced towards the kitchen to where Susan was making a coffee.

I hugged him. 'You made the right decision; she's good for you. Please don't worry, we'll sort something out.' But I still couldn't believe what was happening to us, things had moved so quickly. I leaned against the patio doors, watching people on the avenue: a couple with a child in the man's arms, an old lady leaning heavily on a younger woman's arm, a child being pulled along by a small Jack Russell. Nanna had a saying for when she thought someone was getting too big for his boots or self-satisfied, or even taking things for granted; "God could drop a clog on their head". In other words, watch out, something could happen to ruin everything. I wondered if any of those people walking past had a clog hanging over them.

'It's Sam I feel most sorry for. He blames himself. He thought Albert was paying the rent while he paid the other bills. But I feel I'm as guilty. All those months I sat with Albert and he never said a word. I just don't understand.'

'Neither of you must shoulder the blame, love. Perhaps it was too much for him to think about – or he couldn't. He was dying and he was scared. We don't always do what we should sometimes.'

He was right; I had kept that memory a secret for years, when I knew I should have spoken out.

Chapter Seventy-Eight

2002: Today: 5.00 p.m.

I'm standing by her chair. She's asleep. I turn away.

'Stay.' My sister's voice is firm.

Even though I can't see her, she can see me? That's not fair. And she should be on my side. Why does Rose care so much about Mother? I wonder if being dead stops you remembering what happened in your life. Perhaps Rose has forgotten what I've never been able to.

1981

Time was running out; Mr Parker was repossessing the house in a few days.

We were sitting in the Dropped Anchor, Sam nursing half a pint of mild and me sipping a Babycham, when Brian and Pauline joined us.

'We've got something to tell you.' Brian took a quick slurp of his beer.

Pauline nudged him. 'I'll tell them.' She was smiling but I saw the concerned look in her eyes. I knew immediately what she was going to say but kept quiet. It was her news after all – however I would feel about it. 'I'm pregnant.' She caught hold of my hand and squeezed. The look we exchanged said it all. I knew she understood, especially now, when we had no money and were virtually homeless. 'You okay?'

'I think it's wonderful,' I said. 'Congratulations.' I kissed her cheek. 'I'm so pleased for you.'

Sam thumped Brian on the shoulder. 'So pleased for you, mate,' he said. They'd been trying for a while and Pauline had already been through two miscarriages.

Brian grinned, his face reddening. He took another long swig.

'But what about your plans? About emigrating?' I said. I knew they'd been planning it for months. 'And the house, it's on the market, isn't it?' Was it selfish of me to hope they wouldn't go to Australia after all?

'We've had a thought,' Brian said, putting his pint pot on the small round table in front of us. 'The doctor insisted Pauline packed in work. We don't want to take any chances this time. So we decided to wait to emigrate until after the baby's born. We've taken the house off the market for now and we've talked it over and thought we'd ask if you wanted to come and live with us until we go? Pauline's going bloody mad on her own all day.'

'I am.' Pauline pulled a face. 'I hate being on my own – it's so boring. Honestly, Irene, you'd be doing me a favour.'

'It would be brilliant but I'm still working at the shop until it's sold or rented to someone new and where you live is a bit far for me to get there for the morning papers.' I smiled at them. Besides I was still managing to keep up with my days at Clough Fields and I didn't want to give those up. 'But thank you anyway...' I caught Sam staring at me. 'What?'

'I've already said...'

'You've already said – yes?' I raised my eyebrows at Sam.

'I've cleared it with Mr Wardle.'

'And my days at the school?' How would I get there? I tried not to show my annoyance, but the resentment must have been in my voice. I saw Pauline and Brian look at one another, alarm on their faces.

'I'm sorry, love...'

'We're sorry, Irene. We forgot about the school.'

'Please say yes, Irene.' Pauline looked close to tears.

I took my top lip between my teeth; what was I thinking? They were offering us a home. Somehow I'd have to clear it with Clough Fields.

'This has been planned between the three of you, hasn't it?'

'Sorry,' they chorused. At least they had the grace to look shamefaced.

'No, I'm sorry. It'll be all right, I'm sure.' I'd miss the children but I'd ask Christine Widdecombe if I could go back to the school after our friends had emigrated. I might even manage a day or so there before then. 'I'll ask if I can go in every now and then; see if they can get someone to cover for me.' Perhaps Barbara, Martin's mother would do it; she was only there one day a week at the moment. 'It'll be okay,' I said, finally.

They gave a collective sigh of relief and Pauline leaned over to give me a hug.

'Thank you. I'm sick to death of the radio and all that's on telly is the Pope's visit. But then, when I turn everything off, I can't stand the silence.'

I hugged her back. 'I bet you'll be wishing for some peace and quiet once the baby's here.' Even as I spoke I fought against the twinge of envy. It would be a while until Sam and me could even think about starting a family. We had no chance, not until we had got some money behind us. And that looked as though it would be a long time in the future.

It worried me how I would feel living with Brian and Pauline and seeing them getting so excited about their baby. But I was also aware that was selfish of me and that they were making the offer as true friends. 'If you're sure...'

'That's settled then.' Pauline sat back on the bench.

'What about rent?' We'd need to pay something; we weren't charity cases.

'We'll sort that,' Brian said. He glanced at Pauline. 'We thought a few pounds, food and electric? Twenty a week?'

Sounded fair to me. But still I said, 'And I'll do the housework and the meals – let Pauline rest.'

It didn't take long for us to move in; we hadn't much stuff of our own once most of Albert's things had been given to the cancer charity shop. We went out to Manchester for a meal to celebrate. What would happen when our two friends actually left for Australia, we weren't sure. But we were still on the housing list and, for the time being, all we could do was keep our fingers crossed that we got somewhere permanent to live sooner or later.

Chapter Seventy-Nine

2002: Today: 5.05 p.m.

Breathing in. Out. In. Matching the rhythm of Rose's breath. I feel the brush of air around me.

The man next door comes home. Hear him running up his stairs, flushing his loo, running downstairs. Banging around.

The throb of my heart booms loud in my head. No, it's the blast of noise from his radio.

She'll wake up. I nod towards my mother. 'She'll wake up,' I whisper. She'll create. She'll create. The thought whirls round in my head. If she starts so will he; he'll be thumping on the wall again.

'Sam will be home soon.' The words were whispered.

So Rose doesn't know everything... 'No. he said he'll be late home.' I wonder whether he'll feel Rose in the house now she's begun to talk; will that make a difference?

1981

Pauline's excitement about the baby was infectious, even if it was tempered by the awful morning sickness she still endured during the first month we lived with them.

'I can't take much more of this, Irene.' She slumped to the bathroom floor in tears, her face scarlet.

I crouched alongside her. Even though I'd been holding her hair back while she threw up down the loo there were splatters of vomit on her long fringe.

'How long did the doctor say this would go on for?'

'He didn't, he just said it happens to a lot of women. Just like he said about these bloody things.' She pushed her leg out in front of her and pointed to the varicose veins that bulged in her right calf.

'We don't have to go today, you know. It's stifling out there. I wouldn't be surprised if we didn't have another thunderstorm.'

'We're going. And I'm not having that bloody woman lording it over me in her fancy blouses with oversized shoulder pads and tight white jeans that she can still wear because, "I'm hardly showing, darling".' She mimicked a posh voice wonderfully. 'Bloody cow. Bloody Fiona.'

Pauline's pregnancy appeared to have brought out a lot of swearing in her. She struggled to get to her feet. 'Help me up, will you, Irene? I'll have a shower and then see what to wear for this sodding coffee morning.'

'God, I hate this woman.' We stood at the end of the gravelled drive of the large stone house.

'We don't have to go in,' I said for the tenth time. We'd walked slowly along the few streets it took to get there but we were both sweating in the humid heat of the June day. Thunder rumbled in the distance.

Pauline pulled at the neckbow of her floral baggy dress. 'I feel a right frump.'

'You look lovely. The blue collar goes with your eyes.' She had put quite a bit of weight on despite hardly eating. Fluid retention she said, her doctor had told her.

'Something else to bloody worry about.' She'd thumped her thighs.

'Right. Come on.' I grabbed her arm and we marched as best we could along the drive and around to the back of the house towards the chatter and clink of cups and plates. 'Remember it's for charity,' I hissed.

'Girls!' Fiona greeted us with a wave, which sent the ash from the end of her cigarette in an arc over the quiche and sandwiches on a table by the patio doors of the house.

'Oh, Christ, that's her.' Pauline dipped her head to mutter.

'She's smoking,' I said. 'I thought you weren't supposed to smoke if you were pregnant?'

I felt Pauline's shrug against my side. 'She's a law unto herself. Just don't eat the food.'

There must have been at least thirty women sitting, chatting and drinking, at small tables on the immaculate lawn enclosed by Leylandii trees. Yellow roses covered a tall pergola on a path leading to the patio where others were standing, glasses in hands. A show garden.

As far as I could see most were not pregnant, all wearing floaty dresses and many in large sun hats. Some glanced over at us before turning away to continue their conversations. I felt very self-conscious so goodness only knows what my friend felt like.

'Do you know anyone here, Pauline?'

'I don't think so. I thought there'd be some others from the relaxation class the clinic runs – but no.'

Fiona walked towards us on wedge heels. I hadn't seen her before. She had bright green eyeshadow and mascara, her thin blonde hair carefully arranged and lacquered. As Pauline had forecast she was in tight white jeans and a heavily shoulder-padded top. It was satisfying – for me at least – when I saw she had thick thighs so the jeans made a shushing noise as she moved.

'Darling, don't look so disapproving.' She pouted at Pauline. 'I couldn't manage without my ciggies and I couldn't bear to get fat...' There was no way her glance at Pauline's stomach was accidental. I heard my friend's intake of breath. 'And the doctor told me smoking will keep the baby small.' She gave a high-pitched laugh. 'So a win, win situation all round, I say—'

For you, I thought. Poor kid. The irritation, anger, whatever it was I felt, rose up; I couldn't keep my mouth shut. 'Should you be drinking as well?' I said. 'I read somewhere—'

'Oh tosh, darling, couldn't do without my G and T.'

Who the bloody hell says "tosh" these days?

Pauline had gone very quiet.

'Do you know,' I said to Fiona, 'I don't think we will be staying here after all.'

Her eyes opened wide. I noticed some of the lurid eyeshadow had smeared onto her cheek. 'Why ever not?' She took in a long drag of her cigarette. 'This *is* for charity you know. Some charity my husband's Rotary Club is supporting.'

'Which is?'

She hesitated before saying, 'A good cause...'

I fished into my shoulder bag and pulled out the five-pound note Pauline and me had agreed on and pushed it at Fiona. 'No doubt it will be in the local paper next week.'

We had hardly walked around the side of the house before the sky lit up followed by an enormous crack of thunder and the heavens opened. I pulled out the two pac-a-macs I'd brought with me and we put them on.

'Ever-ready Irene.' Pauline laughed, pulling the hood over her head.

There was a lot of screeching from the back garden. We grinned at one another, linked arms and splashed our way back home.

Chapter Eighty

2002: Today: 5.10 p.m.

The prickle of unease trails up the back of my neck and over my scalp; something's wrong. 'Rose?'

She's gone again.

I'm alone.

The loud rock music from next door gets louder.

Mother's eyes flicker.

Oh god...

Eyes still closed, her mouth opens.

1981

'Let's go shopping.'

I glanced across to the kitchen door. 'Well, I must say, you look brighter this morning.' I dropped the tea towel onto the draining board, leaving the rest of the breakfast dishes to dry themselves. 'It's nice to see you not looking green for once.'

Pauline chuckled. 'Don't speak too soon.' She carefully made her way to a chair and sat down. 'But I do feel okay – so far. Any tea on the go?'

'You sure?'

'I think so.' She leaned back, her hands clasped over her ever-expanding stomach.

'Baby stuff?'

'Yes, if you're up for it. I could do with your help choosing. And you must be sick to death of being stuck in the house with me.'

'Not at all.' Actually, some afternoons, when she was dozing on

247

the settee, I'd have a walk along the nearby canal, enjoy the fresh air. 'And we have had a couple of outings, the relaxation classes—'

'All four of them—'

'The doctors–'

She groaned.

'Fiona's—'

'Don't mention that bloody woman.' But she laughed. 'No, what I want to do is spend some money, buy things: the carrycot, a pram, nappies – anything. Just so we know I'm looking like a whale for a reason.'

'Sam and Brian have made a good job of sorting out the nursery.' I put the cup of tea on the table in front of her and leant against the sink to drink mine.

'I love what they've done.' She sipped at the tea. 'Ah, that tastes good.' She looked up at me. Her voice softened, 'You know, Irene, it might take ages now to sort out the Australia paperwork again.' She held out her hand to me. I put my cup down and took hold of it. 'I'll need you for quite a long time before all that happens. This baby has to put in an appearance first and I can't say I'm looking forward to that bit.'

'You'll be fine. The General is a good hospital.' I gave her hand a little shake. 'Now, let me clear these things away, tidy up a bit and sort something out for us to eat tonight—'

'Oh leave it.' Pauline hoisted herself out of the chair. 'Let's go shopping.' She stopped by the door. 'I'll get dressed. It'll be fun. I could do with a bit of fun after all these weeks. It's time we went out more. Let's talk to the lads tonight, plan a few outings...' I listened to her plod up the stairs and stop on the landing. 'But for now – Mothercare here we come...'

It would be good to get out as a foursome again. Sam and me had agreed that we'd take each day as it came for the time being. Make the most of just being together. Another of Nanna's sayings was, 'It will come and it will go, it always does,' whenever there were difficult times. I had to believe that.

Chapter Eighty-One

2002: Today: 5.15 p.m.

Her lips quiver.

I stand by her side, put my hand on her shoulder.

'Shush. It's okay, Mother.'

She turns her head to bite my fingers. A thought flashes through my brain when she lets go: good thing she hasn't got her teeth in. I pull my hand away.

She lets her head fall back and yells. 'La, la, la, la...' On and on and on. I don't know how to stop her.

1981

The annual fair arrived on the common at the edge of town. Childhood memories of the fun I'd had with Rose and Sam had tugged at me and I persuaded him to take me. Brian and Pauline didn't need any encouragement.

But, to be honest, it hadn't even occurred to me that she'd want to go on everything, let alone the waltzers. It skimmed through my mind that the last person on earth who should be in this screeching, spinning ride was Pauline.

But she'd insisted.

'I'm not being left out of anything.' She'd laughed. 'Come on.' It was a bit of a squeeze getting the bar that fastened us against the plastic of the seats to close over her belly but she managed to wriggle down until it clicked.

'I'm dizzy,' I yelled at Sam, burying my face into his shoulder.

I could barely hear his laugh above the bass of the raucous music that thumped into my skull from every corner, every alleyway of the fairground. Lights: red, purple, yellow illuminated the laughing faces of young men, the screaming mouths of girls being whirled around the other waltzers.

When the revolving stopped, we staggered down the steps of the ride and stood under one of the great arcs of white lights above them.

'My legs feel like jelly,' Sam mouthed at me, laughing.

'And mine.' I held on to him looking upwards. Moths of all sizes fluttered and batted against the round lamps. The sky was black beyond the illuminated haze. In the air the sweet smell of toffee apples and candyfloss mingled with the oil and grease of the rumbling engines of the rides that surrounded them.

Pauline clutched Brian's arm. 'I feel sick now.' She held her hand to her throat.

'I'm not surprised, I told you it would be too much.' In the lull of sound, when the last note ended on the dwindling 'Bennie and the Jets', there was a distinct trace of irritation in his voice. 'It's not just you you need to think of, you know.'

I looked at Sam in surprise, it was the first time I'd heard his friend sound even remotely angry. It was a shock to hear him raise his voice to her.

Sam moved his shoulders up around his ears and leaned towards me. 'Not our business, love.'

'Okay.'

But then Brian held Pauline at arm's length, pretending he couldn't get near enough for her large bump and kissed her full on the mouth and the uneasy moment passed.

'Big wheel?' Sam pulled me across the trampled grass towards the queue with the other two following at a slower pace, arms around one another. Friends again, thank goodness, I thought.

At the big wheel, I climbed the wooden steps to the swinging seat clinging on to Sam's hand and helped by the grinning youth who used the opportunity to pat my backside.

'Watch it,' Sam growled.

The lad laughed. His gold tooth matched the hooped earing almost hidden in the tangle of black curls. He leaned to lock the rail in front of us pushing the back of the carriage. It swung wildly back and forth, matching the movement in my stomach, I yelped. The lad laughed again.

We hung suspended twelve foot in the air. Sam slung his arm carelessly around my shoulders and I nestled against him. But I noticed he tightly gripped the bar with his other hand. It made me smile. As the ride started we waved at Brian and Pauline. They didn't see us; they were too busy kissing. Sam and me did the same and I wasn't sure whether it was the feel of his lips on mine or the swinging of the carriage that made my stomach flip.

It had been a wonderful evening. One that almost made me forget that we'd soon have to look for somewhere else to live; that before long, soon after their baby was born, our friends would be on the other side of the world, lost to us forever in Australia. There'd be phone calls, I thought. But it wouldn't be the same. The fleeting sadness was swept away as, with a shout from Sam, our carriage rose to the top and stopped. The raucous music faded, a breeze, sharper than I expected, blew my hair across my face and billowed my skirt.

Sam's fingers crept along my thigh and under the leg of my panties. I lifted my face to his, enjoying the familiar clench of muscles between my legs.

I love you, Mrs Hargreaves,' he murmured. His lips were warm and firm.

When we made love later that night, I was sure we'd made our first baby.

Chapter Eighty-Two

2002: Today: 5.20 p.m.

She's almost purple in the face.

'Shut up!' I hold her face between my palms. Try to make her look at me. 'Stop it.'

Heavy footsteps on the stairs.

Sam.

Not yet. Not yet. I turn to look. Not Sam. The neighbour.

He yells in my face. 'Shut her up.'

'I can't.'

He pushes past me.

'Get out!'

He's shaking her. 'Shut up. Shut the fuck up,' he shouts.

It's the look of fear on her face that makes me move. He can't do this.

1981

The scream woke us.

'What the hell?' Sam sat up in bed.

I threw back the covers and slid out. 'Pauline?'

'Irene!'

'Coming.' When I ran into the bathroom Pauline was doubled over, her arms wrapped around her stomach.

'Pain,' she gasped, falling to her knees and crouching on all fours.

I saw the swirl of liquid surround her, soak into her nightie. 'Your waters have broken.'

'It's not due for another three weeks.' Brian was hopping around on the landing, trying to put his pyjama bottoms on.

I felt the hysterical giggle threatening to escape and switched to look at Sam. 'Phone the midwife, the number's by the phone in the hall.' I kept my voice sharp; one of us needed to stay calm. 'Brian, help me to get her on your bed.'

'Should we move her?'

'Yes.' I knelt beside her, waved one arm towards Brian and wrapped my other arm under her. Her stomach was tight, hard. 'Pauline, you need to be on your bed.'

'No! I'm not bloody moving.' She took in a sharp breath.

I put my face close to hers. 'Please, Pauline, try to get up. You should be on the bed, not here on the bathroom floor.'

'I. Am. Not. Moving.' She spoke through clenched teeth.

I felt the movement ripple along her stomach; the strangest sensation.

'How long have you been having pains?' I lifted her chin. Her hair hung damp and limp around her face; I smoothed it back and behind her ears. 'Pauline, listen to me, try to slow your breathing down. When the pain starts again, try to relax into it. The midwife will be here soon.' I hoped I sounded calmer than I felt, although I knew what I said about relaxing was correct. I'd been a couple of times with her to the antenatal clinic. 'Pauline – try to remember – how long have you been having pains? And how far apart?'

She shook her head. 'I don't know – a while.' She breathed in deeply. 'I don't know.'

Where the hell was the midwife?

'Irene...' She said my name on a wail. 'It's happening again...'

'Breathe. In. And. Out.' I did the same to encourage her. 'Good girl.' When the contraction faded I said, 'Well if you won't move, love, we can at least make you more comfortable. Brian, get the duvet and pillows off your bed.' He didn't move. I saw him swallow, his eyes fixed on Pauline. I heard Sam on the landing. 'Sam?'

'Yes?' He peered around the door, keeping his eyes on me.

'Bring the pillows and duvet off their bed, will you? Did you get hold of the midwife?'

He hesitated. 'Her husband says she's already out on a call.' He stopped as Pauline gave another wail. 'But he said he knew where she was and he'd get a message to her.' Going into their bedroom he raised his voice. 'Her husband said not to worry, with first babies it can take...' His voice trailed off when he pushed the bedding through the doorway. 'A while...' It was as though he thought Pauline wouldn't hear even though she was only inches from me.

'Oh really? Bloody really.' She glared round at him. 'What the fuck would he know?'

I wasn't sure who she meant but Sam retreated instantly.

'Brian, help me to get her onto the duvet. Pauline, you need to help us.' I shoved the pillows in front of her hands. 'If you're more comfortable on your knees you need to rest your arms on the pillows.'

One hand at a time, she dragged the pillows until they were almost under her chest. The she lowered her head and spread out her arms on them. Between us we arranged the duvet under her.

'That's better,' I said at the same time she started to yell.

'Breathe. Breathe.' I grabbed a towel off the rail and dabbed the sweat off her face.

She lifted her head. 'I need to lie on my back.'

'Okay.'

Brian helped her to lie down and knelt alongside her holding her hand.

She pushed him away. 'Fuck off!'

The front of her nightdress was wet through. She was shivering. I grabbed a couple of bath towels from the shelf in the airing cupboard and covered her as best I could before sitting back against the bath.

For a moment or two none of us spoke. A dog outside began to howl, followed by another. I heard the engine of a car on the road and locked eyes with Pauline. The midwife? The car passed the house. I saw the hope fade in her eyes in the same way I imagined it did in mine.

Pauline raised her legs and let her knees flop open. 'Sorry about the view.' Her voice was hoarse but she managed a faint smile.

Relieved she could joke, I waved a casual hand and answered in kind. 'No worries, seen one, seen them all.'

She gave a breathy laugh. It was a joke we'd shared when we'd gone to one of her workmate's hen party and there'd been a male stripper.

'I'm sorry, sweetheart...' Brian laid his face next to hers.

She twisted away from him. 'Fuck off.'

'If I'd known it was going to be like this...' He was almost crying.

She glared at him. 'Don't be so sodding stupid, I—' her next words turned into a scream. She arched her back.

A gush of brownish liquid flowed from her. I saw her body open. I scrambled towards her.

'I don't think this baby is going to wait any longer.' I looked closer. 'I think I...' my heart was pounding. 'I can see the head, Pauline.' I looked up at her, wiping my eyes with the heel of my hand. 'I can see the head.'

She was panting, her mouth screwed tight.

'I can – I can see the head.' I felt dizzy. 'Oh god...' Pull yourself together, I told myself.

She stared at me between her knees. 'I want to push.'

'I think you can...'

She lifted her buttocks off the duvet and grunted. Blood and liquid flowed as the baby's head slid out of her and stopped. I put my hands under it and Pauline arched again.

The baby, covered in white slime and blood, fell into my hands. So tiny. So warm.

All three of us were crying. Pauline flopped back. Brian leaned over her and kissed her.

'What? Is it okay? What...'

'A girl. A little girl.' But under all the slime and blood, she was blue. I didn't think; I opened my dressing gown and held her to me, blowing on her face, hoping the baby would take in the air. The twisted greyish umbilical cord trailed between her and Pauline. The baby started to cry, a thin warbling cry. I felt the movement of her hands and legs through my nightdress. I gulped, laughed in relief.

'Let me have her.' Pauline held out her arms, her face anxious.

'Sorry.' But my reluctance slowed my actions. I held the baby to my neck for another second.

Brian moved the towels. Pauline took her and placed her on her breast. He covered them up again. I couldn't see the child.

And then chaos. I heard the doorbell, Sam pounding up the stairs. 'The midwife's here.' Heard his gasp when he saw what had happened. I looked up to him. He lifted me up and held me close. I was sobbing.

For the second time in my life I had fallen in love with a baby.

Chapter Eighty-Three

2002: Today: 5.20 p.m.

'Get out! Get out!' I'm yelling at him, dragging on his arm. The fury swirling around in me makes me shake. I don't know how I find the strength to do it but I heave him down the stairs and out of the door before I even realise what I've done. I sit down on the kitchen floor. No more – no more.

'Rose?'

But I'm on my own.

1981

They kept Pauline in the hospital for a week whilst the baby was in the special care unit. When they came home I was so excited.

Pauline wasn't; she was reluctant to touch her and cried a lot. Sometimes she refused to get out of bed.

'He says it's post-natal depression. He's given her tablets, says she should rest,' Brian said one morning, coming back into the kitchen after seeing the doctor out.

'Will you stay home with her?' I asked.

'She says not to. I don't know what to do.'

'We can't let the town council down, it's a good contract and we've only just signed.' Sam frowned. 'Alteration and painting work on the new offices, Irene.'

'No worries. I'll help all I can.' I was only too happy to.

Holding the baby in my arms, feeling the lightness of her tiny body through the layers of blankets, breathing in the milky warmth of her skin reminded me of the times I'd held Rose. The first time I had that thought was a jolt; I studied the baby's face. No slant of eyes, no sign that this child was like my sister. It wouldn't have mattered, I was besotted.

I was in heaven. Pauline didn't want to breastfeed so I made up all the bottles and fed the baby. I didn't even mind the night feeds. At first I struggled to get her to latch onto the teat of the bottle, touching her mouth with it, letting some of the milk drop onto her lips. But once she got the hang of it, she was away.

She was a quiet baby most of the time. If she cried with the wind I gave her a spoonful of Woodward's gripe water which always helped. Except for when it rained or was too cold, I took her out in her pram to make sure she had fresh air. Every evening I bathed her in the little white baby bath to make sure she didn't get nappy rash.

I knew Sam was worried that I was getting too attached to her, but I made sure Pauline looked after her for a few hours each day so I could get on with the housework and making meals. I tried to be very careful; I didn't want Pauline to feel I was taking over in those first few months.

Then, one day, shortly after a Christmas that had passed almost unnoticed, Pauline stopped dissolving into tears and took over with the baby. I can't say I didn't miss looking after her but I'm sure I didn't show it. Most of the time. But Pauline and me were good friends and she understood. And I still made the meals and kept the house tidy.

They'd decided to call the baby Phoebe.

'We can't keep thinking of her as the baby,' Pauline'd said. 'She's going to be called Phoebe, after Brian's mum.' She smiled at him. 'She would have been a good grandmother.'

And perhaps they wouldn't be emigrating if both his parents were still alive. I couldn't stop the thought. But they'd died years before Sam knew him.

Like us, neither of them was religious, so they organised a naming day instead of a christening at an old mansion in its own grounds just outside town.

I hadn't known what to expect when we got inside but it was perfect.

Brian and Pauline had chosen Dusty Springfield singing 'The

Look of Love', to be playing when we walked in. There was a lot of clearing of throats and I don't think I was the only woman who had to blow her nose.

The room was large. The coving on the white walls and the pattern on the ornate ceiling was gilded in gold paint. It offset the red carpet and the red velvet-covered chairs which were arranged in a semicircle. The humanist celebrant, a woman in a navy dress and jacket and high-heeled red shoes was already there. She was standing in front of the large Victorian fireplace which had tiles on either side of the grate decorated with a red and yellow tulip pattern.

We sat down; there were around thirty of us, including Pauline's parents who'd travelled from Australia. The reason, I knew, why our friends were emigrating there.

'Welcome,' the celebrant said, smiling and balancing a folder over her arm. 'Welcome to Phoebe's naming day. My name is Laura. I'll be with you today to welcome Phoebe into the world and to welcome her into your family. But first ... Brian?' She beckoned to him. He handed Phoebe to Pauline and went to stand by her. On a small table, a tall taper candle stood in a brass holder. 'Brian will light the candle to acknowledge and remember those no longer with us. Today we are remembering his parents, his father, who was also called Brian, and his mother, Phoebe, who this little one is named after. The candle will remain lit throughout the ceremony.'

It took Brian a few moments to strike the match and light the candle. I saw his hand shaking. As the flame rose he paused, his back to us. When he turned to walk back to his chair his eyes were red but he was smiling.

'What I will read next is a short piece written by Phoebe's mum, Pauline, and her best friend, Irene, who will be one of Phoebe's guardians.' She gave a small cough.

'Once upon a time, high up in the sky where the stars shone at night, there was a star in the sky that shone more brightly than the other stars. This was because it was not actually a star but a wish, a longing ... a child. A child called Phoebe who was looking closely at all the people in the world, all the people on all the islands and in all the lands of the whole wide world. She took a long time thinking about this, and the journey that life had for her, and then she chose the best parents of all the people on all the islands and in all the lands of the whole wide world. She chose Pauline and Brian...'

I have to admit, it was mostly me that had written it; because I did think our friends would make the best parents. And secretly I hoped there was also a bright star, a longing, a child who was also waiting for the right time to come to Sam and me.

Afterwards Brian gave a speech making us her guardians, despite the fact that we would be on the other side of the world.

'We have chosen Sam and Irene to be the special mentors in Phoebe's life even though we will be in different countries, because of the love they have shown to us as a family. We know they will nurture, love, and guide her through her life...' he turned to look at us, 'however far apart she and they are.'

Sam squeezed my hand and murmured, 'You're doing okay.' Even as we smiled at one another, then at Pauline and Brian, he knew how I felt because I knew he felt the same. Even as we promised that we would always be in touch with Phoebe, our hearts were breaking.

To disguise my sadness I gazed through the large windows. I could see beyond the garden of the large house to a field planted with trees.

At the end we all trooped out into the crisp March afternoon, to where a hole had been dug in the hard ground, ready for Phoebe's small oak tree. In turn we dropped spadefuls of soil around it and each of us read out our chosen wishes for her. Some people had poems they'd written, one or two said prayers. Then we gave them to Brian for him and Pauline to keep for when she was grown-up.

The day was full of friendship, laughter, good food and a feeling that we are all bigger than just ourselves.

In the evening we had a wonderful party at their house with a few friends and Pauline's parents.

'Phoebe.' Brian smiled, putting her into my arms after we'd all

259

made a toast to her. 'You two will be her best auntie and uncle: her guardians.'

Holding her to me, feeling the fullness of her little arms through the sleeves of her white cotton dress and smelling the Johnson's lotion on her skin, brought a hard lump to my throat. Sam putting his arm around my waist and whispering, 'You okay, love?' was the final straw and I burst into tears.

I was going to lose Phoebe. Just as I'd lost Rose.

Chapter Eighty-Four

2002: Today: 5.30 p.m.

The loud bass beat from next door stops.

No sound from upstairs

I make myself stand. I make myself climb the stairs.

1982

'So we're putting the house back on the market and we've arranged everything. We'll be leaving on the tenth of May.'

Pauline's words dropped into a pool of silence. The ripples spread through the air around us in the restaurant. Echoed.

I took a sip of my wine, forced my lips into a smile.

'We wanted to be sure everything was set up before we told you. We thought it only fair.'

I nodded. 'We knew it was on the cards, didn't we, Sam?' My laugh sounded false even to myself. 'We couldn't be your lodgers forever.' In the end my voice was a squeak.

'Well, this deserves a bit of celebration.' Sam spoke in a too-hearty, too-loud voice. 'We'll have to have a leaving party for you at the Anchor.' Under the table he squeezed my leg. 'Pull all the stops out, eh, Irene?'

I nodded again, not trusting myself to speak. I pushed at the steak on my plate, concentrating on cutting it into small pieces.

'The thing is...' Brian stopped. 'The thing is – we can't guarantee the house will be sold by that date. And I'm contracted to start my new job at the end of May. We can't afford not to go, or I could lose it.'

'Good grief, mate, no,' Sam said. 'So you want us to move out so you can rent it?'

'No.'

'No!'

They spoke together.

'We have a favour to ask you.' Brian put his knife and fork down. 'We'd like you to stay on and sort it all out, like. Rent free,' he added, hastily. 'We've arranged to carry on paying the mortgage until it's all settled. The solicitor says we can all go in and get it settled legal-wise until we find a buyer...'

'And you'd trust us to do that?' Sam turned to me and grabbed hold of my hand. 'We can do that, can't we, Irene?'

We could; we'd moved further up the council list and there was a possibility of getting a place of our own in the near future.

But I'd be losing Phoebe.

'Irene?' Pauline took hold of my other hand, stopping my movements with the knife. 'You all right?' Her eyes were anxious.

'Of course.' I was being selfish. 'It's just that I've really enjoyed the last year.'

'Oh, don't set me off as well...' She pulled a handkerchief from the sleeve of her jumper.

We both laughed and snivelled at the same time.

'What they like, eh, mate?' Brian grinned at Sam, but I could tell they were both as upset as us.

'You could always visit us.' Pauline wiped her eyes and dabbed at her nose.

'You never know, you might decide to come out to live in Oz some time,' Brian added

We all knew that wasn't possible. At least not in the near future.

So, suddenly, the make-believe vanished. My arms would be empty again. Phoebe wasn't my child, she didn't belong to Sam and me; we weren't going to be the ones to watch her grow into a young woman.

We had a big leaving party for them at the Anchor and raised a glass to their new life.

When we went back to that empty house I stood in the hall, my arms held stiffly by my side and howled, pressing myself into Sam's body, trying to shut out the pain, the loss. And failing.

Afterwards, when my husband had made love to me and was stroking my hair from my tear-stained face, I buried my head into that familiar hollow between his neck and shoulder. 'I want a baby, Sam. I want a baby of our own.'

'I know.' His voice rumbled low in my ear. 'I know, love.'

Chapter Eighty-Five

2002: Today: 5.30 p.m.

Her bedroom's cold. The fan heater's not on. I don't remember switching it off.

'I need help, Rose,' I whisper. 'I need help.' I'm trying to think what I'm supposed to be doing but I can't. I press the pads of my fingers hard over my eyes. So hard it hurts. But I don't stop.

1983

Eventually, the house was sold. We handed over the keys to the new owners, and went to sign the papers on our friends' behalf at the solicitors. Did what we'd promised. And, at last, everything was falling into place; there was a house waiting for us on a new council estate on the Barraclough site where Nanna's flat had been.

After Pauline and Brian had left, I'd found a job in a local grocery shop and gone back to volunteering at Clough Fields.

The first day I knocked on the door and walked into my allotted classroom it was like I'd never been away. A few of the children who'd been in the class before were still there, including Karen, the little girl I'd sat next to before. She jumped up from her chair and ran towards me to give me a huge hug, looking up at me. Her lovely eyes with the upward slant and laughter lines at the corners as she smiled, her mass of dark hair, reminded me so much of Rose.

'My, Karen, you've grown so much.'

'You have grown so much,' she said.

I laughed, hugged her. 'How old are you now?'

She turned to look at the teacher who said, 'You're twelve, Karen.'

'I am twelve,' Karen told me. 'How old are you now, Miss?'

'Oh, I'm ancient.' I laughed again.

'Funny age.' She clapped her hands. 'How old is... ash ... un...' she halted, stumbling over the word.

'Very old.' I glanced at the teacher. Not Mrs Taylor but a small plump young woman with red cheeks and a wide smile. Miss Ellery, the new head teacher, Greg Allison, had told me. 'Sorry to disrupt the class, Miss Ellery.'

'Not at all Mrs Hargreaves. We knew you'd be here today. Welcome back. Some of the other teachers have told me so much about you. I am so glad you're joining us again.' She waved to the chair at the end of her desk. 'Please, sit here. We're just recording our weekly news on the cassette recorder.' She picked a cassette off the desk, slotted it into the tape compartment and closed it. 'Karen, would you like to go back to your chair, please?'

'Yes.' Karen went to her chair. But, instead of sitting on it she dragged it, with much scraping and huffing and puffing, to bring it next to me.

I looked at Miss Ellery. She smiled, put her head to one side, nodded slightly.

'Okay,' she said. 'You go first, Karen. Would you like to tell the class your news today?' She pressed the play and record buttons and slid the recorder towards the end of the table closer to Karen.

'Yes.' Karen put one hand on my shoulder and leant across me to put the other on the edge of the table to get nearer to the recorder.

'I have news,' she said. 'Today my friend came back to school...'

Chapter Eighty-Six

2002: Today: 5.35 p.m.

My eyes burn. I pull my hands away. Blink. Screw up my face. Blink.

Can't stay here like this. Must do something. When I speak my voice is loud in my head.

'Time for bed, Mother.'

She struggles when I try to lift her from the chair and pinches the loose skin on my arm. It hurts.

Sod it.

I let go of her, straighten up. I could just leave her there. What difference would it make?

1983

'Ready?' Sam pushed the key into the Yale lock. I put my hand on his and we turned it together

Our new house. And it was in Denholme.

It was the second lovely thing that had happened that week. Sam had a surprise of his own...

'I didn't even know this place was here.' I stared around the busy little café and through the arch to where the art studio was.

'Thought you'd like it – only opened Saturday.' Sam smiled, stretching his arm across the table and holding my hand. His thumb smoothed the narrow gold band on the third finger. 'What do you think about the décor?'

Ah, I guessed why he wanted to know; this was where he'd been working for the last month.

'Mmm.' I studied the pale cream walls, the stone floor tiles and the delicate gold filigree on the coving, the landscape paintings and the long mirrors on either side of the archway which helped to make the small room seem longer. 'Mmm?' Finger tapping my chin, I made him wait, tipping my head from side to side. The gold tracery on the coving was a speciality of Sam's; I always marvelled how a man which such large hands could paint something so lovely. 'Well,' I drew the word out, 'I do like the mirrors and the pictures.'

'Huh!' He sat back in feigned indignation and I laughed.

'It's smashing, love,' I said. 'I see they let you experiment with your drawings.'

'Let me?' He raised his eyebrows. 'They positively begged me to do it, said it added a touch of class.'

'And so it does, Sam, you're very clever.' Oh, I was proud of my husband, no ordinary decorator was he. He could turn any old dump into a palace.

The waitress appeared with the coffees and the biggest chocolate éclairs I'd ever seen. Nostalgia swept over me. 'Rose's favourite,' I whispered.

Sam had sat back to let the young woman take the things from her tray and place them in front of us. Now he leant forward again to hold my arm, worry darkening his eyes. 'You don't mind...'

'You remembered.'

'I did. She'd be twenty now.'

It was impossible to think of Rose as a grown woman. I even wondered if she would have reached this age, so many Down's syndrome children didn't. I thought for a moment about Rose's friend from school. Martin Althorpe, Barbara's son. He'd died of a heart attack a year ago.

'It's a lovely gesture, Sam.' I looked at him, saw the tension clear from his face.

'There's something else,' he said. 'Happy birthday.' He took a small blue velvet box from his jacket pocket and flipped open the lid. 'I thought the sapphire matched your eyes.' The stone, surrounded by small diamonds shone in the overhead lights. 'I think it's the right size.' He took the ring from the box and took hold of my finger. For once I didn't care that my hands were on show; I could even say that in Sam's hand mine looked positively dainty. As he pushed the ring close to my wedding band there was a clapping. I glanced around, a few people at the other tables and a group of the staff by the café kitchen door were watching. Just then the waitress appeared with a bottle of sparkling wine.

'Sorry it's only elderflower, Mrs Hargreaves,' a woman called from behind the counter. 'We don't have a licence. But we wanted to join in with the celebrations. Sam told us what he was going to do.'

'Better late than never.' Sam couldn't keep the grin off his face. 'I always promised you an engagement ring.'

'And it's beautiful.'

We kissed to another round of applause and a wolf whistle from the chef, leaning on the counter of the hatch from the kitchen.

I thought I was the luckiest woman in the world, to have Sam for my husband.

Chapter Eighty-Seven

2002: Today: 5.40 p.m.

No, she has to be in bed.

I go around the back of the chair and push, trying to slide it closer. She yelps, tries to turn, tips her head back, side to side, fighting to see what's happening. Then she plants her feet on the carpet and stiffens.

1983

From the front window I thought I could see where Nanna's flat used to be. But it was only guesswork I knew; the site had been cleared of everything, including the big sycamore tree that used to be on the corner of her street.

There was a raised banking of grassed land across from us and a long row of houses above that. From what I could tell they were all much the same: semis with matching front doors (ours was blue), large living room windows, two bedroom windows upstairs, all with white frames and red-tiled roofs. And, best of all we had small gardens, which were fenced, both at the back and at the front.

It would be our first Christmas in our own home.

We spent that first day cleaning the place from top to bottom, Sam polishing all the windows until they gleamed, and me mopping and hoovering. We had a small kitchen table and two chairs, a settee, a radio and a television, both rented from Rumbelows, and the bed. No carpets yet; we'd run out of money. It didn't matter.

That evening we lit the fire in the living room and collapsed.

'Think you'll like it here, love?' Sam slung his arm over my shoulders and rested his head on mine.

'Mmm.' I stared at the flames. 'Our first fire in our own fireplace,' I said, admiring the cream and brown patterned tiles and the photos on the mantelpiece: one of Rose in her school uniform, one of Sam's dad and the one of my family where Nanna had said Mum looked as though she was chewing a wasp. Our wedding photo was in pride of place on top of the television. 'I think we'll both like it here.' I looked down to our clasped hands. 'In fact, I think we'll love it, and so will our children – eventually.' For the first time in a long time I felt settled.

'Children, eh?' Sam nuzzled my neck. 'Well, Mrs Hargreaves, 'appen we'd better crack on with that.' He stood, lifted me into his arms and carried me towards the stairs.

Where he stopped.

'Now then, we have two choices...' He looked up towards the landing. 'I can either carry you all the way and probably do my back in and put paid to any christening of that bed. Or...' He stood me on my feet. 'I could chase you up those stairs and you could have your wicked way with me.'

We'd only had the one night there when the doorbell rang. It took me a few minutes to recognise the woman standing on the doorstep. Mrs Tattersall. The neighbour who lived opposite Mum.

'Can I come in, pet?'

'Yes. Yes, of course. 'I opened the door wider and stood back to let her pass me 'What is it? What's wrong? Is it Mum?'

'It is lass.'

'Is she okay? How did you find us?'

'Your mother said she thought you were moving onto this new estate the other day, so I took a chance.'

I'd told Mum we had got this house; what did Mrs Tattersall mean, "she thought"? An uneasy feeling stirred inside me.

The woman took off her black woollen hat and ruffled her hair. 'Always make my head itch, these things.' I waited while she unravelled her scarf and undid the top buttons of her coat. 'Mind if I sit? I'm that knackered and this cold weather always takes my breath away.'

'Yes. Do.' I ushered her towards the settee and sat next to her.

'I should take my boots off, those roads are caked in mud.'

'It doesn't matter.' I gestured towards the bare floorboards, stifling my impatience. 'And they won't tarmac or put street lamps in until the estate's finished. 'I'm surprised you found us, there are no names on any of the avenues.'

'I just asked at the houses where folk were. Asked if a young couple had moved in over the last day or two. Next door but one pointed me in your direction and—'

'Mother?' Knowing how she could go on for ages, I interrupted the woman. 'What's the matter with her?'

268

'What's up?' Sam had a screwdriver and plug in his hand; he was connecting the new cooker the Council had provided.

'It's Mother, Sam. Mrs Tattersall? Across the road from Mother's?'

'I – we – the other neighbours thought you should know she seems to be struggling. She's looking... The house is looking a bit...' She fixed her mouth into a thin line, frowning. 'I'm not sure how I should say this, Irene...'

'Just say it.' Sam came further into the room. 'Just say what you've come to say, Mrs Tattersall.'

She looked a bit affronted; I had to admit he did sound as impatient as I felt. She straightened her back and looked across towards him.

'Quite frankly, the state of her house is bad enough from the outside, with the guttering broken and the paintwork on the window frames and front door badly needing doing...'

I didn't know whether to feel indignant because of the woman's inference that it was my fault, or ashamed I hadn't even noticed the few times I'd been on Grove Street.

'You said "She's looking..." Mrs Tattersall. What did you mean?'

She shifted towards the edge of the settee and twisted to face me more fully. 'She's let herself go, Irene. She used to be such a smart woman...' I wondered what that really meant; what was behind those words. There had always been a lot of curtain twitching on that street.

'And?' I prompted.

'She's struggling, we can all see that. Been struggling a while but she denied it, told us to keep our nebs out. But this morning I got her to admit she's not coping on her own...' There it was, that first twinge of alarm. Mrs Tattersall drew in a long breath to rush out the next words. 'She asked me to come and see you, to ask if you'd go to see her.'

Chapter Eighty-Eight

2002: Today: 5.40 p.m.

I grab both sides of the back of the chair and pull, twisting it around. I've got my eyes closed so I can't see her. I don't want to see her face, the bewilderment. The fear.

'It's your own fault.' I'm not sure if I say the words aloud.

She holds on to the arms of the chair as, slowly but surely, I'm dragging it nearer to the bed.

She has to be in bed.

1983

We stood in front of the door on Grove Street, the rain drumming on the umbrella we huddled under, and splashing down from the broken gutters. The backs of my legs were being splattered with dirt from the pavement, water ran into my shoes, my stockings stuck to me.

'We don't have to do this,' Sam said, pulling the collar of his jacket further up around his neck. 'The state of the paintwork,' he gestured with the umbrella towards the door where the wood could be seen in places, 'is not your responsibility.'

'I need to see what's going on. It'll be okay, I promise.'

He moved his head closer to mine. 'Are you okay? You're a bit pale.'

'I'm fine.' I wasn't. I lifted the doorknocker; the brass was dull, pitted.

When I heard the shuffle of footsteps, the fumbling of the catch, I straightened my shoulders but I was trembling inside.

'I didn't think you would come...' my mother said, peering around the half-open door.

A long note of silence passed between us; I kept eye contact with her.

'So, are you going to let us in?' Sam lowered the umbrella and shook the rain off to the side of him. He ushered me in front of him.

My mother pushed open the door to the gloomy front room. The chill of the wet November afternoon seemed to have followed us in.

'Why haven't you got the fire lit?' I switched the ceiling light on.

She shrugged in answer to my question. I glanced around the room. Dust was thick on every surface I could see, the net curtains were grey, the carpet covered in crumbs.

'And the cleaning of the place? The hoovering?' I balanced on the edge of the settee, careful to keep my hands away from the upholstery. Sam stood at the back of the room. 'What's happened, Mother?'

'Something wrong with the electrics.'

'So why not get someone in? Or why not ask Sam to have a look at it?'

She didn't answer.

'I'll look now.' As though he couldn't wait to get out of the room, Sam left. I heard him rummaging and cursing under the stairs.

'I need to go for a pee,' I said. I lied; I'd felt a strange need to go upstairs as soon as I'd walked through the front door. 'I'll be back in a minute.'

I ran up the stairs. On the landing I stopped. She was here. 'Rose?' I slipped into the bedroom that Rose and me had shared. There was a sadness in the room. 'Rose?'

I sat on her bed stroking the uncovered duvet. I thought I could smell the aroma of Johnson's baby lotion.

'Hello, love,' I whispered, and closed my eyes. 'I'm here.' On the back of the lids I saw an image of her. Not the last image I had; not that memory, but one of the times I'd watched her running and singing one of her little wordless songs. It made me smile even as the sorrow in the room filled the whole of me. I sensed a gentle touch on my cheek. And thought I heard a sigh. 'It'll be all right. I promise,' I whispered.

271

I brushed away the tear that trickled off my chin and stood, ready to face whatever it was my mother wanted.

When I got downstairs Sam was still bumping and banging around under the stairs.

'What's wrong with the wiring, love?'

'What's right with it, you mean. It's a bloody maze of odd wires. And someone's been messing around with the sodding fuses. I'll need to contact one of the sparkys from work to look at it.' His head emerged from the cupboard, a worried frown between his eyebrows. 'You ready to leave, Irene? Before she drags us into helping her? You know we've got nowt to spare cash-wise.'

'Give us a minute or two?'

When I went into the living room my mother was crying.

'I need help, Irene. I won't go to your dad, so I'm asking you.'

'Asking me what?'

She flung her arms out, taking in the room. 'Look at the place, it's falling down around my ears. I can't look after it.'

And then I knew what she was going to ask next.

'I can't afford to live here on my own anymore. Will you come back? Will you come to live here?'

'Not in a month of bloody Sundays.' Sam appeared in the doorway, his arms folded. 'Irene?' When I didn't answer he moved out into the hall.

'Sam, wait. Please.'

He came to lean on the doorframe.

I gazed out of the window to the flowering cherry tree on the pavement outside. The street lamp lit the bare branches bowing under the torrent of rain. 'How have things got to this stage, Mother?'

'I've left my job.'

'I heard you'd been sacked for helping yourself to stuff you shouldn't have.' The chap she'd had the affair with had long since moved onto a bigger branch, together with his wife and kids, so she'd had no one to cover up for her. But I stopped myself from saying that.

She sniffed. Her mouth pursed but said nothing.

'We can't come and live with you, you know that. It just wouldn't work. And we've only just moved into our own home.' And yet... I closed my eyes for a moment, tilted my head. Listened. Rose?

The harshness of her scorn snapped my eyes open.

'Rented. A rented council house.'

Sam moved to the front door. I could see him from the living room; he stood, his hand on the lock. His shoulders were set and I knew what an effort it was for him to stay there.

'But it's ours. A home we've waited a long time for.'

Did she hear the hesitation in my voice? Because the next thing she said was, 'This is your home.' She pulled her thick, grey cardigan tighter around her, folding her arms over it. She looked from me to Sam.

'Was. Once. It's years since you made me feel welcome in it.'

Her sniff was one she didn't use very often: long and drawn out with a slight nod. 'I know. And I'm sorry.'

'I never thought I'd hear that word coming from you, Mother.'

She blinked, almost smiled, made a dismissive one-shoulder shrug. 'Yes, well...' She bit her lip, gave Sam a sideways glance. 'It could be yours – this house. We could be joint owners? Put your names on the deeds?'

'We've not got money to buy into the place.'

'I wouldn't want money, there's no mortgage on it.'

Thanks to Dad, I thought. 'So what would you want in return?' I met her gaze.

'Irene. Come on, love.' Sam was staring at me. 'You're not seriously thinking...'

'Wait.' I shook my head at him. 'You really mean it, don't you, Mother?'

'Yes, I do. But,' she raised her chin, 'I won't beg. I'm just offering.'

Sam gave a short laugh. 'And what will you do when we say—'

I interrupted him. 'Or if...?' I looked over to him. 'If we say yes?' He was staring at me in disbelief. 'You'd put us on the deeds?'

'Of course. With me,' she added hastily. 'As joint tenants. My solicitor—'

'Your solicitor?' I never knew she had such a thing.

'Yes. My solicitor says it can be done.'

Not as confused as Mrs Tattersall led us to believe, then. 'So, Mother, I'll ask again. What would you want in return?'

'Well, that's obvious, isn't it? The house needs doing up—'

'Or knocking down.'

I heard Sam's comment; he sounded so angry.

'We'll need to talk it over—'

'Irene!'

'But I'm not promising.'

'Thank you.' She actually looked grateful. 'I'd help all I could. You and I could do things together, Irene.'

'Well, that would be a change.' It had been years since that happened. Before Rose. The thought was there unbidden, together with the image that came with it. Could I really trust my mother? Then I remembered that small sigh when I was upstairs.

'Just as a matter of interest, what will you do if we don't say yes?' Sam's jaw was jutted out, his face stubborn. 'What else have you thought to do with the house?'

'I'd sell.'

That decided me.

Sam tipped his head to one side, stared at me, eyebrows raised.

'It's madness, Irene. It would never work. I can't credit you're even considering it.' He looked a different man than the one I'd woken up with that morning, lines of irritation around his mouth.

'I'm sorry.' I couldn't meet his eyes. I rested my elbows on my knee, my chin on my palms. 'It would mean we would have our own home—'

'We have our own home here.' Sam waved his hand around.

'Rented. Belonging to the Council. Not really our home—' I couldn't believe I was saying that. I'd been so excited when we'd heard we'd been allocated this house.

'It *is*. It's what we've wanted for so long, waited for... Somewhere that's ours, where there's just the two of us when we close the front door.'

But not where Rose is.

If my mother does sell the house, Rose will be there with strangers. I can't let that happen. 'I am sorry,' I repeated.

'We'd need to spend a fortune on it. I'd,' he pointed to his chest, 'I'd have to work on it in whatever spare time I'd have off work.'

'But there'd be a lot I could do. And Mum would chip in I'm sure—'

'I didn't get that impression.'

'She would, you heard her. She said she would.'

I saw him shake his head. 'We've waited years to get a place of our own,' he said again. 'Of our own,' he emphasised. 'And now you want to go back to live with your mother?'

'But with you as well—'

'Do you really want *me* to live with your mother? You seem to forget I've known her – known what she's like – all my life. You must be mad, love.'

He called me love. Did that mean he was softening to the idea? Rain slid along the living room window. I crossed the room to draw the new orange curtains I'd only sewn and fitted a day ago. I was so nervous I wasn't sure my legs would keep me upright, so I sat on the windowsill.

How could I persuade him, how could I tell him how important it was for us, for me, to go back to Grove Street?

I couldn't let Mum sell the house. Not with Rose there, I couldn't.

Chapter Eighty-Nine

2002: Today: 5.50 p.m.

'Right. Let's get you into bed.' I'm breathing hard and my heart is thumping by the time we're next to the bed. I go to the front of the chair. 'How are we going to do this, Mother?'

She's glowering at me, her nostrils are flaring in short sharp bursts of breath and her mouth pursed. Nanna's voice echoes in my head: "lips like a cat's arse."

1983

'It'll cost a fortune to do up. And take months.' Sam opened the back door and stood on the step, facing away from me. A cold slice of air filled the kitchen. I hunched over the table, grasping the mug of now tepid tea. I knew I'd disappointed him. It had taken until now to get our own home, and he didn't understand why I was even considering going back to live on Grove Street.

'Come in and sit down, Sam. Please.' He'd said "it will", not "it would". I watched him close the door, saw the uncertainty in his face, even in his movements: the way he smoothed his hand over his hair, slowly unbuttoned his overalls, and let his arms drop to his sides when he sat at the table.

'I can't see any advantage in going to live there—' he said.

'It would be ours, Sam—'

'And hers. Your mother will be there – all the time...'

A headache coiled at the back of my neck; we'd been talking for hours. In fact we'd talked about nothing else all week.

'We could make a list,' I said. 'Reasons to stay here, reasons to move there?'

'The biggest reason for both lists would start with your mother. Yes. No.'

'I know. But we could sort that. We could have either the front room or the kitchen as our own—'

'Which brings us to another problem – mealtimes. I wouldn't want to come home from work every day to face your mother across the table.'

'We could have different times to eat. Mother's had her main meal at lunchtime for as long as I can remember. We'll both be out.' I had a sudden idea. 'We could even make one of the bedrooms into our living room.'

'What about when we have children? A family?'

'We can cross that bridge when we come to it.'

'You're not going to let this go, are you, Irene?'

'I just think it's too good a chance to miss, owning our own home. We wouldn't have to worry about money, about finding the rent when you have no work on—'

'So that's it? You don't think I earn enough?'

I'd made a mistake; I saw the anger tighten his jaw.

'I'm sorry, Sam, I didn't mean it like that. I meant to say it would take the pressure off you to always be looking for the next job, the next contract...'

He stood, pushed back the chair. 'I don't want any tea. I think I'll have an early night.'

I tried to catch hold of his hand but he pulled it away. 'Sam. Please...' He didn't say a word as he stalked out.

Fear hollowed out my stomach, churned inside me. I thought I was going to vomit. We didn't fall out, Sam and me. Ever. What had I done? What had I been thinking? I should tell him I'd changed my mind. It didn't matter; we could stay here. I should go to him right away. I half-rose, sank back on the chair. I'd wait until morning; give him chance to cool down.

'I'm willing to give it a go, Irene. Though what we'll do if it doesn't work out...'

Sam had evidently been sleeping in the tee shirt and underpants he'd worn yesterday, from the crumpled and creased state of them. Or not sleeping; he looked exhausted, dark shadows beneath red-rimmed eyes.

'I shouldn't have tried to push you into agreeing, Sam. I'm sorry. It's a stupid idea—'

'No.' He shook his head. 'I've thought about it all night—'

'I've been stupid.'

'No you haven't. I understand and we'll give it a go.'

'But what if it doesn't work? What if we can't stand it there?'

'Dad always said it's the things you don't do that you regret. It's the chance to have our own house, Irene.'

'With my mother as the booby prize.'

He laughed. 'Well yes, there is that.' He crossed the kitchen, took hold of me. 'I hated falling out with you, love. It's not us, is it?'

'No, it's not.' I leant into him. 'I'm sorry,' I said again. 'Are you sure? We could just forget the whole thing. Tell her no.'

'Hush.' He stroked my hair, rested his palm on my neck. It soothed me, the feel of his hand on my skin. 'I understand, love. You don't want the house where Rose lived to be owned by anyone else. That's it, isn't it?'

'Yes. Yes, it is, Sam.' How could I have thought he wouldn't understand? But I couldn't tell him I felt she was still there somehow. 'I'll make it work, Sam, I promise. And we'll own a share of the house. We'll have our name on the deeds.'

Chapter Ninety

2002: Today: 6.00 p.m.

Silence hangs between us.

She's in bed.

I haven't changed her pad. The seat of the armchair has a wet patch. I should change her pad.

I pick up the duvet and spread it over her. I don't look at her face before I turn and walk away.

PART TWO

Chapter Ninety-One 1990

'What did he say?' Sam helped me out of my coat.

I was beginning to dread the look of expectation and anxiety every time I came back from the doctors. 'Same as before. Stop getting stressed about it.' As though I could, I thought.

'But it's been years.'

'I know.'

The day we'd got the new council house we'd made a big ceremony of dropping my contraceptive pills one by one down the loo of the B&B we'd stayed at.

I could see Mum sitting at the kitchen table reading one of her women's magazines. 'On second thoughts, let's go for a walk. It's lovely out.'

We stood on the pavement, unable to make up our minds which way to go. 'The park?' Sam suggested.

'No.' It would be full of mothers pushing prams, chatting about their kids, making the most of a Monday afternoon before their husbands came home wanting their teas. 'Not the park.' I turned in the opposite direction. 'How about the canal?'

We held hands and walked in silence for a while.

'You should be working,' I said at last.

'Best thing about being self-employed.' Sam bent down and kissed my cheek. 'Giving yourself time off.'

The canal path was dry for once but the earth was rutted with the shapes of past puddles. 'Watch your step.' I could hear the slight impatience in Sam's voice below the concerned words. He was waiting for me to tell him everything the doctor had said. But there was no more to be said.

'I'm fine.' There was the same edgy tone in my voice. I breathed in. 'Just smell those bluebells.' I looked across the water to the wood on the far side. The haze of blue under the trees, moving slowly in lines with the slight breeze, reminded me of the sea. 'Lovely.'

'Didn't he suggest we had more tests of some sort?'

'Yes.'

The canal was murky. Long strands of brown weeds drifted under the surface. The grass on the banking trailed down, the tips of the blades rotting in the water.

'Can I ask you something?' Sam stopped. He put his arms around me but I could feel the tension in him. 'You did come off the pill, didn't you?'

I leant back to look into his face. 'What do you mean? I haven't been on them since we moved. You were there when we got rid of them.'

'I know. But it's just – if you'd gone back on them I'd understand. With the way things are – with living with your mother and everything.'

He didn't say it, but I knew he thought we'd made a rod for our own backs ploughing all our money into Grove Street, leaving little to save. Sam had made the place into a little palace for us and I was grateful. Many times, when I was in the house alone, I talked to Rose. I wouldn't be able to do that anywhere else. And I knew she understood my heartbreak every month when I realised there would again be no child for Sam and me.

The house was now worth far more than when we first bought into it. I knew Sam thought we should sell; the money raised would be just enough for both Mother and us to each buy one of the starter homes on the new site off Travis Road. But each time Sam mentioned it, I changed the subject; I couldn't leave Rose. Even if living with my mother was a nightmare.

Before I spoke again I gazed at the rippling water in the canal. The surface drifted one way, then another with the slight breeze that had risen.

I thought back to the conversation I'd had with her a few months after we'd moved into Grove Street...

'Power of what?' Mother stood next to me with the tea towel in one hand and a dinner plate in the other.' You want to have what?'

'Power of attorney.' I swished my hand around in the soapy water, feeling for the last of the cutlery. 'It's just a form the solicitor – your solicitor, if you like – can draw up.' I waited, choosing my words carefully. 'It's like insurance, you know. So that later – probably not for a long time – years – if something happens and you don't want to be bothered...' I put two forks onto the draining board and pulled the plug in the sink. 'Or can't look after things money-wise – I can do it for you.'

'My money? This house, kind of thing?' She sniffed, a quivering, long, drawn in breath.

'Yes.' I brushed the soapsuds from both arms, looked around for a hand towel. I could sense her temper rising

'Well, that's not going to happen, is it? Me not able to look after my own stuff?'

I took the towel from the worktop and dried my hands. 'It might—'

'Let me stop you there, Irene.' She dumped the tea towel onto the back of one of the chairs without finishing drying the dinner plate in her hand. 'Whatever it's called, I'm signing no form so you can get your hands on any money of mine. And I'm not daft. The day after we sorted out the joint ownership of this place with my solicitor, I had him make up an agreement that he'd look after my affairs. And that includes not selling the house while I'm still alive. As a joint owner, I'll never agree to it. I'll block any attempt you and him...' She jerked her head towards Sam who was setting up his workbench outside with the tins and brushes he'd need to paint the new bedroom window frames. 'Any attempt you and him make to sell my roof over my head.' And with that she spun around and stomped off leaving me to dry the rest of the pots.

I remembered listening to her banging up the stairs to her room, Sam waving at me from the back garden, me lifting my hand in acknowledgement and wondering how I was going to tell him what she'd just said. Knowing, in my desperation to stay with Rose, I'd led us straight into a trap.

Now I cupped his face with my hands. 'I want a baby as much as you, Sam. It just hasn't happened yet.' I stressed my next words. 'I did not go back on the pill. I would never lie to you.' I kissed him. 'Come on, let's get back. Cheese and onion pie okay for tea?'

'Lovely.' But there was still worry in his voice.

'One day – when we have a whole brood of kids around us, we'll look back and laugh at all this mithering.' I tugged on his arm and we began to walk back. 'Like the doctor said, we need to stop worrying about it and it will happen.'

A duck emerged from the banking followed by three small ducklings.

'It'll be okay. This time next year – who knows, eh? You'll see. You'll make a great dad.'

And, if it was a girl she would be called Rose. I'd promised my Rose that.

Chapter Ninety- Two

2002: Today: 6.00 p.m.

The paracetamol have spilled onto the table at the side of the bed. I sit on the edge and pick up the glass. I put two of the tablets in my mouth. The water tastes stale but it doesn't matter.

I'll just rest for a few minutes.

I know it's time. Before Sam comes home; it's time.

1994

'As you know, all the tests we have done over the years have shown that there is physically nothing wrong with either of you. Sometimes this just happens, I'm afraid. For some reason, Mrs Hargreaves, you have been unable to conceive...' The doctor tipped his head to one side.

I felt as though I was a strange but interesting object in a specimen jar he was studying. Or in a bloody zoo.

'So? What now?'

He shrugged. 'I can't really suggest anything else. Except relax, see what happens...' He half-smiled.

I almost saw the voice bubble over his head, "and enjoy trying". I swore to myself that if he said it I would reach over and pull his red bulbous nose.

'What about IVF? Would we be eligible for IVF?'

He leant back until his chair was on the two back legs, and tapped his pen against his chin. 'As you may be aware we, this practice, became fund holders four years ago and since then we have needed to be careful with our budget. We are, indeed, able to purchase suitable care – er, procedures – for our patients. But I'm afraid at one of our meetings we, as a practice, decided that we would – er – could not – fund fertility treatments – IVF.' He leant forward, the chair bumped down on all four legs. 'Sorry, Mrs Hargreaves.'

I thought he didn't look in the least bit sorry. I glanced at Sam who'd been quiet the whole time we'd been sitting opposite Doctor King. He still didn't speak and I needed to swallow my bitter disappointment before I found my own voice.

'Couldn't you make exceptions? Would you – the practice – reconsider?'

'No.' The abruptness, and his next words shocked me. 'Have you thought of adopting?' He swivelled his chair from side to side, tapped his pen on his desk, 'I think you'd be ideal.' He looked from Sam to me a few times. 'Hmm – perhaps not adopting – how about fostering?' He sat forward, elbows now on his desk. 'You'd be ideal foster parents.'

I looked at Sam, couldn't make out what he was thinking. But the idea lit a spark in me.

'Sam?'

He turned slowly towards me, a mix of sadness and hope in his eyes. Now he did speak. 'Not adopting, Doctor King's right.' He shook his head. 'We could try fostering, though. But we wouldn't give up trying for a baby of our own, would we, Irene?'

'Of course not—'

'You'd be giving a home to a child.' The doctor began to rummage through some papers on a shelf next to his desk. 'Just think about it. I have some paperwork here about fostering. I can set up an interview for you...'

'We'll think about it,' I said, knowing Sam needed some time. 'We'll take all the information and we'll think about it.'

By fostering, we would be able to love and look after a child who needed us. Rose would be happy to hear children's laughter in her house.

But I knew we had to talk to my mother about it. After all, it would affect her as well.

'No, I don't want a child in the house. This is still my house.'

'Our house. The house belongs to the three of us, Mother.' And Rose.

She'd kept me waiting for ages while she stared out of the kitchen window, her back to me.

'Well?' I grew impatient. 'You know we've wanted a family for years. Even *you* can't have missed the fact that we've been having tests, seeing a specialist about why it's not happened yet.' The exasperation welled up inside me. 'You must have known that we were hoping to have a family when you were so keen to get us to buy a share of the house? What would you have done, Mother, if I had got pregnant?'

She didn't turn around when she spoke. 'How would you know what you'd get?' I knew what she was asking. I bit down on my lower lip, stopping the words coming out; I'd make her say them herself. 'What if you were offered a child like your sister. Like those you see in the school you go to?' Her voice sounded strange.

'You mean a Down's syndrome child? Why would that be a problem, Mother?'

The pause was even longer this time.

'Why is that a problem?' I pushed for her answer. 'Because you feel guilty?' I waited until the air almost vibrated between us. 'Is that it?'

'Yes!' She spun around. 'Yes! Yes! Yes! But not for what you're thinking.'

'What am I thinking, Mother? What?' The memory hung between us.

She was the first to break eye contact. 'Don't ask me, Irene.' She touched my arm when she passed me and went upstairs.

I didn't understand what she meant.

I lied to Sam; I told him I'd thought long and hard and decided against fostering. He didn't understand; he knew how much I longed to hold a child in my arms.

'Why? You've been so excited by the idea, and now you say you've changed your mind. Just like that?'

'I'm sorry. I've been going round and round in circles thinking about it, and I just don't think it's right for us at the moment.'

'Fostering? Just the fostering idea? Not, not having a child? So you still want one of our own?'

'Yes. Yes, of course.' It wouldn't happen, I knew that in my heart but I didn't say it. Just as I said nothing about my mother making sure that I remembered that the house was still part hers and she'd refused point blank to agreeing to my having power of attorney years ago.

She was very quiet for the rest of that week. I caught her looking at me sometimes as though she wanted to say something. But though I gave her every chance she stayed silent.

Chapter Ninety-Three

2002: Today: 6.15 p.m.

I don't open my eyes when I wake. I hear something, a scraping sound. My skin is crawling, my scalp tight. What was that?

'Sam?'

Silence.

1994

Something went wrong between Sam and me in the weeks following. I didn't know why. When I asked he said nothing was wrong; he was just busy in work, things on his mind about some contract. But, instead of talking about it as he usually did, he became impatient when I pushed to know more. He was distant, quiet. We made love less often. It's a time that we don't talk about.

I was still helping out at the school one day a week. I loved it there. There was another new head teacher, Mr Middleton. He often asked why I didn't go back to college; I was still young enough to have a career in teaching. I think what stopped me was that, if I had, then Sam would know, once and for all, that I'd given up on wanting a family. And, as I said, I felt there was something different, not right, in our marriage.

Besides my time at the special school I also worked part-time at a small grocer's shop on the Barraclough estate. And, although I knew that sometimes Sam regretted buying into the house because of my mother, I didn't; Grove Street was where I felt Rose was.

Chapter Ninety-Four

2002: Today: 6.15 p.m.

I roll onto my side and look around, my eyes settling on Rose's doll on the set of drawers. I'm sure she's moved. She's usually leaning against the glass vase but now she's fallen forwards, one arm across her chest. And her face is turned towards me. Painted blue eyes watching me.

'Caroline?' Fear trails up the back of my neck and over my scalp. 'Rose?'

1995

I knew something was going on with my mother. Sometimes she'd call me Rose instead of Irene. More and more she'd forget the name of things or why she'd gone into the kitchen for something. But I just put it down to her age. Which I suppose I shouldn't have done as she was only in her sixties. To be honest, I didn't take much notice. What did amuse me was that she started quoting some of Nanna's sayings, her favourite being, "old age doesn't come alone", whenever she forgot something. Which was increasingly more often.

More surprisingly she began to visit the neighbours, declaring them all old friends. As far back as I could remember she'd shunned them, calling them all gossips. She'd often come back to our house with gossip of her own, now.

Then, one day, it all came to a head.

I walked in from work to find Sam's mother sitting having a cup of tea at the kitchen table. In almost twenty years we'd seen neither hide nor hair of her and there she sat, bold as brass. 'What's she doing here?' The shock made my voice shrill.

'Ada's an old friend from way back. Before you were born anyway.' My mother sniffed.

'So how come you never told me? How come I suddenly find out Sam's so-called mother is an old friend? I don't believe you.'

My mother sniffed again, lifted her shoulders in a couldn't- careless movement and looked at me over the rim of her cup. 'Ada is one of my oldest friends.' She spoke in that pseudo voice, enunciating each word, torturing the vowels, in the way Dad and me used to chuckle about.

I wasn't finding it funny that day.

'One of your oldest friends?' I realised I was staring with my mouth open and closed it, tightening my lips. 'Utter crap. I don't think so. I want you out.' Ignoring mother I fixed my glare on Ada. After all the years she hadn't worn well; her cheeks and nose were covered in a criss-cross of red veins, the skin loose, raddled. She glowered back at me with bloodshot eyes but said nothing.

Instead, Mother spoke. 'Ada and I have been friends for a long time but we lost touch.' She put her cup firmly on the saucer; we hadn't used cups and saucers for a long time. 'We met again through a friend—'

'What friend? You don't have any friends.' There was no point in asking; she was lying. However they'd found one another it was clear to me that they were up to something; I saw the gleam of triumph in those piggy-eyes of Sam's mother and I recognised the sniff of satisfaction from mine.

'She'll have to go before Sam comes home. I won't have him upset, not by her.'

'I've told Ada she can stay here.'

'Stay here? Why?' I shook my head, hard. 'No. What do you think you are doing, Mother?'

'She's had a difficult time over the years. I know what *his* father did to her.' She jerked her head towards Sam's raincoat hanging on the back door. 'Taking her house off her.'

'Whatever she's told you it's a lie. Albert did nothing to her. She left him and Sam when he was a little boy. She only came back when she thought—' I stopped, refusing to argue. I pulled my coat off and threw it over the back of the nearest kitchen chair and dropped my handbag on the table. 'What's happened?' I said to Ada. 'You fallen out with your latest man, then?' The way she drew herself up in the chair but wouldn't meet my eyes, told me I'd hit the nail on the head.

'Ada can have the spare room. She'll pay rent —'

'Of course I will, I'm not a scrounger—'

'Huh!' I was lost for words at that.

'It'll be a bit of extra coming in. And I'll have someone to talk to when the two of you are out.' My mother stuck her lower lip out and blinked, slowly, in an expression of self-pity.

I clenched the back of the hard chair so tightly I could feel the wood digging into my palms. 'I go to work, Mother. As Sam does. And that's Rose's room.'

'It's an empty room.'

I tried to calm down. Crossing the kitchen to stare out of the window, I took a few deep breaths; a woman walked past on the common land at the back of the house, with a small dog on a very long lead. It ran, snuffling at patches of grass. I spoke without turning around.

'Mother, this can't happen.'

'Why not?' She was querulous now.

'This is as much Sam's and my home as yours – we have a say as to who can live here as well as you. She can't lodge here; I won't have her in Rose's room. And it wouldn't be fair on Sam for her to live here.' I felt sick to my stomach. 'All the work he's put into the house, how much more value he's put on it—'

'And don't think I don't know why. You'd sell the place from under my feet, given half a chance—'

'We wouldn't, I'm just saying—'

'Why do you think I wouldn't sign that bloody paper you wanted me to sign all that time ago – that bloody power thing?'

'Power of attorney. It was only to protect us, to make sure we could stay on here, when you needed looking after—'

'I don't need you looking after me, Rose. I never wanted you...' She stopped, hand to her mouth.

291

'Rose? Never wanted?'

'I just forgot who ... I don't need you looking after me or anyone else.'

'You asked us to live here. You were the one who said you couldn't manage.'

Sam's mother – Ada, as I reminded myself to call her, was calmly lighting a cigarette, watching us through the stream of smoke when she raised her face to blow it out. She was smirking. I wanted to slap her.

Closing my eyes I took a deep breath and forced myself to be calm. 'And do I really have to remind you about us wanting to foster, Mother? What happened then, eh? *You* didn't want us to – so *I* gave in, didn't I? For the sake of peace, I gave up that idea.'

'I didn't tell you to.'

'You didn't have to say it outright. Your reaction was enough. How could I have brought a child into this house where it wasn't wanted by one of the people already living here? Yet another child not wanted.'

'What do you mean by that?'

'You know what I mean. And what you did about it.' The old resentment, the dislike, was swelled up inside me.

'I don't know what you're talking about.' My mother sneaked a sideways glance at Ada.

'Really?'

'Really.'

Standing, my mother folded her arms under her bosom and nodded at me. 'Ada and I could afford this house on our own. We could buy you out.'

It was said triumphantly but I didn't miss the sudden look of alarm that flitted across the other woman's face.

'You really believe that, mother?' I nodded towards Ada. 'I should make that clear to her if I were you. I think she's got other ideas.'

I felt the draught of cool evening air at the same time as I saw her face change: a frown, a lift of her chin.

'What's going on?' My stomach lurched when I saw Sam in the doorway. 'What's she doing here?' Even to me his voice sounded threatening. 'I said what's she doing here?'

'Sam.'

He stopped me by holding up his hand. 'I'm asking her.' He pointed at Mother.

Undaunted she faced up to him. 'I've said she can lodge with us.'

'Over my dead body.'

'I've nowhere else to go, son.' Ada stubbed out her cigarette in the saucer.

I saw Mum frown at such treatment of her best crockery.

'Don't call me that.' His face flushed. 'Don't you dare bloody call me your son.' The muscles at the side of his jaw tightened spasmodically. 'How did you even know where we lived?'

'I've always known. I've been friends with Lily for years.'

Sam looked at my mother. 'Something you forgot to bloody tell us, huh?'

'That's a lie, Sam. They're not friends...' I tried to get him to look at me but it was as though he hadn't heard me.

My mother waggled her head, sniffed sharply. 'None of your business as far as I'm concerned.'

'Like hell.' He didn't even look at Ada when he next spoke. 'I want you to fuck off. Now!'

His sudden shout startled me, he hardly ever swore, and she jumped, pulled her collar around her neck leaving her hands crossed over her throat.

'Lily says I can stay. We're old friends.'

'Crap!'

My mother moved to put her hand on Ada's shoulder. 'She's staying. She's my friend and she needs somewhere to live.'

'Irene?'

I looked at him. 'Sam...' I didn't know what to say; I'd said all I could to them already. I was lost for words.

'Right.' Sam spoke slowly. 'Okay...'

Before I could speak again he'd left the kitchen. I followed. In our bedroom he was throwing clothes into our old suitcase.

'What are you doing?'

'Leaving, Irene, I'm leaving.'

'Sam, she'll probably only stay a few weeks...'

He ignored me. 'You coming?'

'Where? Where would we go?' I flung out my arms. 'Where the hell can we go?'

He didn't answer; he only looked at me for a long moment.

'Don't...' I put my hand on the doorjamb to steady myself. 'Don't...'

'I will not live here with that woman under our roof, Irene. I won't.'

'I'll talk to Dad; he'll make Mother see sense. He'll make sure your – she leaves.'

'What can he do?' Sam threw open the wardrobe doors, dragged out some of his shirts and stuffed them into the case. 'He can't do anything.'

I couldn't stand it. 'Please...' I crossed the room to him. Swallowed. 'I'll make her leave. It'll be all right. 'I'll sort it.'

He hugged me close to him. I breathed in his familiar smell, so dear to me. He was shaking as much as I was.

'Look,' His breath was warm on my throat. I clung to him, 'I've not said anything before now because I hadn't made up my mind properly—'

'What?'

'I was offered a big contract a few weeks ago. I haven't known what to do—'

'Is that what's been wrong? Is that why you've been so distant with me? Why didn't you talk it over with me?'

'Because I already know your answer, you won't leave this house...'

I didn't say anything. I knew he was right; how could I leave? Now more than ever, how could I go and leave Rose with those women?

'I need to give them my decision. Tomorrow. It'll mean me taking on a couple of lads...'

I pulled myself away from him. 'You've already decided.'

'No. But it's a good job. Big money.' The calmness in him seemed to have arrived as suddenly as his earlier fury.

'Where? Where is it – this – bloody wonderful job? Where, Sam?'

'Cardiff.'

So far away. And he'd been considering it without telling me.

He held on to my hands. 'I'm sorry, I should have told you—'

'Yes, you should.'

'Try to understand, Irene—'

'Understand what?'

'What's happened tonight has helped me to make up my mind. I will not be one minute longer near that woman than I have to be. And this is my out—'

'Your out? Your out from what, Sam? Me? Mother? *Your* mother...' I chose the word deliberately. 'Your mother coming here gives you the excuse to leave me? Is that what you're saying?'

'No. No, that's not what I'm saying. I could have turned the contract down weeks ago—'

'But you didn't, you kept your options open and kept it to yourself—'

'Because I knew what you'd say, I knew you wouldn't leave this house – with your mad idea about Rose—'

I felt the chill flood through me. 'I thought you understood...' I turned away from him, stared through the window. For once the road was empty. *I* felt empty. 'Then you had better go, hadn't you, Sam? There's nothing more to discuss.'

He came close to me, his hand on my arm. I shrugged.

'It would be good for us... A new start—'

'Go. Go on, go.'

'This firm, they pay for living quarters. If you came with me that allowance would go towards a flat or something. We'd still have this house—'

Weariness swept over me. 'Just go, Sam.'

'Try to understand – with her here, I can't…'

'Then, like I said, you'd better go.'

'You're obsessed with this house—'

'Obsessed? Obsessed?' Truth hurts. 'Well, I'm sorry you think that, Sam.' I made my voice cold to hide the despair. 'Just go.'

'I'm going.' There was an answering shift in his tone. 'I can't – won't – stay.' He picked up the suitcase, took my hand. Hesitated. 'Please.' His voice changed. 'Please come with me.'

'No.' I looked down at his hand on mine. Shook it off. How to explain? I couldn't; any more than I could leave Rose. I needed her as much as I believed she needed me. And Sam was trying to make me choose between him and Rose.

'It'll be hell, living with those two. You do know that, don't you?'

I didn't look at him. I didn't watch him go.

Chapter Ninety-Five

2002: Today: 6.15 p.m.

'Rose? What's happening?' My knees crack when I stand up, steady myself. Paracetamol tablets scattered next to the empty glass but I can't remember if I took any. I must … I must put Caroline back in her place. Feet so heavy. What's wrong? Standing in front of the drawers. Pick up Rose's doll. Clasp her close to my face; she smells musty. Should have washed her years ago. But haven't, didn't want to lose my sister's touch on it.

1995

Sam had been gone months. Our phone conversations were stilted, terse, each of us resentful of the other.

Once I asked him to come home. I'd been determined not to say it but still I blurted the words out.

'I miss you.'

'And I miss you, Irene. But I can't come back to that house, you know that. Not with her there.'

He was as stubborn as I was. Both angry at one another. Both trying not to show it. Both not giving an inch.

'Come here, check it out. I'm sure you'd love it. Outside of Cardiff there are some lovely little villages. This hostel is a dump. The lads I've hired are a good hard-working bunch but they're a mucky, noisy lot. I wouldn't expect you to live here. Just say the word and I'll find somewhere better for the two of us.'

'No, Sam.'

'Why not? I don't know how you can stand being there.'

'I've got the hospital school, my job – Rose. I'm not here most of the time. Just in the evenings.' I didn't tell him I'd moved into the bedroom I'd shared with Rose the day he left; I couldn't stand the thought of Ada being in there and it was comforting being closer to my sister.

'Find another school. Get another job.' His voice rose. 'Not that you'd need to get a job – I'm earning good money, Irene, and we've been offered another contract here.'

'Another!'

It was as though he hadn't heard me. 'Carry on like this for a few more months and I'll have earned enough for a good deposit on a house down here. We won't need to worry about Grove Street. It'd be a fresh start for us. A new start, a new life for us, eh?'

'No.' He hadn't understood anything. He didn't care how I felt, what it meant to me, being here. With Rose.

That phone call ended with me putting down the receiver. I was so angry that he was considering taking on another contract. So scared our marriage was over.

It wasn't. But it was damaged.

After I refused to go to Cardiff a third time, he didn't ask again. It was a stalemate that we didn't know how to break.

Soon the time between phone calls stretched to once a week. And it was almost always Sam who ended the call.

By then there was a good reason not to move to Wales; something I hadn't told him.

Often I'd come home to find both my mother and Ada snoring on the settee and nursing glasses, an empty bottle of gin on the coffee table. And, when they were both sober, there were some horrendous quarrels, especially when a bill came through the letterbox. Many times I paid the bill from the money Sam sent home each month, just to restore an uneasy peace. I was sure, if I wasn't there, it wouldn't have been long before the house went to rack and ruin and my mother would get so far into debt that she'd need to sell the place. And I couldn't let that happen.

Because something else was happening, worse than the rows between the two women. Now and again, when I came in from work, it was though I was a visitor Mum had to entertain; she'd offer me tea, insist I sat down for a chat with her and Ada. But she never called me by my name. At other times she was back to being her old bitter self. When it first happened, I thought it was the drink. As the months passed, I knew it was more than that. She'd write shopping lists for groceries, buy what was on the list, come home, find the list and go off to the shops again. I'd find food in her wardrobe, knickers in the fridge. It was an endless round of checking what she was doing.

And then Ada disappeared as abruptly as she'd arrived. So did the small amount of savings I had hidden in my underwear drawer. And my best coat.

Mother went mad when she realised two of her blouses had gone as well.

I stripped the bed the woman had used and gave the room a thorough clean.

And then, for my mother, it was as though Ada had never been with us. She never mentioned her again. I wasn't sorry.

I wanted to tell Sam about his mother going. I wanted to tell him he could come back home now. But something stopped me.

As for my mother; I didn't know what to do about her. There was something definitely wrong and I had to get help from somewhere.

Chapter Ninety-Six

2002: Today: 6.15 p.m.

I put Caroline back in her place. There! Straighten her bonnet. Good! But something's wrong. Something I should do... Can't remember. 'Rose?' I wait. Listen. 'I've done my best, Rose. You know I have...' Wait again. 'But I'm tired. Sam's tired. It's not fair.'

The knot in my stomach tightens. Why doesn't she reply?

1995

I didn't want to worry Dad but I needed his advice.

We were sitting on the cast-iron bench on the little patio outside the French windows of their flat. There was a rich smell of coffee coming from the kitchen.

'I know it's not your problem, Dad, but I need some help. It's about Mum.' I smiled at Susan as she handed a large cup to me and then one to Dad. 'Thanks, Susan. I like your dress by the way. Red suits you.'

'Thanks. Debenhams, in the sales,' she said, sitting down with her own drink. 'Help yourself to cake, it's lemon drizzle, made this morning.' She spoke lightly but I caught the cautioning sideways slant of her eyes towards my father.

I knew why: she'd long since had enough of Mum. I was sorry to drag them into the situation now but I needed him to help me. 'She's been acting odd, lately.' An understatement but it was somewhere to start about the mess I was getting involved in.

'Besides being her usual self, you mean?' He helped himself to a slice of the cake. 'Sue's the best cook I know. Try some of this.'

'I will, in a minute, Dad.' I leant forward so he had to look at me. 'She's acting really odd sometimes, doing strange things. I've noticed it for ages.' I stopped, not sure how to explain it. 'She's either all over me like a rash or she's nasty – I mean, I thought at first it was the drink...' It was like talking to a brick wall; he didn't respond. 'I mean, she's always got plenty of bottles of gin in but it's not that. I'm sure it's not.'

Susan touched his arm. Still he didn't speak. 'Derek?' She looked worried.

He nodded at her.

There was something going on I didn't know about but still I persisted. 'I'm sorry, Susan, I know how you feel about Mum but I'm the one who's with her all the time. And I don't know what to do.'

She spoke for him. 'I do understand, Irene.' She kept her hand on my father. 'But your dad's not been on top form lately. I don't think he can cope with your mother just at the moment.'

I'd been so caught up with worrying about how I felt, I hadn't really looked at him. Now I saw what a strange colour he was. And his eyes were sunken, dark shadows around them. 'Dad? What's wrong?'

'Just had a bit of a cold lately, love. Nothing to worry about.'

'Don't lie, Derek.' Susan was sharp. She turned to me. 'He's been dizzy a lot lately. And he won't see the doctor himself. So he's in no state to advise you, Irene.'

I could see she was right. And I was grateful to her in a way; she always put Dad first. 'I'm sorry, Dad. My mother shouldn't be your problem. I'll sort it out. '

'And I'm sorry too, Irene.' He rested his cup on his knee and squeezed Susan's fingers. 'I feel like you've been landed with your mum, one way and another. It's not fair on you, I know.'

'Don't worry.'

300

'She's not your responsibility, Irene,' Susan said.

If she wasn't my responsibility, whose was she?

Chapter Ninety-Seven

2002: Today: 6.30 p.m.

I've done my best. No more. So many long days, longer nights, Rose. You know that; you've seen. Why the silence?

I'm so cold inside I'm shaking. Or is it fear?

I cross the landing. Stand at her bedroom door for a moment.

1996

I made an appointment at the doctors for Mother to be checked over. When we parked outside the surgery she refused to get out.

'Why are we here?' What's wrong with you?' She stopped me undoing her seat belt by clutching on to the lock.

'It's not for me, Mother. I made the appointment for you. It's about your knees,' I lied.

'Nothing wrong with my knees.'

'There is, you're always moaning about them. So come on, it's almost time for our appointment.'

When we walked through the door to the crowded waiting room my mother refused to go near the lines of blue plastic chairs, filled with restless people, reading, talking, staring into the far corner of the ceiling.

'I'm not sitting near all those people, I don't know what's wrong with them. I could catch something.' Her voice was strident.

The muted buzz of chatter paused momentarily, all eyes turned towards us.

I cringed, smiling a silent apology to the room.

The nurse showed us into a side corridor where there were four empty chairs. Nurses in dark blue uniforms, receptionists in smart grey uniforms walked past us, their footsteps squeaking or tapping on the tiled floor. Most smiled at us until Mum shouted, 'Nosy bitch', at one nurse. After that they studiously ignored us; obviously the word had got around.

The cream walls were covered in posters that Mother began to read loudly and repetitively:

'HAVE YOU HAD YOUR FLU VACCINATION?

HAVE YOU HAD YOUR FLU VACCINATION?

DO YOU NEED A HOME VISIT?

DO YOU NEED A HOME VISIT?

REPEAT PRESCRIPTIONS? ASK AT RECEPTION.

REPEAT PRESCRIPTIONS? ASK AT RECEPTION.

COURTESY TO STAFF AT ALL TIMES.

COURTESY TO STAFF AT ALL TIMES.

COURTESY TO STAFF AT ALL TIMES.'

'Be a good thing if they were courteous to us first,' she said when one of the receptionists passed us again. 'D'you hear me? I said – it would be good if you were fucking courteous to us first.'

'Sorry,' I mumbled. The woman smiled, a cool professional movement of her lips.

'Ignorant cow,' my mother said in a loud voice. 'And you can stop staring,' she said as the door opposite us opened and the doctor smiled at us. 'Lilian?' he put his head to one side.

'Mrs Bradshaw to you. Idiot.' She marched past him and sat in his chair behind his desk, pulled her skirt so far up I could see her knickers.

'Mother...'

'You said it was my bloody knees.'

'Don't worry.' He smiled at me. 'I'll just sit here, shall I?' He sat alongside hers and looked at Mother's notes. I knew my letter to him was there, the one asking for these tests. I hoped she didn't see it, didn't recognise my writing.

He gently prodded her kneecaps. 'They are a bit swollen. Touch of arthritis, obviously.' He sat back and picked up a notepad. 'Now Mrs Bradshaw, a few questions if you don't mind.'

Twenty minutes later we were back in the car, my mother's face puce with rage.

'The cheek of the bloody man,' she fumed. 'Trying to make me look bloody stupid. What was the date of my birthday, what year was I born. And what was that bloody business of counting backwards? Saying the months of the year back to front? Bloody daft! All that stuff? About who's the Prime Minister? Who cares?' She pushed me away when I tried to fasten her seat belt. 'And you didn't help.' She turned her head and stared out of the side window of the car.

'I wasn't supposed to.' I pushed her seat belt into the lock without her noticing. 'And you couldn't answer all of them,' I reminded her.

'Stupid,' she said. 'Bloody stupid. You and him.' And sniffed. Dismissive.

She refused to speak to me all the way home. It didn't matter; I mulled over the young doctor's prognosis.

'I understand why you needed to get your mother here,' he'd said, in an aside to me. 'I can see things are a little difficult. And I'm afraid it looks as if you're right. Dementia. Of course, we can do further tests, discover what form of dementia... But, medically, there is little we can do. On the other hand there is a great deal we can set in place that will help you. I think it sensible to get social services involved at this stage.' I was relieved to know I could get some help.

The social services were more than happy to set up what they called 'a package' to help me with Mum. But I knew, as soon as I opened the door to the poor woman that Mum would have none of it.

'Don't want bloody outsiders poking their bloody noses in.'

'Think of Irene,' the young woman said. 'You love your daughter, don't you Lily?'

'Lilian.'

'You don't want her to be ill, do you?'

Mum shrugged. 'I don't ask...' Mum struggled with the words. 'I don't need...' She scowled at me and then at the young woman. 'Fuck off.'

Chapter Ninety-Eight

2002: Today: 6.30 p.m.

There's a chink of light from the street lamp coming through the vertical blinds. It spreads across the duvet on my mother's bed and onto the pillow next to her head.

I reach up and pull the curtains closer together. The faint line of light is still there, but blurred around the edges.

Which is how I feel, blurred around the edges. Except, for me, there is no light...

1996

I told Sam what was happening to Mother. I heard the hesitation in his voice when he said they were still in the middle of the contract.

'How bad is it?' he asked.

I wasn't going to plead with him.

'Bad enough, but I'm managing with her.' I didn't tell him I'd had to give up work and, worse still, the school. I didn't tell him I'd cried the day I walked out of the gate at Clough Fields for the last time. I still hadn't told him Ada had gone. 'I don't suppose you'll come home for Christmas?'

'No.'

His answer, so abrupt, so definite, angered me. 'She's gone...'
The long silence that followed told me he'd understood.

'Why didn't you tell me?'

'Why have you never asked?'

'I'm sorry.'

I kept quiet.

'Look, Irene, it's impossible; we're on a tight schedule and we'll only be having the day off. We moved on to another branch of the company's store in a different part of Cardiff. They want it open by spring.'

Another contract? 'So I won't be expecting you to come home anytime soon then... Oh, for god's sake...' I'm watching Mother putting the dirty cups and plates from lunch in the cupboard without them being washed.

'What?'

'Not you, Sam. Oh, just wait a minute.' I cross the kitchen, tucking the phone between my chin and shoulder and start taking the plates out. She slaps at my hands. I give up and go into the hall.

'What's happening, Irene?

'If you came home you'd see.' *But you won't and I won't ask you to...* I run my forefinger along the ledge over the living room doorframe and it comes away covered in a layer of dust. I don't want him to come home because he thinks it's his duty; I want him to be here because he loves me.

'It wouldn't be worth me coming home for just a day. It's too far, you know that.'

Not even for me? 'So you say.'

'What's that mean?' Even through the poor reception of my mobile I heard the crisp tone. 'I'd no sooner be home than I'd have to turn around to come back—'

'I haven't seen you for over eight months, Sam—'

I didn't intend to say that and I was sorry the moment he answered.

'You could have come down here, Irene.'

Mum shuffled past me, muttering. 'Lavvy.' Her knickers were around her ankles; she took the stairs one at a time, awkwardly at first and then stepped out of them. I looked at them through the bannister. They were sodden.

'Is there someone else?' It was a question I'd wanted to ask for months.

There was a long pause. I strained to hear him.

'I don't know how you can say that, Irene.' He spoke quietly. 'There's only you, there's only ever been you. I'm here earning bloody good money. For us.'

I knew that. He was still sending me a cheque every month, more than I needed. But I closed my eyes at his next words.

'Look, I've almost got enough for a deposit on a house. I can't be there for Christmas but I promise I'll come back when I've made enough. If you won't come to Cardiff, I'll come back to Denholme. But...' He stopped. I heard the long breath he took. 'I won't live with your mother anymore. I've had enough. Even with – her – with Ada gone, I can't come back to that house.'

And I can't leave.

Chapter Ninety-Nine

2002: The Day: 6.35 p.m.

And now there is no Rose. I can't feel her with me anymore.

Why? Why was she here all the time in the past and gone now I really need her? Why did she speak to me and is now silent?

1996

Christmas Eve. Despite what Sam had said in the past, I'd still hoped he'd change his mind and come home. But the phone call that morning had convinced me he'd no intention to. When we spoke I heard the clatter of work, men whistling and calling out behind his voice.

I'd felt the stab of bitterness when he said, 'We're trying to finish an hour early, go for a pint...' before he stopped, as though realising what he'd said.

'Well, won't that be bloody wonderful for you.' This time it was me who put the receiver down first. 'Sod you, Sam Hargreaves. Fucking sod you,' I muttered. I picked up my mother's knickers and, in the kitchen, threw them into the sink. I went upstairs to find a pair of clean, dry ones for her.

I was in the shopping centre in town looking for a pair of pyjamas for Dad and something for Susan. I'd just come out of Marks & Spencer when I saw Mum. She was standing under the memorial statue of the soldier on a horse, her shopping bag on the floor near her feet. And she was crying. People were swerving around her, not looking.

I'd left her at home; how had she got into town?

'Mum?' She didn't have a hat or a coat on even though it was bitter cold. 'Mum? What are you doing? Where's your coat?'

She sobbed, the tears dripping off her chin, her nose all snotty. But it was as though she couldn't see me, even though her head was turned in my direction. I moved closer and saw she was trembling. Taking my coat off and shoving her arms through the sleeves I hissed, 'Are you drunk? Breath on me –come on – haw on me.' She was breathing into my face anyway. There was no smell of alcohol.

'What the hell are you doing?'

What she said, then, frightened me. 'I don't know ... I don't know where I am.'

It was ages before I succeeded in stopping a taxi. It started to snow but I had to stand, shivering, on the edge of the pavement, frantically waving at each one that went by, with the rest of the traffic speeding past, spitting up wet slush. She was crying and I was almost sobbing myself. But I couldn't let her shelter in one of the shop entrances in case she wandered off.

Our heads and shoulders were soon covered with a layer of snow and attracting a lot of curious stares. Just as I was beginning to think it would be easier to get to the nearest bus stop, a black cab pulled up. Blow the expense, I thought, squinting, glancing up through the large flakes at the dense grey cloud.

I needed to get both of us home as fast as possible.

It snowed for over a day. Christmas Day afternoon, it stopped. Nothing was moving on the street outside. The man next door had covered his car with a tarpaulin and it lay hunched like a camel under a mound of white. The pavements were still untrodden but, as I released the little top window in my bedroom to shake off the covering of snow, I heard the excited laughter of children, saw them dragging their sledges back and forth along the street. The deeper tones of their fathers – I presumed it was their fathers – supervising them. The silence in our house made me feel even lonelier: the television programmes were a constant round of happy family shows. I hadn't been able to get through to Sam; the mobile connections were constantly busy. Mum hadn't been up all day and I'd made my excuses to Dad and Susan.

'Dreadful migraine, I'm sorry. Have a nice day and I'll see you tomorrow. Probably...'

Not sure whether they believed me but they accepted it.

The doorbell rang. I had no idea who it would be. I peeped in at Mum, she was asleep, a snore opening and closing her lips. I shut her bedroom door quietly and ran downstairs.

When I opened the front door, the snow was piled almost as high as my shoulders. It stayed there for a moment, like a peak on top of a mountain. Then it collapsed into the hall. We both stared down at it.

'Sam!'

'I'll get a shovel,' Sam said, and stepped over it. I stood back to let him pass and watched him stride along the hall.

I'd only spoken to him on the phone yesterday. Now, here he was, brushing snow from my hall back onto the path.

'I'll put the kettle on – make a brew,' I said.

He said nothing. Just nodded.

My hand shook as I filled the kettle and switched it on. I stared out of the window at the flat crust of whiteness.

I felt his warmth behind me and leaned back. 'I didn't think you'd ever come back to me again,' I said, turning into his arms.

Chapter One Hundred

2002: The Day: 6.35 p.m.

I fill my lungs with air and slowly breathe out through my mouth, telling myself I'm not frightened.

I glance at the clock with the extra large numbers, bought when she could still tell the time. Now it's just something else for her to stare at, to puzzle over. I'm cold – and tired. It's actually twenty-seven hours since I slept properly, and for a lot of them I've been on my feet.

I move around the bed, straightening the corners, making the inner softness match the shape of the outer material, trying to make the duvet lie flat but, of course, I can't. However heavily her head lies on the pillow, however precisely her arms are down by her sides, her feet are never still. The cover twitches until, centimetre by centimetre, it slides to one side towards the floor like the pink satin eiderdown used to do on my bed as a child.

Like the pink satin eiderdown on Rose's bed used to do.

1997

Dad wasn't well again; nothing he could put a finger on, he said, just not on top form. Susan made him stay in bed.

I'd not been in their bedroom before and it felt odd to be sitting on the large squashy armchair by the window watching the covers rise and fall over him in that king-size bed – as though I was intruding on a private part of their life. I glanced around. Unlike Mum's bedroom at Grove Street, this was light, modern, the wardrobes built-in so there was more space to move around. The curtains and bedding were white. I stared out of the window at the avenue, watching an elderly couple walking, holding hands, the man's head at an angle towards the woman, as though he was listening intently to what she was saying. And then he laughed. I couldn't hear the laugh, but he threw his head back and his face was so – so joyful, I smiled, even as the tears prickled the back of my eyes. I didn't even know why I was crying.

'Irene?'

'I'm here Dad.' I drew the chair over to him. 'How are you feeling?'

'Not so bad. Tired.'

'Susan told me the doctor said you've a chest infection.'

'Apparently.'

'Can I get you anything? A drink?'

'No thanks, love.' He shuffled himself up against the pillows, reached over, patted my hand. 'I need to talk to you.'

'Wait until you've had another sleep.' Even as I said the words I remembered that other time, almost the last thing I'd said to Nanna. And then it had been too late. I would never know what she wanted to tell me. So I said, 'What is it, Dad?'

'Where's Susan?'

'Gone grocery shopping, she won't be long,' I reassured

him. 'Did you want her for something?'

'No.' His voice was so low I had to lean forward to hear him. His mouth worked as he tried to get the words out. I waited.

'There's something I've been meaning to ask you. Should have asked you a long time ago...' He slid his tongue across his lips.

I could see how dry they were. 'Let me get you some water.'

'No.' He raised his hand. 'What will you do, Irene? When your mum gets too bad...' He faltered.

I'd told him long ago how she'd made it impossible for us to sell the house, even though Sam and me were joint owners.

'Hush, Dad, it'll be fine. We'll be fine.'

'I worry what will happen to you.' His breathing quickened. I could hear the phlegm rattling in his chest. 'She can only get worse. It's not fair on you. You shouldn't have to be the one stuck with her.' He lay back against the pillows, beads of sweat on his upper lip.

'Well, we couldn't inflict her on anyone else.' I forced a laugh. 'Can you imagine her in a care home anyway? Having to sit cheek by jowl with strangers?'

He closed his eyes. 'She'd empty the place,' he whispered.

'Or,' I said, thankful to see his smile smoothing out the lines of pain and worry, 'or, worse still, sit by Mrs Hardcastle,' I said. 'Can you imagine the uproar that would cause?'

'Oh dear, your mother's arch-enemy, was Edith...'

'I know. All those homemade biscuits and fairy cakes she used to put in your coat pockets.'

He moved his head, slightly nodding. 'At choir practice in chapel. It wouldn't have been so bad if she hadn't included all those little notes as well...'

'"Billy-ducks," Nanna called them.' I laughed. She told me Mum had fastened one of the *billets-doux* to the back of Mrs Hardcastle's hat with her hatpin so everyone could read it at morning service. 'Nanna said Mum called her a Jezebel.'

'She did. Poor Edith.' Dad's laugh ended in a coughing fit. When he got his breath back he said, 'The worst time was the Sunday she asked Minister Hulley if she could read out a notice for the WI AGM...' he stopped.

I took over the story. 'And then told the whole congregation what Mrs Hardcastle had been doing. And poor old Jack Hardcastle was sitting right next to her.' I giggled, remembering that moment of horror and hilarity Nanna and me had shared.

Dad lifted his head to look at me. 'Got it in the neck from your mother for weeks. Just for eating the darn cakes.' He fell back against the pillow, exhausted, even as he gave another breathy laugh. 'So...?'

'I'll get social services in again,' I said, trying to reassure him. 'If Mum gets worse.'

He closed his eyes in agreement but still said, 'you tried that before...'

'Well, she'll have no choice this time.' I didn't want this conversation. I leaned back. 'Let's just get you better, eh? Stop mithering about her.' I heard a car draw up. A rush of fresh air blew through the bedroom and the front door closed with a crash.

'Here's Susan now,' I said, relieved.

We waited for her to come into the bedroom. The silence between us was filled with unsaid words.

Chapter One Hundred and One

2002: Today: 6.35 p.m.

In the end I yank her feet up and tuck the duvet underneath. Tonight of all nights I want her to look tidy. I want everything to be right.

I want everything to be right, Rose. For you.

My mother doesn't like my moving her and opens her eyes, the thick lines of white brows drawn together, giving up the pretence of being asleep. Lying face upwards, the skin falling back on her cheekbones, her flesh is extraordinarily smooth, pale. Translucent almost.

I wait by the bed. I move into her line of vision and now it's as though we're watching one another, my mother and me: two women – trapped.

Have you felt trapped in this house, Rose?

1997

Overnight, Dad was taken into hospital with pneumonia.

I sat by the side of his bed where he was propped up by a mountain of pillows. The top sheet was folded neatly around his waist, the covers tucked firmly around him. Tucked up like a boat. The memory of that suddenly came back to me. That's what I used to say to him when I was little and he came to kiss me goodnight: 'Tuck me up like a boat, Daddy.' And he would go around my bed pushing the blankets tightly under the soft mattress until it curved underneath me. It made me feel so safe, even though I could hardly move.

I wished I could make him safe now.

Susan and me had taken turns to keep an eye on him since he'd been admitted. We ignored the pointed stares and comments about 'proper visiting times' from the nurses. We weren't leaving him alone with strangers for anyone.

He'd had a bad day; his breathing was rasping and the harsh cough racked his body. Three times one of the nurses had placed the oxygen mask over his nose and mouth for a few minutes to give him some relief. And, although the collar and the front of his pyjama jacket were wet with sweat, his hand in mine was cold and clammy. The fluids and antibiotics that had been dripped into the vein in his arm over the last three days and nights didn't seem to be making any difference.

I closed my eyes. Come on, Dad, fight this. We need you. I need you.

313

A sudden clatter startled me. I watched as the ancillaries pushed the trolley around the ward, piling up the dirty crockery from the end of each bed. They wheeled past us without even looking at Dad; he hadn't eaten since he'd been brought into the hospital.

The ward was being tidied up, ready for visiting time. I was waiting for Susan to come in and take over for a few hours while I went home to get some rest. And to give Sam a break from looking after my mother.

I lifted a hand to attract the attention of the nurse at the next bed. 'I wonder if we could draw the curtains while the visitors are here – give my father some privacy?'

'Well, it's not usual for us to do that.' She came towards us, a slight frown on her face.

She was only young and she looked harassed. Her badge read Kylie Moore RN.

'We did ask for a side ward but there wasn't one free,' I said. 'He really shouldn't be in a general ward. I'm only asking for him not to be on show.'

'I can ask Sister.' She checked the clock on the wall above the door. 'Perhaps it will be...'

It was the way she stopped that made me look quickly back at Dad. His eyes were open; he was looking at me. I felt the slight squeeze on my fingers.

'Dad? Are you okay?' The pulse in my throat quickened. I could feel the panic rising in me. I twisted around to look at the nurse. 'Is he all right?'

'I won't be a moment.' The nurse swiftly pulled the curtains around the bed and went through them. I heard the squeak of her shoes as she hurried away. As she went through the ward doors I heard the buzz of voices, of the relatives outside in the corridor, waiting for visiting time. They'd have to wait now, the thought came automatically. Surely the staff would make them wait?

What was happening? I stood up, leant towards my father. 'Dad? Dad.'

I felt a touch on my back.

'What's happened? What is it?' Susan's voice trembled. 'Irene ... I ...'

I heard the chatter again as the ward door opened. The curtains swished open. The nurse had come back with a young doctor.

'Can I?'

We moved to one side to let him get nearer to my father and watched in silence as he examined him. All the time, Dad's eyes were fixed on us.

When the doctor straightened up he looked at us, smiling. 'Chest seems a bit clearer. Looks as if Derek is back with us again.'

'I am.' Dad's voice was croaky but his mouth twitched into a small smile.

The rush of relief must have hit Susan and me at the same time; the next minute we were sharing the chair, precariously balancing on the edges and laughing and crying at the same time.

'We'll keep you on the antibiotics and fluids for another twenty-four hours, Derek, and then see how you are.' The doctor pressed his hand on Dad's shoulder before turning to us. 'He'll probably sleep now. I suggest you two ladies go home for a rest. We'll keep an eye on him.'

I looked at Susan. She shook her head. 'We'll stay,' she said.

'Up to you.' The doctor glanced at his watch. 'It is visiting time. But after that...' He pulled his eyebrows together in an obvious attempt to look stern even as he smiled. 'You'll leave him to get a good night's sleep. Okay?'

'Okay.'

He pushed his way through the curtains.

'I'll get you another chair,' the nurse said.

We stayed poised on the chair, arms around one another, staring at my father who'd closed his eyes again. He looked exhausted.

'Oh, Irene.' Susan rested her head on my shoulder. 'Thank god.'

'I know.' I heard the chatter and scrape of chairs. 'I'll ask if we can keep the curtains closed.'

'Yes. And I'm staying after visiting. I don't care what they say. But you must go home to get some rest.' She paused. 'And to rescue that lovely husband of yours.'

'Bet my mother's been leading him a right merry dance,' I said with a wry smile. 'I'll go if you're sure you'll be okay here?'

'I – we'll be fine.'

The young nurse came back with a chair. 'I'll leave the curtains,' she whispered.

'Thank you – Kylie.'

She grinned. 'My pleasure.' She studied Dad for a moment. Despite the dark smudges under his eyes and the unhealthy pallor of his skin, he did look a little better. 'I'm glad for you,' she whispered.

After visiting time was over I walked out of the hospital and into a taxi. I cried all the way home.

Chapter One Hundred and Two

2002: Today: 6.35 p.m.

'I'm sorry, Rose.' Again my words float away, unacknowledged. Does she know how the guilt has stayed with me? How that memory has never gone away? I should have stayed with Rose that day.

'I can't do this anymore, Mum,' I say. 'I can't, Rose.'

1997

The trees across the fields at the back of the house were now black jagged shapes against the pink and gold of the sunset. Starlings were gathering in long ribbons and coils.

'How do you feel?' Sam stood alongside me, holding my hand.

'Better than I was a week ago.'

'And he'll be okay?'

'That's what the doctor said. They wouldn't have let him home if not.'

'It was a close call.'

I shivered. 'Don't. I can't bear to think about it.'

'You go round to the flat whenever you want to, love. I'll see to your mother.'

I kissed him on the cheek. 'Thanks, Sam.'

'You need to catch up on your sleep now.'

'And you don't?' I jerked my head towards the house. 'You're not telling me it's been easy for you these last few days.'

'Your mother is my biggest fan. She's no trouble for me.' He laughed.

'Some days,' I said.

'Well, let's just be glad your dad is getting better and things will go back to normal.'

I could hear the chatter as the starlings swooped and circled, the sounds matching the tumult of thoughts in my head. I held my fingers to my temples. 'Back to normal,' I said.

Chapter One Hundred and Three

2002: Today: 6.35 p.m.

'I can't go on, Mother.' I lift my arms from my side, let them drop: my hands too substantial, too solid to hold up. They're strong – dependable, Sam always says. I just think they're like shovels and I've always been resentful that I didn't inherit my mother's slender fingers. After all I got her fat arse and thick thighs, why not the nice bits?

2000

Things were getting harder day by day. I didn't know what else we could do except to manage as best we could.

And there was no chance of me having a child. It wasn't something I talked about to Rose anymore.

The celebrations of the Millennium meant nothing to us. We watched all the programmes about it on the television: the daft debates about it being the end of the world, the promotions of millennium goods, the news of various forthcoming festivities and we tried to find some enthusiasm. But we were so tired we slept through the fireworks displays.

Mother gradually got worse. There was one particular day I remember because of the change in her afterwards...

'Give me my money.' Her face was red and twisted up in fury.

'I haven't got your money, Mum.' Not this again.

'My purse ... here ... here.' She thumped the table. 'Bloody thief.'

I carried on ironing. She'd emptied all the cupboards; the kitchen looked as if a bomb had hit it.

'Get out,' she shouted, 'get out ... my house. Sod off ... you.'

I wished I could.

'Don't need you.'

And I wished that were true. I finished pressing the collar of her blouse and handed it to her. The woman from the social services office that I talked to sometimes for advice said we had to let her do as much as possible for herself. 'Do you want to put this on a hanger for me?'

'Fuck it.' She crumpled it up and threw it on the floor.

I'd had enough. I unplugged the iron and put it on the worktop, collapsed the ironing board and carried it to the cupboard under the stairs. I wasn't gone a minute when there was an almighty scream.

I ran. 'What? What's happened? What have you done?'

She was holding out her hand and crying. There was a burn right across the middle of her palm. The iron was on the floor – broken.

I manhandled her to the kitchen sink.

'It's okay, it's okay. It's not too bad. Hold your hand under the tap.' The water gushed over both of us, the sleeve and front of my jumper was soon soaked.

'Cold – cold,' she yelled, pushing her face right up to mine. 'Cold.'

'I know.' I moved my hand across her back in small rubbing actions, like you do when you're comforting a child. 'It'll make it better. We'll put some ointment and a plaster on it.'

It took me an hour to calm her and get her to lie down on the settee for a rest. I sat on the floor next to her. I was jerked from a doze by a smack on the back of my head.

'What? What this?' she shouted, ripping the plaster off. 'Get away...go...away. Where's my money.... Bloody thief.'

That night Mother had a slight stroke. The doctor called it a TIA. But she didn't speak properly after that.

Chapter One Hundred and Four

2002: Today: 6.35 p.m.

She's awake. Was Rose awake when this woman murdered her? Were you awake, Rose? Did you know what she was doing? Were you frightened? I listen for the answer, bringing clear my memory of that day; it strengthens me to do what I have to do. You know I'm doing it for you, don't you, Rose? Did she stand clutching the pillow in the same way she held on to the hatred of you? Like me? It's time.

Why won't you answer me?

Chapter One Hundred and Five

2002: Today: 6.35 p.m.

Is there anything left in her brain that will form words? Or thoughts. Or memories? Does she remember that memory? The memory I've carried around for so many years.

Her eyelids flicker. 'Rose,' she says, as clear as that. She's lifted her head and she's looking beyond me to the door of the bedroom. The pulse in my temple quickens, goose bumps rise on my arms. I lower the pillow and twist round to follow her gaze.

I see her. I see Rose: her shock of black hair, the flecks of white deep in her irises. She's cradling her doll, Caroline, in her arms but she's studying me, her head to one side as if willing me to understand. She's in the outfit she was buried in, the white cotton dress with small red strawberries dotted all over it and the lacy white cardigan Nanna had knitted for her. Around her chubby wrist is the silver bracelet I'd bought for her out of my Saturday wages and – tucked under it – a white handkerchief folded to show the embroidered R in one corner, just below the lace edging. On her feet she wears white ankle socks with lacy tops and red sandals. No, not sandals– one sandal. 'Rose.' I lift my hand. She takes a step back. The landing light seems dim. She's more difficult to see in the gloom. 'Rose.'

And then she's not there anymore. I can't see her. But I hear her voice; a soft whisper. 'Don't, Iwene.'

'I don't understand...' The trembling starts in my legs, sweeps through my body. When I drag my eyes away from the doorway and look down at my mother she's asleep again, her breathing barely moving her lips.

I drop the pillow onto the armchair and walk away.

Is that what Rose wants; to stop me, for me to walk away? I don't understand. What happened? I sit on our bed and gaze around.

I would have killed my mother; I thought I should. Because she killed Rose.

My eyes rest on Caroline; the doll Rose had just been holding. How can that be?

I pick her up. Her bonnet is dusty. I wipe my palm over her face and then rub the grime off on my sleeve. I want to sleep. Lying on the bed I put her on the pillow alongside my head. The painted-on blue eyes stare, unblinking, at me. The glaze on the hand has gone, sucked down to the grey clay by Rose when she was a toddler. I touch the red woollen dress, notice how grubby it is, feeling guilty that I haven't looked after Rose's doll better. The legs are cold, one foot is missing from the time Rose had bounced Caroline on the back step and it broke off. Dad had tried to mend it but the glue didn't stick.

I sit up. The movement makes me sway, my head dizzy. I'll wash the dress. Rose will see me washing it; it'll make her happy. I unbutton it and pull it off.

Caroline's stuffed canvas striped body looks strangely vulnerable with the string drawn up around her neck, fastening the body to the head. I hold her close to me, hugging her. The head rattles. I hold the doll away from me, studying it. The body is stuffed with soft kapok. I poke it. Nothing. Shake it. There is a whisper of a noise. A slight crackle inside the head. I pull at the string and the head falls onto the bed. I pick it up and peer into the neck; there's something inside. Pushing two fingers into the neck I manage to hold on to it and slide out a tightly folded piece of paper. My fingers tremble when I begin to straighten it out because I can see the writing; slightly faded but still decipherable. The rounded letters are shaky but it's Nanna's handwriting.

My dear Irene,

I'm hoping I will have chance to tell you where to find this note. But, if not, I hope you will find it when I'm gone. I know Rose's doll is the one thing of hers you'll keep. I've seen you holding it many times. It is the toy that she loved most, after all.

And I'm hoping so much that you will forgive me. I let Rose go. It was me.

"Let Rose go"? Nanna? Nanna killed Rose? I drop my hands to my lap, holding the paper slack between my fingers. I loved my grandmother. I thought she loved me, loved Rose. I've clung on to the memory of that day I saw my mother murder my sister. Believed I saw my mother murder my sister. This is the first time I've doubted what I saw; I was so sure. I've had a lifetime of resenting, even hating, a woman for something she didn't do.

I made myself read on.

I want you to know Rose didn't suffer. She was asleep. I'd given her some of your mother's sleeping tablets in her afternoon milk.

So it was planned. The bile that swirls in my stomach makes its way into my throat. I swallow. It's bitter.

How to make you understand?

The acidity rises again and burns my mouth. I rush into the bathroom and heave over the rim of the lavatory. When there is nothing else to spew out I slump to the floor. The note is crushed in my hand. I smooth it straight.

I worried for such a long time. I knew I was ill, before any of you. I believe I did the right thing. You have your whole life in front of you. I hope it's with Sam. I like him, he's right for you. I heard you and him talking once, heard him say you shouldn't be responsible for her. He was right.

No he wasn't; she was mine to look after.

I couldn't chance you losing him. I can't let you be responsible for her, it wouldn't be fair.

It would have been my choice, Nanna. My choice.

And I know my daughter, your mother, wouldn't look after your sister. She's too weak. Perhaps that's my fault too. And yet she's been strong about this. She would never let me tell you. She said you needed me more than her. That's why she let you blame her all these years. But I can't go without trying to put things right between the two of you. I'm sorry I've only had the courage to do it this way. I hope you can find it in your heart to forgive me, Irene.

I can only say I am soon to meet my God and that he will judge me. I bow my head to that.

I'll always love you.

Nanna xx

I don't know how long I've been sitting here. I cross the landing towards my mother's room. What do I feel now? I don't know. She's lying still for once. I study her face; she looks relaxed, unusual these days. I can't change this mixture of dislike and pity; the years have been too hard, too filled with resentment.

But still I say it. 'I'm sorry, Mother – Mum.' And I am. My voice is loud in the silence that surrounds us.

She doesn't move. I bend over her, watching for the movement of her mouth, her nostrils. She isn't breathing. A cold breeze moves over my skin. I straighten up, glance at the window but it's closed. When I look back at the door there is a flicker of a shadow. Then it's gone.

PART THREE

There's a queue at the bus stop. I count the people: two women about my age, deep in conversation, a teenage boy, his face hidden by a hood, head bobbing to some unheard music, a young mother, wriggling toddler tucked under her arm as, frowning, she tries to fold up a buggy. Slightly apart, one man sways from foot to foot, cigarette in one hand, mobile phone in the other. Every now and then he stares at the phone, then along the street towards the direction the bus will come. He looks anxious, much like I feel.

There's a slight cramping in my stomach; I think I need to go to the loo again; third time in the last half hour. I don't seem able to breathe deeply enough; anything other than a shallow intake of air brings on a coughing fit.

A bus arrives, the queue shuffles on. I notice the man with the phone carries the buggy for the young woman. The child is still wriggling in her arms but now she's smiling.

I move around the living room, plumping up cushions, straightening the photos on the shelf and picking up the one of Mum and Dad, me and Rose. To me, Mum still looks as though she's chewing a wasp. The thought makes me smile but when I look into the mirror above the fireplace I see it's a half-smile. There's always sadness when I reflect on our relationship; I'd held on to that image of her standing by Rose's bed for so long. But over the last few months since she's been gone, I've wondered if things might have been different if I hadn't seen her then. Wondered if, as time passed, would we have grown to like one another? Pondered why Rose took so long to let me know the truth? Was it because she knew it was Mum's turn to go?

The label at the back of my jumper is scratching my neck and I consider if I've time to cut it out and then dismiss the idea; taking the jumper over my head will spoil my hair and it's taken ages already to get it to look right.

I go to sit on the stairs and gaze at the front door.

When the doorbell rings it makes me jump. I stand up, step off the last tread of the stairs, check my reflection in the hall mirror and rub at the back of my neck where the label chafes. A strand of hair stands up from the crown of my head and I lick my fingers to smooth it down. The bell is rung again. Impatient. This is it; there's a quiver of excitement in my stomach. I'm grateful to Sam for letting me do this alone. I know he and Dad and Susan are as thrilled as me. Pulling at the cuffs of my jumper, I take a long breath and, twisting the lock, pull open the door.

And there they are. Their mother is in prison for twelve months; it's a short term fostering. It was what we wanted to do; look after the children until the family can get back together. Challenging – but not as challenging as the life I've had so far. These thoughts are flashing through my mind, even as I beam and back into the hall to let them in.

I've got to know the young social worker, Sally, over the last few months; she takes her work very seriously. Quite rightly. I just wish she smiled more, relaxed a bit.

'This is Alison,' she says, nodding towards the girl, ushering them in.

'Ali...' The girl glowers round at her before fixing me with a stare. Her mouth tight, holding in her anger.

'Hi, Ali.' I don't attempt to reach out my hand to her, to touch her. I know she's ten, that awkward age before leaving childhood behind to face the unknown of growing up.

Her shoulders, hunched up, now slump and she lets her lips part as though to speak but, before she can, Sally says, 'And this is Auntie Irene,' in a bright determined tone.

'Irene,' I say, hunkering down to Ali's level so our eyes meet. I grin. Her mouth quivers, fighting against a smile. Conspirators. I nod. She hasn't let go of the little boy's hand who stands close to her. 'And this is...?'

'Oliver. I'll get their bags.' Sally tip-taps across the pavement to the car. I don't look up.

'Olly.' Ali leans towards me and whispers, 'He's six – he's special...'

'I know,' I reply. 'Hello, Olly.'

He doesn't answer, just shuffles closer to his sister, his face turned into her chest. That's okay; I know how he must be feeling. I wait. Outside, behind them, Sally is speaking on her mobile, occasionally glancing towards us. She always seems to be rushing on to the next thing she needs to do; always hassled.

Olly is peeping at me. I hope my smile doesn't look strained but I desperately want him to feel safe. Seconds pass before he lifts his head completely. I hope Sally stays on her phone; I don't want this moment broken.

And then he's looking at me, studying me. I see the broad forehead, the flat cheeks, the slightly upward-sloping, serious eyes and my heart surges.

'He's special,' Ali repeats, her forehead creasing. She strokes his spiky auburn hair, all the while watching for my reaction.

'I know,' I say again and, standing up, hold out my hand. It's as though I've stopped breathing. Then his hand is in mine. Soft, chubby fingers.

I lead them into our home. In the living room I show them the photograph. 'This is my sister, Rose, she was special too.'

ABOUT HONNO

Honno Welsh Women's Press was set up in 1986 by a group of women who felt strongly that women in Wales needed wider opportunities to see their writing in print and to become involved in the publishing process. Our aim is to develop the writing talents of women in Wales, give them new and exciting opportunities to see their work published and often to give them their first 'break' as a writer. Honno is registered as a community co-operative. Any profit that Honno makes is invested in the publishing programme. Women from Wales and around the world have expressed their support for Honno. Each supporter has a vote at the Annual General Meeting. For more information and to buy our publications, please write to Honno at the address below, or visit our website: www.honno.co.uk

Honno, 14 Creative Units, Aberystwyth Arts Centre
Aberystwyth, Ceredigion SY23 3GL

Honno Friends
We are very grateful for the support
of all our Honno Friends.

For more information on how you
can become a Honno Friend, see:
https://www.honno.co.uk/about/support-honno/

Also by Judith Barrow and available from Honno Press

The Howarth family series
Pattern of Shadows
Changing Patterns
Living in the Shadows
A Hundred Tiny Threads

THE MEMORY